Praise for the Novels of J. Carson Black

Dark Side of the Moon

"*Dark Side of the Moon* takes you on a perilous descent into a shadowy underworld where light cannot reach, trust can be fatal, and the deepest truth is only another lie. Once again J. Carson Black delivers a harrowing nonstop thrill ride that will eclipse every other suspense novel you read this year!"
—Michael Prescott, *New York Times* bestselling author of *Mortal Faults*

Darkness on the Edge of Town

"Black's multidimensional debut is a first-rate procedural that will keep readers up until the wee hours. . . . This white-knuckled thriller has a gritty realism, especially as Laura must exorcise ghosts from her past to complete her present case. The crux of the mystery is filled with plenty of red herrings that will leave readers guessing until they reach the fascinating, suspenseful conclusion."
—*Romantic Times*

"A well-crafted, suspenseful police procedural, rich in characters, plot, and setting. J. Carson Black gets it right, and mystery fans couldn't ask for more."
—Michael McGarrity, national bestselling author of *Slow Kill*

"J. Carson Black is a . . . genre treasure. Like Michael Prescott, Black can make you believe she's the first person ever to use the material she does."
—*Chicago Tribune*

"A superb debut . . . compelling and crisp. The characters will haunt your thoughts. Welcome to a strong new voice in American crime fiction."
—T. Jefferson Parker, author of *California Girl*

continued . . .

Dark Side of the Moon

J. CARSON BLACK

A SIGNET BOOK

SIGNET
Published by New American Library, a division of
Penguin Group (USA) Inc., 375 Hudson Street,
New York, New York 10014, USA
Penguin Group (Canada), 90 Eglinton Avenue East, Suite 700, Toronto,
Ontario M4P 2Y3, Canada (a division of Pearson Penguin Canada Inc.)
Penguin Books Ltd., 80 Strand, London WC2R 0RL, England
Penguin Ireland, 25 St. Stephen's Green, Dublin 2,
Ireland (a division of Penguin Books Ltd.)
Penguin Group (Australia), 250 Camberwell Road, Camberwell, Victoria 3124,
Australia (a division of Pearson Australia Group Pty. Ltd.)
Penguin Books India Pvt. Ltd., 11 Community Centre, Panchsheel Park,
New Delhi - 110 017, India
Penguin Group (NZ), cnr Airborne and Rosedale Roads, Albany,
Auckland 1310, New Zealand (a division of Pearson New Zealand Ltd.)
Penguin Books (South Africa) (Pty.) Ltd., 24 Sturdee Avenue,
Rosebank, Johannesburg 2196, South Africa

Penguin Books Ltd., Registered Offices:
80 Strand, London WC2R 0RL, England

First published by Signet, an imprint of New American Library,
a division of Penguin Group (USA) Inc.

First Printing, January 2006
10 9 8 7 6 5 4 3 2 1

Lyrics to "Those Feat'll Steer Ya Wrong Sometimes" © 1990. Written by: Paul Barrere,
Craig Fuller, Richard Hayward, Bill Payne, and Fred Tackett

 REGISTERED TRADEMARK—MARCA REGISTRADA

Printed in the United States of America

To Liz Gunn

Sometimes, all you really need is a good whack
between the eyes with a two-by-four—and
some damn good advice to follow it up.
Thank you

ACKNOWLEDGMENTS

Thanks to Leslie Boyer, MD; Tracy Bernstein—who knows good Tohono O'odham frybread when she tastes it; John and Doreen Bransky; Karen Brichoux; Sinclair Browning; Tony Copeland; Pat D'Antonio, MD; Mike and Ani DeHart; Leonard Fieber, MD; J. A. Jance and Bill Schilb; Kallie Johnson; Judy Layton; the incomparable band Little Feat—Paul Barrere, Sam Clayton, Craig Fuller, Kenny Gradney, Richie Hayward, Shaun Murphy, Bill Payne, and Fred Tackett—and Andy Martin at Deep South Entertainment; Janet Loeb of *Casa de Sueños*; Jennifer and Billy Lopez; Carol Davis Luce; Cliff McCreedy; Jean McCreedy; Jane Bunker Overy; Elizabeth Owen; Ziggy Pawlowski; Michael Prescott; Sharon (Kat) Putnam; Scott Shackelford; Barbara Schiller and Darrell Oliver; TPD sergeant Jim Schneden; Jen Stead and Orville Wiseman of Wiseman Aviation; Pam and Wayne Taylor; Jeremy Thompson; and the Amazing Alice Volpe. And thanks to my compadres in crime: Sheila Cottrell, Elizabeth Gunn, J. M. Hayes, E. J. McGill, and Susan Cummins Miller. Thanks especially to my husband and First Reader, Glenn McCreedy; my mother, Mary Falk; and to John Cheek of Cops n' Writers, DPS detective Terry Johnson, and TPD detective Phil Uhall—as usual, you guys went above and beyond.

Have you ever seen true evil? I mean looked it in the face and recognized it for what it is? I have. And you know what? It's a face like any other.

1

Thursday—Pahrump, Nevada

Because of the mineral show, which he had not expected, Bobby Burdette had to stay in a little hole-in-the-wall called the Mercury Motel. The Mercury Motel had a pool full of screaming kids and a plate-glass office that arrowed out toward the street in a triangle—the kind of space-age dump the Jetsons would have stayed in. The motel sign, a thermometer, lit up at night: red neon mercury climbing up to the boiling point over and over again.

At least that wasn't a lie; even in September, it was ninety degrees after the sun went down.

The Mercury Motel was situated between a defunct filling station and a date-palm orchard. The dates fell over the fence into the parking lot and onto the wax finish of his classic Dodge Challenger—the Mean Green—and got picked up by people's shoes. At any given moment there were a half dozen of them littering the walkway in front of the motel rooms like squashed cockroaches.

Bobby told himself he didn't have to put up with the poor accommodations and the sickening smell of dates much longer. If things worked out the way he expected, he'd never have to stay in a shithole like this again.

There was a good side to Pahrump, though, one he

hadn't considered when he blew into town earlier today. For one thing, the plate-glass office had nickel slots.

And, the town had a whorehouse.

And, it was legal. It was called the Bambi Ranch.

Bobby planned to bag one of those Bambies.

He'd seen it on a cable show once, how the girls would parade into the parlor and line up—blondes, brunettes, redheads, wearing different outfits—and you could pick the one you wanted just like at Red Lobster. There was something about it that just got to him, somewhere deep. Like that feeling you get in your gut when you ride a roller coaster.

The sun was going down below the far mountains when he drove the Mean Green out of the Mercury Motel parking lot, the sun flashbulbing him in the eyeballs. For such a little town, the traffic in Pahrump was hellish; mostly crawling RVs with satellite dishes on their roofs, the street lined with booths and a herd of people on the sidewalks, sometimes walking right out in front of him.

For a minute he wondered if the Mean Green was the right car to be seen in. The lime green paint and chrome wheels weren't exactly camouflage. But everyone was so busy looking at cases full of minerals or watching their own feet they probably wouldn't notice a circus driving through.

Besides, he liked how ballsy it was—hiding in plain sight.

The Bambi Ranch was out of town; he knew that was a requirement of all legal brothels in Nevada. He was surprised at the size of the layout—there were five narrow buildings, like temporary offices they had at schools, only this was no school. All of them were painted lavender. As he drove over the cattle guard into the parking area, he noticed an airstrip to his right, the wind sock sticking straight out like a condom. There was also a satellite dish on a balding Bermuda lawn surrounded by a white picket fence.

The place was lit up like a Christmas tree. Tiny white bulbs strung up in the Aleppo pines, colored lights all over the front office, and not the kind you got at Kmart, either—these were professional quality, the kind you'd find on the front of the casinos in Vegas. All that light power on these little sorry buildings. Like the crown jewels on a ten-dollar hooker.

He'd wanted to savor the event but it didn't turn out that way. The women outnumbered the men, and they sure didn't line up like he'd expected. More like they converged on him like sharks on chum.

"You want me, don't ya sweetness?" a handsome woman in her thirties said, practically getting him in a half nelson. She smelled of heavy perfume, breath mints and gin, but her skin was smooth and her boobs were huge.

Another one said, "With me you buy one, you get one free. Redeemable anytime." This chick was younger, with black hair and purple lips. Pale as a fish's belly.

Then there was the brooding Russian woman who tried to smile. At least he thought she was Russian. Pale, washed-out, sad. Most of them, though, they flounced and strutted and ran their fingers through his hair. When the door opened and another man came in, three of them made a bee-line for him. They reminded him of the catfish he used to feed as a kid at Lake Mead: boiling up the water, their mouths avid.

The one who remained was the young chick. She had a stud in her eyebrow and looked kind of skeletal, but her skin was like cream. And she didn't reek of booze like the older ones. She caught his look and nodded to the menu on an easel near the counter—a list of services and their prices, all nicely written up in fancy calligraphy on white poster-board. He opted for basic cable, so to speak, and paid the bored little man behind the counter in cash.

The Goth girl motioned him to follow her. She led him outside into the warm night, across the cracked walkway to the first trailer, down a hallway to a small dark room, paneled with walnut veneer.

The minute they got through the door, she removed her

clothes. If you blinked, you missed it. She had on boots that zipped up the insides and a flimsy skirt with an elastic waistband. Zip, zip, and the boots were off, and then she shimmied out of the skirt and her bottom half was naked as a jaybird. She clasped her arms around his neck and pulled him down on the bed without a word.

It wasn't as fun as he thought it would be. In fact, he found his mind drifting, thinking about tomorrow and all the days after that. Playing it out in his head. He seemed to hear her from a distance, moaning and groaning, doing her level best to get him to finish up.

But he wasn't into it. It wasn't anywhere near as exciting—as dirty—as he had expected it to be. The whole idea had been huge in his mind, but this—this was paltry. And so his mind wandered to something he saw on the road on the way up here today: an abandoned airplane hangar baking in the desert sun. The Goth woman whimpered about how good he was—he noticed she worked herself into more of a lather the longer it took, like jockeys whaling on their horses as they neared the wire—but his mind was on the checkpoint trailer at the California border, the two Homeland Security agents in their protective vests and their dark clothing, the sun bouncing off their sunglasses, the big German shepherd between them.

He liked their look. Easy enough to approximate. All he needed was a haircut and the right kind of sunglasses.

"Oh—my—*God!*"

Bobby wondered if he should fake it like his girlfriend did, or just quit. But he was stubborn; he wanted his money's worth. So he decided to put his mind to it, and with intense concentration, managed to put it over the top, just as the egg timer by the side of the bed rang.

It was the hardest work he'd done all day.

Feeling good about getting it done, he said, "How was that, sweetness?"

"Oh, it was *great*."

The way she said it made him want to slap her. That tone

in her voice. He'd heard that tone all his life, and every time it said he wasn't worth talking to or listening to or even lying to. The way women could put you down just by the inflection.

Just once, he'd like to see something on a woman's face besides contempt, disappointment, greed, or want.

"The tip jar's over there," Goth said.

For a moment he saw himself picking up the jar and tossing it into the mirrored closet doors, but then he remembered that he shouldn't do anything memorable. He had to think about the big picture. He wanted to be like those two agents—anonymous in their dark glasses and their clipped haircuts.

He put a dollar in her jar and said, "Sorry to overtip you, but I don't have any loose change."

She slammed the door after him with her foot.

The Mean Green sat patiently outside, his only friend.

Well, his girlfriend thought she was his friend. She thought she was more than that. But the more she loved him, the less he felt like loving her. Human nature was funny that way. It had always been like that with him. He knew it, but still he kept digging himself into these holes. Now he was going to meet her in Vegas, and he knew what was coming. *All these wedding chapels going to waste.*

He had other plans for his life.

His mother would have socked him one for even thinking that. Her favorite expression was, "Don't blow your own horn." But ever since he was a little kid, he was certain he'd make a name for himself. Sure, if you looked at it from the outside, if you were a stranger, you wouldn't think much of that prediction. But he was just getting started.

He cruised back down the highway through the warm velvet dark, the Mean Green's windows open. Singing along with a Little Feat CD, shouting the lyrics into the desert air: " 'When the Feats are on the box the speed just slips my mind, I start to sing along, tap my toe and slap the dash in time.' "

The ranger in the song who stopped the car telling the guy: "Son, those Feat done steered you wrong this time." Easy to get steered wrong; life surely was a slippery slope. He himself had spent most of the second half of his life trying to get out of the trouble he caused for himself in the first half.

But when God blew through your soul and told you it was *your* time—you heard it. And if you were any kind of man at all, you did something about it.

Back in Pahrump, he hit the slots at the casino. Thinking of all the people on the street and in this place. Wondering: Did they know how it could all change for them in an instant? Did they have any concept of God's stern and unyielding judgment coming for them, rolling down the highway?

More than likely, they had their blinders on, like everybody else on the planet. Looking around at the people here filling their time, throwing their money away with both hands, he knew that was true. All most people did was try to get from one hour to the next.

Bobby quit while he was slightly ahead and went back to his room. Looked at his maps, thought about what he'd do the next day. Scouting, mostly. And planning.

He thought about Death Valley just across the line—how appropriate was *that?* And the desolate stretch of road, the airplane hangar rotting in the sun, stark against the desert brush—noticeable and unnoticeable at the same time. And he, Bobby Burdette, looking cool and tough in his dark glasses.

2

There were two cops at the campsite when Laura Cardinal arrived at the scene, one of them looking at the tent as if he were trying to figure out how to pack it up.

The opening to the red, two-man dome tent was unzipped, the nylon door piece lying on the forest floor like a tongue. From this angle, Laura could see at least half the interior. The backside of the tent glowed orange-red where it was lit from behind by the sun. Sunlight poured in through a fist-size hole in the fabric. She could see little of the tent floor, but what she saw was empty and soaked with blood.

Warren Janes, the sergeant who had accompanied her to the scene, had to walk fast to keep up with her. "This is the second time something like this's happened," he said. "A kid drowned in the lake at the beginning of the summer."

Laura was half listening. Her instincts had kicked up into high gear, and what they were telling her wasn't good. Something wrong here. Not that there wasn't plenty wrong to begin with—two college kids shot to death while sleeping in their tent.

"What happened?" she asked, her gaze still fixed on the campsite.

"Well, that's the weird thing. Kid was with his teacher,

Mr. Garatano, late at night. What Mr. Garatano said was the kid wanted to swim so he dove off of the boat. He never came up."

"How old was the kid?"

"Fourteen."

She stopped. "What were they doing out in a boat late at night?"

Janes shrugged. "He *said* they were fishing, but we all wondered about that. Mr. Garatano got fired not too long after that. We investigated, turned out the kid got tangled up in some weeds and drowned."

Interesting, Laura thought, but she had other worries. Despite the perfect late-summer day, and the reasonable assumption that the Williams PD cops had preserved the scene, Laura had the feeling there was something she didn't know. And then it came to her.

She voiced her suspicions to Janes. "The bodies are still in the tent, aren't they?"

He cleared his throat.

At that moment she saw the younger cop reach down to pull one of the tent pegs out of the ground.

"Officer! Don't do that!"

He straightened up, uncertain. Little more than a kid—maybe only a year or two out of high school. He stepped back from the tent as if it were a snake, his movement quick and athletic.

The older cop started in their direction, as if trying to ward them off. "The ME's people were just here. I tried to stall them, but they couldn't wait any longer."

"They took the bodies," Laura said. She wanted to punch a wall—or something. Or someone.

The cop had stopped in front of them, hands on his hips, as if the altitude bothered him. "They were so busy in Flag this weekend—there was a pileup on the freeway—this was the only time they could cut someone loose to come get them."

Laura resigned herself to the reality of the situation. This was bad, but she would have to work around it. She and Victor, her usual partner, had a saying when things went wrong at a crime scene: *That's showbiz.*

Laura motioned to the younger cop to join them. She noticed he was careful to follow the prints the officers had made entering the scene, adhering to the "one way in, one way out" rule. This surprised her. After seeing him reach for the tent peg, she'd expected him to be impulsive.

Sergeant Janes made the introductions. "This is criminal investigator Laura Cardinal with the Department of Public Safety," Janes said. He glanced at her. "Have I got that right?"

"Detective's fine." Thinking: *Where the hell is Richie?* If he'd been here earlier, he could have stopped them from taking the bodies.

The two officers were Tagg and Wingate. The older cop, Tagg, smelled of cigarette smoke. Wingate seemed on edge, adrenaline running through him like a muscular river. Laura guessed this was the first time he'd seen anything like this.

Janes said, "I want you to give her and her partner everything you've got."

Tagg was looking at her as if trying to place her. "I've heard your name before. Aren't you—?"

Laura didn't reply directly to his question. Instead, she motioned toward a blue truck parked behind them on the forest road, just outside the campground gate. "Is that the victims' vehicle?"

"That's right," said Janes. "Thought we'd leave it for you to process."

"I'll need a warrant." Even though the truck belonged to the crime scene, Laura wanted to be on the safe side, go ahead and get the warrant. Depending on where they were, even crime scenes required warrants, which Laura thought was just plain nutty. "Is there a justice of the peace or judge you like to go to?"

Janes motioned to his patrol car. "I have his number on the computer. We can do it telephonically."

"Do we have photographs?"

"The medical examiner's office took some, but they're in Flagstaff."

"I took some Polaroids," Wingate volunteered. He trotted up the red cinder road to one of two Williams PD police cars and returned a moment later.

Four Polaroids. "That's all the film I had."

Laura held each one of them in the shade of her body, squinting against the brightness.

Hard to tell what was what; the colors were faded and the shapes indistinct. Yellow hair in a tangle. Pale flesh clotted with blood. The boy behind the girl; half-in, half-out of the sleeping bag. Spoon fashion, his right arm over her body. The sleeping bag and walls of the tent soaked with blood.

The top of the boy's head gone.

All four Polaroids had been taken through the holes in the tent, from different angles.

"Is that one sleeping bag, or two?" Laura asked.

"Well, technically, there're two," Tagg said. "They zipped 'em together. You can do that with Cabela's."

Tagg added, "Double-ought buckshot. Shot right through the tent flap and two other sides."

"He didn't see them, then?"

"He could've seen them through the holes in the tent, but he didn't bother to open up the door flap. We had to open it to get the bodies"—Tagg glanced at Wingate—"the victims out."

"Josh's the one who found them," Sergeant Janes explained. "He knew Dan."

Josh Wingate was staring at the tent. The high-voltage energy field surrounding him had not abated; in fact, it seemed to be getting stronger. "We were best friends in high school," he said.

Laura looked at him with new interest. No wonder he seemed so off balance. His eyes were like shards of cut green glass, pulverized with hurt, but she noticed that his posture was straight and he held his chin high. Almost defiant.

She remembered a shabby kitchen in Florida, how it felt to see someone you knew die right in front of you. "I'm sorry."

"It's bad," Josh Wingate replied, "but I'm okay."

Laura had her doubts about that. "You found them?"

"My mom lives up that road." He pointed to Country Club Road behind them. "I was on my way over when I saw his truck."

"How'd you know it was his?"

"We used to camp out here a lot when we were kids. Plus, the bumper sticker."

Laura glanced at the truck, a generic late-model GMC, the same medium-blue sheen as Cataract Lake. A common enough color in trucks. The bumper sticker said "COWBOY UP." There was an NAU sticker on the windshield. Dan Yates and Kellee Taylor both had attended Northern Arizona University in Flagstaff.

"They weren't supposed to be here," Sergeant Janes said. "The campground's been closed since Labor Day for repairs."

It was the third week of September now. Laura looked out at the quiet lake, the pines. The grass going tawny, the palette of wildflowers fading to tarnished glory. After Labor Day the north country seemed to give up on tourists until ski season. "We're kind of far from town, aren't we?" she said. "I would expect this to be the sheriff's jurisdiction."

"The city annexed this area last year—there's plans to build at least one hotel and restaurant around here, what with the lake and all."

Laura continued to stare at the lake. Wondering again, where was Richie Lockhart? Sergeant Janes hadn't heard from him, and neither had she.

Well, she didn't have the luxury to wait for him. Whatever she did now, she had to do right. Her crime scene—she always thought of a crime scene as hers—had been com-

promised by the removal of the bodies. She had to go with
what she had.

Officer Wingate had been the first on the scene. He was
friends with at least one of the victims, which might influence his memory in ways she couldn't fathom, but he was
still her best bet. He would have to be her eyes and ears.

3

The first thing Laura did was clear out a space in the dirt. She said to Officer Wingate, "Why don't you step right here?" He looked at her, uncertain, then planted his foot on the ground. Laura put a red-and-white ruler beside his footprint, then photographed the print and the ruler with her thirty-five-millimeter camera. Then she cleared another space in the ground and placed her own foot in the center and photographed that.

"I see what you're doing," Wingate said. "Now we'll know our own footprints."

As they entered the area inside the crime scene tape, one thing was clear to Laura immediately. She said to Officer Wingate, "Look at the ground. Do you see anything unusual?"

"No, ma'am." And then, "Wait." Careful to stay on the path trampled by the Williams PD officers, he hunkered down and scanned the ground. "Looks like they covered their tracks."

She nodded. A large area had been smoothed over, probably with a push broom. The random pattern of pine duff carpeting the ground had been replaced by a layer of ponderosa needles and dirt mixed together, the grama grass and purple asters and few green strands of meadow grass poking up dusty, dispirited heads. She took several photographs of the ground.

Laura scanned the area, looking for the glint of metal, and saw none. She guessed that whoever had covered his tracks had picked up his shell casings, too.

She breathed in the sun-warmed tang of pine. This altitude, the sun was hot on her back, her neck, her hair. She wished she had a hat.

"Let's backtrack, see how far this goes."

She followed the path back out, and ducked under the tape, Wingate her quick shadow.

They walked just outside the perimeter of the swept area. The killer had been thorough and tricky. There were several places where pine duff had piled up underneath the trees. At any one of these spots he could have walked out on the hard-packed needles. They followed each possible trail, radiating outward like spokes on a wheel—but found nothing.

Officer Wingate took his cue from her, sticking close, but sure to walk behind her, in her footsteps, keeping his thoughts to himself. She could see out of the corner of her eye that his legs were shaking. Adrenaline. His body finally getting the message, the aftermath to finding his best friend from high school shot to death.

Amazing what guns could do. All the shotgun deaths she'd seen, she never got used to it.

She had already formed at least one impression of the killer. Unfortunately, that impression was mixed. Shooting into a tent without opening the flap pointed at a killer who didn't know his victims. She thought there was a lack of curiosity, as if he couldn't care less whether the people in the tent lived or died. The fact that he didn't open the tent, didn't look inside to make sure they were dead, that pointed to someone who had no stake in the outcome. That pointed to a random shooting.

But if it was a random shooting, why go to such pains to obliterate his presence?

It was almost as if there were two different people at work here.

They now stood directly behind the tent, approximately fifteen feet away, on mildly undulating ground. Officer Wingate careful to stay behind her.

It looked to Laura as if the killer had shot three times; one round going through the front flap, one on the right side, and one in the back. Judging from the size of the holes in the tent, she guessed he'd shot from about this distance: fifteen feet give or take. She pictured him circling the tent, walking and shooting, walking and shooting, walking and shooting.

She said to Officer Wingate, "People would have heard the shots." Even though it was a rural neighborhood, there were houses scattered around the area.

"Yeah, but they'd probably think someone was jack-lighting deer."

She almost stepped on a partial print, realized it belonged to Wingate. "What time did you spot the truck?"

"This morning, around seven. Maybe closer to seven thirty. My mom wanted me to help her unload some hay, and then she was going to make me breakfast."

"And you stopped then?" she said as she took several photographs of the ground and the tent. "Or did you stop on the way back?"

"It was on the way to my mom's—I never got there." He motioned up the road to the gate. "I parked right behind his truck."

"And then what did you do?"

He told her how he had gone around the gate and walked down toward the lake. "Their tent was the only one here. It wasn't hard to figure out it was them."

"You recognized the tent?"

He looked at her, confused momentarily. Trying hard to be accurate. "No. I mean I knew it belonged to whoever had the truck."

Trying hard to be precise. He reminded her a little of Andrew Descartes, although his hair was close-cropped and blond and Andy had been dark.

They worked their way in toward the tent. Laura asked, "Which way did you come in?"

He pointed to the stampede of tracks. "That way, just down from the road. I made note of where I went in and went out the same way."

"I see that. It's made my job easier."

"Thanks." His eyes brimming over with pain.

She tried to ignore that. "Then what?"

"The tent was torn like that—my first thought was bear, but then when I got closer I knew it was gunshot."

"Then what did you do?"

He stared into the middle distance, as if seeing it all again. "I just stood there, tried to get my bearings. My first thought, was that they—Dan—went somewhere, and somebody used the tent for target practice. You know, vandals."

Laura understood that. Despite overwhelming evidence to the contrary, it was almost impossible for the human mind to make the logical leap that someone you knew could be dead.

"But I think I knew, even then." His voice seemed to come from high in his chest—agitated.

"What did you do then?"

"I called Danny's name a few times. He didn't answer. So I walked over and checked it out."

He paused, but Laura didn't prompt him. The hot sun pounded down on her head as she waited for him to continue.

"That hole in the door flap—thing was hanging by a thread. I looked just enough to see they were dead. Then I backed away from there and made the call."

"Did you recognize them?"

"I knew it was Dan." He cleared his throat.

"Can you show me where they were?"

He did so, using his hands to illustrate. Laura could see

it. The sleeping bag had started out in the center, perpendicular to the tent door. The top half of the bag had been skewed sideways, though, as Dan and Kellee rolled to the right. Burrowing into the tent wall, as tight in as they could get.

Laura looked in through the front, took pictures of the floor, the walls. Then she carefully zipped up what was left of the front flap, so she could look at the hole. She looked at each of the three holes in the tent, thinking trajectories.

Narrowing her focus down to the two people trapped inside, their movements, even their thoughts. Their terror seeping into her own soul like poison gas.

She knew about terror—felt it now, rising like a high-water mark in her chest—something that happened these days at the drop of a hat.

Kellee Taylor had come to rest against the edge of the tent, curled into a fetal position, her face shoved down into the tent floor. Dan Yates's body surrounding her, partially covering her with his right leg and arm.

He had done his best to protect her.

They'd had enough time between the first shot and the second to move as far to the right as they could, hoping they could evade the next round.

Laura guessed that by then the killer was already walking around the tent to the right.

By reacting the way they did, Dan and Kellee had unwittingly put themselves directly into the line of fire.

4

A stray breeze fluttered a fast-food receipt poking out of the trash bag. Laura had set the bag on the ramada picnic table near the campsite, and had been going through its contents. Suddenly she felt a twinge in the small of her back—a leftover from a car accident when she was in the Highway Patrol. She massaged the spot with a latex-gloved hand.

Officers Tagg and Wingate had been dispatched to canvass the houses along the road near Cataract Lake Park to find out what the neighbors had heard or seen last night. The sergeant, Warren Janes, remained behind. At the moment he was leaning against his patrol car, eating his lunch. Content to let her do her thing.

Laura knew he'd been told by the Williams police chief, who was currently on his way from an interrupted fishing trip in Montana, to "render unto Caesar." Caesar, in this case, being the state law-enforcement agency she worked for, the Department of Public Safety. Apparently Sergeant Janes had no trouble with that, which surprised her. Usually the cops she dealt with in small towns wanted in, not out.

Still no sign of Richie Lockhart. Calls to his cell phone netted only his voice mail. He didn't answer his pager.

Laura thought about calling her sergeant, but she didn't want to bother him, or worse, let him think *she* was bothered. Telling him she couldn't keep track of her own partner wouldn't look good. Something her old mentor, Frank Entwistle, had drilled into her: Never show weakness. Her squad was just like grade school—all the subtle forms of tyranny, petty triumphs and slights, subtle but clear.

Lately, though, everyone in the Criminal Investigations Division had been nice to her. Too nice, actually. Solicitous, tiptoeing around her as if she were a new-laid egg. Jerry Grimes, her sergeant, had given her two soft assignments in a row—white-collar crimes.

Taking her out of the game.

She closed her eyes against the sun, which had slowly moved through the ramada as morning turned to afternoon. It was going on three thirty. The air smelled of pine duff, warm earth, blood, and garbage.

Carefully, she replaced the stone over the trash bag and walked out into the clearing. She stared at the lake—a blue sliver cutting through the pale green-gold grasses sloping down from the pines. She needed to breathe the air, feel the sun on her back, give her mind a chance to absorb what she had learned so far.

Today was Saturday and it *felt* like a Saturday. When Laura was a girl, she loved Saturday mornings. On Saturdays the world was full of possibilities. She was free for the whole weekend, she could do anything she wanted. But by Sunday afternoon the small white cloud was on the horizon; she knew the storm was coming, that her freedom was about to end. By dinnertime the cloud was bigger and darker, and by nighttime, the whole sky was black.

The next morning it was back to school to face the bullies.

With this job—with this *calling*—she had finally found her clan. She'd always considered herself one of the boys. Now she was one apart again, and she didn't like it. She especially didn't like coming around a corner and running into friends and colleagues who immediately stopped talking midconversation.

Laura could smell a charcoal grill somewhere. A warm

Indian-summer day in the high country, the droning of lawn mowers, people taking care of the stuff they'd had to put off all week. Saturday.

Saturday had a meaning in this case, because it was the weekend, and Dan and Kellee had used the extra time to travel. She wondered if they had cut classes on Friday to come out here and spend the night, or if they had waited until the end of the day.

She absorbed the sun, thinking about what she had found so far in Dan Yates's truck: a tea-length dress, cream-colored, hung in a garment bag from the window of the extra cab, along with a man's suit. Cream-colored pumps to match the dress. A man's dress shoes had been shoehorned behind the front seat, rolled-up dark socks inside. A tie lay on the backseat. Sometime on this trip, Dan Yates and Kellee Taylor had gone somewhere where they'd had to dress up.

Put that together with what she had found in the top half of the garbage bin near the ramada—a cardboard box containing remnants of white frosting and chocolate cake, a boxful of candles, sandwich wrappers, an empty bottle of sparkling cider, and two plastic screw-on champagne glasses—and she was beginning to see a pattern.

A dress-up, and a celebration.

A breeze ruffled the impassive face of Cataract Lake, shadows combing across the shimmering blue surface. She thought it would be beautiful at night, too. She wondered what it was like out here the night the boy drowned.

Lakes were deceptive. This lake, in particular, appeared open and friendly. And tiny. It would seem to be an easy task to swim across Cataract Lake. But underneath the placid blue surface were weeds, rocks, fishing line, and junk.

Laura glanced at the sky: So blue it seemed to pulsate. The golden grama grass threading itself through the shadows of the ponderosa pines. A wood chipper alternately droned and whined somewhere to the north, changing its tone depending on what was being devoured.

It was clear that Dan and Kellee had not just gone out on a camping trip. They had been somewhere where they had to dress up. Afterward, they had changed back, Dan discarding his tie on the backseat, rolling his socks and sticking them in his shoes. They had come here to camp. She guessed that the pink cake box, the sparkling cider, were theirs.

The rest of the evidence was more straightforward. There were the usual items you'd want on a camping trip, all of them packed haphazardly in the black duffel inside the tent, one edge soaked in blood. A green cooler. A college text of *Oedipus Rex,* Kellee's name and phone number neatly written inside the front cover. Her purse—a couple of credit cards, some money, a few receipts, hairbrush, and so on—nothing earth-shattering but worth noting, including a stub for a roll of film. Like the photos taken by the police early this morning, the film had gone to the local Safeway.

Unfortunately, Dan's wallet was missing, and Laura got confirmation from Janes that one of his officers had checked it, then returned it to the pocket of his jeans. It had gone off to the medical examiner in Flagstaff.

It was the first time she'd come even close to losing it. She didn't, though, just calmly asked him to send an officer to drive up and get it, and reviewed with him that it must be put into an evidence bag, signed and sealed, and brought back to her. Janes had been pretty annoyed at her walking him through it, but to his credit he didn't say anything.

She finished up with the trash bag, sealing and marking her finds in plastic or paper evidence envelopes, depending on whether the garbage was wet or dry. The old paper-or-plastic question, with a twist: Wet stuff, like blood, went into paper; dry into plastic.

Lots of blood in the tent. Which reminded her, she needed to figure out how to transport the tent to the Department of Public Safety crime lab in Phoenix.

She'd just started working on that problem when the silence was shattered by a loud car engine reverberating through the forest. She glanced up and saw the sun flash off the windshield of a red Monte Carlo as it turned off the road into the Cataract Lake campground.

Richie Lockhart, her new partner, was here at last.

5

The engine fell silent, the quiet returning to the forest like a soft snowfall. A car door slammed, loud in the open space. Briefcase in hand, Richie Lockhart started down the road, the sun catching his prematurely white hair.

He was short and shaped like Gumby, his body the same thickness all the way down. His face open and sunny. He didn't walk; he *sauntered*.

The anger simmering inside Laura all day threatened to boil over. She'd clamped the lid down tight, because she had never worked on a case with him before and wanted to keep an open mind. But now she was mad. Two people were dead. You didn't treat it like a walk in the park.

Sergeant Janes detached himself from the fender of his patrol car and walked up the road to meet Lockhart. They met on the cinder road, then started walking down together. Richie stopped next to Dan Yates's truck, looking it over, his admiration obvious.

The two men were talking when Laura reached them.

Warren Janes looked at her with new eyes. "Now I know where I heard your name," he said. "Nice work."

She didn't know if he was referring to her capture of a serial sexual predator and killer named Musicman, or the effect his capture had on DPS, the ramifications radiating outward like circles in the wake of a rock thrown into a lake.

She had thrown the rock.

"I wouldn't want to be you, though," Janes added.

Richie beamed. "I think it's fair to say that all of us—to a man—are proud of the way Laura here stepped up."

Laura said to Richie, "I thought you were flying here."

"The plane had mechanical problems. I waited all morning, at *least* two hours, before they told me to go ahead and drive up."

She didn't ask him why he'd turned off his mobile and didn't answer his pager.

"So what've we got?" Richie asked.

Laura ran it down briefly: the young couple, college kids, killed by a shotgun in their tent.

Richie was turned slightly toward Janes in such a way that he was cutting Laura out of the loop. Or at least that was how it looked. "Why did they camp here?" he asked Janes.

"The boy—Dan—his family lives here. We think it was someplace familiar; they probably camped here because they have before." Janes was talking to Richie but looking at Laura. Wondering, perhaps, what it was like to be a standout in an agency that encouraged invisibility.

"Anything else I should know?" Richie asked.

Laura said, "The bodies are gone."

That threw him. He wiped the back of his hand across the salt-and-pepper stubble on his chin. "There much left to see?"

Laura told him about the cake box in the garbage can, the dress-up clothes in the truck. The bloody tent. As Laura described the scene, her mind, which had been working on how to move the tent, suddenly came up with an answer.

She turned to Sergeant Janes. "Can you get me a body bag?"

Janes looked uncertain. "A body bag? I guess so, sure."

She took out the small notebook she always carried and

wrote down a list of things she'd need, and handed it to him. "I'm going to need a DPS officer to transport it to the crime lab in Phoenix."

"No problem there." He nodded in the direction of Interstate 40, a corridor Laura had once worked when she was in the Highway Patrol Division of DPS. "We're thick with them—you excuse the expression."

"Good. We want to get this done before dark."

"What's this about?" asked Richie, falling into step with her as she walked back toward the campsite.

"We have to move the tent."

"Yeah. So?"

She stopped to explain. "I want to get the tent floor, so we can diagram where each pellet went into the ground."

"I know that," Richie said impatiently.

She ignored his testiness. "So we roll it up, as loosely as we can, and put it in a body bag."

"Why can't we put the whole tent on a flatbed?"

"On the freeway? Going seventy-five miles an hour? The thing is falling apart."

For a minute she thought he was going to argue, but he just shrugged and said, "You da boss."

It didn't take them as long as Laura thought it would. With spray paint, they marked circles around each gunshot hole in the sides of the tent before cutting around them and placing them on a picnic table to be transported separately. Next, they cut the tent body away from the floor.

"Oh, shit!" Richie said, looking at the swipe of blood on his elbow. "I hope neither one of them had AIDS." He glared at Laura. "We should have thought of this."

Meaning *she* should have thought of this.

Although they wore gloves, it was impossible to avoid getting some blood on their arms and clothing, even though most of it was dry or nearly dry. Laura could have asked the Williams PD or the sheriff's department for HazMat gowns and masks, but hadn't wanted to wait; she'd wanted to get the tent floor out of here before dark. And so she had taken a calculated risk that Dan and Kellee were AIDS-free.

This was not like her. Like most cops, Laura was overly cautious by most lights. But lately she'd been taking little risks—in traffic, attempting fix-its at home that could and did backfire on her. She had garnered an impressive array of cuts, bruises, and blood blisters in the last few weeks.

She'd been impatient lately. With herself and with others. Little things got to her more, and she wanted to burn through the day-to-day boring stuff of life as quickly as possible. But when it came to this case, she needed to slow down and let herself think. Do something off-the-wall here, and you could never go back. Evidence was easy to misplace or mess up, and she didn't want to create a loophole for the killer's lawyer to exploit down the line.

They marked all four sides of the tent, starting with the area where the door was. Then they marked the corresponding points on the ground with little colored flags on wires. After the fabric of the floor was rolled up—loosely, to avoid friction—Laura deposited it into the waiting body bag, zipped it up, sealed it, and wrote her name on the evidence tag.

"I have hand cleaner in the 4Runner," she said.

"A little after the fact," Richie grumbled, but he followed her up to her car.

As he scrubbed his hands with the liquid antiseptic hand cleaner, he said, "They're gonna look at that thing and wonder what kind of body is *that*. Looks like a goddamn iguana."

By this time it was going on six o'clock and the rays of the sun slanted and flashed between the trees. The Highway Patrol officer—her nameplate said Marty Fields—was waiting for them up on the road. If all went well, the tent would be at the DPS crime lab in three hours.

Richie glanced at the lowering sun. "Looks like it's notification time."

Laura opened the driver's door of the 4Runner, expecting Richie to ride along with her.

"Let's take my car," he said.

She looked at the red Monte Carlo, black and chrome strips running down the sides, a stylized silver "8" on the right front fender.

"I've got all my stuff in here."

"We could move it."

"I'd feel like Starsky and Hutch riding around in that car." Aware that Warren Janes was watching their interaction. "We'd better go in mine."

His face turned stony. "Tell you what. We'll caravan."

She watched him scurry to his car and get in. He started it up and revved the engine, the Monte Carlo's deep-throated roar drowning out the peace of the forest. Motioning to her to lead the way.

Laura realized they'd be driving separately all around town, first to Safeway to pick up Kellee's photos, then to notify the families of the victims. That did not sit well with her. Her parents had been children of the Depression and didn't like waste, and neither did she. "Wait!"

Richie powered his window down but kept revving the engine, forcing her to walk over to him.

"I'll go with you. Let me get my stuff."

For answer, he popped the trunk.

Sitting way down in the bucket seat, peering out past three stickers on her side of the windshield, "1," "8," and "15"—no doubt they carried some deep mystical meaning—Laura avoided looking at Richie. She didn't have to. Self-congratulation rolled off him like the Canoe cologne her first boyfriend wore for the high school dance.

They followed the road back through the mouse-hole tunnel under the railroad tracks, then over the freeway into Williams, where the road split into two one-way streets: Railroad Avenue going west, and one block over, old U.S. Route 66 going east.

Modeling itself as a tourist town, Williams had two main attractions: stores exploiting the Route 66 nostalgia craze, and the Grand Canyon Railway. The Grand Canyon Railway shuttled tourists back and forth to the Grand Canyon for the day. Route 66 . . . just *was*.

The late-afternoon sun glowed off the walls of the Main Street buildings up the way. Many of them had been made of rock quarried near here—a mosaic of reds, golds and dark browns held in place by a Krazy Glue of cement. Driving through town this morning on the way to the police station, she had counted mostly curio shops and antique stores—a shop with old cameras in the window, another selling ancient radios of every description.

Williams's one supermarket, Safeway, was situated on the west end of town, not far from where they came in. Laura noticed a shop off to the side on one end of the parking lot. One window displayed a mannequin dressed up in cammos, wielding a paintball gun; the other, a mannequin in a white wedding dress. Red letters that would glow at night spelled out the name KITTEN'S JOY SEWING SUPPLY AND DRESS SHOPPE.

Richie disappeared while Laura waited under the harsh fluorescents at the photo kiosk for the clerk to find Kellee's photos. Halloween decorations were already up. She'd just opened the flap when Richie returned, holding a jelly doughnut. He craned his neck to look at the photo on top, a candid shot of Kellee Taylor, looking young and healthy. "My, my."

Laura said, "That's the female victim."

"Oh."

Then: "She have a sister?"

Cop humor. Laura ignored him, bringing her focus down to the photograph. Shutting everything else out. Well, almost everything—she did notice the powdered sugar from Richie's doughnut raining down on the sleeve of her navy jacket.

She'd shared a squad room with him for three years, but

suddenly the whole Safeway was too small for the two of them. Something about him—his body language, his jelly doughnut, his *presence*—distracted her. She ignored him harder.

Richie was right about one thing: Kellee Taylor was a knockout. Fresh-faced and golden-skinned, her blond hair pulled back into a ponytail under a ball cap, she wore an NAU baseball shirt with dark sleeves over denim shorts. She stood in front of Hoover Dam, radiating health and happiness.

Her whole life ahead of her.

Laura thought of Josh Wingate's Polaroids, the color and the life drained out, the vibrant cornsilk hair turned dull and greenish yellow from the flash, clotted with blood.

Laura had no idea how long ago this picture had been taken, whether it had been from this trip or from an earlier one, but it could mean that Dan and Kellee had gone to Hoover Dam as recently as yesterday.

With the next photograph a puzzle piece clicked into place. The sign above the door said: FORGET ME NOT WEDDING CHAPEL.

That explained the cake and the champagne glasses.

Dan and Kellee stood in bright sunshine, Cupid's arrow lit up in green neon behind them. Kellee wore her cream-colored dress, and Dan looked uncomfortable in his suit. Kellee held a single red rose.

Richie Lockhart wiped his hands with the little tissue that came with the doughnut and breathed over her shoulder. "What do you know? They tied the knot."

"We've got the beginning of a time line," Laura said, thinking out loud. "That picture at Hoover Dam. What time do you think it is?"

"Could be morning or afternoon."

"Well, let's think about this." She recognized the road and the way the dam curved—it was facing the Arizona side. If her calculations were correct, the shadows were thrown by the eastern sun, not the west. "I'd say nine, ten in the morning at the latest."

"Could be."

"Look where the shadows are coming."

"Okay, sure, I can see that."

"And at the chapel it could have been as late as one or two." In her mind she let it play out. "They were killed sometime overnight . . . unless this picture was taken the day before, on Thursday."

"Uh-huh."

It occurred to her that she had one answer right here. She glanced at the sticker on the envelope. The date stamped there was: 9/15, 4:38 P.M.

September fifteenth. Yesterday.

"Yesterday morning they drove to Vegas, got married, and made it to Williams before five." She went through the snapshots again—a party at an apartment that Laura assumed belonged to either Dan or Kellee, and one or two of Dan that could have been on the Northern Arizona University campus. Only four photos of their wedding trip, including one outside the chapel, a group shot. People milling around. Many of them—including the bride and the groom—had their backs to the camera. A candid shot.

Whoever the photographer was at the chapel, he wasn't a pro.

As Laura waited for Richie to pay for the jelly doughnut, she toyed with the time line. If her calculations were correct, Dan and Kellee had left early yesterday morning to get married in Las Vegas, possibly on an impulse. They'd come back to Williams, left the roll of film at Safeway—probably bought the food for their celebration there—then settled in at the campground.

Did they go by to see Dan's parents?

The celebration was for two, though: two champagne glasses, two sandwich wrappers, a small cake.

She wondered if they had kept their wedding a secret.

Richie finished paying for the doughnut and motioned

toward the restroom. Laura took the opportunity to talk to the three checkers. They were all extremely friendly and helpful, but none of them remembered the young couple. She got the name and number of the woman who had worked there yesterday, then went looking for Richie. He wasn't in the store and he wasn't outside.

Probably still in the bathroom. She knew he had prostate problems—like everything else, the state of his urinary health was fair game. He was the squad practical joker. The good thing was, he didn't mind laughing at himself.

From the parking lot, Laura took another look at the old motels on Main Street. Parked along the street were plenty of beat-up old trucks, the kind construction workers drove. Hammering rang in the clear air, punctuated by the whine of a circular saw. This part of town was as busy as a beehive, even though it was after Labor Day and Laura hadn't seen many tourists. Despite the Indian-summer heat, the area felt closed-up to her, fall in the high country, which made for a strange juxtaposition with the frenetic noise down the street. The town was in the throes of a renovation boom, lots of old motels getting makeovers but keeping the same nostalgic neon glow of their glory days.

Laura wondered how much of that activity a small tourist town could support. Whoever was building wasn't worried.

The shadows were beginning to slant across the parking lot, the light turning the houses, trees and cars the color of apple cider. She watched the cars cruising Route 66, absorbing the beauty of this late-summer day. A nice quiet town, lots of old houses, small yards, picket fences, and tall trees. But many of the houses had seen their best days, and most of the vehicles she saw were old and beat-up.

"That's a relief," Richie said at her elbow. "You could say it made a vas deferens in my life."

Laura's laugh was obligatory; she'd heard him say that at least a dozen times before. Her mind was still on Kellee, by the dam. The girl, looking confidently into her future, unaware that she would be dead in less than twenty-four hours. That for a few terrifying moments between one shot and the next, she would be huddled against the side of the tent, her heart chugging like a runaway train, the man she had married trying—and failing—to protect her.

6

Chuck Yates's house was the last in a grid of streets dead-ending at vacant land opposite the Holiday Inn. Across a field of meadow grass and sunflowers, Laura could see the big trucks on I-40, moving like items on a conveyer belt. Seeing the last rays of the sun sparking off the tractor-trailer rigs, Laura felt a yearning to go with them. Even though she had been a Highway Patrol officer for several years, she had never gotten to the bottom of her love of the road. Which was why, so often, she volunteered for out-of-town assignments.

The Yates house—blue with gray trim—looked cramped and forlorn despite a new roof. On the left side, a paddock took up the equivalent of one lot, a buckskin gelding inside. Small but well put together, a quarter horse. In the open land across the street from the Yateses' house, someone had set up a barrel pattern—three oil drums forming a triangle. From the looks of the hard dry ground, no one had run the pattern in a long time.

The unkempt front yard of the Yateses' house was dominated by a tall apple tree. Fallen apples, not much bigger than golf balls, littered the walkway and the patch of grass in the front yard. The yard was enclosed by a waist-high chain-link fence matted with morning glories. A GMC work truck was parked face-out in the driveway, a horse trailer backed up next to the carport.

A little boy, couldn't be more than three years old, pedaled a Big Wheel over the cracked front walk. A toddler stood in a yellow playpen, alternately chortling and shrieking at the older boy's antics.

At the sound of Richie's loud engine cutting off, Laura saw a figure materialize behind the screen door, then dash outside.

For a minute Laura thought she was looking at Kellee Taylor come to life. But the hair was a shade darker, the features different, although they held a similar girl-next-door quality. This must be Dan's sister Shana. According to Josh Wingate, Shana and Dan were twins.

The girl reached down into the playpen and picked up the baby boy. She looked at them with open curiosity.

This was the part of the job Laura hated most, where you walked into someone's life and with a few words blew that life to smithereens.

Every time she did it, she was yanked back to the time and place where she had received news just like it. Sometimes she wondered what it was about her, what perverse part of her nature made her revisit this hideous ritual over and over again.

The girl, Shana, sensed something. Laura could tell by the protective way she held her little boy.

"Are you Shana Yates?"

The girl nodded, plainly wary.

Laura introduced herself and Richie. "May we come in?"

The girl looked diffidently from the baby to Richie, then nodded. She led the way into the house, holding the screen door for them. As Laura passed her she sensed the girl knew something was wrong. Could feel it, suspended on a taut wire of tension.

After the bright late-afternoon light, the house was gloomy. Laura's eyes adjusted quickly, though, drawn to the eight-by-ten framed photographs cluttering the wall near the brick fireplace: Shana on the buckskin horse. In most of them, Shana posed on the horse with ribbons, belt buckles, even a saddle. Some showed Shana and the horse—Mighty Mouse, according to the plaque—leaning deep into a barrel in a rooster tail of dust.

Now, in her early twenties, she was the mother of two children. Too busy to run the barrel pattern across the street?

Laura took a deep breath. "Are your parents here?"

Shana set the child down on the couch and sat beside him, holding on to his wriggling body. "They're in Flag for the day. What's going on?" She looked at Richie, who was transfixed by the fish tank underneath the photographs.

Richie looked at Shana. "Did you know that your brother was in town yesterday?" Richie asked. "Did you talk to him at all?"

"My brother? What about my brother?" Looking from one to the other, her nervousness quickly turning to panic. "What's going on?"

Experience had taught Laura that the sooner she told Shana, the better it would be for her. She knew it was no mercy to draw it out. She had to be clear, so there was no room for doubt. She walked over to Shana and squatted on her heels, looked her in the eye. "Shana, it's important you listen to me. Your brother Dan was shot and killed last night. Dan and Kellee both, they're gone."

Shana stared at her, her mouth moving. Looked at Richie. She stood up abruptly, letting go of the little boy. "Omigod. What hospital—"

Laura caught her hands. *Steady.* "He's gone, Shana. He was killed. Kellee was killed, too. Is there someone you can call?"

Shana breathed through her mouth, tiny little gulps of air. Staring at nothing, or some drear inner landscape. Then she transferred her gaze to Laura.

"My brother's dead?"

"I'm afraid he is."

"What happened? Was it a car accident?"

Shana was still trying to absorb what she'd been told. Her whole world had been blown to bits, and she was feeling her way toward the truth. In many of Laura's death notifications, families asked about car accidents, even though they had already been told their loved one had succumbed to a homicide. A car accident was something anyone could assimilate.

Laura said, "They were shot to death. Is there any way you can get in touch with your parents? Maybe you should call them so they can be here."

"I can't tell them—"

"No, you don't have to tell them. You could just ask them to come home. Or if you want, I could call them."

Shana was starting to shake. Her eyes red-rimmed, tears getting ready to fall. "No, they'd know the minute you— Oh, *no!*"

She collapsed onto the couch, grabbing at her hair, which had been caught up in a barrette at the back of her smooth neck. Pulling on it, wrangling it back and forth. "I can't get this *thing* out of my hair!"

"Do you need anything? We could get you a glass of water."

"Water? Sure, why not?" Her voice rising. With one last wrench, the barrette came out.

"If you don't want to talk to your parents," Laura said, "is there somebody else?"

She opened her mouth, almost said something. Then she started to cry. Just leaned her head on Laura's shoulder and sobbed.

The little boy was standing on the couch now, leaning against the back. He knew something was wrong. He slipped, fell to his knees, and clamped on to Shana's thigh, his face screwed up, ready to cry. Which he did with a burst—long, braying sobs.

Richie said, "It's not fair to let your parents—"

"Richie, could you go get Shana some water?" She said it politely, as Shana's warm tears seeped into her jacket.

"Sure." He disappeared into the kitchen and Laura heard him slamming around the cupboards, pouring water.

Just then a truck pulled into the driveway. Laura saw it through the window, out of the corner of her eye, as she continued to hold Shana.

Laura heard truck doors slam, voices, a little boy's shout. "Is that your parents' truck?" she asked Shana.

Shana looked at her numbly, nodded.

Richie appeared in the doorway with the water, looking toward the door.

A key turned in the lock and the door opened.

They sat around the kitchen table: Chuck Yates, his wife Louise, Laura and Richie. Shana leaned in the doorway of the kitchen, arms folded, watching and listening. Looking as if someone had slapped her face raw. Occasionally shouting at the little boy, Justin, to "quit running around and for God's sake stop *screaming!*" The baby, Adam, had been put down to sleep.

The notification had not gone easier with her parents. Mrs. Yates stubbornly refused to believe that her son Dan was dead. She resisted quietly, with dignity. She didn't argue, just refused to believe it—would not even let the possibility in. They had made a mistake.

That meant that after a while Laura had to address all her questions to Chuck Yates.

If Louise Yates refused to hear, Chuck Yates saw it coming and met it head-on. She saw him as an aging knight, tall as a redwood, facing the enemy and taking the blows—the killing blows.

"I guess I have to go identify him."

"We don't require that anymore," Richie said. "We have more than enough for identification."

"What are you saying?" Rubbed his grizzled forehead with one ham hand.

"You don't want to see him," Richie said.

His words took the air out of the room.

Laura glanced at Louise Yates. Her mouth was grim, her chin stubbornly set. Holding the line.

Laura said to Mr. Yates, "Do you know anybody who would want to do this to your son?"

He stared down at the yellow cheesecloth covering the round oak table, shook his head.

Shana said from the doorway, "What about Ray Simms?"

"Ray Simms?"

Shana shoved her fist under one red eye to catch more tears. "He used to be on the football team with Danny. He had it in for him because Danny was starting quarterback. He *hated* him."

"How long ago was that?"

She took a deep ragged breath. "Five years ago."

Laura dutifully wrote down Simms's name. "He still lives in Williams?"

"I think so." She tightened her arms around her chest, not letting anything in or out. Defiant.

"Did you see them yesterday?"

"I didn't even know they were in town," Chuck Yates said.

"That's not like Dan," Louise said. "If he was in town, he would have called."

Richie said, "Did you know about the wedding?"

He might as well have lobbed a bomb. Stunned silence radiated throughout the room.

At last Louise said, "Wedding? Whose wedding?"

Laura said, "Dan and Kellee got married yesterday. In Las Vegas."

Louise's face clamped down. "That can't be."

"It's true," Richie said. He handed her the photographs.

She glanced at the top photo, Kellee and Dan in front of the chapel, then put the stack facedown on the table. "I don't believe it."

Richie said, "Why's she in a dress like that? Why's she holding that rose?"

Laura looked at Richie and cleared her throat.

Richie saw her expression and hiked his shoulders: *What are you going to do?*

"I'll bet it was a play," Louise Yates said. "Kellee has a drama class."

Richie opened his mouth to say something, but Laura gave him another look.

Chuck Yates reached over and touched his wife's hand. She jerked back as if he had dashed boiling water on her instead. The look in her eyes as she regarded her husband—Laura could swear there was loathing there.

"Louise—"

"Don't you say a word. Dan would tell us. He wouldn't go behind our backs like that. It's just not true."

"Why would they tell us this if it wasn't true?" Chuck asked.

"They made a mistake, is all."

Richie mouthed to Laura: *Denial ain't just a river in Egypt.*

She ignored him. Her gaze strayed to Shana. The girl had straightened up against the doorjamb, and Laura could swear she saw alarm in her eyes.

"Shana?" Laura asked her. "Did you know Dan and Kellee were getting married?"

The shutters came down. "Huh-uh."

"Dan didn't say anything? A hint, maybe, something you might have misinterpreted?"

She shook her head and recrossed her arms. "Nope."

Louise stood up. "Would you like coffee?"

Laura smiled at her. "That would be nice."

She smiled back. "Dan got me a coffee grinder for Christmas. I have a macadamia-nut—"

"That would be fine."

Richie turned to Chuck. "Anyone else you'd consider an enemy?"

"Dan mentioned some kid had a crush on Kellee."

"Oh?"

"He didn't think much about it, but the kid was pretty obvious." She thought he was going to say something else, but he only stared at the refrigerator.

"You know his name?"

"Jamie Cottle. His dad owns Shade Tree Mechanics here in town."

The coffee grinder roared to life, drowning out all other sounds.

"Honey," Chuck said. "Could you stop that? We're talking."

The sound rose to a grating shriek, then stopped suddenly, like the abbreviated cry of an animal taken in the night.

Louise's eyes darted from one to another—everyone in the room. Her eyes small.

"I won't believe it. Not unless I see for myself."

7

At the briefing, Laura met the Williams police chief, Peter Loffgren, who had arrived late in the day. It was Loffgren who had called DPS early this morning to ask for assistance. The Phoenix DPS—much closer to Williams—had been unable to send anyone, and so the directive had gone down to Tucson.

The shape of the chief's head—his receding hairline, lack of chin, and thin neck—made Laura think of a lightbulb. He must have stopped off on his trip back to don his uniform. She liked the fact that his eyes, which at first glance seemed lazy, missed nothing.

Six of them took up the small conference room—Chief Loffgren, Warren Janes, Ben Tagg, Josh Wingate, and Laura and Richie.

Laura had already looked through Dan Yates's wallet, which had been brought back this afternoon from the ME's office. In it were several receipts and one credit card. Something else had gone with Dan to the medical examiner's office: the marriage license, still in its stiff envelope. It had been tucked into the inside pocket of Dan's jacket. Laura wondered if he had kept it there, on his person, so the two of them could look at it whenever they wanted.

The discussion centered on the canvass of the houses near Cataract Lake.

According to Tagg, a few people had heard three or four (there were conflicting stories) shotgun blasts around ten o'clock at night. The time was generally agreed to because two families in houses just north of the campground had been watching the local news at ten.

Tagg said, "The people I talked to heard it but they didn't do anything."

"Why not?" Laura asked.

Tagg shrugged. "A lot of hunters around here. The locals hear plenty of gunshots in rural areas."

"At ten o'clock at night?"

"There's folks that've been known to jacklight deer."

What Josh Wingate had said.

"Plus, a lot of people hear gunshots, they try to talk themselves out of it," the chief said. "They're not sure they're gunshots, tell themselves it's a backfire."

Laura knew that was true. She also knew most people hearing gunshots would stay inside for safety reasons. Because they didn't go out to see if it really was gunfire, they were often too embarrassed to call it in. No one liked to be thought of as a busybody.

After the police officers left for their shift, Laura, Richie and the chief sat down and talked it through. She gave the chief what she knew—the rough time line of the events, the fact that Dan and Kellee had gotten married and had not told Dan Yates's family.

"The parents had no idea they were in town," Richie said. "They cooked up this whole thing and their family didn't even know."

"I think Shana knew," Laura said.

Loffgren said, "You do? I know they were close. Dan was always looking out for her. Little things you'd see. Dan was in and out of our house a lot when he was a kid, and a lot of times he brought her along."

"I bet that went down well," Richie said.

"She had one hell of a fastball as I remember," Loffgren said. "So what do you think this is? You have any ideas?"

"Could be a stranger," Richie said. "Somebody just did it for kicks. It happens."

"Kids?"

"Could be," Laura said. "Although whoever it was sanitized the scene. That doesn't sound like kids."

"Could it be a serial killer?" Loffgren asked. "Random shooting for whatever reason, but he covers his tracks? Maybe this is his ritual."

They'd already run it on VICAP, but had found nothing similar. Random shootings, yes, plenty of them. But nothing like this. "If there were others, it could point to that," Laura said. "We don't have enough information at this point to know. You're aware that agencies only report to VICAP if they're in the network—and a lot of the smaller agencies aren't."

"We just got on ourselves, last year."

Laura said, "The kind of guy who'd walk around a tent shooting inside without looking to see if his victims are dead doesn't fit with the cunning it would take to cover up tracks, take his shell casings. Unless he knew them *too* well, and didn't want to see what he'd done."

Richie rubbed the tip of his nose. "I notice you said, 'guy,' Laura. Why be exclusive? It could be a female."

"It could."

"But unlikely," Loffgren said.

Richie leaned back and clasped his hands behind his head. "I don't know. Women these days are as capable as men. That female serial killer in Florida, the one they made the movie about? And on our side, you know, what Laura herself did."

"That was good work," Loffgren said.

"You know it. She makes the rest of us look bad."

Laura ignored that. "Chief, I don't think it's a woman running around with a shotgun. Sure, there are women out there who could do it, like from the military, maybe some-one from one of the ranches around here, but it's a less likely scenario than the other. While I wouldn't rule anything out, going down that road too far would be counter-productive, in my opinion."

Loffgren looked from one to the other and sighed. "We've got to put our backs into this. Dan was a good kid—the best kind of American—and from what I hear, so was Kellee. They didn't deserve this."

"I agree," Richie said.

"It's hit our family pretty hard—hell, everybody in town is upset about this. This is a small town and everybody knows each other. I want whoever did this."

He didn't say it, but Laura got his intention loud and clear.

Whatever's going on between the two of you, don't let it get in the way.

One thing you could say for Richie Lockhart's car: It could corner. Laura found herself enjoying the curvaceous drive down off the rim in and out of the moonlight shadows alongside Oak Creek.

At the northern end of the canyon where the trees were thickest, they bottomed out in a turn. Before them, on the left, a wooden sign grew out of an island of zinnias and petunias, lit from beneath: TAYLOR'S CREEKSIDE CABINS.

A rustic country store faced out to the road. Laura guessed that at one time there had been gas pumps out front.

The sign above the door said, TAYLOR'S CREEKSIDE COUNTRY STORE: EST. 1924. Behind the store were several cabins reached by landscaped paths, the thick ground cover shining from recent watering. Fanning out, the farthest cabins stood among a smattering of ponderosa pines—she could see the cozy glow of lights here and there. Judging from the cars in the parking lot, the place was full up.

They stepped out into the crisp night air. Laura could smell earth and flowers and hear the sound of the crickets. The nicest thing, though—she looked up and could see the stars.

Looking around, Richie said, "Quaint, huh?"

Laura prepared herself as they walked up the steps to the store. Two notifications in one night—a great introduction to hell. The bell over the door tinkled as they walked in. A pretty, middle-aged Asian woman sat on a stool behind the high counter on the left of the tiny store, underneath a buzzing Marlboro sign.

Laura glanced around: There were three aisles stocked with condiments and snacks—the condiments all in small jars and bottles. A cold drink case spanned the wall on the opposite end from the counter—beer, wine, soft drinks, bottled water. She noticed a revolving paperback rack and a tiny section for video rentals. The videotape boxes were faded from the sun. A white four-door cold case took up half the wall to the right of the cash register. It could have been original with the building. One of the doors was cluttered with snapshots of fishermen displaying their catches, hunters holding up the heads of deer who could no longer hold them up for themselves, and a man posing with a red, white, and blue plane: FLY THE GRAND CANYON—HIGH PINES CHARTER FLIGHTS—GLENN TRAYWICK, PROPRIETOR.

Richie asked the clerk if they could talk to Jack Taylor.

"What is this about?" the woman asked, eyes wary.

He showed her his wallet badge. "We need to talk to him about his daughter."

"Kellee? What's wrong?" The woman leaned against the counter, the whole of her small body taut. "Is she all right?"

"That's really a matter for—"

Laura said, "You know Kellee well?"

"She's my stepdaughter. Is she all right?"

Her face was pale, her black hair like silk, tiny blue threads catching the light.

"We'd like to talk to you both—can you reach your husband?"

In the fish-belly-white glare of the Marlboro sign, the woman's face looked stark with fear. She picked up a walkie-talkie from under the desk. "Jack? Jack, come to the office—there's . . . someone here you need to talk to."

An older man's voice, amiable and slightly hoarse, said, "Be right up."

His voice comforting; the kind of voice that automatically allayed fears. The woman held the walkie-talkie to her ear long after he had signed off.

Her hand was shaking, her eyes dark. She watched as Richie wandered to the back of the store to look at videotapes, then turned to Laura. "I have to know. She's dead, isn't she?"

Laura had to answer her. "I'm sorry, Mrs. Taylor—"

A weak smile. "Megumi." She held out a soft white hand—decorum in the middle of grief. "So she is dead."

"Yes, ma'am. She died last night."

"I had this feeling."

"Why? Why would you have that feeling?"

"I thought it might have come back."

Laura was about to ask her to elaborate when the bell above the door rang. A tall, seventyish gray-haired man entered, ducking his head to avoid the lintel. "Megumi? What's going on?"

He had an open, tanned face, lined from sun. Blue eyes that held a degree of calculation in them. He wore a plaid flannel shirt tucked into gray trousers, a hand-tooled leather belt with a sand-cast silver-and-turquoise buckle in a wheel shape—Navajo. Arms loose at his sides, he looked like someone who was used to hard physical work. He reminded Laura of her father, a schoolteacher who could fix anything and loved outdoor work.

Laura told the Taylors everything. When and where Dan and Kellee were found, the fact that they had eloped to Las Vegas.

Richie remained at the back of the store, engrossed in old videotapes. Letting her do the heavy lifting.

The man, Jack Taylor, didn't react the way she expected.

He accepted it immediately, seeming to have skipped part of the spectrum—shock, denial, anger—and landed on sad.

"It's ironic," he said.

"Ironic?"

"Kellee nearly died three years ago. She had a brain tumor. The diagnosis was—they said—it was inoperable."

"What happened?"

He opened his hands. Calloused and rough; hands used to work. "It went away. Like that. Just . . . evaporated."

"They did so many tests," Megumi Taylor said. "MRI, CAT scan, blood tests. But it was gone."

"The doctors couldn't explain it," said Taylor. He leaned against the counter, sagged. A big man bending under the weight of the unthinkable. Except he *had* thought about it, thought about it a lot. "It always felt like we were living on borrowed time. We even had a plot picked out in the cemetery in Sedona. She wanted us to celebrate her life, to have a life afterward."

Megumi said, "She's—she was Jack's only child."

"My wife died when she was little. She grew up here, helping me around the place in the summers, and then she went to college—" He wiped at his nose. "She landscaped this place, you know that? Just a kid in high school."

His tears falling on the counter.

Laura waited, feeling that familiar sinking in her heart as she absorbed the pain of others. *I'm like a shock absorber*, she thought. *One that doesn't work so well.*

Richie had stopped browsing, and stood quietly. Listening to the pain in Jack Taylor's voice.

Laura asked them if they knew Kellee was planning on getting married.

"I knew she wanted to," Taylor said. "She loved Dan. He was a nice kid. You could do a lot worse. Responsible, serious. Although I worried about the religious aspect."

"Religious aspect?" Richie asked.

"The Yateses. Chuck is very active in the Southern Baptist church. Nothing wrong with that, but." Jack Taylor took

Megumi's hand in his. "We're not big on religion. We both think—" He looked at her. "There's been so much misery in the world because of religion. Although, you could say what happened to Kellee was a miracle."

Laura thought, but didn't say, that it was strange that God had spared Kellee from death three years ago, only to allow her life to be taken now. Laura understood their ambivalence. Although she believed in God—she just *did*— she had a hard time understanding where He stood on things.

She'd seen the unspeakable. Hard to fathom, a loving God.

Jack Taylor did not look up, but stroked Megumi's tiny hand with a giant, calloused thumb. "Now I'm glad they did get married. Maybe that was what Kellee was waiting for."

They stopped off at a freeway exit for some fast food and sat in the car under the sodium arc lights of the Burger King. Laura tried to eat healthily at home, but whenever she went on one of these trips, all bets were off. On the road, a McDonald's Big Mac or a Jack in the Box Supreme Crescent offered unique comfort. Even the smell of fried food acted on her like a soporific drug.

Laura was glad Richie was driving. On the way back to Williams, she closed her eyes and listened to the deep, throaty engine, to the hum of the tires on the freeway as they left Flagstaff and drove out onto the high northern Arizona plateau, feeling the accumulated psychic weight of this day.

When they drove into Williams, it was going on eleven. Too late to call home. Tom got up early—a habit for both of them. What Laura really wanted to do was ask him about this morning. She wouldn't do that, though. How could she frame it without sounding whiny and insecure?

Laura was convinced that if she just heard his voice, she'd know immediately if he just hadn't been in the mood—which was fine—or if it went deeper than that.

It was too late to call, so it was a moot point. She was re-lieved, but also just that little bit more anxious, because not calling put off the moment of truth a little longer.

On the way into town they detoured by the Williams PD. The yellow-brick building on the main drag was quiet, the lighted alcove open to the street, one lonely guy behind the window inside. He recognized them, though, celebrities that they were.

"The chief called in a while ago," Officer Donnelly said. He had thick glasses that magnified his pale eyes and a comb-over of dyed brown hair. He handed Laura a While You Were Out slip with Loffgren's home number on it. "He said to go ahead and call as late as you want."

She called from the station, Loffgren picking up on the second ring.

"Thought you should know about this. There have been three reports of road-rage incidents between here and Las Vegas in the last couple of months. One on 93 just north of Kingman, two on I-40. The Mojave County sheriff's department investigated all three. The investigator's name is David Fellows. He's on duty tonight. I'll give you the number."

"Two of the incidents were pretty typical," David Fel-lows told her when she reached him. "Someone gets cut off, the other guy flips the bird, it escalates. Fortunately, noth-ing came of either one of them.

"The third one, though—that's another story. A woman was turning onto 93 toward Vegas, just outside of Kingman. Guy came right up on her tail, almost clipped her. Both the driver and passenger yelling obscenities. The victim says the passenger waved a gun at her."

"What kind of gun?"

"She said it was big. A rifle of some sort. She didn't get his license, it happened so fast. I can fax you the report."

Laura got a description of the vehicle—a black truck, newer model. The woman couldn't describe it any better than that.

"Road rage could fit," Richie said when Laura hung up. "Dan pisses somebody off on the way back from Vegas, guy gets mad, follows them all the way to Williams. Bang."

"But why wait?"

"Yeah, you've got a point there. They got here, what? Four thirty? What was the guy doing between then and ten o'clock that night?"

"I'll check it out tomorrow, anyway." Laura was starting to drag. Now that she had made her decision about calling Tom, all she wanted to do was get her stuff into a motel room and go to sleep.

Most of the motels on the main drag were built in the forties and fifties, many of them renovated but still looking the way they had in their heyday.

They settled on the Pioneer, an L-shaped motel on a newly resurfaced parking lot, a covered-wagon sign out front, and a line of pink neon running along the eaves just under the roofline. HBO and a coffeemaker in every room.

8

What a relief.

All day she had been building it up in her mind, what in retrospect was an incident of no importance at all—the way Tom had warded her off this morning. Her fears had proved baseless. Tom showed up at the motel shortly after she did. He had everything packed in his truck—tent, wine, bread and cheese for a midnight snack. Now here they were at Cataract Lake. After some torrid lovemaking, they lay entwined, drowsing in each other's arms.

The whole incident forgotten.

As Laura lay in the shelter of Tom's body, she understood that everything had changed. She, who prided herself on her independence, realized that she had committed herself to him. The commitment was clean and hard and pure, and she didn't want to go back to the way it was before. You couldn't unring a bell, and Laura found that she didn't want to.

Luxuriating in his closeness, she felt his breath on her shoulder, his sides rising and falling in sleep. And she smiled. Drowsed.

The crunch of a twig startled her into full wakefulness. In an instant, every muscle, every nerve, every synapse was on alert.

A laugh. Or was it the wind rustling through the trees way up?

No, a laugh. Barely there, crude and insinuating.

She huddled in the tent, stone-scared, Tom beside her still deep in sleep. Her heart pounding.

A shoe scraped on dirt. Laura braced herself, knew what was coming next, but for some reason, couldn't move. But Tom did. He erupted from the sleeping bag and took hold of her, dragging her across the tent with incredible force, covering her with his body just as the first volley blasted through the tent like a rocket booster.

Shot peppering the inside of the tent, exploding in the ground beside her. Three loud blasts. She must be hit but was still in shock, the organs of her body no doubt already breaking down—

Tom's grip loosening suddenly, Laura squirming in his arms, trying to see him, his blood raining down on her face. The realization that he was dead barreling through her, dousing her in sweat.

An excruciating cramp in her calf.

Automatically, she shortened the muscle in her leg. The pain vanished in an instant. The harmonica chord of a passing train sounded close by. She realized she was in a motel room in Williams, on old Route 66, alone. No Tom. No one shooting at them. The sheets plastered to her with sweat.

The train horn again. The desert where she lived outside Tucson was two miles as the crow flew from the railroad tracks. The train tracks here were only a block away.

She sat up in bed and got her bearings. A generic motel room, the yellow porch light from the walk outside creeping in around the curtains and staining the round table by the window. As the train horn receded, Laura noticed a *ping-ping-ping* sound coming from down the street. The pain in her calf gone completely, she got out of bed and looked out, isolating the sound: the chain on the flagpole outside Williams PD, pinging every time the flag unfurled in the wind.

It was windy. She could hear it, scrabbling in the corners of the motel, gusting through the trees, the scraping branch on the bathroom window. A restless night.

Flicking on the light, she went into the bathroom and stared at her face. She looked the same. Just another bad dream in a string of bad dreams.

"Seems to me you've been having a lot of those, lately."

Laura stared past her own reflection through the bathroom doorway at Frank Entwistle, sitting in the chair by the door.

She said, "It goes with the job."

"You know it." The retired TPD homicide cop, recently dead, crossed one leg over his knee at the ankle. She could see a spot where his wife Pat had darned his socks. Who darned socks anymore?

It occurred to her that she hadn't visited Pat since Frank's burial. This made her feel guilty.

Entwistle lit a cigarette. Laura could swear she smelled it, dry and slightly cloying, like the wind chuckling at the doorjamb outside.

"What do you think about this guy, Dan? Quite the hero, huh? First instinct was to save his wife. Kid had guts, shielding her like that."

"I know."

"I bet you'd do anything to get the guy who did this."

"You've got that right."

"You'd do anything to get him, and that's good. But the way you're going about it . . . ." He shook his head.

"What do you mean?"

"Lorie, you think you can fool me? This isn't about Dan Yates and Kellee Taylor. It's about you."

She felt as if he'd pried up something, a piece of wood over a window, just the edge. Just warping it a little, enough to let in a pinhole of light. "How's it about me?" she asked, aware that her voice sounded weak and high.

Entwistle rubbed the bridge of his nose, the cigarette dangerously close to his eyebrows. He did not look good.

His face was the unhealthy pink of a glistening ham, and his white hair was almost translucent. Appropriate for a ghost.

"You're not helping anybody, the way you're going."

"That's bullshit."

"What's that Bible quote? Take the log out of your own eye before trying to take the mote out of someone else's?"

"What does *that* mean?" She grabbed a washcloth, saturated it with water, started going over her arms and legs to rid herself of the dried sweat. "This is ridiculous."

"Just a piece of advice, kiddo. Work the case because it's your job."

"I'm planning on it."

He stood up. "This place is starting to fence me in. I'm gonna take a walk." He opened the door and looked back at her, his eyes sad. "You know what they say, though. People in glass houses shouldn't throw stones."

Another damn cliché. If she had to be haunted by a ghost, why couldn't she have one with a fresh thought in his head?

Entwistle pointed his finger at her. "And you're the one in the glass house."

He walked out into the restless dark, the wind tugging on the top piece of the hair that looked like a toupee but wasn't, and shut the door behind him.

Laura went to the door and opened it.

As she'd expected, the parking lot was empty.

9

The air had a chill to it when Laura turned out of the Pioneer motel parking lot a little after five the next morning. The place was dead quiet on a Sunday morning, the street empty except for a crumpled-up fast-food wrapper scudding along the curb.

She stopped at Circle K on the main drag for coffee, parking beside an old International Scout with the engine running and a hunting dog in the back. Two guys in cammos holding a six-pack of beer and snacks nodded to her as they got in.

Feeling out of balance and mildly depressed, she dog-legged over to First Street to avoid the one-way street, and took the road out of town.

She and Richie had decided to split up for the day. He would drive to Northern Arizona University in Flagstaff and talk to Dan's and Kellee's friends and roommates. Laura would retrace the young couple's movements to and from Las Vegas.

On the seat beside her was a photocopy of a gas receipt from a Circle K in Kingman, photos of Dan and Kellee from the trip, and their marriage license.

She doubted the answer would be found in Vegas, but she couldn't ignore the one detail in the Route 93 road-rage incident—the passenger waving a rifle. Laura didn't like the lag time between Dan and Kellee's drive back and the time they were killed, but there could be an explanation. She'd seen stranger things in her career as a detective.

On the way, Laura found herself thinking not about the case but about what Frank Entwistle had said about glass houses.

She knew she was brittle, that in some ways she was barely hanging on. She acknowledged that this was why Tom's lack of interest yesterday morning had wounded her so deeply. In a world where every little thing seemed to get to her, she'd counted on Tom Lightfoot as the only person in her life she could depend on. Maybe she depended on him too much.

Laura knew about needy people. She didn't like them herself, so why would she expect Tom to? Tom had spent a large part of his life alone, living his life his way. That was part of what attracted her to him—a man in his mid-thirties who wrangled horses and tourists on a guest ranch. She didn't want someone who would make too many demands on her. At least she'd *thought* she didn't.

Initially, she'd resisted letting him move in with her. Now it turned out that the situation was reversed, and she was the demanding one.

The realization struck her: When it came to sex, she was always the initiator. Always. What did that say about their relationship?

If they were on a seesaw, she'd be the one up in the air.

At Kingman she got off at the exit with the Circle K where Dan and Kellee had bought gas.

The clerk at the Circle K didn't recognize Dan or Kellee, even though she had worked Friday morning. Laura wasn't surprised. There were probably fifteen people inside at the moment, and a line of six waiting to pay. The clerk's eyes kept darting nervously to the people behind Laura.

Laura turned around, looking for the surveillance camera, and found it situated in the corner of the store opposite the counter. "I'd like to talk to the manager."

The clerk picked up the pager and called for Reggie Fortin, clearly relieved that Laura was now someone else's problem.

Reggie Fortin led her into the small cubicle that served as the office. He was college age, probably ten years younger than the clerk, and had an ever-present smile that looked as if it were held up by invisible wires.

"How long do your surveillance tapes go?"

He leaned back and clasped his hands behind his head. He wore a short-sleeved white shirt frayed around the collar, and ghosted with yellow stains under the arms. "One VCR tape lasts twenty-four hours. We store the tapes for thirty-one days."

"You have, what, two cameras?"

"We don't have an outside camera at this store."

Laura asked to see yesterday's. He asked if she had a warrant—something a lot of people did these days. What with all the cop shows on TV, a lot of people liked to prove they knew the drill.

Laura said, "I don't have a warrant."

That stopped him. He sat there, tapping his shoe, pretending to think it over. She let the silence stretch; she wasn't about to help him.

"Okay," he said at last. "I guess it wouldn't hurt. This a murder investigation?"

"It's important, or I wouldn't ask."

Thinking as she said it that this whole trip was probably pointless. What was she hoping the videotape would show? A black truck pulled up to the pumps, two guys with shotguns picking a fight with Dan?

He put the tape in the VCR and cued it up to eight A.M. Laura figured that eight would be the earliest Dan and Kellee would get to Kingman; it was a hundred-and-fifty-mile drive from Flagstaff. Judging from the shadows on the dam, Laura was pretty sure they didn't get to Hoover Dam before nine o'clock.

She watched a parade of people coming into the frame to

pay the clerk. Had to stop a couple of times, but none of
them looked like Dan or Kellee. No suspicious-looking
black trucks, either. She was up to ten o'clock now. That
was cutting it close.

"Let's go back. Start it at seven this time."

Dutifully, Reggie Fortin ran it back. She watched again,
trying to keep her mind from wandering.

Then she saw the blond girl. She had passed over her before because she wore jeans, not shorts.

"Stop."

He hit the remote and froze the girl in the frame, diago-
nal lines shimmering across the top.

"You want me to go back?"

"Just a minute."

The girl wore jeans and a camisole top, her hair pulled
up loosely in a barrette.

"Go back," she said. He rewound the tape for a few seconds, then forwarded it again.

"Stop."

The view of the counter came from the far corner of the
room, so mostly Laura was seeing the customers' backs.
But the blonde turned back to look at someone behind her,
said something to him.

Laura knew her.

The blonde was Shana Yates.

The Forget Me Not Wedding Chapel was a Tudor-style
cottage set back from a side street just off the strip, aproned
by a close-shaved lawn, the same glitter-green as indoor-
outdoor carpeting in the harsh Vegas sun. At the right time
of day, the chapel would be swallowed up by the shadow of
one of the behemoth hotel-casinos on the strip.

The sign out front, shocking pink, depicted the silhouette of a bride. She had her hand up to her mouth in a way
that Laura thought was sly.

The hostess who greeted her was fortyish, with wild
hennaed gypsy hair. She wore a long-sleeved white lace

dress that flounced down to the tops of white cowgirl boots. It was an outfit straight out of the 1980s, right down to the shoulder pads. Her nameplate said AUDREY.

Audrey reached out a ring-encrusted hand and grabbed Laura's wrist, hauling her into the cramped anteroom. A mullioned bay window with three window seats took up half the room. Each window was dressed with swagged gray velvet over lace, and cute little knicknacks were propped or hung everywhere—all of them dangling tiny price tags.

"What kind of wedding are you thinking of?" Audrey asked, her large mascaraed eyes sizing Laura up. "We have a very good special going on right now, only a hundred and twenty-nine ninety-nine, it includes photos, video cam, witnesses, limousine service, a rose for the bride, a boutonniere—"

"I'm not here for a wedding." Laura displayed her badge wallet and introduced herself, wondering what it was about her that made Audrey offer her the cheapest package. She showed the woman the photographs of Dan and Kellee.

"I remember them. A really cute couple. Let me go get my wedding book." She bustled out of the anteroom, rose scent trailing in her wake, and returned with a massive white leatherette binder festooned with ribbons and bugle beads. She sat down, the book across her knees. "Ah. Here it is." She turned the book around for Laura to see.

It was a description of the wedding service package Dan Yates and Kellee Taylor had chosen, "Promises," for $199.99.

The most expensive package, for $499.99, was called "Forever."

"It says here the 'Promises' package includes photos and video. Do you have them?"

"The photos haven't been developed yet, and our videographer is editing the tape. We contract all our photography out to one wedding photographer. The same with the video; that's—let me think—I-Cam Video Productions. The photos should be done by Wednesday and sent to the bride and groom. . . ." Suddenly, she touched her wine-red lacquered nails to her wine-red lips, the realization dawning that something might not be well with the bride and groom. "They're all right, aren't they? Nothing's happened to them?" Her eyes widened. "The shooting at that campground! That was in Williams, wasn't it? My girlfriend lives there, and I thought of her when I heard about it—"

"Ma'am, may I have the number for the photographer?"

"It *was* them, wasn't it?" Her expression both stricken and avid. "She was such a beautiful bride. Both those girls were just gorgeous."

"Shana Yates?"

"I think that was her name. The sister. She could have worn something other than jeans, that's for sure. So it's true? The young couple in the campground—I saw it on the news this morning."

Laura didn't see the point in denying it. By now, Dan's and Kellee's names would have been released to the press. "The sister was a witness to the wedding?"

"Her and her boyfriend." Disapproval in her tone when she said, "boyfriend."

"Boyfriend?"

"I assumed he was her boyfriend, but he could have just been the best man."

"What gave you the impression he was her boyfriend?"

"Just the way she acted around him. There's a word . . . proprietary."

"Like she owned him?"

Audrey nodded. "Pretty girl like that, you'd think she could have anybody. This guy was no catch."

"Could you describe him?"

"He was older than her—I'd guess at *least* mid-thirties. Hard years, too. He just seemed low-class."

"Why is that?"

"His clothes. There's no smoking in the chapel, so he

kept everybody waiting while he finished his cigarette outside. I mean, why bother being a witness at all?"

"He sounds self-centered."

Her eyes lit up. "That's it, you put your finger on it. It was all about him."

"Do you know his name?"

"Just a minute. We always have the witnesses sign for the license and the book."

She came back with a small slip of paper, a name scribbled on it. A name Laura didn't recognize: Robert Burdette.

10

"What's that?" June Burdette demanded as her son pushed the dolly holding the oversize box up her walkway, doing his best to avoid one of her hundred garden gnomes and whirligigs.

"You'll see."

"It's not another washing machine, is it? That last one you bought was junk. I hope you didn't go and spend even more money on a replacement. I'm used to it now."

"It's not a washing machine." Bobby Burdette tipped the dolly expertly up the two steps of her front stoop—his years of driving for a moving company were good for something. "Hold the door for me, will you?"

His mother took her sweet time. He noticed she was wearing a new housecoat, which looked just like her old ones, except the colors weren't faded.

With a big sigh, she held the screen door open. "Hurry up, the doctor says I shouldn't hold my arm in the same position a long time, my rotator cuff's gone—it's just bone on bone. Watch the recliner!" She let the door swing shut behind them and followed him in. The room, as usual, was as gloomy as a cave.

"I don't know why you have to keep buying me things. I don't want any more clutter."

"Wait until you see this."

"I'll wait in the kitchen. I'm watching *Days of our Lives.*"

Ten minutes later he went into the kitchen. She was sitting at the Formica table, hunched over the thirteen-inch TV he'd had in his room when he was a kid.

"Come and take a look."

She heaved herself to her feet. "What is it this time?"

"It's a surprise, Ma."

Her mouth squinched up in distaste. "You don't have money to throw away. If you ever did earn a decent living, you'd spend it all in a weekend."

He could feel his blood pressure rising, took a deep breath. "It's a present. For your birthday."

"My birthday's a month away."

She was getting old and ornery; he had to make allowances. "It was on sale now," he said patiently.

June Burdette got up and followed her son into her living room. The forty-inch wide-screen TV looked out of place in a room that had not changed since the 1950s—Early American furniture and throw rugs on brown linoleum. The old set had actually had red yarn tied in bows on the rabbit ears. *Rabbit ears!*

"What's that?"

"It's a TV. A DLP—what they call a projection-screen TV. It's got a wide screen so you can watch your basketball games."

"I like my Magnavox. Where is it?"

"I put it out front."

"Well, bring it back in. I don't want this thing. It's ugly."

Ugly? Her house was ugly. Her housecoats were ugly. Her bald spot was ugly. The way she looked out of her eyes was ugly—she never saw anything good.

"Did you hear me?" she was saying. "Bring it back! I don't want your stupid big-screen TV. Take it back where you got it."

"If that's the way you want it." Clenching his teeth to keep from saying more, Bobby stalked outside and picked up the old Magnavox. He wanted to hurl it out into the yard, take off the heads of some of those fucking garden gnomes. He wanted to throw it on the ground and stomp the living shit out of it.

Instead, he brought it back inside and placed it on the floor.

"Don't hurt it. That TV set has lasted twenty years. Unlike you, I can't afford to go around spending money like it's going out of style."

"I bought it for *you*."

"Well, I don't want it."

He turned the new set on.

She stared at the set. "It sure is clear. I thought these big things were hazy."

"It's DLP—as good as it gets."

"Well if that isn't a good picture. Almost as good as the Magnavox. Hmph." She touched it with the toe of her slip-on moccasin. "Well, it's here now. You might as well leave it here. No point you taking it back now. Where's it from, one of those big box stores? That's the only place you could afford to buy something like this. You know what they'll do, don't you? They'll charge you a reboxing fee. That's the problem with those places—they sell you something cheap and hope that when you get it home you won't be satisfied. Then they get extra money for nothing." She picked up the remote, still sheathed in plastic, her little bird eyes bright as she traced over the buttons. "If you take it back it'll just be throwing good money after bad."

"Then you want it?"

"It's here now. I don't want you to have to make another trip."

Every time, every single time, she did this to him. He'd come over, think that maybe just this once she'd be appreciative, she'd give a little instead of take, take, take, and every single fucking time he was disappointed.

"I'm just saving you another trip. Seems like you're always making two trips: one to buy, and one to repent. Why can't you just once think before you act?"

"I can think all right."

She snorted. "You never had an original thought in your life. I've always had to look out for you. Why you can't be more like Steven—"

"Steve's a damn junkie, Ma."

"Don't use that kind of language with me. He got through high school, didn't he? What have you ever done?"

He wanted to tell her what he was about to do, but kept his mouth shut. "You want me to take the TV set back or not?"

"You can leave it here."

"You could thank me."

She looked away.

He wanted to ask her why she had to be so mean to him, why she never once cut him any slack. Why she treated him like he was a dog turd she'd picked up on one of her moccasins. "What's so hard about saying thank-you?"

"I thanked you."

"You did not."

"I did."

Sometimes he wanted to wring her chicken neck.

"Your problem is," she said, "you don't listen. You don't listen and you don't follow anything through. A normal person would ask me what I wanted for my birthday. Like Steven—"

"I don't see you getting anything from him."

"He'll come through. He always does."

Suddenly he flashed on his Bible class at the First Pentacostal Church his mother used to take him to—how the teacher told them they could pick any Bible story they wanted and draw a picture. He had chosen Cain and Abel. And just like Cain, the gifts he had to offer her were never good enough.

He didn't know why he bothered.

"Another thing—you said you were going to take care of

that tree out there for me. One of these days it's going to fall on the house."

"I said I will and I will. As soon as I get some time."

She folded her arms. "See? That's exactly what I mean. You're always saying you're going to do something, then find some excuse not to."

"I've got to go." He started for the door.

"What about the Magnavox?"

"What about it?"

"You going to throw it out? You know how my back is, I can't do it."

He wanted to tell her she could shove the fucking Magnavox, but he didn't.

He took it with him and threw it in a Dumpster on his way back home.

11

It was going on three o'clock in the afternoon when Laura got back to Williams. She bypassed the motel and turned onto the street where Shana Yates lived.

When she arrived at the Yateses' house this time, no children were in evidence. Out front, the two-horse trailer was hitched to the beat-up old truck and Shana Yates was in the process of loading Mighty Mouse. Shana draped the lead rope over the little horse's back and he dutifully walked right in. Shana ducked into the horse trailer to tie him up, then opened the side window. Immediately, Mighty Mouse's nose poked out, nostrils fluttering as he pulled in the scents, a green straw of alfalfa already sticking out of his mouth.

Shana looked good in jeans and a green long-sleeved blouse. When she saw Laura, uncertainty flitted across her face, as if she had encountered someone who was out of place. "Hi," she said, the smile not reaching her eyes.

"Hi, Shana. Can we talk?"

Shana gestured to the trailer. "I'm kind of busy."

"Going to a rodeo?"

"Rodeo?"

Laura glanced at the cleared land across the street. "You're a barrel racer, aren't you?"

"Well, actually, I don't ride anymore."

"Oh?"

There was an awkward silence. Then Shana said, "Well, I've got to go."

"Can I come along?"

"Uh. I might be gone for a while."

"I've got time. There are a few more things I need to get cleared up." She added, "Finding out who did this to Dan."

Shana looked torn. She obviously didn't want to talk to Laura, but she loved her brother. The love of her brother won. "Okay."

Laura got into the passenger side of the truck, which looked as if it had been hit by a bomb. Papers, fast-food wrappers, magazines, a halter that had seen better days, an old cowboy hat, water bottles, candy bars—all sharing space with her feet.

"Where are we going?" Laura asked as they pulled slowly out onto the street.

Shana paused, her face drawn. Then she said, "I'm selling Mighty Mouse."

That stunned her. "Is there some special reason you're selling him now?"

Shana's shoulders rose and fell. "It's just time. I'm a mom now."

"How're Adam and Justin?"

"Good. They're with Ronnie."

"Who's Ronnie?"

"Their dad." She glanced at Laura. "I know what you're gonna ask next. We're divorced."

"But you still see each other?"

"Why would you think that? I hate his ass."

"I thought your ex might be the guy you were with in Vegas."

Shana colored. "I wouldn't go anywhere with him." She glanced in her rearview mirror as she shifted down for the turn onto Cataract Road. At last she said, "So I knew about Dan and Kellee. What's the big deal?"

"Nothing, except maybe your parents would have liked to know."

"That was up to Dan, wasn't it? You can leave me out of it."

"But you're in it. You knowingly lied to me. Do you think I'm just playing around here? This is a murder investigation, and we're talking about your brother's death."

Shana slapped the steering wheel. "Okay. Fine."

"How long did you know about Dan and Kellee's wedding plans?"

"A couple of weeks."

"You have any idea why they kept it secret?"

"I might as well come clean, huh? Isn't that what they say on TV? Dan and Kellee got married because she was getting sick again."

At that moment the truck jounced into a pothole. Laura felt her heart sink, too. "You mean the brain tumor?"

Shana wiped at her eyes, sniffed, trying to keep the tears at bay. "You know about that, too? You *are* a good detective."

Laura could understand the sarcasm. It was a coping mechanism—she'd used it herself. Had to, the only female detective in four squads at DPS. Shana reminded her of a kitten, hair standing up on end to make her seem bigger.

"Kellee's brain tumor was coming back, so she and Dan decided to get married?"

"Well, what would you do?"

Laura tried to picture the situation, put Tom into the middle of it. A few days ago she would have been more level-headed. Now she thought that getting married was exactly what she'd do in a case like that. "I'm sorry," Laura said. "It's such—"

"A waste? Oh, yeah. It's that, for sure!"

Bitter.

Laura realized what a roller coaster Shana had been on in the space of forty-eight hours. First a wedding, now a funeral. Laura realized it wasn't so strange that Shana was selling her horse. When faced with a death in the family, people often did something drastic, hoping that by taking action—any action—they could somehow change the dynamics of their broken lives. Laura, herself, had done something similar. She had married Billy Linton a few weeks after her mother and father were killed.

She thought of the parallels between her own life and that of the Yates family. When faced with Kellee's bad news, Kellee and Dan had decided to get married. Laura wondered if, had Dan and Kellee lived, it would have worked out better than her own hasty marriage had.

Laura recognized the route they were taking. The road they were on passed the north entrance to Cataract Lake before coming to a T-stop at Country Club Road. They turned right, which would lead them past the section of campground where Dan and Kellee were found. Laura noticed that Shana kept her eyes forward, concentrating on the road. Not even a flick of the eyes as the Kaibab National Forest sign marking Cataract Lake flashed by.

Her knuckles white, though, holding the steering wheel in a death grip.

"Shana, do you have to sell your horse now?" Laura asked.

"I want to."

"How long have you had him?"

"Seven years."

"How many ribbons have you won on him?"

"I dunno, close to thirty? I almost won a horse trailer once, missed by a fifth of a second."

"Sounds like he's been a friend to you."

Shana looked at her. "How do you know?"

"I had a horse once. She was a friend to me."

"What happened?"

"The woman who owned her wanted her back."

"I thought you said you owned her. How could—"

"To tell you the truth, it's still a sore spot with me. I do know I missed her. She was in many ways my best friend."

Shana kept staring straight ahead, but her shoulders started heaving. She kept swiping at her nose, but this time the tears came and she couldn't stop them. "Oh, God, I can't see!"

She pulled over to the side of the road in a cloud of dust. Laura glanced back and was reassured by the shape in the horse trailer's front window.

Shana laid her head down on the steering wheel. "He's gone. I can't believe he's gone!"

She held on to the wheel, crying. Hitching breaths, ragged sniffles. Laura had a pack of tissues in her purse and handed them over. Shana blew her nose, gulped. "He . . . he was my best friend. He was more than a brother." She swiped at her nose again. "We were twins. I was the older one, by two minutes, but he was always my older brother— and now he's gone. All I have left is Mighty Mouse. . . ." Which started her crying again. At last, tears and snot wiped away, she put the truck in gear and headed out again.

"You could call whoever it is—"

"No. I said I'd come by. Her granddaughter's there and she wants to ride. . . ."

Laura realized it wasn't her place to say any more.

The blacktop curved to the left and became Double X Ranch Road, although Laura saw more golf carts than cows. Abruptly, the artificial green of the golf course gave way to fenced meadow. Off to the left was a sprinkling of ranch houses, backdropped by the Bill Williams Mountains.

Shana slowed the truck and turned onto a cinder lane that was little more than two tire ruts. One car-length in from the road was a five-bar gate bracketed by fence posts made from naked tree limbs. Hammered to one of the posts was a metal sign that said, UNICORN FARM.

"Can you open the gate?" Shana said. Laura did so, waited for Shana to drive through, then closed it behind her. "Why's it called Unicorn Farm?" she asked as she got back into the truck.

The girl shrugged. "Mrs. Wingate likes unicorns."

"Wingate? Any relation to Josh Wingate?"

"His mom."

So this was where Josh Wingate had been going when he saw Dan's truck.

Up ahead, in a scattering of ponderosa pines, a Wedgwood-blue house topped by a brown shingle roof dreamed in the sun and shadows. The roof stretched down past the house, doing double duty as a porch covering, running all the way across the front. To the right of the house up a slight rise was a long, low building, small square windows running along the side high up—a barn. A few chickens out front, near a triangular chicken coop. The lane branched right and left through a last-gasp riot of sunflowers. They took the right fork toward the house.

A woman stood on a wet flagstone walk in the yard, watering the flowers bordering the bright green grass fronting the house. Up close the place showed signs of disrepair: A few shingles were missing, the roof was matted with pine needles, and the house paint had faded. The words "genteel poverty" came to mind.

The woman watering the pansies was heavyset, her ponytailed blond hair showing two inches of roots. In shape, she was an apple, not a pear. She wore white capri pants and a pink T-shirt that swelled around the bulge in her waist.

Shana pulled up and asked Laura to roll down her window. She called out, "Hi, Suzy. Where's Barb?"

The woman paused to bat an ash from her cigarette. "Down at the barn with those horses again, last I saw."

Shana put the truck in gear and they drove to the barn. Laura watched Shana, the set of her mouth, her eyes squinched up against something hurtful. Almost said something, but didn't. Shana was over twenty-one; she had a right to do anything she wanted, even if it appeared she was acting impulsively. For all Laura knew, this wasn't an impulsive act at all.

Shana got out and walked into the barn, calling out Barbara Wingate's name.

Laura watched her stalk around the side of the barn. There was a manic quality to her voice. Grief or anger.

Or fear?

It came to Laura all at once, the overwhelming sense that Shana was scared.

Scared of what? It could be as simple as the fact that she was facing her own mortality. Her twin brother—big, handsome, strong—had just been wiped out in an instant. That would scare anybody.

Shana tromped back over to Laura. "She's not around. I don't know what she's doing. She told me she'd be here!"

Moving rapidly into tantrum mode.

Laura caught a movement in the corner of her eye—a figure in the pasture to her left. "Could that be her?" she asked.

Shana followed her gaze. Her face fell into lines of relief. She called and waved. The woman, wearing jeans and a long-sleeved shirt, waded toward them through the shin-high grass, followed by three horses.

Judging by Josh Wingate's age, Barbara Wingate must be at least in her midforties, but looked much younger. She wore a gray felt cowboy hat with a flat crown, clapped down over reddish-gold hair pulled back into a ponytail. A few loose strands, torched by the afternoon sun, framed her heart-shaped face. She had a figure that was both slim and generous. She looked like the kind of woman you'd like to share morning coffee with on a sunny deck. Hell, she looked like an *ad* for a woman you'd like to share morning coffee with on a sunny deck.

She stripped the heavy leather gloves from her hands and tucked them into the belt that cinched her small waist. "Shana! How are you doing?" Her voice was as melodious and attractive as her person.

"I brought Mighty Mouse."

As Laura reached over the wire fence to shake Mrs.

Wingate's hand and introduce herself, something crunched underfoot—the wing of a dead raven. Laura stepped back quickly, noting the ants riddling the shiny black carcass, the empty eye socket.

"You're with the Department of Public Safety?" Mrs. Wingate asked. "Josh told me all about you. He was very impressed with the way you work."

That caught her off balance. "Thank you."

Shana repeated, "I brought Mighty Mouse."

Barbara Wingate frowned. "You know, Shana, if you don't want to sell him, we could lease him for a few months. That way, if you change your mind—"

"I won't change my mind."

"Well, then, I'll go get Erin." She climbed through the fence with desultory grace and walked toward the house.

Shana watched her go. Three ravens dipped and flapped through the clear sky, their wings a rush of air, their voices harsh. Brothers to the dead raven by the fence? Laura said to Shana, "Did you drive up to Vegas with Dan and Kellee?"

"Uh-huh."

"So it was you, Bobby, Dan and Kellee?"

"As a matter of fact, I met Bobby there."

"Who'd you come back with?"

"Bobby. Why? Is it important?"

Laura stifled her disappointment. She'd been hoping Shana had come back with Dan and Kellee. She might have seen something if they'd encountered trouble on the road. "Did anything happen on the way up?"

"What?"

"Anything unusual."

"What, like someone was following us? You think whoever— No. At least *I* didn't notice anything."

"No one cut you off in traffic, anything like that?"

"No."

Laura sighed. It had been a long shot. "You don't know of anyone who disliked Dan or Kellee?"

"I told you before, Dan was liked by everybody. Except for that one guy, a long time ago."

It appeared that Shana didn't know any more. "What about Kellee? Was there anybody you know of who didn't like her?"

"God, I dunno. To tell you the truth, I don't spend a lot of time thinking about Kellee."

"You didn't like her?"

Shana hiked her shoulders, stared sullenly out at the pasture. "Got a cigarette?"

"Sorry."

"Figures." She continued staring out at the pasture and the mountains beyond.

Laura had exhausted this line of questioning. She wouldn't get anything else out of Shana. So she ignored Shana's cold shoulder, ignored the stink of the sun-warmed raven carcass, and watched the horses.

They were Thoroughbreds. One of them had a knee the size of a honeydew melon, but all of them were well conformed, beautiful to Laura's eye.

"What's the story with him?" she asked Shana, nodding to the horse with the bad knee.

"Mrs. Wingate takes in retired racehorses and tries to find them homes. She puts photos of them up on the Internet."

"That's good of her."

"Yeah. She's a pretty cool person. She works with little kids, too, ones that have problems. She gives them riding lessons—you should see it, it's really kind of cool."

"Will she do that with Mighty Mouse?"

"Probably not. He's pretty hair-trigger. Not a beginner's horse." Her voice held a certain pride. "She's going to save him for her granddaughter."

"Erin."

"Uh-huh."

A screen door slammed and two figures emerged from

under the porch. Barbara and a thin girl Laura guessed to be eight or nine years old came toward them.

Laura was surprised that the girl—Erin—hung back. When faced with the prospect of a new horse, most girls that age would be excited to the point of hyperactive.

Erin was very slight, and there was a strained look to her eyes.

"Is Erin sick?" she asked Shana.

"Uh-huh. I think she's got mono."

"Mono?"

"Or it could be something else. I don't really know."

It was clear she didn't really care, either.

Barbara Wingate stopped, looked back, said something to the girl, who hurried up. Barbara rewarding her with a beatific smile.

Laura stood off to the side while Shana backed Mighty Mouse down the ramp and tied him to the trailer. Apparently, Shana was making a clean sweep; she pulled out a saddle and a bridle, then dumped a pile of grooming equipment on the ground, as if she couldn't wait to be rid of them.

She stripped off the shipping bandages and saddled Mighty Mouse. Laura watched Barbara Wingate and her granddaugther. Erin stood there listlessly, as if she were watching a TV program she wasn't much interested in. Barbara Wingate's hand touched Erin's back—offering comfort? When Shana was done, Barbara leaned down and said something softly to Erin. Erin nodded. Barbara helped the girl into the saddle.

It was clear Erin knew how to ride. She dutifully trotted Mighty Mouse up the dirt road a ways and loped back, easily able to pull him up. She circled him one way and then the other, neck-reining him. Mighty Mouse looked like a million dollars.

Glancing at Shana, Laura saw the pained expression, tears glittering in her eyes.

Erin looked at Barbara for permission, then slid down to

the ground and led Mighty Mouse over to them. "Nice horse," she said. But her voice was flat.

She started to cough.

Her grandmother squatted down next to her. "Erin, do you want to go inside now, honey?"

"I'm okay."

She didn't sound okay.

Shana checked her watch. "I've got to go."

Barbara dug into her jeans pocket and handed Shana a check. Laura caught the amount: over twelve thousand dollars. Shana tucked the check into her own jeans pocket and walked briskly for the truck. "Where do you want the trailer?"

Laura and Barbara Wingate exchanged looks. Sadness in the woman's green eyes, the lines around them wrinkling in sympathy. "Go ahead and back it up next to the barn," she said.

"Are you coming?" Shana yelled to Laura. "Or do you want to walk home?"

Laura said the usual—"It was nice meeting you, hope Erin enjoys Mighty Mouse"—then got into the truck.

Shana backed the horse trailer expertly back into a slot between the pasture fence and the barn, got out, and un-hitched it. She got back in and floored the truck so hard the tires slewed in the dirt.

Laura looked back in the sideview mirror at Barbara Wingate and her granddaughter, watched them dwindle down to tiny dots.

On her way back from Shana's house, Laura drove by a car repair shop. The sign outside said SHADE TREE MECHANICS—the name of the garage Jamie Cottle's father owned.

Jamie Cottle was the boy who had a crush on Kellee.

Even though the place looked closed for the day, she pulled into the parking lot. The sun's last rays glittered redly through the boughs of the massive elm tree out front, possibly the shade tree in the garage's name.

Laura unclipped her cell phone from her belt and punched in her home phone number in Vail. She realized by the fourth ring that the answering machine would pick up. Thought about leaving a message, but ended up disconnecting instead.

She looked at the garage. Shade Tree Mechanics was a converted filling station from the Mother Road days. Two bays buttoned up tight, the glassed-in office papered with posters for the Grand Canyon Railway and a faded one from the Williams Rodeo, a year old. She peered in through the office and could see through the window in the door to the service bay. A couple of cars were parked inside.

Up against the far back wall, she glimpsed part of an industrial-size tool chest; more tools on the pegboard to the left. The cherry-red tool chest was grimy and scuffed from years of use, much bigger than the one at the Chiricahua Paint Company warehouse. That had been the kind you got at Sears.

The Chiricahua Paint Company had burned to the ground a little over a month ago. She had been inside. And the tools—

Suddenly Laura got that aspirin taste in the sides of her mouth and under her tongue that she got before throwing up. She clamped her mouth closed and swallowed, willing whatever wanted to come up to go back down. *Think about something else—Tom? No.* The bobcat kittens who lived on the roof of her desert house. She concentrated on that, and after a few moments the feeling went away.

Not good, though. She couldn't react like this every time she saw a tool chest.

It looked like the owners of the Pioneer motel were having a yard sale, card tables set up on the walkway outside the office and the first two cabins. Not much left, except a couple of cases of cheap-looking jewelry and old computers, printers, a coffeepot decanter. Richie Lockhart's car was still gone; Laura wondered if he was still interviewing the roommates in Flagstaff.

A large woman in a wheelchair kept a sharp eye on two boys packing stuff up as she chatted with the young woman who had given Laura her key last night.

The young woman was tall with long dark brown hair that fell to her waist, wearing jeans and a blue tunic top that Laura had seen on nurses and orderlies. She was leaning down to talk to the woman in the wheelchair. A black chow wearing a purple bandanna sat patiently under the card table nearby. The boys were in the process of stowing fold-up chairs into a pickup truck. Laura noticed that one of them was college age. A contemporary of Dan and Kellee?

She went up and introduced herself to the group.

The dark-haired girl's nameplate said, WENDY BAKER. "I thought you were detectives," she said. She turned to the woman in the wheelchair. "She's investigating what happened to Dan and Kellee."

The woman nodded sagely. She had very pale skin, her face pear-shaped and somehow amorphous, black hair stringy. But when she smiled it was hard not to smile along with her. She held out a soft white hand ending in perfectly lacquered nails. "Glad to meet you. My name's Donna. These are my boys, Matthew and Darrell."

The boys both nodded to her politely. Shy?

The chow rose to her feet and walked over to Laura, standing in front of her as if to say, You may pet me. Kind of like the queen of England saying, "You may curtsy."

Laura held her hand out for the dog to get a whiff of her—a precaution in case she was wrong.

"That's Chelsea," Wendy said. "Don't worry. She won't bite."

Laura ran her hands over Chelsea's luxurious coat, then massaged the dog's back just above one hip. The chow leaned closer, eyes closed in ecstasy. Laura smiled; she

knew all the good spots. "Did you sell much?" she asked
Donna.

"A few odds and ends," Donna said. "We've been set up
all weekend, and tell you the truth I'm kind of disappointed.
Locals came, but there aren't many tourists left this time of
year. They're the ones who'd buy the jewelry."

Most of the jewelry in the glass cases looked like knock-
offs of delicate Zuni work. The colors were silver,
turquoise, coral. Lots of little birds strung on chains.

Small town, everyone knew each other. Wendy could be
Dan's age or a little older, and Darrell could be a high
school senior or a college freshman. Laura said, "I guess
everyone's talking about what happened at Cataract Lake."

"Been all over the news," Donna said. "Shocking. Such
nice kids, both of them. Darrell's friend Jamie worked with
them at the Mother Road Bar and Grille, isn't that right,
Darrell?"

Laura straightened. "Jamie Cottle?" She looked at Darrell.

He cleared his throat. "Uh-huh."

"Is it true what I've been hearing? Jamie had a thing for
Kellee?"

"He liked her. I don't know if I'd go so far as that."

"I'd like to talk to him. Does he still work at the Mother
Road?"

"Nuh-uh. He works for his dad now, at Shade Tree."

"Have you talked to him since the shooting?"

He shrugged. Giving her the clear impression he wanted
to be anywhere but here. "We talked on the phone."

"Where does he live?"

Donna broke in. "On Oak, across from the high school.
You think he could have hurt those two kids?" She took a
handkerchief out of her purse, shook it, snapped the purse
closed, and rested it on her ample lap. Wiped her face with
the handkerchief. "Still hot, can you believe it? If you're
thinking Jamie Cottle did this, you're barking up the wrong
tree. I know him and I know his parents. He's a good kid,

been a real good friend to Darrell. In fact." She glanced at Darrell. "Weren't you two out together Friday night?"

Darrell nodded.

"What were you doing?" Laura asked him.

Another shrug. "Not much." Looked meaningfully at the street as if to say, *I rest my case.* "Just hung out. Did a couple of loads of laundry."

"You usually do laundry on a Saturday night?"

"If my clothes're dirty. He was the one washing clothes. His dad works him so hard he doesn't have time to do anything."

"You do it at his house?"

"No. Sandoval's Seventy-six. They have a Laundromat."

With a little urging, he explained that they started a load of laundry around nine or so at night, then cruised for a while. Came back, moved it to the dryers, and cruised some more. Both of them too young to go to bars.

"Were you driving or was he?"

"I was."

"When did you drop him off?"

Darrell said he wasn't sure. Maybe midnight, maybe a little later. No one saw them at the Laundromat, although somebody did dump his first load out of the dryer, leaving it on top of a washer. "Pissed us off, whoever did that."

"Why would they? Do that?"

"The other dryers were out of order."

Donna said, "I'm telling you, that boy wouldn't hurt a fly. Not after what happened to his family earlier this year."

"What was that?"

Donna's eyes looked like black currants, set deep in unrisen dough. "His younger brother died. The whole family's been devastated."

Wendy said, "His brother was Terry Cottle—T.J."

Laura looked from one woman to the other.

Wendy said, "T.J. was the boy who drowned in Cataract Lake."

*   *   *

Laura waited a little longer for Richie Lockhart, then walked to the Mother Road Bar and Grille for a quick dinner. In a way she was glad to be alone; there was a lot to think about. Shana's evasiveness, the fact that she'd gone to Las Vegas and lied about it, the act of selling her horse and trailer a day after her twin brother was found shot to death in a tent with his new wife. Pocketing twelve thousand dollars, closing the door on her old life. Reasonable explanations for all of it, but Laura felt Shana was hiding something.

And Jamie Cottle. She asked about him at the Mother Road. Nice kid, good guy, quiet; one of the waitresses called him "sensitive." All of them commented on the tragedy at Cataract Lake earlier this year, when his brother, accompanied by his high school coach and math teacher, dove into a dark lake late at night and never resurfaced.

Common knowledge that Jamie had a crush on Kellee. But he'd never acted on it, as far as anyone could tell. The waitress who called him sensitive, a girl named Lilly Brawley, mentioned that he never said anything, but the crush was painfully obvious. He would blush and stammer when she talked to him. He had it bad, Lilly said, but she couldn't see him doing anything overt to even get her to notice him. And she knew Dan; Dan worked there, too, and it was laughable to even picture them as rivals. Dan was an adult. Jamie was a boy, despite the fact that there were only three years or so between them.

Jamie Cottle either was or wasn't tied to this case. On the surface, he didn't seem capable of an act like that, but one thing bothered her: the coincidence. Jamie's brother had died earlier this year at Cataract Lake. Dan and Kellee had been shot to death at the same lake. Superficially, the two cases didn't appear to be linked; the boy had drowned early in the summer, and Dan and Kellee had been shot to death. T. J. Cottle had been accompanied by a teacher in suspicious circumstances—a man and boy out on a lake late at night. According to Richard Garatano, the teacher, T.J. had dived into the lake voluntarily.

Wildly different cases.

But Frank Entwistle had taught her that there was no such thing as a true coincidence. There was always a link somewhere, even if it was tenuous and unimportant, and it was her job to track that link down and decide if it had merit.

Back at the motel, she divested herself of her gun and phone, placing them on the bed, and turned the local TV news on low. She caught the tail end of a report on the shooting at Cataract Lake, a glimpse of stock footage of the lake itself.

She glanced at the phone on the bed. Tom would be done for the day, the horses fed and taken care of, no more tourists to wrangle. She made a move for the phone but stopped herself.

What did he say just before she left? "I'll call you." But he hadn't so far. She'd heard the "I'll call you" line countless times during her single years, and they never meant it. But Tom lived with her. She wondered if he'd said it just to placate her. Or maybe out of guilt?

He said he'd call her; let him call. She wasn't going to give him the satisfaction of going first.

A loud rumble reverberated off the motel walls, punctuated by one earsplitting roar before clean silence.

Laura heard the car door slam, heard Richie unlock his door and go inside, heard the TV come on. Some thumping, the sound of the shower turning on.

Not long after that, he knocked on her door.

He leaned against the doorjamb, the look on his face triumphant. "Got something," he said, walking past her into the room and sitting in one of the chairs by the window. He crossed his leg over his knee, wriggling his foot. Wired. "We've got a witness."

"We do?"

"Yup. Some guy slept out by the lake, saw the whole thing."

"Where'd you hear this?"

"Somebody heard him talking and reported it to Williams PD. A Sandra Bell, B-E-L-L, heard him bragging about it outside the Mother Road B and G last night." He shifted in his seat, pulled out a crimped notepad from his jeans pocket. "Guy's name is Luke Jessup."

"You have an address?"

"According to my notes, he's a drifter—does odd jobs for folks. Delivers water."

"Delivers water?"

"You see all those tanks around town? In the back of pickups, people hauling them around on little trailers? Place has a water shortage in the outlying areas. People outside the city limits have to come in for water. Fill up their tanks just like they'd do with propane."

Laura remembered the tanks. White ones, mostly, some shaped like propane tanks, only they looked plastic. She wondered why Richie had noticed that and she hadn't.

"Has an old truck, a 'sixty-seven Chevy, pals around with a guy named Dave Soderstrom. I do have *his* address."

On the way to Dave Soderstrom's house, Richie gave her the rundown on Dan's two roommates.

"He just moved in a month ago. They had no idea he was getting married, and from what I gathered, one of them— that'd be Steve Banks—wasn't a happy camper. Took it personally that Dan was planning to split and didn't bother to mention it." He shrugged. "Either way, they're looking for a new roommate."

"Did you get a look at his room?"

"Wasn't much there—Danny boy hadn't gotten around to unpacking. Looks to me like they threw his things— clothes and toiletries and stuff—in the boxes he already had and hauled them all down to the garage."

"That was quick."

He turned onto a road leading out of town. "Life goes on, I guess."

He described what he had found in the boxes. Dan's financial statements, credit card information, checkbook, phone records, etc. Posters and things he never got around to putting up. Sports equipment, college texts, clothing, CDs.

"Usual stuff for a college kid. I was surprised there was only one credit card, though. College kids love the plastic. I've got it all in the trunk of my car. So then I went to Kellee's apartment. Her roommate—Amy—she's a piece of work. She knew they were getting married but was sworn to secrecy. I looked at Kellee's room, pretty much what you'd expect. Left it the way it was, put a seal on the door."

"Amy's a piece of work? What makes you say that?"

Up ahead was a small, shabby trailer court called the Rainbow's End. They turned onto the first lane and Richie looked at mailboxes.

"I dunno—just a feeling I got. She acted like it didn't affect her at all. Of course, Kellee hadn't been there long. She and Dan worked all summer at the Mother Road. Maybe Kellee and her roommate met through a college ad. Here we are."

They pulled up in front of a yellow house trailer with a patch of yard. A GMC truck of similar vintage to Shana's was parked out front on a scabby bit of lawn.

As they emerged from the car, an earsplitting cry cut through the night air—a baby.

Richie sighed. "Just like home."

Richie and his wife had five children, one just recently out of the baby stage.

Richie pushed the bar up on the gate and they walked up to the trailer and knocked. The baby wailed, a counterpoint to a boom box somewhere, a thumping bass. Butter-colored light fell from the curtained window on one side of the door.

A harried-looking woman in shorts and an extra-large T-shirt with an American flag on it shoved the door open, jiggling the baby on her arm. Cute little guy. At least Laura *thought* it was a boy, but she could be wrong; she was going by the blue blanket. The woman was large, tired, and pale, with stringy brown hair pulled up in a clip that had big, nasty-looking teeth.

"We're looking for Dave Soderstrom," Richie said.

"He's in his room. Last door."

Music coming from behind the door. Or rather, the bass beat. Laura couldn't hear a tune.

Laura said, "Have him come to the door."

The woman looked at her funny, but then yelled up the hallway, "Dave, get out here!"

The music turned down abruptly and a couple of moments later a string bean of a man with a ponytail and a goatee appeared in the doorway. He looked to be in his mid to late thirties.

The smell of pot rolled off him. He wore a frayed Hawaiian shirt and flip-flops despite the chill in the house. Red nylon running shorts—circa 1980—peeked out from under the shirt.

He smiled vaguely and said, "Hi, there."

Richie showed him his badge and introduced himself and Laura. The woman, who had retreated into the trailer, suddenly reappeared. "Aren't you going to take out the trash?"

"Sure."

"Now?"

"Okay." He sounded just like a teenager. "You mind?" he asked, motioning for them to follow, tramping down the uneven carpeted floor to the cluttered kitchen area. He opened a cupboard and pulled out a kitchen bag from its box, and walked with deliberate slowness around the trailer emptying wastebaskets, Richie and Laura trailing after him. He pulled out the full kitchen bag—a Top Ramen wrapper on top—and painstakingly twisted a tie around it and the other bag, then motioned them to follow him outside.

He led them through the gate and up the lane toward a Dumpster under a poplar tree at the end. The tree shimmied overhead, fat heart-shaped leaves mirroring the light on the pole above them.

Richie asking him questions about his friend Luke Jessup.

"Luke?" he said, hefting the second of the two bags into the Dumpster. "Is this about what he saw? Those kids getting shot?"

"That's what he said?"

The man leaned against the Dumpster and scratched his nose, oblivious to the garbage smell. Shook his head. "Ol' Luke. I hate to say this, but he's usually full of shit. Nobody listens to what he says. But this was something you just can't discount."

"You believed him?"

"He did seem unusually worked up. I told him he shouldn't cry wolf like that, but he kept talking about it, like he felt he had to convince me."

Richie asked, "What did he tell you?"

He swiped at his nose. "Sometimes he drives down to the lake and camps there. He was just getting to sleep when he heard a shotgun blast."

"Just one?"

He rubbed his jaw deliberatively. "More than that. He said maybe two or three. He sits up and he sees this guy walking around, shooting into a tent. Just shooting into it, you know? I mean, that's just not cool."

Laura asked, "The guy walked? He didn't run?"

"That's what Luke said. That's what made it so scary. Somebody who's that cold, man. You know?"

"Where does Luke live?"

"Right now, nowhere. He's kind of a mountain man. Goes wherever his feet take him."

"Does he work?"

Dave shrugged. "Odd jobs. A couple of people around here hire him by the job, but it's kind of hit-or-miss."

Richie asked, "Is there *anything* he does regularly? Someplace he goes to eat? Someplace he crashes?"

"He never misses church."

"Church?"

"It isn't much of a church. More like a ministry. The Staff of Life. It's over on Third Street."

On the way back to the motel, Laura called the Staff of Life Ministry. As she'd expected at this time of night, she got their voice mail. She left a message, then glanced at Richie. Might as well try to get along with him, since they had to work together. "That was a cute baby," she said. "Couldn't tell if it was a boy or a girl, though."

"It was a girl. I'm surprised you couldn't tell that."

"But she had a blue blanket."

He rolled his eyes.

"How's yours doing?"

"Oh, man, she's a little pistol. Cutest little kid you ever saw. Sleeps through the night. Always has, which is a great thing for Gail."

"That's good."

"Yeah. Gail and I are having so much fun with her. I'm telling you, you don't really grow up until you have kids."

Laura didn't reply to that. She thought she was a grown-up now.

"How's your boyfriend? Tom, right? You thinking of tying the knot?"

"That's not even on the radar."

"You should think about it. There's nothing like being married, having kids. I wouldn't trade it for the world. I mean, sure, it's a lot of work. But it's worth it. These kids, they can make you so proud. Did I tell you Chris is the star of his soccer team? Kid's gonna be a natural on the football field. Wide receiver. You can take that to the bank."

Laura glanced at Richie, short and built like a rubber eraser. She couldn't picture him running down any field, let alone a football field.

"Our anniversary is coming up," Richie was saying. Looking at her, actually engaging. "I want to go to Colorado, but Gail's got her heart set on San Diego. She's always wanted to stay at the hotel on Coronado Island, you know, the big old one? I'll probably give in, as usual."

He talked about his family all the way back to the motel—his three girls, his two boys, Gail dragging him to an opera and how he'd actually kind of liked it. Listening to him talk made her wish for a family of her own—something she normally didn't think about. "Family" had not been part of her lexicon for the past eleven years. She realized she had forgotten what it was like to be part of a family, to have someone who loved you no matter what. That mainstay had been gone so long that now she barely felt its absence; her life had evolved into something else. Like an old road, the memory of her own family had been almost erased by time and neglect. What would it be like to have that kind of support system again? Someone who was always there for you?

She'd hoped Tom would be that someone, but now she wasn't so sure.

Richie parked in front of his room, yawned. "I'm dead. Let's reconnoiter tomorrow morning and see where we're at, maybe check out that church."

But Laura couldn't sleep. After lying awake for what seemed like hours, she was wide-eyed. Maybe the mountain air would make her sleepy. She got up, pulled her jeans on under her nightshirt, put on her shoes and walked outside into the chill night.

Cigarette smoke permeated the air. She could see the tiny red glow over by the office across the way. Someone sitting in one of the plastic chairs outside the first room, the manager's office. A slim woman with dark hair, waving at her.

Laura walked over. She wasn't crazy about cigarette

smoke, but the idea of company trumped the potential bad effects. Wendy said, "Pull up a chair."

Laura did so, careful not to tread on the sleeping chow.

"You making any headway? On the case?" Wendy asked.

"Not really," Laura said truthfully.

Wendy put out her cigarette in the sand-filled coffee can at her feet. "I knew Dan a little. From what I could tell, he was a really nice guy. This is just incredibly sad."

Laura silently agreed.

Wendy caught her long brown hair, brought it over one shoulder, and stroked it absently. "Poor Shana. Who's going to look out for her now?"

"You know Shana?"

"We were on the quadrille team together in high school."

"She sold her horse today."

Wendy stared at her. "Mighty Mouse? Are you kidding me? She *loved* that horse."

"She sold the horse and horse trailer to Barbara Wingate."

"Wow. That's unbelievable." Wendy stared straight ahead, working it out in her mind. "She must have been really upset. People do weird things when they get upset. Stuff they wouldn't normally do."

"I suppose she has other things on her mind," Laura said. "Dan's death. Her children. Her boyfriend."

"She still running around with that creep?"

"You mean Robert Burdette?"

"That's the one." Wendy shook another cigarette from the pack sitting on her lap, stuck it between her lips. "Although sometimes it's hard to keep track. Shana always did run through men like babies through diapers."

Laura closed her eyes, enjoying the cool air on her cheek. She heard the flare of a match and smelled the smoke. Turned her head so she didn't breathe it directly in, even though it probably didn't make any difference.

Wendy said, "Barbara Wingate must have bought

Mighty Mouse for Erin. I hope it perks her up. Maybe it will get her mind off everything she's been going through."

Wendy moved her hair to the other shoulder, and Laura noticed the gold-colored nameplate pinned to her tunic catching the light. The nametag said, WILLIAMS HEALTH CARE CENTER above the name WENDY BAKER.

"Are you a nurse?" Laura asked.

"No, I do intake. Part-time."

"Is Erin very sick?"

"If she isn't, she sure gives a good imitation of it. Nobody knows what's wrong, though—there are so many different symptoms. All she's been through, and Mrs. Wingate's just beside herself."

Chelsea the chow stretched, groaned, and went back to sleep.

Wendy added, "I can tell it's beginning to wear her down. She's a real fighter. So persistent, always asking questions, being real proactive, you know? That's important. When it comes to patient care, a lot of people don't realize they've got to ride herd on the health care providers. I could tell you stories . . ." She shook her head. "At least Barbara Wingate knows what's going on, how important it is to watch out for Erin. She should, considering."

Laura was about to ask Wendy what she meant, but the moment passed when Wendy motioned to Richie's car. "My cousin has a Monte Carlo just like that. Same color, only he's got the eight on one side and the three on the other."

"What do those numbers mean?" Laura asked.

"Number eight is Dale Earnhardt Junior's car."

Laura had heard the name. "Is he the guy who died in that car race a few years back?"

"No. That was Junior's dad, Dale Earnhardt. The Intimidator. His car was number three." She put out the second cigarette, only half-smoked. "I hope switching out the sets worked out for your partner. He is your partner, isn't he?"

"Sets?"

"For when he was watching the NASCAR race—the re-

ception was driving him crazy. We traded him a set from the
room on the other side. He didn't come back around, so I'm
assuming it was okay."

Laura's gut tightened. "He was watching a car race yesterday?"

"Uh-huh."

"How long do NASCAR races usually go?"

"Usually? Barring crashes, four hours."

Laura and Richie went by the Staff of Life Ministry the
next morning. Laura was still steaming over the idea that
Richie had spent a large part of yesterday watching a
NASCAR race. No point in saying anything, though. Working closely with him had illuminated his character in a way
she hadn't noticed previously: He could be passive-
aggressive, especially when cornered. He'd love it if she got
bent out of shape over the car race—it would give him a
chance to trot out his favorite defense mechanism. As much
as she'd like to confront him, it would not move the investigation forward, and with homicides, momentum was
everything.

The church was headquartered in a brick bungalow with
colorful posters of Jesus and his disciples taped to the
walls. A plump, pleasant-looking woman at the desk told
them that she hadn't seen Luke Jessup for a couple of days.

Her brows knitted with worry. "It's pretty strange. He
missed teaching his Bible class yesterday. That's not like
him."

"You mean, he's pretty punctual?" asked Richie.

"I mean," she said, staring at Richie hard over her reading glasses, "he has never missed a worship service or a
Bible class in the five years I've known him."

As they left, she added, "If you find him, let me know,
will you? I hope he's all right."

The back-to-back autopsies at the Coconino County
medical examiner's office in Flagstaff were both deeply

disturbing, and routine. The post on Kellee Yates confirmed the resurgence of her brain tumor. Maybe the news would be a comfort to her parents. Hard to know.

After the autopsies, Laura and Richie split up; Richie went back to Williams to look for Luke Jessup, and Laura remained at the ME's office to meet Chuck and Louise Yates.

Laura saw their truck pull in off Fort Valley Road and met them out front. Chuck came around to open Louise's door, but she was ahead of him and nearly mowed him down. Laura got the impression the door opening was something new, a deference to his wife's grief.

Louise Yates bulled her way to the walkway out front before stopping dead. She stared at the beige building set back into a stand of ponderosa pines, looking at it as if it were the first circle of hell. Andrew Whitcomb, the forensic investigator for Coconino County, joined Laura. He introduced himself and led them all around the walkway to the back.

They entered through the back door into a sparsely furnished room, fifteen by fifteen feet—red-tile floor and bare white walls. Laura noticed the refrigerated cases where corpses were kept, and hoped Chuck and Louise Yates wouldn't.

Louise immediately saw the sheet-covered gurney parked along one wall. She gasped.

A chair had been placed next to the gurney. The chair was coral red and made of nubby material. Laura noticed that Louise Yates held Andrew Whitcomb's hand as if she had known him all her life. He had clearly done this many times before, and inspired confidence with his gentle, respectful demeanor.

Andrew let go of Louise's hand long enough to push the sheet up away from the young man's arm, which lay just inside the rim of the tray on which he had been stored.

Louise groaned.

Behind Laura, Chuck Yates muttered, "Dear God."

Andrew Whitcomb returned to Louise's side, said something Laura could not hear, something for Louise's ears alone. Louise nodded. They crossed the few feet of distance to Dan Yates.

"Do you want to sit down?"

Louise shook her head. She was staring down at her son's hand, which was palm-up and slightly curled. The sheet had been pushed halfway up his forearm, mercifully covering up several pellet wounds Laura had seen during the autopsy photos.

"Why don't you stay with him a while?" Andrew said.

She turned to him, panic in her eyes. "But what if it isn't Dan?"

Chuck spoke up. "You know what they said. They matched his fingerprints. His fingerprints from that time he worked at—"

Louise hunched her shoulders and Chuck stopped talking.

Time stretched. Louise kept staring at Dan's arm. The room went completely quiet. Louise's expression was flat, unreadable, but her fingers seemed to move of their own volition, almost as if she were playing piano in the air by her hips. Laura wondered what she would do. Wondered if she'd bolt.

"I don't want to touch him if he's not my son," Louise Yates said into the silence.

Andrew Whitcomb stood with her. He said nothing, but he was there.

Suddenly, Louise bent at the waist and picked up the arm. Shocked at the weight, or maybe the feel of his flesh, she nearly dropped it back on the metal gurney, caught herself just in time. "He's cold," she said.

"Yes, ma'am. That's true."

"Like he was in the refrigerator."

She held his hand limply, at the wrist. Staring at the arm, uncertain. Laura could see the struggle that went back and forth behind her eyes: She didn't want him to be her son, but instinct told her he was, and this would be her last chance to touch him.

Abruptly, Louise Yates sat down in the chair and covered his hand in both of hers.

She started to cry, hugging the hand to her cheek, her tears falling on the pale flesh. Running her fingers over his palm, his knuckles, his fingers, exploring the only part of her son she was allowed to see.

Memorizing the weight, the mass, the feel of his skin against the time when she would never have access to him again.

12

Mark Sproule was early. He usually was. Every time he met someone he'd get to a place anywhere from fifteen to five minutes early, and even though he'd tried many times to recalibrate his timing, it never made a whit of difference. The result this time was that he found himself standing outside the Mineshaft Coffee Shop in Shoshone, California, the early-morning chill seeping through his jacket, watching the sunrise. Hands stuffed into his pockets; he'd forgotten his gloves.

I'm too old for this, he thought as he stared out at the mountains. The mountains stood out like crisp blue cutouts against the pale morning sky, just a hint of lemon between two low peaks. He'd just driven all the way to Indiana and back, a turnaround of four days, and all he wanted to do was go home.

By thirty-seven years of age, you'd think I'd have a stable life like everybody else. But all that had been shot to shit a year ago. Now Rhonda had taken Sarah back to the family home in Indiana, and he was left out here, alone, except for his tortoises.

His tortoises and his friends. If they really *were* friends. He was beginning to have his doubts. How well did he really know any of them?

He flashed on his four desert tortoises, Hambone,

Colonel Klink, Bubba, and Landshark, their ancient, shriveled faces, their wise eyes. They weren't really his, but the state gave him a permit to care for them. That was because he was considered a law-abiding citizen. He'd gotten the first two for Sarah. Now she wasn't here to enjoy them.

He'd have to figure out how to give them back without raising any alarms. Tell the government he was moving to Indiana, which was true.

Stamping his feet in the cold desert light, he wondered for the hundredth time: *How'd I get into this?* He still wasn't sure. Considering what he knew about the PATRIOT Act, knowing that without any explanation they could deport *U.S. citizens,* how had he allowed himself to get involved in this mess?

He thought he must have just slid into it.

They kept telling him his part was minimal, but he knew deep inside that you could never be one hundred percent sure of anything. He'd learned that the hard way.

Mark rubbed his hands for warmth, lit a cigarette. Used to be he'd laugh when anyone said the government was out to get people. That was for those wing nuts in Kingman, places like that, where they stockpiled weapons and dug themselves bunkers and laid in the old MREs, spicing up their diatribes with Ruby Ridge and black helicopters.

But now he knew. The United States—the country of his birth, the country he had pledged allegiance to as a schoolkid—was only as good as the people in power at the time. Like any and every other government in the world.

Look at Yucca Mountain. Those two words sent shivers up his spine. Pretty soon the U.S. government would start transporting nuclear waste on the highways and rails from every corner of the country and bury it out here, in this pristine desert.

But it was the nuclear plants that scared him the most. For the first time in over twenty-five years, the government was seriously talking about building new ones. If there was a nuclear plant accident like the one at Chernobyl, it would take twenty-five thousand years to recover from a major plutonium meltdown.

He'd seen a documentary on Chernobyl—people's homes, blackened and rotting, falling back down into the toxic earth. The sarcophagus housing Reactor Four, supposedly made to contain the radiation, was just a Band-Aid and was a prime candidate for a nuclear explosion. The Zones of Exclusion covered only a radius of nineteen miles. If the thing exploded, it would destroy Russia, Belarus, the Ukraine.

And these assholes were planning to do more of it here.

So here he was, taking a risk that probably wouldn't change a thing in the long run. But he had to do it.

Plus, there was the money. *Don't forget the money.* Not a whole hell of a lot, but enough to get him to Indiana, get him set up in an apartment, see him through the first six months. Enough to let him be near his little June Bug. And maybe what he did here could start a national dialogue, get people to wake up and see what was happening before it was too late. He knew from his own experience that a person needed a jolt every once in a while if they were ever going to learn anything.

An old blue truck pulled into the parking lot. Bobby Burdette driving, Glenn Traywick leaning his elbow on the passenger-side window.

"Hop in!" Bobby Burdette yelled.

Mark threw his cigarette on the walkway and ground it out under his boot, walked over and squeezed into the cab. "You sound happy this morning."

"I am happy. I found the perfect place."

As usual, Glenn had that serene, sunny-seeming demeanor, but his blue eyes were neutral—you could never really tell what he was thinking. He wore stiff dark denim head to toe, his jacket collar pulled up to hide the strawberry mark on his neck, the blocky gimme cap with a lightning bolt and the words GLENN ELECTRIC on it pulled low over his grizzled eyebrows. Guy had his own business, and he was doing this—Jesus.

Glenn always wore the hat. Mark was there when Glenn saw the cap at an electrical repair shop, couldn't resist that his name was on it. When he wrote letters to the paper he signed himself Glenn Electric.

Bobby, Mark noticed, was sporting a new haircut. Military short, with whitewalls. New, mean-looking sunglasses, wraparound, that you couldn't see into. He looked like a cop. All he needed was the mustache.

Bobby pulled out of the parking lot, and Glenn Electric's Styrofoam coffee cup spilled onto Mark, not scalding, but bad enough.

"Shit! I'm sorry. These damn lids never do what they're supposed to."

"Rag on the floor," Bobby said.

Mark stared at the red rag under his feet. It looked like it had been left out in the elements for months, stiffened into frozen whorls and crusted over with oil. What was he doing with these people?

He used to teach fifth-grade biology, and now here he was with a guy who wore a hat labeled GLENN ELECTRIC and someone who looked and acted like a poster boy for *Soldier of Fortune*. He might just as well be stranded on the dark side of the moon.

Twenty minutes later, they reached Micaville. Or at least the sign for Micaville. Some poor taxpayers had paid good money for the green reflector sign, but there was nothing in the road except a broken foundation in the weeds, lined by a foot-high parapet of stacked wafer-thin flagstones, and one toasted brown Joshua tree.

Bobby pulled off the road in a funnel of dust.

Mark said, "This is where we're gonna meet?"

"No," Bobby said, pointing out the window to the left. "We're gonna meet over there."

Mark squinted against the bleached whiteness of the landscape, the puffs of dusty sage like dirty sheep, saw the orange-slice shape way out there, corrugated metal dulled by the sun.

"What's that?"

"Hangar," Bobby said.

At that moment, Mark felt his bowels wanting to let go. They really meant it. It wasn't a game. They were serious, which meant so was he. He sucked it up, literally, willing the cramp in his gut to go away.

It did. But the airplane hangar stayed where it was.

The apartment Kellee had rented in Flagstaff was red brick accented with wooden beams and a shingle roof. The Swiss Chalet Apartments were neatly laid out around a common area. A walkway wound between snippets of bright green winter lawn and tamed bushes. Flower boxes filled the lower windows, and brown wooden balconies containing the detritus of college students—beach towels, bicycles, grills.

Apartment 409C was on the second floor. She didn't have to knock; the door was open and some song she didn't recognize floated out. The male voice was deep and scratchy and meandered tunelessly.

She called out, "Is someone home?" Had to shout three times, louder and louder.

A barefoot brown-haired girl in short shorts and a skimpy top appeared in the doorway. Her hair was held up over her neck in a big clip. Pert nipples poked through the thin material of her top. Laura concentrated on the girl's face, which was pretty despite a row of pimples across her forehead and a good paving-over of base makeup. "Can I help you?"

Laura showed her shield and introduced herself.

The girl hung on the door, confused. "I talked to a detective the other day."

"This is just a follow-up."

"Oh." She left the door open and walked into the apartment. After turning down the music she threw herself onto a cream-colored couch.

The room was mostly white or cream, with dark brown rattan furniture that looked as if it had been bought all at once. Aside from several large textbooks, notebooks and loose paper, the place was neat and well cared-for. Laura sat on a chair opposite her.

Amy answered her questions intelligently and thoughtfully. She would be a perfect witness. Laura got the impression that Amy was a very smart person, and was using her intellectual capacity to distance herself from the trauma of losing her friend and roommate. She was dry-eyed, articulate, and helpful. Offering her opinions on the relationship between Kellee and Dan ("They both were old souls, but nonetheless there was a naive quality to them"), on her own relationship with Kellee ("I saw her more as a sister than a friend—we were, like, family") and on Kellee's family ("Kellee and I spent a couple of days down at their cabins this summer").

Laura remembered what Richie had said, his conclusion that Kellee and Amy had just recently met. He'd been wrong about that.

"How long have you known each other?"

"Since psych class last year."

"But you only became roommates recently? Why did she move in with you if she was planning on getting married?"

"It came up suddenly. Even though they dated all last year, Kell never mentioned marriage before. So when I suggested she move in with me after my other roommate left, she jumped at it."

"Must have been a shock when she told you."

"Tell me about it. All of a sudden, it was, like, 'We're getting hitched!' That's what she said, the night they both came back here and announced it. *I* think"—she unconsciously touched the pimples on her forehead—"they got all jazzed-up and decided, you know, 'It's now or never.' It was like they fed off each other's excitement."

"Why weren't you her maid of honor?"

Again, the touch to the forehead, feeling along the row of zits as if it were Braille and she could read some answer in them.

"She asked me, but I couldn't do it. I had an exam Friday, the first of three mandatory exams. If I missed one, it would bring my whole average down. She knew that. She knows how important school is to me. I'm in premed—I plan to be an orthopedic surgeon."

"You knew about the brain tumor? Do you think that's the reason they decided to get married?"

"Well, that's the logical conclusion. People often act impulsively when faced with their mortality."

Analytical. Almost pompous in her pronouncements. Laura had a feeling this girl was riding for a fall—when the shock wore off.

"Anything you can tell me about that day?"

She shrugged. "Dan showed up about seven. Kellee grabbed her stuff and they took off."

"Anything else? Something that sticks in your mind?"

Amy looked inward, scanning her memory banks. Wanting to be as helpful as she could.

"Nope. Just that Dan said they needed to hurry—they were picking Shana up on the way."

"Do you know Shana?"

"I met her once."

Terse. Disapproving.

"So they were picking Shana up on the way? Did anyone mention Shana's boyfriend?"

"Bobby? I know Dan didn't want him there. At the wedding."

"Why?"

"He didn't like him. Neither did Kellee, but she gave in when Shana insisted she wouldn't go unless he could be in the wedding party—such as it was. Kellee's—was—like

that, a peacemaker. She'd rather give in than have any un-
pleasantness."

"So Kellee and Dan didn't like Bobby Burdette?"

"*That* was pretty clear. Kellee couldn't understand what
Shana saw in him. She thought he was a bad influence."

"How so?"

"Something Kellee said. She was worried about Shana
getting in trouble. When I pressed her on it, she wouldn't
say anything else." She shrugged. "Sometimes Kellee could
be like that—she'd just clam up."

"Did you ever meet Bobby?"

"Just the one time I met Shana. I didn't like him, either.
Kellee was worried about it, but if you ask me, it was just a
transition thing."

"A transition thing?"

"The transition from adolescent to adult. The end of high
school, trying to decide what to do? It hits all of us in some
way or another. Even people who have it all together and
know what they want to do. So many rules you grew up
with now don't apply—college is your first great freedom.
Unfortunately, a lot of kids abuse that freedom and get into
trouble."

"You think Shana was in trouble?"

"What do you think? Twenty-one years old, she's already divorced with two kids. *Forget* college. In my opinion, that girl painted herself into a real corner."

Laura ignored the holier-than-thou tone and pressed on.
"Kellee ever mention that? The fact she wasn't going to college?"

"Oh, no. Kellee was the kind of girl who respected people's privacy. She tried very hard not to appear judgmental.
Besides, I think it was just a general worry. Dan probably
didn't like the fact that Shana was so dependent on his parents. Here they are, they've already raised *their* children,
been responsible adults, you know? And then they get saddled with—maybe 'saddled' is too strong a term; there's
something in it for everyone in these kinds of family

dynamics—but Dan was such a stand-up guy, you know? The kind that didn't lean on anybody, and Kellee was the same way. It had to bother him, on some level."

Laura added to her notes and then said, "I need to look at her room again."

"The other—" She stopped herself and smiled. "Just a follow-up, right?"

"Right."

"Her parents already came and got her stuff."

"I'd like to take a look anyway."

"Why not?" she said brightly.

As Laura looked through Kellee's room, she contemplated the byzantine tunnels of Amy Dawson's mind. "Forget orthopedic surgeon," she muttered. "You should be a psychiatrist."

Laura drove back to Williams and stopped by Shade Tree Mechanics on the way back into town.

As she opened the door to the glassed-in office, she noticed a young man in a blue-gray jumpsuit slamming his palm against a soft-drink machine. Big kid. His movements ponderous, like a bear's, as if standing upright wasn't all that comfortable for him.

"Jamie Cottle?" she asked.

He turned to look at her, blinking furiously. Freckled bovine face, unusually thick jaw.

"No, I'm Walt."

"Is Jamie here?"

He turned his attention back to the machine. "It *always* does this." He kicked the vending machine hard. Coins trickled down into the tray and he scooped them up. "Jamie's not here on Mondays. He working on your car?"

"No. Where can I find him?"

"He lives with his folks on Oak."

The house on Oak Street yielded nothing except the perception of the kind of people who lived there. A blue spruce dominated the front yard, a few stray pinecones littering a neat green lawn as perfect as velvet. The house was a pale yellow ranch with a shingle roof, a travel trailer tucked up along the side. A satellite dish up top, a flag hanging from a pole attached to the garage. No answer to the illuminated doorbell. A brown shepherd mix with one ear up and one ear down stuck his head through the vertical blinds and barked once. Laura left her card, with a note on it for Jamie to call her.

Laura's phone rang the minute she got to her car.

"I've got the tent back," Richie said. "How about we meet at the lake in twenty minutes?"

When Laura got to the lake, sunlight was bouncing off the water and into her eyes. Normally, there would be fishermen standing at the edge, fishing lines catching the light as they whizzed out through the air. There would be a soft *plunk*, the egg sinker quickly falling down through the water. Not much more noise than that, maybe the sound of a cooler lid coming off, a rattle of a paper bag or Saran Wrap unwinding from a sandwich, the scrape of a shoe on dirt as someone shifted hindquarters to a more comfortable position—all sounds magnified by their proximity to water.

A solitary sport done in the company of strangers, easygoing but insular.

That was what this lake should be.

Or maybe there would be kids splashing and chattering and screaming. The smell of charcoal smoke drifting over the water. But today there was no one. Just a police car parked across the entrance, and yellow crime-scene tape quivering in the breeze.

It seemed strange, as if people had not just deserted the lake but the world on this silent early afternoon.

Laura remembered the times she and Billy had gone camping up on Mount Lemmon near Tucson. They had a red tent just like Dan and Kellee's, the kind a young couple might get at Kmart. She remembered what it was like to be a college kid off camping with her boyfriend, the world full of promise, madly in love and burning from it. The world revolving around them.

The same age as Kellee and Dan.

Dan and Kellee's tent had been reduced to a forlorn circle of nylon, the vibrant color bleached away but not enough to banish the ghost map of their blood, the material punctured in several places—grouped shots.

Laura and Richie spent an hour marking the places where the buckshot had penetrated the tent floor, then digging in the ground for pellets, putting each pea-sized piece of shot into pill vials, bedding them in cotton.

They worked in silence. Laura finally asked Richie why he wouldn't ride in her car.

He sat back on his heels, looking at her as if it were self-explanatory. "It's a Toyota."

"What's wrong with a Toyota?"

He shrugged.

"No. Really. What's wrong with a Toyota? They're the most reliable cars there are. I have a friend who owns a Camry, it's still going strong at two hundred thousand miles."

She saw both pity and smugness in the look he gave her. *You don't know anything.*

She almost said something about the NASCAR race, but didn't. Instead, she stood up and ironed out her back. Hurting again. She sat down on one of the big rocks of the fire ring, watching as Richie rolled up the tent floor. Clasped her hands around her knees, pulled them to her chest, felt the pain in her back ease. Her eyes focused downward on the dirt, the slightly charred look to it, the white and gray rock surfaces bright in the sunlight.

She dusted her hands together, feeling gritty. Placed her hands on the rocks on either side of her, straightened her back, stretching.

Richie glanced at her as he carried the tent floor up to the car, the bag containing the buckshot vials in the other hand. "You coming?"

"I'll be along in a while."

"Wish this thing would wind up. It's my kid's birthday. I don't like being away on their birthdays."

"I know." Feeling weary herself.

He rubbed the back of his neck, which had a healthy sunburn—high altitude. "I've got a feeling about Jessup. I spent the morning asking around about him while you were at the ME's. It's like he disappeared into thin air. If we could find him, I'd bet he'd give us something to chew on. Oh, well." He started for his car. "See you back at the ranch."

Laura heard his car start up, the roar startling a flock of ravens. Then he was gone, and she had the lake and the campground to herself.

She closed her eyes and absorbed the good feeling of the sun on her face. Thinking about Luke Jessup disappearing. Thinking about Shana selling her horse and trailer for a good bit of cash. Thinking about Jamie Cottle and his brother. Looking out at the smooth blue surface of the lake, wondering where T. J. Cottle dove in. Maybe there was more to the story—an argument, maybe, between teacher and pupil? She looked down at her hand, palm flat against the big rocks. Her nails were dirty from crawling around in the dirt and picking out buckshot from the ground.

She made a mental note to ask for the file on T. J. Cottle's death.

Looking at her nails again, her eyes straying to the crack that resulted from the juxtaposition of three big stones, a wedge of darkness that looked perfectly round.

So round she had the childlike urge to put her finger down it. Her finger would definitely fit; the hole was the size of a man's finger. But she didn't. There could be anything down there—specifically spiders. Having suffered the effects of a black widow bite, she sure as hell didn't want to go there again.

She got up and headed for her car.

13

The layout of the Blue Lagoon Hotel and Casino was an endless labyrinth that always delivered you to the same place—or at least it *looked* like the same place. Easy to get lost, each room a cacophony of repeating chimes and pelting coins, all embedded into clockless, busily patterned areas designed to keep people there as long as their money held out. The blue-green color and shifting lights that were supposed to represent water reflections were all part of the theme, along with the repeating coconut palms on the carpet and the water slide from the third to second floor. Plenty of jungle stuff—vines hanging from the ceiling, themed restaurants like the Keel-Haul Saloon, little grass huts for the cashiers, roving cocktail servers dressed in loincloths or grass skirts, depending on their sex. Pretty girls and even prettier boys. All of it blurring together in Bobby Burdette's mind.

Work first: Scope out the parking lots, get up on the roof of the Mirage next door. Reluctant to give up the helicopter idea, but it was looking more and more like he'd have to. It would look great in a movie but it was problematic; there were too many ways for them to cheat. Best to do it the smart way, even if it wasn't dramatic.

The goal was to survive. Survive and thrive.

Still, he went up on the roof—managed it quite easily.

Security wasn't what it was cracked up to be, even though he saw his share of men in suits bending into their collars and touching their earpieces.

All for show. Just like Las Vegas itself.

After the reconnaisance tour, it was time to lounge by the pool, play the slots, hit the craps table, and eat as much shrimp cocktail as he could.

He'd earned a vacation.

He managed to lose himself in the games for a couple of hours, but when he came out from under them he thought about Shana again.

When he called her yesterday, she'd seemed distracted.

It wasn't his imagination. She was definitely trying to get off the phone with him, making transparent excuses. He'd even mentioned that he was going to spend the following night at a brand-new Las Vegas casino, knowing she'd ask if she could meet him there. But she didn't.

"I thought you were in Kingman," was all she said.

"Nope, I'm having a minivacation. Don't ask if you can come—I'm only going to be there one night."

She didn't say anything.

Unlike her. She always said whatever came into her empty head, which was one reason he was glad he'd never told her what he was planning. Bad enough what she *did* know.

The main reason he stayed with her was she was so hot-looking. When she went out with him, other men turned their heads to watch her. He knew they were thinking what it would be like to spend hours in the sack with a girl like that.

Plus, she had been in on this harebrained scheme from the beginning. Another good thing about her—he'd been able to let his guard down, not watch his words, at least about *that* part. But since he'd come up with his alternate plan, even that advantage had gone out the window. He had to school himself to think one way whenever he was with

her—the way that led to Cottonwood Cove. Like that was
the goal.

But now he sensed that something had changed between
them.

He lay on a chaise, watching the parade of beautiful
women modeling bikinis from Island Fashion, the hotel's
boutique. Shana would look good in one of those.

What was going on with her? She'd mentioned her
brother three times.

A cocktail waitress in a grass skirt asked him if he
wanted a refill. "Sure, doll," he said, holding up his empty.

Her made-up face smoothing over into that still expression women got when they felt insulted.

Watching the water, watching the girls, but his mind on
Shana. Thinking her brother's death might have unhinged
her.

How close was she to the edge?

Twenty minutes later he was packed and standing in line
waiting to check out, thinking he'd better stay close to
home from now on.

Back at the motel, Laura took her second shower of the
day, more to cool off on a hot Indian-summer day than anything else, then took out her files and reviewed them, looking for anomalies—anything that might stick out. As usual,
she went into a mild trance, only vaguely aware of the com-
ings and goings outside her window. When she finished
going through the murder book, it was a couple of hours
later.

She went outside to stretch her legs and noticed that
Richie's car was gone. Peering into the window of his
room, she spotted the motel key on the table.

People left their keys inside a room when they checked
out.

She called his cell. He answered, his voice almost blot-
ted out by wind and traffic.

"Where are you?"

"Gas station in Flag."

"Flag? What are you doing there?"

"I'm taking the tent back to the lab."

"In *Phoenix?*"

"Uh-huh. Then I'm going home."

"Why?"

"Sheriff's deputies nailed Hector Lopez at a trailer in San Simon. I've got to be there."

"What about this case?"

"You're doing pretty good on your own."

"Did you clear this with Jerry?"

"What do you think? Look, I've got to go. Looks like I'll get to see my kid tonight after all."

"You could have told me—"

But he'd already hung up.

In retrospect, Laura thought this might be a good thing. She and Richie hadn't spent a lot of time working together on this case; he had gone his way and she had gone hers. So there was already something of a disconnect. Now she had the whole enchilada. A double check with her sergeant, Jerry Grimes, verified that Hector Lopez, a big-time people smuggler—a *coyote*—had been captured today. Lopez had run a one-stop shop that moved large numbers of illegal aliens over the border, providing them with forged documents and licenses. He had also held some of the illegals hostage, charging their families exorbitant prices to release them. A couple of his people had gotten into a gunfight on Interstate 10 with a rival gang of *coyotes*, resulting in the death of a citizen whose car had been caught in the cross fire.

Jerry said, "It's Richie's case. We need him—is that going to be a problem?"

"No problem I can see."

"That's good." She heard the relief in his voice. "To tell you the truth, we're kind of stretched thin at the moment.

Everybody's doubling up. Are you anywhere near wrapping this thing up?" His voice hopeful.

"You need me now?"

"No," he said hastily. "Just hoping we can get a solve on this. I mean, two college kids . . . you know."

"I have some things to work on."

"The lieutenant says whatever you need, within limits. This is an important one."

Laura wanted to say every case was important, but she knew better than to argue with him. The idea of two young college students being ambushed as they slept in a campground would make everyone nervous. The sooner they found whoever did it, the better. And Jerry was a good guy, the best kind of sergeant. He let her do her thing, even if sometimes her thing was unconventional. He depended on her, trusted her. Maybe the only one left in the department who *did* trust her.

So Laura said, "I'll do my best," and left it at that.

She walked three blocks to the Safeway and bought some supplies: a couple of sheets of white posterboard and two dolls, Barbie and Ken, on sale for $4.99 each.

Laura had never played with dolls when she was a little girl, never even owned a Barbie. But tonight Barbie and Ken would suit her purposes perfectly.

As Laura walked back outside into the almost-dark, she felt the stress of the last few days easing. She wasn't surprised at the little tug of excitement. She savored the feeling.

An only child, Laura had always been good at doing things on her own, so used to entertaining herself that she didn't need anyone to bounce her ideas off. It was her version of the nesting instinct. Some women liked to clean house; she liked to get all the materials she needed to do her work and burrow down into it. She looked forward to doing that now.

Laura stopped at a fast-food place and, instead of ordering what she really wanted—something loaded with fat and grease—got a salad that tasted like cardboard. She even used the low-fat dressing. It filled her but didn't satisfy her.

Back inside the room, she taped the two posterboard sheets together, overlapping by about a foot, and spread it out on the round table by the window. She put the notes she had taken from the autopsy and from the work she and Richie had done mapping and collecting buckshot on one of the two chairs, and sat in the other.

She drew a large circle, representing the tent, on the contact paper. Then she removed (with difficulty) Barbie and Ken from their respective boxes and placed them inside the tent, their feet toward the tent entrance. She put Ken on his back and Barbie on her side, facing him. Laura tried to raise Ken up on his elbows, but the plastic limbs were resistant. She guessed that he had heard a sound and raised up on his elbows just before the first shot blasted through the tent. From the evidence, it appeared that after the shotgun blast, after the buckshot had penetrated his foot, Dan had moved quickly, shoving Kellee to the right side of the tent. There had been little blood in the area where their feet would be, just a small blood trail as he whipped his leg to the side.

The ME had gone through all the wounds with her, Laura charting them on a legal pad: three rounds, nine projectiles each, sixteen of twenty-seven shots accounted for.

The killer had shot through the front of the tent first, from approximately fifteen feet away. Laura marked the shots this way:

1-1   took off male victim's right big toe
1-2   shatters right shin
1-3   tears right calf
1-4   goes through right heel into floor of the tent

She added the other five shots that had not hit Dan, but penetrated the tent floor:

1-5   hole to the right

1-6   ditto
1-7   hole to the left
1-8   ditto
1-9   ditto

She rearranged Ken and Barbie, pushing them over onto their sides, nudging them up against the line representing the right edge of the tent. Turned the contact paper one quarter turn clockwise. Now the couple was horizontal to her, and she was in the shoes of the killer.

She logged the rounds Dan and Kellee had received this time:

2-1   severs female victim's carotid
2-2   breaks female's right collarbone
2-3   female—chest below collarbone
2-4   male, below right nipple, destroys heart
2-5   through his forearm and into female victim
2-6   into her Adam's apple
2-7   through her right arm, passes alongside bone, into his right rib cage, breaks rib, travels back and embeds in male's spine
2-8   below her right nipple two inches toward mid-line
2-9   back of male's right hand, into her chest cavity, lacerating her aorta

According to the ME, all nine shots stayed inside the bodies.

This was the killing round. Dan Yates's heart destroyed, Kellee's carotid severed.

Kellee's aorta lacerated.

Buckshot lodged in Dan's spine.

Buckshot lodged in Kellee's throat.

Once again, she moved the paper. This time she was facing the tops of the victims' heads.

She filled in the last round:

3-1   into the ground to the right of Dan Yates
3-2   ditto
3-3   ditto
3-4   ditto
3-5   ditto
3-6   ditto

All of these shots missed the victims, penetrating the floor of the tent and the ground. Laura had recovered all of them.

Shots 3-7 to 3-9 were grouped, within the radius of a tennis ball, and all hit Dan Yates in the back of the head.

3-7   rode the curve of the brainpan and back into the brain stem
3-8   shattered the back of the skull
3-9   also penetrated the back of the skull

With shots 3-8 and 3-9, there was a large outshoot—lots of blood and brain matter spraying the floor and sides of the tent.

She stared at her diagram, the list of shots.

The numbers on the sheet of paper looked cold, clinical, but the effects of the damage piled up. It spread out like a poisonous lake in her stomach, a flat hard pain. The salad felt like crumpled paper, all rough edges.

Amazing what guns could do. She'd been to so many scenes where someone had shot in anger, before they had a chance to think, to realize what they were doing. Homicide detectives actually liked these cases because they were easy solves.

Laura hated them. She hated seeing ordinary people, people who thought of themselves as good, suddenly confronting an evil in themselves they could not previously imagine. Coming face-to-face with the kind of damage they could do, there was inevitably deep shock. Shock and anguish. A decent person up until then, now desperately wishing he could call the bullet back.

People who would have to build, in their minds, a whole new house for their souls.

That was not the case here. The message she got from this guy was, he didn't care.

He didn't care, but then again, he did.

He didn't care enough to look inside the tent, but he cared enough to make sure they were dead. That was where the overkill came in.

He had walked all the way around the tent and shot into three sides. This struck her as deliberate, methodical. But there was a rage component, too.

Thinking about it, looking at the damage, Laura was sure he had known them.

The room was airless. Laura got up and opened the door. A cool breeze slipped in, eddying around her bare ankles, and she thought of Frank Entwistle. No sign of him tonight, even though he might have made himself useful, brainstorming with her as he did in the old days whenever she had a case that bothered her. Even though he was TPD retired, and she was a detective with the state police—rival agencies—Frank had always been her mentor. But these days, Frank Entwistle appeared where and when he wanted to, and there was no way Laura could conjure him up. The man who boasted that he was related to Peg Entwistle, the young starlet from the 1930s who committed suicide by jumping off the H on the Hollywood sign, liked to make dramatic flourishes of his own.

Laura sat back down and stared at the outline of the tent, the two dolls, pretty and blond like their human counterparts.

If it was true that he knew them, the most obvious motive was jealousy.

Which brought her back to Jamie Cottle.

She knew that sometimes love—and rejection—could

grow in a person's mind until it was bigger than anything else.

The people she'd talked to thought Jamic was incapable of violence; that he was shy and quiet, unable to even tell Kellee how he felt. But they couldn't see inside his head.

There was something that bothered her, though. How did the killer know where to find them? Dan and Kellee had run off to Vegas on a lark. Would this person, the killer, follow them all the way to Vegas, and then to the Cataract Lake campground? If that were true, he'd have to pick them up in Flagstaff.

She stared at the circle, trying to empty her mind, create a vacuum for a fresh thought to come in, but all she saw was the dumb circle.

The circle bothered her.

She'd tried to draw a perfect round circle but it hadn't turned out that way. It bulged out on one side. Laura had never had a steady hand for that kind of work. She sketched well, but drawing a straight or curved line—it must not fit in with her personality.

She felt the urge to touch it up, make it more even.

Thinking: *You wouldn't find a perfect circle in nature.*

She sat still for a moment, frozen in place by the thought. Then she grabbed her fanny pack, gun and flashlight, and headed out to her car.

14

Megumi Taylor awoke to an empty bed. Outside she could hear the patter of the sprinkler on the lush ground cover near the cabin. Usually, that was a soothing sound. But there was something big behind the sound of the sprinklers, something outsize and bloated whose shape she sensed but could not articulate.

It took a few minutes for her mind to catch up with the pain inside. When it did, she felt as if she had suddenly stepped on a shard of glass, it was so sharp and piercing.

The sharpness was followed by a dull void. The feeling that there was no future.

She knew that was not true. She had Jack. Jack was her life. But she also understood that their marriage, as she knew it, was over. There were no longer three of them; they were no longer whole. Whatever happened now, it would not be what it was.

Megumi thought she had prepared for that long ago, but now she understood you could never really prepare. As she couldn't with her father and then her mother. There was no preparation for the ghost pain of someone you loved who was no longer there.

Jack's being gone from the bed was nothing new. She knew he had a secret life, friends he corresponded with on e-mail, talked to on the phone. She also knew it had noth-

ing to do with her. She knew it was not another woman.
Jack was not made that way.

Her girlfriends—if she had any left—would have
scoffed at that. Would have told her that she had her head in
the sand. Those were the kind of girlfriends she had when
she lived in San Francisco—skeptical women. Always
looking for the con behind every kind man's act.

No, Jack loved her. But he needed something else, something that belonged to the silence late at night. It was his
restless nature. He needed to move around in his skin, he
needed to reach out to other friends. He used to have a ham
radio. Now he had the Internet.

Silly woman, her friends would say. *Where there's
smoke, there's fire.*

Through the crack in the door, she saw the light on, as
she had seen it countless times over the years of their marriage. She heard his voice, muted, on the phone. The clock
said one fifteen.

Tonight she wanted to go and see if he was all right. She
knew that would break the unspoken bargain between them,
but it was something she needed to do.

She sat up on the bed, her bare toes touching the rag-rug
carpet on the polished pine floor.

Feeling the cool air insinuate itself through her nightgown, caress the back of her calves. She rose, walked
across the gleaming floor, and pushed the door open. It
creaked.

He was sitting in the living room, under the old-
fashioned hurricane lamp, talking on the phone. His back
hunched over the phone, but she saw him stiffen slightly.

She said nothing. He knew she was here and he did not
require her comfort. Sometimes being a wife was lonely.

She walked back into the bedroom. Stood at the window,
looking out at the parking area, the flower border, all
leached of color, the arc of silver water jetting across the
grounds.

As she looked out, the light around her grew.

He stood in the lighted doorway.

A tall silhouette, his arms hanging useless at his sides. For a moment she felt a hard fear rip through her heart— there was an alien quality to the way he just stood there.

He said, "Megumi."

His voice alien, too.

Then he fell to his knees, his hands clutched to his face, and broke into hoarse sobs that came from his depth.

She ran to him, embarrassed and scared at the same time. His wife, the one he turned to, always. She held his hot wet face against her breasts, saying soothing things, some of them in her almost-forgotten language.

He clutched at her and poured out his soul.

15

Laura thought: *This is stupid.*

But she was here now, slowing down for the turn into the Cataract Lake campground. She'd learned long ago to go with her instincts, even if they seemed unreasonable.

To the right she saw headlights on the lane leading out of the campground, bouncing off the trees—a car coming out. The gate to the lake was still closed, but the lane ran a couple hundred feet to that point.

She pulled onto the verge just before the campground entrance to let the car come out. A small car, white. Young man at the wheel, a flash of concern in his wide eyes as the car jounced past her and turned left on Country Club Road. Laura glanced in her side mirror, trying to see the license plate, but it was too dark.

Her heart rate already going double-time.

She made a U-turn and followed the car, which turned on Cataract Road going east. Followed him along the railroad tracks, under the freeway overpass, recording her impressions. The white car was the kind kids who didn't have a lot of money drove. It had a Chevrolet decal on the back window and no hubcaps. Cheap but made to look kid-cool. Possibly souped-up. She radioed in the license plate and got her answer: The car belonged to Jamie Cottle.

Small world.

She followed him toward town. A car pulled off a farm road in front of her, slowing her down, but on this flat terrain, she could track the white car's taillights as it turned onto Seventh Street and headed toward the main part of town.

As she turned on Seventh, the taillights seemed to blink out. She sped up, almost drove right past him. The car was parked under the elm at Shade Tree Mechanics, the kid sitting on the hood.

Laura pulled in so that the car and the kid were in her headlights. She remained inside, assessing the situation. Kid leaning back, cross-legged on the car hood, hands behind him and palms flat on the car. Looking at her.

She stepped out of the car, her right hand close to the SIG Sauer in the paddle holster on her hip. "Police," she said. "Let me see your hands."

He shifted forward, raised his hands up high.

Using her left hand, Laura played her flashlight over him. Kid was tall and sinewy, a thin face bisected by the dark bang of hair falling down over thick brows, the hair parted at the side. He wore a jacket over jeans. Diamond stud in one ear. She couldn't see his expression, but he had cooperated with her immediately.

"Are you Jamie Cottle?"

He cleared his throat. "Yes, ma'am."

Laura identified herself as a DPS officer. "Get down off the car, turn your back to me, and put your hands behind your head. Clasp your fingers together."

He didn't argue. He slid to his feet, turned so his crotch was up against the side of the little car, hands behind his head. Back stretched, an attitude of patient waiting.

"Do you mind if I search you?"

"I guess not."

She patted him down, asked him if he had anything in his pockets that might hurt her. "No, ma'am."

Nothing except a wallet and a couple of sticks of gum. When she was done she asked him to face her.

"Are you aware that Cataract Lake is a crime scene?"

He nodded. "Yes, ma'am."

"What were you doing there?"

A fraction of a pause before he said, "Mourning."

"Mourning."

"Yes, ma'am."

She looked at his face. Pale, stoic. His eyes holding hers. "Can I move now?"

"Yes."

Before she could react, he had the car door open and was sitting in the bucket seat, one long jeaned leg stretched out as he reached for something.

Laura withdrew her weapon and assumed a shooter's stance, her gun locked in both hands and aimed into the car's interior. Every sense was heightened: the scrape of his sneaker on the asphalt, the light falling on his neck as he leaned for the floorboard of the passenger side.

"Let me see your hands."

He didn't react as quickly as he should have. Laura tensed, ready. He could have a knife or gun under the seat.

Jamie Cottle straightened, his hand coming up. "I have to show you this," he was saying.

Holding a sheaf of paper.

He saw the gun leveled at him, and his eyes widened. "Shit."

Laura returned the SIG Sauer to her holster.

"Oh, man." He swallowed. "I just wanted to show you this."

"Go ahead and step out of the car."

He did as he was told. Watching her, his expression unreadable. She held out her hand and he gave her several sheets of paper, stapled. Apricot-yellow in the sodium arc streetlight above. Printouts from Internet sites—news pieces.

She hadn't seen these particular articles, but she knew what they were about.

One of the headlines: *Arizona DPS Detective Nabs Serial Killer.*

Kid looking at her. "That's you, isn't it?"

"Yes, that's me."

"What you did—-that took a lot of guts. I admire you."

What game was he playing? "Why do you have these?"

He brushed at the bangs on his forehead. "When I heard there was DPS here, I recognized your name. I looked it up. I knew what you did in Tucson, how you caught that guy." He flicked his eyes from the printouts to her face. "How are you doing? Do you have any suspects?"

She ignored that. "What were you doing at Cataract Lake?"

"I told you, I was mourning. I went to be at the place where Kellee's soul left this earth." He brushed at his hair again, which had flopped back in place over one eye. "Isn't that what you would do? If it was you?"

This kid knew how to frame the debate. Laura admired his quickness, but it only added to her distrust. "Could you tell me what you were doing Friday night?"

He touched his chest. "Me? You think I would hurt Kellee?" He walked around in a circle, slapped his thigh, looked at the sky. "I can't *believe* that." He came toward her, his shoulders hunched, and Laura's hand tensed again as she stepped back to give herself room to draw the gun if she had to. This was what police work did to you. It made you think about killing or being killed several times a day.

"I would never hurt her!" Cottle was saying. "How can you think that? I would never, ever, harm a hair on her head!"

Turning away from her, walking some more, hands in his pockets. "No way would I do that to Kellee. How could you think that? I love her!"

She consciously softened her tone. "Granted, you love her. But she's dead, and I need to know what you were doing on the night she was killed. To eliminate you as a suspect, if nothing else. You understand that, don't you? I bet you know the statistics. How women are most often killed by their lovers."

"I was *not* her lover. Get that straight. We never, ever

were lovers." His eyes holding hers again. Dark pinpoints in his head, but she could see something wild and untethered behind them. The tip of her thumb hooked over the belt holding her holster, just in case.

"What are you going to do, *shoot* me?"

"Just tell me where you were. How hard is that?"

"I was doing my laundry, okay? While somebody was out there shooting the woman I love—" He stopped. Shook his head.

It looked like real grief to her.

The only problem was, in domestic situations where loved ones were killed, the killers often expressed remorse.

Jamie Cottle was sucking it up. His face impassive, now. His voice neutral. "My friends and I were hanging out on Friday, I had laundry to do so we did it at Sandoval's Seventy-six. I bought a candy bar. Maybe the lady there saw me. In between we cruised, hung, Darrell got some guy to buy us beer at the Circle K. Now I wish it was me who talked to him."

Laura asked him a few more questions, which he answered satisfactorily. She let him go. His last words to her as he climbed into his little car were, "Let me know when you catch the motherfucker. I'll be there!"

He laid scratch out of the parking lot.

Back at the lake, her headlights picking out the pines on either side, the moonlight turning the cinder lane the color of putty. Laura flicked off her lights at the entrance to the campground and cruised in, coasting stealthily down the slight decline, gravel popping off the tires.

Adrenaline just now kicking in. The kid slipping into the car so fast, Laura a hairbreadth away from shooting him. Shooting or being shot.

You never knew when death would come up and hit you in the face. Most people didn't understand that simple truth, but cops did.

She put it out of her mind and thought about Jamie Cottle in a more clinical way. She believed he loved Kellee. But she had no idea how that love might manifest itself. There was something wild about him. It could be that two traumatic blows, so close together, had unhinged him a little bit.

But there was a calculating side to him, too. The way he had gotten her to play on his terms, even if it was only momentarily.

Whichever way you looked at him, Jamie Cottle was a strong kid. Laura was sure there was something he wasn't telling her. She doubted she'd ever get it out of him if he didn't want to tell.

Outside, the night creaked with crickets. She stared up at the indigo sky above the black cutouts of the pines: incredible. The stars spread out above her like an Appaloosa blanket, so close it was dizzying.

The air chilly, the first harbinger of fall.

Laura let her eyes adjust to the darkness, then walked down the road to the campsite. She came to a stop at the fire ring, the small boulders coming up about shin-high. Ran her flashlight beam over the rocks, over the cracks *between* the rocks, looking for the perfect circle.

And there it was, just as she remembered it.

As she played the beam over the crack between the rocks, Laura could make out a thin round rim, a little smaller than the circumference of a quarter. Rubber? Plastic?

You wouldn't see it in the shadow, but with the flashlight beam directly on it, the rim was red.

Laura squatted down, pulling the tweezers and evidence bag out of her jacket pocket. She grasped the rim with the tweezers and tugged gently. Lost her grip and had to do it again. Slowly drawing the red plastic tube upward, already knowing what it was.

A shotgun shell casing.

She put it in the envelope she'd brought with her. Felt herself grin with satisfaction. She glanced around, feeling the chill more than ever now. The level area where she and Richie had worked on the tent floor looked different. It lay in a pool of black shadow from a giant ponderosa pine, but there was something there that wasn't there before, about knee-high.

She walked over.

A makeshift wooden cross, shored up by a pile of rocks, had been erected on the spot where the tent floor had been. Kellee's name was cut into the crossbar.

Laura paged Richie in Tucson. He called back immediately.

"What are the odds?" he said, when she told him. "Talk about your million-to-one shot."

"It must have fallen faceup into that crack. If it was dark when he was cleaning up, there was no way he'd see it."

"He must've been sweating it big-time. Interviewed any nervous nellies lately?"

A few of them, she thought. Maybe Jamie Cottle had put up the cross and spent the rest of his time looking for the cartridge. "You know what I'm thinking? We should have had someone there night and day. I'll bet whoever did this came back looking for it."

"Well, if he did, we weren't there. And he didn't find it. So give yourself a gold star."

Laura said, "I'm sure he knew them."

"What makes you think that?" His voice skeptical.

"The thoroughness. The fact he covered up. Shooting into three sides of the tent, making sure they were dead."

Another pause. Then, "It could just as easily be a random shooting. You said so yourself."

"It could be, but I don't think it is."

"For all we know that shell casing's been there for years."

"No, it was fired recently."

"Okay, so we've got the evidence. Now all we have to do is find the guy who did it."

16

In her dream she was back at Alamo Farm. A blood-orange sun sank low in the sky, melting into the big dark trees in their full summer green. Laura was on her way back to the barn, sitting easy in the English saddle, slightly weary from the work in the ring. A good weariness, though. Calliope, her mare, walking quietly, "on the buckle." There was a small buckle that connected the two separated reins, and when a horse was on the buckle it meant that the rider just let the reins lie flat on the animal's neck, let the horse steer its own way home.

Her feet were out of the stirrups, a relief from the hot pins and needles in the balls of her feet. She leaned down to smooth Calliope's dark velvet neck. Looking between the divining-rod ears, the soft fall of the mare's short mane with each strike of a hoof on ground.

She rode past the tennis court. Jay Ramsey, whose mother owned Calliope and Alamo Farm, was busy hitting tennis balls. Tanned, white-shorted, his blond hair catching the light, he scrambled back and forth, whacking at the lime-green balls shooting out of a machine at one end. Faster and faster, the motorized wheelchair zooming and swooping. so many balls Jay had to catch them in his lap, many of them bouncing to the court floor. Suddenly, the machine stopped, and he turned his chair to watch her go by.

He looked lost.

Another goddamned nightmare. Laura awoke to the motel room in the dark, alone.

She didn't want to be alone, but she was.

The image was strong, almost physical, the way she had reached her hand down and smoothed the mare's rich dark neck with one palm, the delicate tracery of veins underneath. She could smell the slightly wet coat, taste the bloom of dust in her mouth. And the image of Jay Ramsey, young and strong except for the wheelchair, had been vivid; her mind had added the wheelchair in the disjointed way of dreams. When she first knew Jay, he could walk, run, and play tennis. This had been before he was paralyzed in a drug-related shooting.

Not long ago, Jay had helped her with the Musicman case. Now he was dead. More fallout from the case—the gift that kept on giving. The place Laura remembered so vividly from her childhood would also soon recede into the past with nothing to physically hold it to the earth. Jay was gone, Calliope was gone, and Alamo Farm would soon be up for sale.

Laura was aware of music—faint and country. She looked out the window and saw Wendy sitting outside the office across the way.

Suddenly, she wanted company—wanted it badly. She pulled on her clothes and went out to say hello.

"If Shana was going to sell him, I wished she'd've asked me first." Wendy Baker ground another Marlboro into the coffee can sand.

The subject at hand was Mighty Mouse.

"You know what she got for him?" Wendy asked Laura.

"I didn't ask." Laura had seen the check, but she had no

idea what percentage of the twelve thousand dollars had been for the horse, and what had been for the trailer.

"I doubt Mrs. Wingate would sell him, if she bought him for Erin. My little sister is just starting the circuit. She's good but her horse isn't the best, and he would be perfect for her."

Laura reached down to let Chelsea sniff her hand, then rubbed her luxurious neck, thinking about the Thoroughbreds on Barbara Wingate's farm. "That's a nice thing she does, taking in those horses."

"She and her husband were both such good people. Really cared about the community—events, charity drives, you name it, she's on it. She basically runs the rodeo." Wendy lit another cigarette and blew a long stream of smoke into the air. "The kind of person you'd think would get a break from God—if there really is a God. But, shoot, it didn't work out that way. First her husband, then Kathy." Wendy saw Laura's puzzled look and added, "Kathy was Josh's older sister. She and her husband Mike died in a car wreck. Huge shock. They were both doctors at the Health Care Center—Mike delivered my niece. That's how come Mrs. Wingate's bringing up Erin."

"That must be tough," Laura said.

"Never once did she complain or ask for help—and Erin's got her share of problems. Mrs. Wingate's pioneer stock, that's for sure. The backbone of this community, people like that. Like my mom and dad. My dad lost a hand in Vietnam, but he came back and bought this motel, raised five kids, and none of us got in trouble." She flicked an ash. "When I was a kid, I wanted to be like her—Mrs. Wingate. She used to teach catechism at Mother of Sorrows, and she was so beautiful I thought she was one of the angels when I was little. Kind of like those sixties westerns that are always on the movie channel? Like Hayley Mills, only older? I even dyed my hair so I could look like that." She touched her long dark hair. "*That* was never going to happen. Besides having dark hair and skin, I was a real string bean. Flat as a board."

She reached down and stroked Chelsea. "Are you any closer to finding out who did it?"

"Not really."

"Josh Wingate was the one who found them, wasn't he?"

The small-town jungle drums were going night and day. Laura had looked at the papers, and there had been no mention of who had discovered the bodies. "He was first at the scene. By the way, do you know a guy named Luke Jessup?"

"Luke? That street preacher who pesters the tourists? To tell you the truth, we've had to run him off a few times—he scares people away. You know, when they're trying to check in? Why?"

"We want to talk to him."

Wendy looked at her with new interest. "Why? You think he did it?"

"No. I just want to talk to him. You don't know where I can find him?"

She tipped the chair back so she was leaning against the wall. "Are you kidding? Nobody ever went looking for him before. Everyone's always tried to get him to go away."

The sun was just up, mist clinging to the pines and rising off the surface of Cataract Lake. Earlier in the investigation, Laura had taken six rolls of the scene and the surrounding area. Now she took another two, paying particular attention to the wooden cross Jamie Cottle had left at the tent site.

Cottle had placed the cross on the leveled area where the tent had been. Anyone could walk into the campground; crime-scene tape wouldn't keep them out. Laura wished she'd thought to post someone here day and night. Just another example of how she wasn't firing on all cylinders.

She'd ask the Williams PD if they could spare someone for a day or two, just in case Jamie came back.

On her way here she'd stopped by the Cottle house. Jamie's white car was in the driveway just outside the garage. No lights on, no sign that anyone was awake. Laura had not slept the rest of the night, even though she and Wendy parted company around two. She'd spent a lot of that time wishing she could pick up the phone and call Tom.

She'd taken Polaroids of Jamie Cottle's car from all four angles. She would canvass the area around here again and ask if anyone had seen the car that night. Wondered if she should retrace her steps back to Las Vegas. She didn't remember seeing a car like Jamie's on the videotape at the Kingman Circle K, but her memory could be faulty. Maybe Jamie had followed Dan and Kellee to the wedding chapel.

She also wondered how Jamie Cottle knew where Kellee had died. He could have seen the colored flags they had planted into the ground marking the tent's four sides. Even so, he had planted the cross on the right-hand side, where Dan and Kellee had come to rest.

Had he done it unconsciously?

Laura stared out at the lake, thinking about Jamie Cottle and T. J. Cottle. What happened when your brother was killed and the man who was with him managed to avoid serious consequences? Would that push you deeper into fantasy? Laura could see Jamie putting all his needs and wants onto Kellee's shoulders. She could see him fixating on her, the one good thing in his life, the one hopeful thing.

What would happen when he found out she was married?

In her briefcase on the picnic table was a copy of the T. J. Cottle file. It was thin, and there were gaps. No charges had been filed against Richard Garatano, not even for marijuana possession or providing a minor with alcohol.

According to the file, a forest ranger named Brent Stabler had been patroling the campground when he saw a man pulling his boat up onto shore. The man yelled to him, told him he needed help. He sounded panicked.

"I think my friend drowned," the man said. "I can't find

him anywhere. I've been out there a half hour looking and he never came up."

The forest ranger's report said the man, whom he recognized as the Williams High School football coach, smelled of pot and beer.

The next day, divers found T. J. Cottle's body wrapped in the weeds. According to the autopsy, T. J. Cottle had drowned with both marijuana and alcohol in his system. The autopsy had also shown there had been no overt evidence of sexual activity, a mercy to the parents.

Garatano was fired two days later. Laura learned he had since left town with his wife and newborn son.

Garatano, the source of Jamie Cottle's anguish, had left town. Where would that leave Jamie? Where could he aim his anger? If other things went wrong in his life, how would he react?

Jamie might think that Kellee's marriage was the ultimate betrayal.

Laura had mixed feelings about Cottle. There was something about him, something she couldn't quite get at. It bothered her. There were parts of him that reminded her of an apparent empty space on a computer's hard drive: unknowable. But who knew what was really lurking there?

His grief seemed genuine, though.

But he also seemed like the kind of kid who would hold on to what he wanted like a pit bull.

17

When she got back to her room the phone was ringing. Laura put down the sack she'd gotten from the bakery—a butter croissant and a Styrofoam cup of "gourmet coffee"— and grabbed the phone, making note of the time: eight fifteen.

"Is this Detective Cardinal?"

A woman's voice, high, scared, breathless. Laura recognized it immediately: Louise Yates. Babbling.

"Chuck doesn't believe me, he says she's probably just with her boyfriend, but it's been two days and she always calls in—"

"Take a deep breath; take your time. I'm right here."

Louise paused. Laura thought she heard a little whimper.

"Shana's gone. She's been gone for two days, her bed hasn't been slept in, and she was supposed to pick up the boys today. I *know* that!" She said this last to Chuck. "Chuck says she's done this before, and that's true, and she can be undependable ..." She was babbling again, her voice kiting higher and higher, disconnected from her body. "But she wouldn't do that to the boys, she's a good mother. . . . I just know something's wrong."

"Did you call the police?"

"Chuck thought it would be better if I called you. That way, if she turned up, we wouldn't have caused all that trouble—you know, getting them to write up a report? I thought because you've been so nice, the things you've done, and . . ." She suddenly wound down.

"You need to call them and make a report."

"But—"

"It's important you do that. The Williams Police Department has access to all the databases, and they know their town." She paused. "But I'd like to come out, if I may."

Her voice almost drowned in relief: "You will?"

"But you've got to report it, okay? Tell them everything you can think of, where she might have gone, who her friends are. I'll be there as soon as I can."

When Laura arrived at the Yates house, Louise burst out the screen door and hurried down the steps. "Thank God!"

Laura glanced at the carport. "Is your husband here?"

"No, he went down to talk to the police. I'm so glad you're here." She bit her lip. "First Dan, and now . . . maybe, do you think it's connected?"

"I doubt that. Let's go in and sit down, okay?"

Laura noticed that the woman kept glancing at the street every time a car came up this way, her expression hopeful. "Can we stay out here? At the picnic table?"

"Sure."

They sat down at the table next to a rusted swing set that must have been used by Dan and Kellee when they were kids. The jungle gym beside it was yellow, red, plastic, and new. Bought for Shana's children by doting grandparents?

"When did you last see Shana?"

Worried, hooded eyes. "Last— No, the night before last. She had dinner with us and then said she was going out for a while." She had picked up the hem of the faded vinyl tablecloth and folded it back on the planks of the table, was rolling it as tightly as she could, letting the roll loosen and drop off, and then starting over again.

"She didn't say where she was going?"

"She never does. Sometimes it seems like she's just a

boarder. No, I shouldn't say that. She's just careless—you know, weren't you like that when you were her age?"

When I was her age I was spending my days in a Tucson courtroom. She had faced her parents' killer day after day for three weeks. Her only ally was the big man who sat with her, TPD homicide detective Francis X. Entwistle.

Louise Yates said, "I just thought she needed to get away. She has lots of friends, and I'm sure she needed to talk to her . . . her peers. She's just been wild. She and Danny were so close. He always looked after her, and now she's all alone. She's so angry, but you know that's just hurt."

"Did she leave with anything?"

"I didn't notice. I haven't been noticing much. She just slammed out of here, saying she had to get—she said, 'get the hell out of this stupid house,' those are her exact words. She didn't eat anything; I didn't either. . . ." A car went by, and her eyes followed it. "She got into fights with her dad. Neither of us had the energy. I know we're supposed to take care of her—she's our *daughter*—but it was like . . ." She swallowed. Close to tears again, but she managed to hold them down. "It was like—for me, anyway—it was like a balloon and all the air went out. No air at all. I just couldn't cope. Couldn't help her at all. And Chuck's no use. Sometimes I think he's afraid of her." She'd rolled the tablecloth up tightly about a third of the way, let it roll back down, kinking.

"Is there anything missing from her room?"

"I don't know. I just looked in and saw the bed wasn't slept in. She doesn't like me poking and prying in her room. She has a suitcase set," she volunteered. "I got it for her when she was in high school choir and they had to go on a trip—" Her eyes widened. "You think she left on purpose?"

"She could have."

"She wouldn't . . ." Louise stopped, covered her mouth with her fingertips.

"She wouldn't what?"

"Leave her sons."

"Maybe she just needed to get away for a few days."

Louise caught her eye, her gaze hopeful. "You think so?"

"It might be her way of coping. She's been through an incredible trauma. You all have. Is there someplace in town she'd go? A friend's place, maybe?"

Louise frowned, the lines etched like fork marks between her eyebrows. "She's got some girlfriends. And then there's her boyfriend."

Stressing the word "boyfriend." A distasteful look on her face.

"Bobby Burdette?"

She fluttered her hand. "I don't think it's serious." She cleared her throat. "You'd have to meet him, to know why. For one thing, he's too old for her. Thirty-eight if he's a day."

"What does he do?"

"I think he drives a truck. A bread truck?" she asked herself, then answered. "Holsum or Goodness Bakery—one of those. I remember she told me that. Used to drive cross-country, a truck driver. I think it's just a phase," she added hastily. "She's planning on going to college, she's planning to enroll at Grand Canyon College next January."

"May I look at her room?"

Laura wondered how Louise had known Shana's bed had not been slept in. The room looked as if it had been hit by a hurricane; more of a high school girl's room than that of an adult woman with two children.

At first sight, there was nothing to indicate the presence of those children, except for the edge of a baby book sticking out beneath a couple of framed photographs and a fuchsia Victoria's Secret bra. The subjects of the photographs were not visible; they had toppled underneath the weight of the landfill of styling brushes, makeup, perfume bottles, and bra.

Louise had told her the boys lived with their father and

his family, which essentially meant they were being raised by their grandparents.

She wondered at the dynamics. The younger child couldn't be more than a year old. Who had made the decision where the children would be raised, and how did that sit with the family on the other side of the equation? There was a lot more she needed to know about Shana Yates—her relationship with her brother not the least of it.

As Laura walked through the room, she pondered the situation. Despite the fact that Shana was twenty-one, she was not far from being a kid herself. Laura wasn't surprised that the grandparents were raising her children, especially in the aftermath of divorce. Still—and maybe it was old-fashioned and sexist—she would have thought that the daughter's parents would be the ones to raise the child.

Tucking her hands under her arms to avoid touching anything, she made a slow circuit of the room, just looking. Lots of junk, but a picture emerged. Shana was sloppy, immune to dust mites, liked pink, and was a closet environmentalist.

The calendar on the wall was from the World Wildlife Federation. Two posters on the wall: one of Eminem, and one of a wolf. A look at Shana's bookshelves (many of the books piled one on top of the other instead of standing on end) yielded a book by Aldo Leopold and *The Monkey Wrench Gang,* by Edward Abbey, stacked on top of a dozen or so copies of *Cosmopolitan* and *People* magazines.

There were a few other books, mostly youth-oriented self-help, from *He's Just Not That Into You* to *Christian and Young.* A book on feng shui—judging from the state of this room, Laura doubted Shana had ever even cracked the spine—and a book on horse training: *Lyons on Horses.* A dusty case of Avon products with her name on the label— was she an Avon lady?

Country music and hip-hop stacked haphazardly in a plastic bin. The country music CDs were from a few years ago, the hip-hop, which was on top, the most recent. As if

Shana had suddenly turned off country and switched to rap music.

All over the map.

A portable file box next to the bookshelf, a WWF decal on the side.

Donning latex, Laura opened the box. Three files, two of them labeled in Shana's bubblelike script. Laura opened the one marked *Clippings*. On top was a cutout from the *Williams News* on a fire at a Williams car dealership. Three SUVs had been burned to the ground. A black-and-white photo accompanied the article, showing an SUV engulfed in flames against the night sky, firefighters launching a thick stream of spray from their fire hoses. The article was dated June 13.

Laura scanned the article. An accelerant had been used—gasoline—and an environmental group, the Earth Warriors, had sent an e-mail to the paper claiming responsibility.

The Earth Warriors. She'd never heard of them. She glanced around the room, at the nature calendar, the posters, *The Monkey Wrench Gang*.

Was Shana a member of the Earth Warriors?

Laura went back over her conversations with Shana, and couldn't remember one reference to the environment. If you went by stereotypes, Shana would have more in common with the ranching families than environmentalists. She grew up here in Williams, not a bastion of liberal thought, and her off time had been spent at horse shows and rodeos.

Which reminded her. Something was missing.

There were no photos of Mighty Mouse. No ribbons, no silver bowls, no belt buckles.

Had Shana taken them with her? Or had she decided to put that part of herself away? Sometimes it was less painful to close a door, so you didn't have to think about the life you once led. Laura was no stranger to that. In the eleven years since her parents' death—after she had sold the place and stored her parents' possessions—she had gone by the house exactly once, on an impulse.

Shana had sold the horse, the trailer, all her tack to Mrs. Wingate.

If she had closed that chapter in her life, was she about to close another? Could she have left for good?

Laura had searched the room, the closet, and had found no luggage, matching or otherwise. Shana had definitely planned to stay more than one night, and her closet was only a third full, her dresser drawers close to empty. Planning for an extended stay?

She had taken off without telling anyone.

Laura looked at the file box again. There were no other clippings other than a follow-up article on the SUV burning.

She looked at the two other files. One was marked, *Someday*. Inside there were more clippings, but these were more in keeping with a twenty-one-year-old woman-child prone to dreaming big about the future. There was a photo of a Porsche Boxster, bright yellow, and one of a grandly rustic cabin—more like a lodge—overlooking a pristine blue lake, cutout from a glossy magazine. The place was called Big Bear Creek Lodge, situated on the Big Bear Lake in Montana. There were also sumptuous pictures of the interior—cowboy chic—and other photos of rooms taken of homes in Los Angeles, the Caribbean, and Aspen. There was a Hinckley picnic boat yacht, a swimming pool where you almost couldn't tell where the water left off and the bay began. Expensive clothing, the kind of stuff you'd get on Rodeo Drive. Beautiful women walking down a red carpet, giving off the aura of untouchability. Laura recognized them: movie stars.

Shana thought big.

The last folder was unmarked, but contained magazine articles about recent environmental setbacks throughout the country. A depressing litany of dying rivers, toxic beaches, lost species.

Laura looked back at the *Someday* file. There was a schism between some of the things Shana wanted for her self (the rustic lodge, a moose head staring glassily from the wall coming to mind) and the atrocities to the environment.

Shana knew how to compartmentalize.

"She'd tell me if she was going to leave," Louise Yates said.

"Her suitcases are gone."

Louise touched her hand to her mouth. "I can't believe I didn't know." She sat down on the brown tweed couch facing the fireplace, her face ash gray.

"I found her address book," Laura said. "Can you go through it with me and tell me who she might have gone to stay with?"

Armed with Shana's mobile-phone number and the numbers of a half dozen of Shana's friends, Laura drove to the Williams PD to compare notes with the officer who took Chuck Yates's statement.

Officer Wingate, who had taken down the information, had just gone out on patrol. Laura arranged to meet him outside the Dairy Queen.

He was sitting in his car when she approached, but got out and they sat down on a low wall that divided the parking lot.

"How are you doing?" he asked her.

"I should ask you that."

"Okay, I guess." He shrugged, looked at his feet.

Laura noticed he was freshly scrubbed, but the flesh beneath his eyes was bruised-looking and his eyes were red.

He added, "It would've been worse a couple of years ago. Because he lived in Flag. Him going to NAU and me to the academy and becoming a cop. We didn't see each other much, except in the summers."

Trying to put space between himself and Dan. Laura understood why he had to do it. "I read your missing-persons report on Shana. That's what I wanted to ask you about."

"Not much to tell. She probably just took off to clear her head."

"Did you know her well?"

"Nah." He ran his hand over his short-cropped hair. "When we were kids she used to tag along sometimes. Kind of funny, because they were born a couple of minutes apart. If you didn't know them, you'd always think of her as Dan's little sister."

"Dan looked out for her?"

"Yeah. Of course there were times he saw her as a monumental pain in the ass."

"They were still close?"

"Probably. He was always the one she turned to if she needed anything. I wouldn't say she was a clinging vine, exactly, but she usually got him to do what she wanted."

"How so?"

"She was kind of a drama queen, you know? Used emotional blackmail to get her way. More than once Dan had to go rescue her. Get her out of some scrape or another." He scratched his neck. "One time she got stranded at a bar when the guy she was with drove off and left her. Neither one of them were of legal age yet, but Dan had to go into the Buckhorn Bar to get her."

"Do you have any idea where she would go?"

"To tell you the truth, I didn't know her all that well. She had a friend named Heather she used to hang around with."

Laura looked at her list. Heather was on it.

A small car went by, stereo thumping so loudly it resonated in Laura's gut. The back windshield emblazoned with the Virgin of Guadalupe.

Josh Wingate said, "I heard you found a shell casing. That ought to help a lot."

"Only if we have a suspect."

"That's what I figured." His eyes continually scanned the

street: a cop's eyes. Always on alert. "You have anything else? I'm really hoping you can catch this guy."

"Not much. You heard about Luke Jessup. I'm still trying to find him."

"You know I was the one who took the report on that one, too?"

"No."

"I wouldn't put too much stock in what he says. Sounded to me like he didn't see much, if he saw anything at all."

"You don't think he'd make a good witness?"

He shrugged. "Just the feeling I got. I've seen him around town. He's always buttonholing people about something. Usually it's about being 'saved.'"

Laura said, "Why did Dan major in forestry?"

"I don't know. I suppose it was a natural."

"Because he cared about the environment?"

"He wasn't a tree hugger, that's for sure. But he loved to hunt and fish, be outdoors. But I wouldn't call him an environmentalist."

"What about Shana?"

"What?"

"Was Shana an environmentalist?"

"Shana?" He looked at her, snorted. "I never heard her talk about it, if she was." He wiped his sleeve across his face. "Of course, I haven't seen her lately. Any wind could blow her—she was always getting excited about some damn thing or other, like, this was *it*, you know? This was what she was going to do. When she married that guy, the one she had those kids with? He belonged to est or eck or something like that—she was convinced that was the be-all and end-all. Threw herself into it headfirst."

"She still into it?"

"I doubt it. That was just one in a whole string of fads. She was gonna join AmeriCorps, but nothing ever came of that. Usually it was because there was some guy involved."

"You mean in the group?"

"Yeah. Dan was always worried about that. How she

didn't seem to have any core. He said the only thing she ever stuck to was barrel racing. But that's not totally true. No matter what was going on in her life, she always stuck to Dan."

Back at Williams PD, Laura asked to see the report for the arson at Jimmy Davis Ford. While she waited, she made some phone calls, with limited results. Heather Olson, the friend Josh Wingate told her about, apparently didn't own an answering machine. After eight rings, Laura hung up.

Heather lived in Flagstaff and attended NAU. Maybe Shana was staying with her. A nice thought, but things rarely worked out that way.

She tried two others of Shana's friends, and got voice mail messages for both. When she called Bobby Burdette, she got an answering machine. She hung up. Next, she ran him on NCIC. Two convictions: one for domestic violence—he had pleaded out and spent three months on probation—and one for a series of small-time burglaries. He'd spent two and a half years in prison for that. He'd graduated from Florence three and a half years ago, presumably walking the straight and narrow since then.

Domestic violence. According to the records, he had grabbed his girlfriend and shoved her head in a toilet.

Why a girl from a nice religious family would put up with someone like that, Laura didn't know. From what Laura had heard, Shana was needy, but she also called the shots when she wanted to. Using her vulnerability to get what she wanted. She certainly controlled her brother that way.

Go figure. Love—or what passed for love—manifested itself in strange ways.

Officer Tagg appeared with the report on Jimmy Davis Ford. "Not much to it," he said apologetically, and left.

The report was pretty straightforward. Although the Earth Warriors had contacted the Williams paper to take credit for the fire, there had been no arrests.

Laura looked at the lab report. The accelerant used was gasoline, but the special kind of gasoline used for boat engines. The three torched SUVs were all Ford Excursions, brand-new, each one estimated at $36,000 to $50,000.

The name Earth Warriors had been run on NCIC and VICAP, but there were no matches. Was it a new group? Or a made-up name to throw the investigation off?

Back at the motel Laura fired up the laptop and looked for the Earth Warriors on three different search engines. She came up with only one reference, and that was a blog by a guy named Peter Sage, who apparently had a limitless appetite for writing about everything and anything, none of it the least bit interesting. Laura was almost cross-eyed by the time she found the words "Earth Warriors" buried in a two-page paragraph.

". . . a guy named John something-or-other. I heard he was in an ecoterrorist group called the Earth Warriors or some such thing, in the *sixties,* if you believe that. Janet said he loved avant garde art, her stuff in particular, and bought several pieces. . . ."

She backed up and read the beginning of the sentence. Janet, apparently, had sold a house in Ojai for the man named John. From the context of the blog, she got the impression that this had happened sometime in the early nineties.

She scanned the blog for further references, but after learning more than she ever wanted to know about waterlily cultivation, gave up. She did send Peter Sage an e-mail asking him to contact her.

So, going by what she had just read, there had been an Earth Warriors ecoterrorist group in the sixties in California. Laura wondered if the new group had stumbled on the name somewhere or if they came up with it on their own. Either way, she doubted the 1960s Earth Warriors were still going, especially since she hadn't found any references in legitimate media.

Laura had a prelunch meeting with Bobby Burdette's parole officer—prelunch because he kept looking at the clock of his tiny gray cubicle and mentioning how hungry he was. He had little to offer except an unflattering mugshot of Bobby, his current address, reports he photocopied for her with considerable reluctance, and a piece of advice. Clasping his hands over his prodigious paunch, he swiveled back and forth in his chair and regarded her sadly. "Whatever you do, don't get him riled. He doesn't like women, and you seriously don't want to cross this guy."

Laura went by Bobby Burdette's house, a cheap but neat gray clapboard house on Edison near Seventh Street. Two big box elders dominating the dirt yard surrounded by the ubiquitous chain-link. An aluminum johnboat sat beside the short cinder driveway, under a portable carport—white cloth stretched into a pitched metal frame. Laura didn't see an outboard motor, but from the marks on the boat, she assumed there was one somewhere, maybe in the metal shed nearby. Boat fuel, too. Hopefully, she could come back and take a good look later, if things went well and she got a warrant.

She debated leaving her card in his screen door, but decided she would rather make it a surprise.

A call to the Goodness Bread bakery depot headquartered in Flagstaff yielded the information that Bobby Burdette was a relief driver for a route franchise that covered Kingman, Williams, and the outskirts of western Flagstaff—that whole stretch of I-40. In a stroke of good luck, he was currently just up the street unloading baked goods at the Williams Safeway. Laura found him in the bread section, unloading hot-dog buns from plastic bakery baskets stacked up on a fifteen-foot-high rack. As she approached, he paused to add up something on a machine that looked like a cross between a clipboard and a calculator.

Laura lingered at the other end of the aisle, in the greeting card section, getting a good look at him.

He looked like his mugshot: thin and seedy-looking, the same dead look in his eyes. His hair was solid black and clipped military-short. He had naturally dark skin that had been damaged by the sun. He was shorter than she imagined. He wore a short-sleeved shirt and dark purple tie, putty-colored slacks over work boots. The short-sleeved shirt barely cut off the tattoo of an eagle, poorly rendered. It looked like a jail tat.

She watched him work. His movements were smooth and precise, no action wasted. A good worker.

Laura tried to picture him with Shana, though—hard to do. Hard, too, to see him through Shana's eyes, what he might represent to her. He was older, so maybe it was a father thing. But this guy didn't seem anything like Chuck Yates, at least not in looks.

She hung back, thinking about how she wanted to play it.

Straight. She cleared her throat. "Are you Robert Burdette?"

He stopped midrustle, cocked his head at her. She saw that his eyes were dark brown, and the irises seemed to jiggle. "Who wants to know?"

"Laura Cardinal, Department of Public Safety." She pushed back her light jacket so he could see the shield hooked to her belt.

"Let me see that."

Laura handed it to him and he studied it, eyes darting back and forth—little tiny shudders. Some kind of physical problem? Or drugs. Taking his time. She wondered if he had problems reading. Finally he handed it back to her. "This about Dan Yates?"

"I understand you came back from Las Vegas with Shana."

He moved a step closer to her, his shoe squeaking on

linoleum, and Laura took a step back, freeing up her body in case she needed her weapon.

He saw that and smiled, knowing why she did it. In no way intimidated. "I did come back with Shana, then I turned right around and went back to Kingman. Had to be in bed early because I had to get to the bakery outlet by four A.M."

"Long drive, isn't it?"

He kicked his toe lightly into the side of the cart. "I'm used to long drives."

"Why did you come back with her?"

"I wanted to give the lovebirds some time alone." The way he said "lovebirds," it could have been something nasty. Still standing close, his chin tipped up so he could look her in the eye. "Plus, Shana and Kellee didn't get along that well, had a little tiff about something. You know how *that* can be. So I volunteered to take her back and drop her off."

"Have you seen her lately?"

"No. Should I?"

Trying to intimidate her, put her on the defensive. Clear to her that Bobby Burdette had done time.

"No reason," Laura said, purposely lowering her voice so he had to listen to her. "Except that her brother's dead and you have a relationship with her."

"Is that what she said? We have a relationship?"

"Am I wrong, sir?"

He shook his head as if he didn't believe what he was hearing. Those jumping-bean eyes fixed on her, hard to look at. "In her head, we do."

"What are you saying? You and she—"

"Shana thinks it's more than it is. I'm not saying we haven't had our fun—but even that wears thin after a while. There's nothing there, you know?"

Laura asked, "How'd you two meet?"

"I don't see that's any business of yours."

"In the Earth Warriors?"

For just an instant his hard-shell eyes flickered. "What's that?"

"An ecoterrorist group. You heard about those SUVs burned at a car dealership here in town a couple of months ago?"

"Oh, yeah."

"Did you know Dan well?"

"Not really."

"How about Kellee?"

"Nope."

"But you were a witness at their wedding."

"Nothing wrong with that, is there?"

Laura tried another tack. "Is Shana into the environment?"

He shrugged, his eyes shutting down.

He was not going to tell her anything. She debated asking him where Shana was now, but her instinct told her not to. She didn't trust anything he said, and if he didn't know Shana had taken off, Laura didn't want to be the one to tell him.

"Look, I've got to be in Kingman by two. It's noon now." He motioned to the half-filled rack. "I've got a living to make."

Laura handed him her card. "If you have anything more to share, you can call my mobile."

"Like what?"

"Anything—maybe something you forgot about Dan and Kellee."

As she turned away, she heard him snicker.

A block away, on Seventh Street, was Jimmy Davis Ford. Half the lot was taken up by humongous sport-utility vehicles, most of them navy blue, black, or tan. Triangular flags shivered on lines stretched around the lot—red, white, and blue, to go with the large flag high up on a pole next to the office.

Laura was looking for Dave Lonigan, the assistant manager. He had been the one who first saw the fire from his home and called the fire department. According to his account, the SUVs were engulfed in flames by the time he reached the dealership.

An overweight, thirtyish man with wren-brown hair and plain features approached her. Kmart shirt and tie combo, small gold nameplate that said, DAVE LONIGAN.

"May I help you, ma'am?" he asked.

She introduced herself. "Is there a place we can talk?"

"Sure." He led the way into the showroom, mostly plate glass, past another shiny black behemoth and into a small office that barely held a desk and two chairs. Lots of olives and purples, fabric walls.

Laura asked him several questions about the SUV arson, and he answered her patiently, although he kept one eye on the parking lot. It must have been her day for swivelers; he swiveled back and forth in his purple chair and tapped the pencil of his pen and pencil set against the blotter, a closet drummer. He basically told her things she already knew from the report.

"You were first on the scene?"

"I saw the glow—I only live a few blocks from here." Everybody lived a few blocks away from everybody else in this town. "I called nine-one-one and then I jumped in the car and headed over there."

"Did you know it was the dealership?"

"I had a pretty strong feeling."

"Why was that?"

Swivel. "Location—where the fire was coming from. "And—" He reached into the top desk drawer, withdrew a sheet of paper, and pushed it across the desk at her with a flourish that she suspected he used to get people to sign on the dotted line. Laura noticed he wore a Williams High School class ring and had manicured nails.

She looked at the paper, a photocopy. It was a memo from Jimmy R. Davis, the owner himself, warning his employees to report anything or anyone suspicious on the grounds.

"Somebody sent Mr. Davis a note basically threatening to do something like this," Dave Lonigan said.

"Do you have a copy of the note?"

"No, ma'am. Mr. Davis does, but he's not here right now."

"Where is he?"

"He's got another dealership in Pinetop. He's there right now."

Laura made note of that.

Dave Lonigan's sharp eye caught a potential customer looking at a new Mustang. "Is that all?" he asked.

"For now."

They both stood up, Lonigan eager to get out there. She followed him through the door, saw him stride in the direction of the lone woman. The woman took one look at him, made an about-face, and hurried to her car.

Lonigan stopped, looking resigned.

"That happen often?"

"With women it does. Some of them like to poke around for a while without anyone looking, get their bearings first." He shook his head. "She didn't look like the type, but who knows?" He looked at her. "You're investigating Dan Yates's murder, am I right?"

She nodded.

"Does that have anything to do with this? The arson?"

Laura was about to answer when he added, "The reason I asked, Dan Yates was here not two weeks ago, asking me about the same thing."

"Dan Yates was?"

"Yes, ma'am. He wanted to talk to Mr. Davis. I think he wanted to see the note Mr. Davis got."

"Do you know if he got to see him?"

"Not really. Mr. Davis wasn't here, but he could have come back."

Laura had put away her memo pad but brought it back

out again, turned a fresh page. "What did he say to you, exactly?"

"He just wanted to know about the fire. He asked if we had any warning, and I told him we did. You don't think someone shot him because of this?"

She ignored that. "Did he say anything else?"

"No. I had a customer."

"What was his demeanor like?"

"He seemed, I don't know, grim? Determined. Come to think of it, I bet he *did* talk to Mr. Davis. He had that look in his eye like nothing was going to get in his way."

18

Tickled Pink, a clothing boutique on Aspen Street in downtown Flagstaff, was squeezed in between two other shops in a row of storefronts. The store on the right was called The Cliff's Edge, an outdoor/sporting goods store catering to mountain climbers. The shop on the left was a soda fountain, tourists wearing shorts and flip-flops on this Indian-summer day. Laura noticed a whole crew of girls about nine or ten years old, taking up the four wrought-iron tables and ice-cream-parlor chairs, chattering animatedly. Most of them wore tights and leotards under short skirts that barely skimmed their behinds. The girls who were standing seemed to naturally splay their feet out. They had unusual grace, most of them slim but not haggard. Hair pulled back. From their name tags Laura assumed that they were part of a dance class on an outing, probably at NAU. There were also several women Laura assumed were their mothers, in their thirties and forties, looking like older versions of their daughters.

In between the young dancers and the specialized clientele of The Cliff's Edge, the Tickled Pink staked out its own territory.

In the windows were translucent mannequins wearing pink—tank tops, lowriders, miniskirts. All shades of pink interspersed with other colors in paisleys, plaids, and flowers. One of the short skirts flying above the waist, in a racier version of Marilyn Monroe on the grate.

Everything that wasn't translucent pink was mirrored, creating the effect of a hall of mirrors at a carnival. It gave Laura a headache.

According to her roommate, Heather Olson was supposed to be working today. A college-age girl sat behind a tall counter, wearing a pink blouse that showed off a large bust. Laura wondered if wearing pink was a requirement of the job. The girl's face was pretty but forgettable, her dark hair parted in the middle, healthy and shiny as a seal's coat.

She held up pink-lensed cardboard glasses. "Want to wear these? They make everything pinker."

"That's the last thing I want." Laura glanced around the store. Empty. Maybe this place wasn't as cool as advertised. "I'm looking for Heather Olson."

"That's me."

Laura approached, showed her her shield.

Heather's expression changed to pained. "Is this about Dan?"

"About Dan and Shana. Has Shana contacted you?"

"No."

Something about the way she said it. A coolness?

"I understand you're a friend of Shana's?"

"Actually, I'm not." Her voice a little high, her breath a little quicker. Not agitated, but it was clear that Shana's name affected her—adversely.

"You're not friends? I got the impression you were."

"How'd that happen?"

"Her mother gave me a list of six or seven of her closest friends."

"I doubt she's got *one* friend, let alone six."

That surprised her. "But you were friends, right?"

"In high school."

"Is there anybody you can think of who she'd go see if she were in trouble?"

Heather jumped on that like a pouncing cat. "She's in trouble?"

"I'm not saying that. She's certainly upset over her brother's death. I just need to talk to her."

"God, that's awful about Dan. He was such a good guy."

"But Shana wasn't so great?"

"She's a backstabber."

"She backstabbed you?"

"Me and everybody else."

"Can you tell me what it was about?"

"Oh, why not? There was this guy I really liked. She knew how I felt about him, but she went after him anyway. Even though she was living with someone—"

"The someone she was living with, was that her husband, Ronnie?"

"Yeah, before they got married. I know she got pregnant just to get him to marry her."

"I thought kids today were beyond that kind of thing."

"Williams is a small town. Lots of white-bread people there, you know what I mean?"

"So she took this guy from you."

"She didn't take him. He wasn't *mine*. She threw herself at him and he responded—what are you going to do, someone flaunts it in your face? That was the thing about Shana. Everything was a competition. She only wanted something if she couldn't have it."

"Did you ever meet Bobby Burdette?"

"Who?"

"A guy she's seeing. You've never heard her talk about him?"

"I haven't talked to Shana in three and a half years."

Laura produced her list of names and numbers. "Do you know any of these girls?"

"All of them."

"Would Shana go stay with any of them?"

Heather hunched over the book, her brows knitted together. "Maybe Jillian."

"Jillian?"

"Jillian North. They were pretty thick, after she and I had our fight. Shana always found somebody. She went from friend to friend—like they were interchangeable. As long as she had someone to get through the day with. And when she got a boyfriend, she'd just leave you hanging."

- "Sounds like she put you through the wringer."

"I'm not the only one. The school halls were littered with the bodies of 'friends' she walked over. I mean, I lasted longer than anybody else, but I've got eyes. She'd make friends with someone, spend all her time with them, and then she'd dump them and it was on to the next one."

"But you think she might still be friends with this Jillian."

Heather Olson shrugged. "Jillian lives in Tucson now, so if they were still friendly, it wouldn't have the wear and tear, you know? Shana really builds you up, makes you feel like you're the most special person ever, but after a while, it's like, she realizes you're human and you make mistakes like everybody else.

"When she starts to see you as a real human being, you'd better watch out."

Leaving Tickled Pink, Laura reflected that Heather Olson wasn't over her experience with Shana Yates. She was about to try Jillian North's number when she heard a sudden commotion next door—the screech of a wrought-iron table being pushed back against the flagstones, someone saying; "Give her room!"

One of the girls sitting on the ground, head down to her knees, gulping air.

Laura said to one of the mothers, "Do you need any help? I'm a police officer."

The woman spun around. "I think we're okay. She just needs to catch her breath—it's happened before."

Suddenly there was a loud *whoop,* and an ambulance glided up to the sidewalk.

Laura stepped back and watched as the paramedics approached the girl. She was now sitting on a chair. Head down, but she was nodding as they crouched beside her.

She looked familiar. It took Laura a few moments to realize where she'd met her before: Erin, Barbara Wingate's granddaughter.

Barbara Wingate was crouched down alongside the paramedics, her face drawn with concern. Hard to believe she was a grandmother and not a mother—she fit right in with the mothers.

The woman beside Laura—blond ponytail, white capri pants, a shell with small horizontal stripes—said something.

"I'm sorry?"

The woman looked to be in her mid-forties. The only thing that showed her age were her lips, which were tight and crimped under a cake of peach-colored lipstick. "I said, it's a shame, but I don't know if Erin is cut out for this. It seems like every time there's a little excitement, it gets to her."

Laura watched as the paramedics helped Erin to her feet and walked her toward the ambulance.

"This has happened before? Like this?"

"She's got some kind of illness—Barbara has told us what it *isn't*. The doctors don't even know. Lately it's been pretty scary—I heard she actually vomited blood. Poor thing." She shivered. "I don't want to sound uncharitable, but this is the third time this has happened, and it spoils—" She stopped herself. "It doesn't spoil it, but the girls were supposed to have a good day, and then *this* happens. . . ." She trailed off, giving up on trying to explain it, shrugging her muscled, bare tanned arms. "It's just frustrating, that's all."

Barbara Wingate was talking to the paramedics outside the ambulance, the diesel engine vibrating, too loud to hear what they were saying. The planes of her face cut into sharp lines of concern, arms folded.

Finally, one of the paramedics nodded and led Barbara around to the back. They closed the doors behind her and slowly drove away.

"Well, that's that," said the woman beside her.

"Are you here from Williams?"

"How'd you know that?"

"I've met Barbara Wingate before."

"Oh. We're here for the day—there's a master class at the university. In fact, it was Barb who arranged it. She knows some high muckety-muck on the board at NAU, so they invited our class. Julie!" she called. "Over here. You need money for lunch?"

A tall girl waved gracefully and toed her way through the crowd.

The woman flashed a nervous grin at Laura. "Don't think I was being mean-spirited about Erin. She's a nice girl and everyone really likes her, and Barb's been fantastic. The moment just kind of got to me." She walked over to meet her daughter.

As Laura walked back to her 4Runner, she tried the number Louise had given her for Jillian North in Tucson. An answering machine picked up. A man's voice said that she had reached a certain number and added, "We can't come to the phone right now, but if you leave a message . . ."

Smart enough not to identify themselves for potential scammers or telemarketers. Smart enough to have a man's voice on the machine.

Laura left a message asking Jillian North to call her, hit END, and immediately punched the number in again. The answering machine came back on. The speaker sounded older, like a man in his forties or fifties, but the human voice could be deceptive.

She heard the ambulance pull out into traffic, no lights. Looked like Erin would be all right. It must be tough on a little girl, trying to get on with her life, do things that other girls did, and then have this happen.

She thought of the mother in the striped top and wondered if the rest of the mothers and the girls resented Erin's health problems for getting in the way.

Laura found one of Dan's roommates, Steve Banks, washing his car in the driveway of an old Craftsman bungalow fenced by a low wall made of volcanic rock. The car was small and black with a decal on the back window—Calvin urinating on the word "Dodge."

Steve Banks was a tall guy with short dark hair, wearing only a pair of long shorts and flip-flops. His pale skin was turning pink, and even at his age he already had a little roll over the rucked waistband of the shorts.

He talked as he sprayed the car with a hose. "I already talked to you guys."

"Humor me."

He sighed, turned the hose off. "I don't know anything about what happened with Dan. We hardly saw each other."

Laura went throught the same questions Richie had asked, and some new ones of her own. "Were you here that Friday when he left?"

"No, I was at my girlfriend's. You'll have to talk to Brandon about that."

Laura glanced at the notes Richie had left with her. Brandon Terry. "When can I reach him?"

"He's around most afternoons. He has a lot of early classes this year."

"Did Brandon say anything to you? About that day?"

"Nuh-uh." He scratched at a white bump on his ankle—an ant bite. He looked down, saw the line of ants on the driveway, hopped backward. "Oh, man!" Stepped onto the grass, pulling off his flip-flops, shook them.

Laura waited while he slipped his flip-flops back on. She circled her cell phone number on her card and asked him to have Brandon call her.

He was still scratching his toe when she left.

*   *   *

Bobby Burdette walked out of Tickled Pink and into the sunshine, but he did not feel it. He did not feel much of anything, except numbness.

He should have tended to business. Instead he'd diddled around, lounging by the pool in Vegas, coming back here, acting like the bread job was his *real* job. Like he was content to subsist by making sure Joe Blow had enough hotdog buns for his cookout. And because he didn't prioritize, he had almost blown it.

He should have gone to see Shana first thing when he got back, but he had gotten busy. The date had been moved up, which had caught him flat-footed. He'd hit three different feed stores in three towns to get the fertilizer. Thinking that the amount of ANFO he had probably wouldn't make a dent, but knowing if he bought more he'd have to rent a U-Haul to tow on the back. That was too complicated, especially since the whole idea was *not* to use it at all.

He'd go with what he had and not worry about it.

But now Shana had taken off, and he'd missed running into that smart-ass female detective by twenty minutes.

Twenty minutes earlier, and they would have had a nice little conversation. *You looking for Shana?*

Yeah, you?

Dogged bitch.

Bobby had not expected her to follow through. She was supposed to be investigating Dan Yates's death, not looking for missing persons. But somehow, she'd connected the two. She had decided it was worth her time to go looking for Shana Yates. How far would she go? Would she drop everything and drive down to Tucson looking for Jillian North?

He had to act as if she would.

He got onto I-17 going south, a new idea already forming in his mind. By the time he got to the exit for the Wal-Mart the whole thing had crystallized. He liked the simplicity of it, how it could work with everything he already had in place.

It might even be the thing that would close the deal.

In the Wal-Mart he picked up a pick, a shovel, a sheet of plywood, some PVC pipe, a case of Dasani water, two big cartons of energy bars, and a twelve-roll package of toilet paper before joining the shortest line. Which put him behind some old fart who took forever to write a check. Stocky, riddled with liver spots, a baseball cap over those dark wraparound sunglasses that made him think of industrial goggles.

Bobby checked his watch. Getting late. He pushed his cart up, almost edging the old guy in his Bermuda shorts.

The old guy stopping just beyond the checkout, looking at his receipt, rubbing his neck and blocking the way.

Bobby had a long way to go and a lot of stuff to do, and this old fart was—

And then, *unbelievably,* the old man tottered back to the cashier. "I just can't let this go. I've been over it twice, and I have to object. You shorted me a penny."

A penny?

The cashier rolled her eyes at Bobby, told the guy she would have to get someone with a key to open the cash register, they would have to go through it all again. . . .

"That's okay, I'm not going anywhere."

Yeah, but I am, you stinking old fart. Bobby reached into his pocket and found a penny. "Here," he said with false cheeriness to the cashier. "I've got a penny."

The old guy waved it away. "I don't want a penny from *you.* I want it from them!"

Bobby thought about stuffing the penny up the old guy's nose. Steaming, he waited while another cashier came with the key, and they went through the whole damn thing again, finally giving the old fuck his goddamned penny.

Later, he found that his rage fed into his work, and it was the easiest and fastest manual labor he had done in his whole life.

*   *   *

On the drive back to Williams, Laura finally reached Don North in Tucson. She introduced herself as a criminal investigator with DPS and asked him if he had a daughter named Jillian.

She could almost hear him stiffen to attention, his voice wary. "Is there something wrong?"

"No. I'm actually trying to locate a friend of hers. I was hoping she might be staying with Jillian."

His relief was palpable. "Jillian's in Mexico. I thought maybe something had happened."

"I'm sorry to have given you that impression, sir. Is Shana Yates a friend of your daughter's? I'm wondering if Shana might be with Jillian."

"If she is, I wouldn't know about it. But I can give you Jilly's cell. We heard about her brother. We've been following it in the papers."

"How long has Jillian been in Mexico?"

"About a week. We have a place in Rocky Point. Jilly's been going through a rough patch and needed a place to be alone."

Another dead end. "She wouldn't want Shana there, then?"

"My guess is, she's probably getting lonely by now anyway. She has three brothers and sisters, so she hasn't been alone her whole life. I could see her wanting company after a couple of days, to tell you the truth. Especially now, going through the divorce."

Laura was amazed at the information people volunteered. "Have you ever met Shana?"

"No—I'm Jillian's stepfather. Jilly grew up in Williams, and when her mother and I married she stayed with her dad to finish high school. She came down here to go to college last year."

Laura tried Jillian's number and got her voice mail. She left a message for Jillian to call her, without identifying herself as DPS, keeping her tone neutral. Too much information might spook her. She'd be more likely to call if she was curious.

Next she called Louise Yates to see if Shana had shown up. She hadn't, but Louise did have something to tell her. Bobby Burdette had called, looking for Shana. He didn't know she'd taken off.

Laura wondered if Bobby could be the *reason* she took off.

On an impulse, she punched in her own number. Her answering machine picked up. For a panicked moment, she thought about hitting the END button, but she hung on for the beep. No point in hanging up anyway; she had caller ID. After listening to her own voice she said, "Tom, I might be coming home tonight. I'll let you know if my plans change." Talking to empty air.

After disconnecting, she sat on the bed and said to the room, "Am I being overly sensitive?"

But there was no answer. Frank Entwistle must be out haunting somebody else.

19

Jillian North did not return Laura's call, so she tried again. This time a young woman answered, her voice breathless. "Hello?"

As if she were hoping for something—or some*one*.

Laura burst her bubble. "This is Laura Cardinal—"

"I was just about to call you."

Laura didn't believe that for a minute.

"Do I know you?" Jillian asked. "Your name sounds familiar, but . . ."

Laura identified herself and asked if she could speak to Shana.

"Shana? She's not here."

"Is she out somewhere? Is there some way I can reach her?"

"Uh, no." Laura could hear the girl's mind racing. "She's not here. I could give you her number in Williams."

"I thought she was staying with you."

There was a pause. Laura got the impression that Jillian North wasn't used to lying. "She's not here. In Las Conchas, I mean." Warming to it. "I don't know where she is, you should check with her parents in Williams."

"When was the last time you heard from her?"

"I don't know . . . Would you mind if I called you back? I'm waiting for an important phone call."

She hung up.

Now Laura knew for sure why Jillian hadn't returned her call. Shana was staying with her, and Shana didn't want Laura to know where she was.

When you had a friend who was a bad liar, that kind of strategy could backfire.

20

As soon as her wheels hit the *Bosque Escondido*—Spanish for "the hidden forest"—Laura's heart sped up with anticipation.

In a few minutes she'd know for sure that everything was all right between them. Tom would still be her lover, the man she knew, tall and strong and quiet, and he would fold her into his arms and kiss the top of her head the way he liked to do.

"Hey, Bird," he'd say. "I missed you."

A few more minutes and all her fears would blow away as if they had never been.

She drove through the desert, glad to see the saguaro cactus and mesquite and prickly pear, the spidery branches of the creosote bushes, a busy tapestry of shapes against the pale moon-blanched ground.

Ahead to the right she saw the glow of the luminarias ranged along the high wall surrounding the the Spanish Moon Cantina. The Spanish Moon was where the ranch guests ate Mexican food and drank margaritas, sore from a day's ride out on the horses Tom cared for.

She came to a fork in the graded dirt road. To the right were the cantina, the main ranch house, and the newer *casitas* for the guests. The road to the left meandered through the desert, visiting a sprinkling of houses where the ranch workers lived. Laura stayed here rent-free. A friend of the guest ranch's owner, she provided a law-enforcement presence—including directing traffic and providing security at the weddings.

She drove down into the shallow, sandy impression made by the Agua Verde Wash. During the monsoon rains in the summer, the wash would run swift and deep—so deep it would leave her stranded at home anywhere from ten minutes to a couple of hours until the water receded. Her car windows open, she felt the cool dankness of the wash and the shadows of the mesquites interlocking overhead. Up ahead was the whitewashed house, a lot like the Mexican row houses in the downtown Tucson barrios, except here it stood alone. Almost as if it had been sawed off on one end and cast adrift among the mesquites.

As she was coming out of the wash, a pair of bright green-gold eyes glowed in her headlights: mama bobcat crossing the lane. The bobcat turned her head to look at Laura before casually continuing across, walking as if she were wearing big furry bedroom slippers.

Laura parked and opened the iron gate and walked up on the brick paving of the porch, worn by almost a century of boots.

No lights.

The place closed up.

Damn.

Laura glanced at the clock for what seemed like the hundredth time. Almost twelve thirty. Tom got up early, like she did. He had to feed the horses. That was something he had to do every day, no matter what the weather.

She'd come in through the darkened house, feeling her way to the light switch. There was no note on the kitchen table, none on the refrigerator, or her pillow, or her desk. The answering machine light was blinking. She played it back and heard her own voice, surprised at how tentative she sounded.

As if she were waiting for a boulder to fall on her head. She'd never sounded like that before, had she?

Laura took a shower. By then, Tom would be back.

But he didn't come back. She readied herself for bed, even slipped in under the covers and turned out the light. But she got tired of listening for the scrape of a shoe on the worn brick, the rattle of a key in the door, so she turned on the television. HBO was playing *The Sixth Sense*. She watched for a while but she'd seen it before and couldn't concentrate on the story, turned it off just as the ghost of the little girl handed Haley Joel Osment the box with the videotape in it.

Laura removed her nightshirt and pulled on jeans and a clean shirt. She pocketed the key and walked down the road to the Spanish Moon, taking the horse trail that meandered over by the corrals. Tom's truck and trailer were gone. That could mean anything, but it came as a shock to her.

What's the matter with me?

She realized she had no solid evidence to go on that anything was amiss. Just this feeling in her gut. And she'd discovered that sometimes the feeling in her gut could be wrong. So she might as well relax, have a drink at the cantina, and enjoy this beautiful moonlit night.

The Spanish Moon Cantina was built sometime in the twenties, Laura guessed. The plaster had receded with age and the weather, so that the adobe bricks stood out in relief. Mina said she'd like to stucco it over "before it melts down like a Fudgsicle," but Laura liked the look—it gave the place an authentic feel.

Laura went through the cantina and outside to a table near the old outdoor bar. The bar looked as if it predated the cantina, scrap wood hammered together to create an enclosed area where the corraled bartender served drinks on a low counter lined with bar stools. Rusty signs were nailed to the old wooden bar, advertising products like Philip Morris cigarettes and Barq's soda. Old picnic tables were scattered around the clearing. Laura chose one closest to a copse of mesquite trees. Other than a middle-aged couple absorbed in each other, Laura was the only patron here.

Mina, five feet tall and built like a battleship, sailed out in her gypsy skirt. Frizzy gray-blond hair and round wire-rimmed glasses dominated her face. She set down chips and salsa for Laura and stood over her, her motherly figure somehow comforting, exuding the confidence that everything was all right now that Mina was here.

"You want the usual? We've got something new if you'd like to try it. Yellowtail, from Australia. Merlot or cab sav."

Laura ordered the cabernet.

Mina remained. "What's got you looking so down in the dumps?"

"Just this case."

"Right. Just this case." Mina had trouble radar that would not quit.

Laura said, "Two college kids shot to death while they were sleeping in a tent. They'd just gotten married."

"That's bad, all right, but you can handle it. Too bad you didn't come earlier so you could have a good meal. The kitchen's closed now, so you'll have to settle for chips." She swept away the menu and set sail for the cantina door, came back a few minutes later with the Yellowtail cabernet. Laura felt like knocking it back fast, like tequila and lime, but made herself sip it. Again, Mina remained. "You hear about the hiker?"

"What hiker?"

"Some girl got herself lost in the Rincons. Been gone two days now. Tom's out looking for her now."

"He is?" That was why his truck and trailer were gone. "How long has he been out?"

"Since early this morning. They've got Search and Rescue all over the place. Ron Bransky? The sheriff's deputy? He asked Tom to help. He knows the area like the back of his hand."

Mystery solved. So Tom was out looking for a lost hiker.

Now all Laura wanted to do was drink her wine and enjoy the moonlight.

But Mina stood there, implacable. Mina thought that every employee on the ranch needed to listen to her take on things. In her mind they were all her children and she could tell them what to do. She dispensed advice freely, and her pronouncements rang with absolute conviction, giving you the impression that she knew more about you than you could ever hope to know about yourself. "What you need is a man," she'd say. Or, "Your problem is, you're too shy. You need to get out more, see some people."

Now she cocked her head at Laura. Movement behind her eyes; Laura could almost hear the gears grinding.

"Thanks, Mina. I've had a long drive, so I think I'd like to just have this wine and—"

"You look like hell," Mina said flatly.

"Well, thanks. I really like hearing that."

"You been sleeping well?"

"I'm fine."

"No, you're not. Something's bothering you. Ever since that thing at the warehouse. It's not natural to bounce back from something like that. Tom being good to you?"

"Of course he is."

Mina looked dubious. "Well, something's going on. I can tell from your aura."

"I'm okay," Laura said. But the flickering candle in the cheap little net-covered bowl on the table seemed to intrude on her vision on the right side. Her eye felt watery, but when she reached up to wipe her eyes, there were no tears. Just a shimmering brightness wavering at the edge of her vision. Strange.

Mina leaning forward, scrutinizing her. "You okay?"

"I'm fine."

Mina sniffed. "One of these days you're going to accept help when it's offered." Then she walked over to the other table.

Lights blinking at the edge of her right eye. The

strangest sensation. Laura closed her eyes but the lights kept jiggling and flashing.

Something like this had happened to her before. Once at a motel when she was investigating the Musicman case, and once on the plane back from Florida. But both times it went away, so she just forgot about it.

She took a gulp of wine, felt its warmth coursing down—comfort. She closed her eyes against the watery light, and willed it to go away this time, too.

By the time she got back to her house, her vision was fine.

Had to be stress-related.

The wine made her drowsy. She fell asleep, and woke up to an empty bed. Tom must still be out looking for the hiker. Now that she knew where he was, she was fine with it. He didn't leave her a note because he didn't know she was coming back. That simple.

She walked into the alcove between the bedroom and kitchen where she kept her home computer, turned it on, then continued on to the kitchen and made herself some coffee and toast. On the Google home page she typed, *vision problems and lights.*

A slew of articles came up. Laura felt a tightness in her chest as she read the descriptions—diabetic retinopathy, macular degeneration, detached retina, migraine, blindness, *brain tumor.*

Scaring herself.

She logged off. It was just stress. She'd had a scare with Jamie Cottle, the way he slipped into the car so fast, catching her off guard.

Seeing her death just before he pulled out those papers.

Something every cop lived with—every *smart* cop, anyway. You never knew when you left the house if you would be coming back.

But Laura knew she was jumpier than usual, and Mina

was right about her lack of sleep. When your job depended on alertness, that wasn't good.

Maybe Frank Entwistle was right. Maybe she did live in a glass house.

She heard scuffling on the roof. The bobcat kittens, playing again. They were getting big. Hector, the guy who looked after the houses, was worried about the wiring, that the cats might be tearing it up.

The wiring in the house is fine, she thought. *It's my wiring that's out of whack.*

Laura turned on the local TV news while she got ready for work. She had grown up with TV and was used to having it on in the background when she was doing something else—a habit. She hardly heard it.

But today she was listening for news of the hiker. Ironing a pair of blue slacks—she had seven pairs of navy and black pantsuits hanging in her closet—she heard the promo, a blond female anchor with a perky voice: "The hiker lost in the Rincon mountains has been found."

Laura set the iron upright and sat down on the bed, watching the television.

When the segment came up right after the break, she was surprised to see it was night. Harsh camera lights spotlighted a young woman, a bit scraped-up and dirty, walking with assistance. Tom Lightfoot holding her arm, his attention on her.

She leaned on him. Exhausted, no doubt. The voice-over saying she had been located around ten o'clock last night.

The camera seemed to linger on the girl, probably all of twenty-five years old. And drop-dead beautiful, despite the smudge on her chin and the glazed look in her eyes. She had wavy black hair that made Laura think of Polynesian dancers, and an exquisite face. And that face was tilted up at the hero of the day, Tom Lightfoot, capable and strong, his shoulders wide enough to carry the world, and he was looking back at her as if he'd discovered something rare and expensive in a handful of dirt. His hand guiding her, as he had guided Laura through doorways when they went places together.

Then he looked into the camera and Laura saw a smile she had never seen before. As if he couldn't believe his own good luck.

Ten o'clock at night.

This had happened at ten o'clock at night, and now it was morning and he still wasn't here. Maybe he had gone to the hospital with her.

It wasn't her imagination. He *had* put her off, sexually. He was losing interest. Seeing the way he looked at that beautiful girl, she felt something dissolve in her chest.

The something that replaced it was hard and it was cold.

She wouldn't let him reject her.

She would be the one to do the rejecting.

21

The Department of Public Safety building was located on a busy corner one long city block from the Tucson International Airport. A two-story putty-colored edifice with three flagpoles out front, the building was a relic from the sixties. At the time it went up, DPS was brand-new and considered the elite law-enforcement agency in the state. Now they had to fight for money like everybody else—and were often on the losing end.

Laura drove up to the parking area, produced her ID for the rolling gate, and drove through. Holding the hurt to her in that miserly, self-righteous way that imbued her with an odd serenity. On a logical level, she knew she was acting like a martyr. She understood, too, that she had gone into a different zone—a stubborn, hurt place that bore little resemblance to actual reality, but she was in it now and she was going to enjoy it. When she got back from Rocky Point she'd tell him to move out. He would ask her why, but she would just say, "It's clear to me this isn't working out."

She'd refrain from mentioning the girl with the Polynesian hair.

It was over, done, kaput.

She used her ID again to get into the building, taking one last look at the cerulean-blue desert sky. With any luck, she'd be on the road in an hour or so, heading for Rocky Point, and she'd get to see more of it.

First, though, she wanted to check out the box marked YATES, RECORDS, from the evidence room. While she was at it, she signed for Dan Yates's laptop and took it over to Charlie Specter, their systems analyst and also their chief computer guy, and waited while he turned it on.

"That's what I like to see," he said, as the computer booted up to the desktop. "Nice and straightforward—just your regular home computer. I'll bet it provides the password automatically to log on. Anything in particular you're looking for?"

Laura thought about it. "Bookmarks. I want to know if he's been checking out ecoterrorism sites."

His fingers rattled over the keys. "Key words?"

Might as well. "Earth Warriors."

Laura detoured by Jerry's office, but he wasn't in. She'd check back in a little while; she was anxious to get at those phone records.

As she entered the squad room, she saw all the detectives either on phones, at computers, or rummaging through papers, looking up at her with harried smiles. Always busy, always going a hundred miles an hour. Home again. She checked her plant, gave it some water, and started right in on Dan's phone records.

Richie's back to her, feet up on the desk, talking on the phone.

Victor Celaya, the guy she partnered up with most often, hanging up his own phone and coming her way. Italian shoes, eight-hundred-dollar suits. His uncle's clothing store for men had been going strong in Tucson for sixty years.

"Long time, no see," Victor said.

"I've been tripping the light fantastic in Williams, Arizona."

He gave her awestruck. "You mean the Gateway to the Grand Canyon?"

"The very same."

"How's about breakfast in a little while? I'll buy."

"What's the occasion?"

He shrugged. "Just can't get enough of your pretty face."

She liked the "pretty face" part, but didn't believe it. Victor had his hands full with a wife and a mistress. "Wendy's or McDonald's?"

"Mickey D's, unless you're particular."

"Sounds good to me. Give me a half hour, okay?"

She sat down at her desk and immediately became immersed in Dan Yates's phone records. It didn't take her long to see that Dan Yates had called one number more often than any other in the last few weeks. A couple of the calls lasted up to twenty minutes, but a lot more of them ended after a minute. She noticed that with some of these, he called the same number back again immediately.

Somebody hanging up on him?

Laura had a good idea who he was calling. She crossreferenced the number with the phone numbers she already had. Bingo—it was Shana. Dan had called Shana several times in the last few weeks, but he had called her rarely before that. And it looked as if Shana had hung up on him more than a few times.

Laura didn't like to leap to conclusions. But she did have a feeling, and that feeling was that Dan had somehow figured out that Shana was involved in the arson at Jimmy Davis Ford. It was a trail worth following.

Now Shana had taken off. The question was, why?

She'd taken off without Bobby Burdette. Did that mean she was running from him?

Scared of him?

Laura thought about this as she went through another box, this one holding all Dan's correspondence and financial records. Maybe he had told someone what he suspected, but she doubted it. Shana was, after all, his sister.

She spent the hour looking through the box: plenty of textbooks, photos of his family, some photos of Kellee, including a couple of her topless out in the boonies. Straitlaced Dan and Kellee had a wild side. She looked through the plastic file case holding his bills. He had the one credit card, carrying a zero balance—as Richie said, just not natural for a college kid. His car loan, his Internet and cell phone bills—all were neatly filed. Everything accounted for, each bill marked off *paid in full*.

A responsible guy.

Also among his possessions: a cigar box full of odds and ends. A cigar box. It was the kind of sappy relic Opie would keep his baseball cards in.

Inside the cigar box were a few greeting cards, most of them romantic in nature, signed *your beloved* and *your fair lady*.

Kellee must have been a true romantic. But weren't most girls that age? Laura remembered how she used to send cards to Billy Linton on every occasion, or on no occasion at all. She'd see a card in the store and it would just grab her. Sometimes she'd give him two or three cards at once. Those were the days when she would write in beautiful handwriting simple notes like *I love you*, and she would never sign them. At the time, that kind of minimalism was important to her, although now she could not recollect why.

Laura thought that the cards people picked out to send usually reflected what kind of cards they themselves wanted. If that was true, Kellee saw herself as a medieval damsel. One of the cards showed Rapunzel in the tower, her long golden hair unfurling down to the knight below.

Did Kellee look at Dan as her rescuer? Did she feel that she was locked in some kind of tower, waiting for her prince to save her? Maybe it had something to do with her cancer.

And sometimes a cigar box is just a cigar box.

When she knocked on Jerry Grimes's open door, he looked up at her and smiled. There was something behind the smile, though, that she didn't recognize. Fleeting, and it was gone. Then he was the same old, same old—his fatherly self.

"How are you doing on the Yates case?"

She told him about Shana and her possible link to the Earth Warriors.

"Rocky Point, huh?" Jerry sitting in the cheap red chair at his desk, rubbing his neck. Looking grizzled and sunburned and old, except for his lively Irish eyes.

Laura shrugged, not wanting it to seem like it mattered that much to her. Even with Jerry, she had to play the game. "It's the best thing I have so far."

"This guy, this Bobby Burdette? You think he killed them?"

"It's a theory. If Dan found out what was going on, you know he'd try to protect his little sister. The way things are these days, terrorism isn't anything to fool around with—even ecoterrorism. Bobby's already been to prison and he's still on parole.

"Plus," she added, "he met them in Vegas and drove Shana back. If anyone would know where they'd be, he would."

"You think Shana will admit to any of this?"

"It's worth a try."

He sat back, regarding her with those bright blue eyes. At last he said, "You want your per diem in pesos?"

She laughed at his joke, even though it was lame. "Hopefully, I'll be back by tonight. All I need is a couple of bucks for lunch."

"You're sure she's there?"

Laura thought about Jillian's painfully contorted answers. "Oh, yeah. Bet the farm on it."

Jerry clasped his hands behind his head. "You know the rules."

"No guns, no pepper spray, no—"

"You got it."

Laura turned to go, but he said, "Wait a minute."

She turned back around.

She had seen his concerned expression before. "Maybe after this case, you could take some time off. Get your sea legs again."

"You think I'm not doing this job right?"

"No, you're going by the book."

"So what am I doing wrong?"

"Nothing." He paused. "That's the problem. You're just going on with your business like nothing happened."

"Everything that happened—they said I did it right, remember? I was completely cleared of any wrongdoing."

"I know. But you could take some time to smell the roses. You know how this job can burn you out."

"Okay, I'll think about it."

"Good. That's all I ask."

"You look like the cat that got the canary," Laura said to Victor as she tucked into her Egg McMuffin. Clearly he had something he wanted to tell her, something he could barely hold back. Victor loved to gossip.

"We live in interesting times."

"What's so interesting about them?"

Victor sipped his coffee, made a face. Looked at her. "Why you drinking Coke with an Egg McMuffin?"

"Judging from your face, the coffee's not all that great. What do you mean about interesting times?"

"I ran into Richie's wife at the grocery store yesterday."

"So?"

Victor leaned forward. "You know how Richie's always talking about his family? Like we don't all have families of our own—well, you and Todd Rees don't, but the rest of us do. He acts like he's living the Father Knows Best–Full House kind of thing, you know?"

"Uh-huh." Thinking about her own relationship going down the tubes. *Put a fork in it, it's done.*

"Well, here's the thing. Turns out they've been separated for three months."

"Separated?" That hit her in the gut. For a moment, all

she could do was stare at Victor. Then she said, "You're kidding. He just came down for his son's birthday—"

"He's pretending they're still together. He's been pestering her, though, and when she saw me she told me all about it—I guess I must look like a priest or something. She wanted me to give him a subtle warning that if he doesn't stop bothering her, she's gonna get a restraining order."

Laura tried to absorb this. Richie had always been crazy about his family—one of the few things she'd admired about him. Their marriage had always seemed rock-solid.

If Richie and his wife could split up, anyone could. "But they seemed so happy."

"I don't know what to tell you."

"He's been lying all this time? Didn't he know it would catch up with him sooner or later?"

Victor shrugged. "I don't know what he's thinking. Gail's pretty upset. If he's not careful, it's going to come back and bite him in the ass."

Before she left for Rocky Point, Laura divested herself of her gun, her backup gun, her knife, and her Mace, and stored them in the bottom drawer of her desk. She didn't dare take them into Mexico; they had very strict laws about that. Then she went to the restroom to freshen up. Her mind on Richie, what lengths he'd gone to to pretend his home life was hunky-dory. Understanding it, in a way. She didn't want to let anyone know about her problems with Tom. It was tough admitting failure when it came to love. So many people seemed to get it right—all those happy couples and families all over the place—that when you were alone, you felt like the odd man out.

It made Richie seem more human to her.

Looking in the mirror of the ladies', she saw what Mina and Jerry and everyone else had been seeing: dark circles under her eyes. Her skin puffy under the fluorescents.

She'd taken the paper Coke cup with her, now down to a rattle of brown ice. She took two of the cubes and, holding them with paper towels, pressed one under each eye. Kept them there until the upper part of her face was numb. She wished she had concealer but she had never used it before, had never bought any because she had her doubts about how natural that stuff looked. The ice would make the swelling go down; it had worked before.

On her way out she ran into Richie.

"Heard you're on your way to find Shana."

"Hope she's there," Laura said in the warmest tone she could muster. No sense in kicking a man when he was down.

"I've got the Hector Lopez case pretty well wrapped up, so I can go back to working this case."

"That's okay, Rich. I'm doing fine on my own. I'm sure you've got a lot of loose ends to tie up."

Her warm feelings turning to annoyance.

He dug his hands in his pockets. "I told you, I've got it covered. Plus, I'm hot on this Luke Jessup thing. I think he's the answer to this whole case."

"Maybe you should go back to Williams, then."

He looked as he usually did: an Oxford shirt with white collar, wide plain-colored tie, jeans, and desert boots. Laura wondered how he could tell such tall tales about his marriage, how he could lie with such aplomb. Cops were good liars—they had to be, to get confessions—but the fact that he had used that ability on her and everyone in the squad was a jolt to the system.

"That's what I'm planning. Jerry wants me to go up there."

"The more the merrier," Laura said, although she didn't mean it. She already thought of this case as hers and hers alone. Walking to the car, she wondered why Jerry wanted Richie up in Williams. Because he thought she couldn't do it on her own?

Or maybe to get Richie out of town and away from his wife.

*   *   *

From the Department of Public Safety she backtracked to I-10 and worked her way over to Ajo Road. Ajo Road turned into State Route 86, which crossed the Tohono O'odham nation. When she was a kid, the Tohono O'odham people had been called the Papagos—another Indian tribe's deprecatory word for "bean eaters." Now the "bean eaters" had changed their name and ran three lucrative casinos.

It was a beautiful drive—lots of desert and mountains and few signs of civilization, except for the crosses.

The last time Laura had been out this way, she'd counted over a hundred roadside crosses between Tucson and the town of Why, Arizona. Most deaths were due to alcohol or speeding or both—the road shared by illegal aliens, pot smugglers, border patrol, tribal members, and college students driving down to Rocky Point for spring break. At the trading post in Gu Achi, besides the rack of potato chips and shelves of condiments and cold cases of drinks, there were shelves upon shelves of wreaths, crosses, and flower arrangements.

A cottage industry.

22

Laura didn't make it as far as Why, though. She ended up in a Chevron station somewhere in the sticks, staring at the cracked mirror in a tiny bathroom that smelled of cleanser. A high sash window cut into the whitewashed brick was open, and a navy curtain blew inward along with the sound of tires on pavement outside.

Laura heard the noise but her attention was on the mirror, because—

Half her face was gone.

That wasn't exactly true. One side of her face looked normal, but the other was like smooth, flesh-colored clay. If she squinted hard she could see faint etchings in the clay where her left eye should be.

The watery light was back, bouncing around the edge of her vision. Closing her eyes didn't do her any good.

What was going on? She'd managed to push down her worry last night at the Spanish Moon, and it had gone away. She'd ridden it out. But now half her face was a featureless mask.

Take a deep breath. Don't panic. It had gone away before; it would go away again.

She walked into the bathroom stall, closed the toilet seat lid and sat down. Kept her eyes closed. The lights, blinking on and off like a neon sign, hammering brightly, a curved shape, like a salamander.

The words running through her mind: macular degeneration, detached retina, blindness, *brain tumor.*

Somebody outside, jiggling the door handle.

The lights blinking.

She got back up and stared at the mirror. It looked the same. Her features wiped away; half her face like flesh-colored plastic.

The person outside knocked on the door.

"Somebody's in here!" Laura yelled. Thinking how incongruous it was, saying somebody was in here, when she was the somebody. Talking in the third person, as if she were watching herself from above.

Panic taking over. She couldn't drive. She was stuck in an old Chevron halfway between Tucson and the Mexican border, and she couldn't drive.

Shit.

Time going by. Her breath coming high in her chest, sweat breaking out on her face, the lights going on and off at the edge of her vision.

She'd bought herself some time, but eventually whoever was out there would knock again.

It came sooner than she expected.

She rinsed her face, opened the door and nearly ran over the small woman with the tiny dog standing there, poised to knock again.

"Took you long enough," the woman said.

Laura ignored her and walked across the asphalt to the 4Runner. She got in after several tries with the key, leaned back in the seat and closed her eyes.

Ride it out.

"You need to get that looked at," a voice said next to her.

She opened her eyes. Frank Entwistle sat in the passenger seat, his elbow cocked on the passenger door.

"What's going *on* with me? Do you know? Because if you know, please enlighten me."

"I *don't* know, kiddo. But it's not good. You need to see a doctor."

"Well, I can't do it now." Was it her imagination, or were the lights starting to go away?

"No, you can't do it now, but the problem with you, Lorie, is once this thing clears up, you'll try to forget it ever happened."

"No, I won't." But she knew it was true.

"That's the way people are. They go from crisis to crisis. They do just enough to get by, and then when things pile up and the bad shit happens, they wonder why. But you're worse than most. You know that, don't you, kiddo?"

She glanced at him, sitting in the passenger seat, wearing a white guayabera shirt and those old-man polyester pale blue slacks, white shoes. His "retirement clothes."

The lights beginning to calm down. She leaned up and looked in the rearview mirror, and was relieved to see that she now had two eyes, a nose, and a full mouth.

Relief poured over her like warm water.

Entwistle stared straight ahead.

"You're like that guy in *The Sixth Sense,*" she said. "He didn't know he was dead either."

"Hey, I'm not stupid."

"Then why are you here? Aren't you supposed to move on? What's holding you here?"

Entwistle shifted in the seat, pulled down the sun visor and looked at himself in the mirror there, smoothed back the loose wave of white hair over his forehead. "I know I'm dead. That's the difference between you and me. I know when it's time to face facts."

"Facts," Laura said. The lights were now officially gone. She looked at her watch: It had lasted twenty-five minutes. She was all right now. According to Frank Entwistle, she was now cleared to cruise onward until the next crisis.

"You been thinking about what we talked about before?"

"What, you mean about not throwing stones? What's that supposed to mean?"

"The glass house, kiddo. Thing is, you're vulnerable. You're sitting in there in your glass house and everyone can see in, but you don't seem to know that."

"You're talking in riddles."

"No, I'm not. You need to slow down, figure this out, before it takes you over."

"What? What's going to take me over?"

"Your fear," he said.

23

Sonoyta, on the Mexican border, was a hot, dusty, noisy town. Driving through it was like driving through the middle of a chariot race. Following the signs, Laura bore left and then right over the Rio Sonoita Bridge, following the right-hand side of the Y, which turned into Mexican Route 8, a two-lane asphalt road arrowing south and west through the desert. The signs were in Spanish, the distances marked in kilometers. The speed-limit signs were also dependent on kilometers rather than miles, so Laura erred on the side of caution and went slower, as the speed-limit laws in Sonoyta were strictly enforced. Waiting for the lights behind her eyes to come back, relieved when they didn't. As she drove toward the coast, the land became dryer and more barren. She passed a roadside shrine to the Virgin at the base of a cinder cone. A green and white *Angeles Verdes* pickup was parked in the turnabout. The Green Angels patroled the highway to help out motorists.

The ground on both sides of the highway turned sandy, choked with dusty-looking saltbush. To her right, although she could not see it yet, was the Gulf of Mexico. Soon vendors appeared along the road in the shade of makeshift ramadas. Then came a few houses, then businesses: The beginning of Puerto Penasco—Rocky Point.

It was getting late in the afternoon when the highway

turned into the the busy, palm-lined thoroughfare, Juarez. She drove past brightly colored houses, strip malls, and little parks, and turned left at the police station.

To get to Las Conchas, an Americanized community outside Rocky Point, Laura had to take a graded dirt road. Late afternoon, the golden light distilled from the heat of the day hung like a haze over the pale saltbush clogging the roadsides. At this time of day, the undulating dunes looked like crystallized salt. The dunes seemed to stretch all the way to distant mountains, which were blue cutouts pasted against the dusty cerulean sky. She drove up to the gatehouse and explained without showing her badge that she was here to talk to Jillian North at Casa del Mar.

The slight Mexican man in his security guard uniform nodded and waved her in. She followed a maze of wide roads through more dusty-looking shrubs, this time interspersed with squares of green indoor-outdoor carpeting and poles with flags—a golf course. To her right, beyond the two-story Spanish-style beach houses, she could see tantalizing glimpses of ocean, shimmering like a pale blue satin ribbon under the lowering sun.

The houses were expensive but eclectic—every place was different. Money was no object, but in many cases taste was. Turrets and winding stairs and tall stucco walls, rooms that looked like add-ons, Spanish tile, lots of white and blue—everyone had built his or her own dream house. The result was a sort of Rube Goldberg version of a Mexican village.

But the ocean, brimming in between the tall blank walls of plaster—the ocean was perfect.

Laura found Casa del Mar on the road closest to the estuary. She parked on the sand out front, crunched her way up to the walled courtyard, and rang the bell in the gate. Casa del Mar was a modern version of a Mediterranean villa, grandiose but too new to be taken seriously. Cobalt-blue tile on the roof, blue tile lining the rosette-shaped windows.

She heard a door squeak open and light footsteps.

One side of the door pushed open, and a sunburned blond girl in her early twenties peeked out. Her nose was peeling.

"Jillian North?"

"Yes." Then her eyes widened as she realized who Laura was. She actually started to push the gate closed.

Laura put her foot out. "May I come in? It was a long drive down here."

Jillian stepped back. Petite and pretty, with long bleached hair parted in the middle, she wore a lime-green flowered bikini that showed all her curves.

Laura entered a bricked courtyard, a closed garage on the right and the front door on the left. A bougainvillea grew in a large olla, tied to a stake.

Jillian led her into the house, asking her to wipe her feet first. Sand was everywhere.

The door let onto a huge room. The air conditioner was on high. Pigskin equipale chairs, copper pots hanging over a kitchen island, Mexican masks on the walls, Talavera vases and sink bowls. Decorated by Jillian's parents, no doubt. Photos on the wall, mostly of children from several years ago—Jillian and her siblings? But what dominated the room was the wall fronting the ocean, French doors set into a bank of picture windows. A deck outside, and steps down to the beach, the ocean only forty feet from the entrance, rolling in, deep, dark blue in the slanting evening light.

Beach towels stretched out on the chaise longues on the deck. Two of them.

"Where's Shana?"

Jillian backed up a step. "She's not here. I told you—"

"I know what you told me." She nodded toward the chaises. "You use both those towels?"

"Uh-huh." This kid was not a good liar. She was even worse in person than on the phone, her face turning red.

"I know she's here."

"No, she's not. She just left."

"Left?"

Jillian nodded vociferously. "A couple of hours ago."

"To go into town?"

"No. For good. She's not coming back."

"You tell her I was looking for her?"

The girl rubbed one lacquered-toed foot against the other. "She knew you were looking for her, but that's not why she left. We—she didn't think you'd come all this way—she wasn't worried about you."

"Why'd she leave, then?"

"Bobby came and got her."

"Bobby Burdette."

"Uh-huh." Jillian sailed over behind the cooking island. "Can I get you something to drink? Ice water? I think there's some sun tea somewhere."

Laura glanced at the granite counter. Three blown-glass margarita glasses, their dark green rims frosted with salt but otherwise empty.

"Margaritas look good."

Jillian glanced guiltily at the glasses.

"How did Bobby know where Shana was?"

"She called him." Mild defiance.

"*She* called *him?* I got the impression she was trying to get away from him."

"Why would you think that?"

"I thought Shana was scared of Bobby." A shot in the dark, but what the hell.

"If you mean they had a falling-out, well, yeah."

"What do you mean by a falling-out?"

"He, uh, slapped her. She said that was it as far as she was concerned. So I asked her if she wanted to stay with me for a while, and she said yes."

Something wasn't right here. "If that was it, why did she call him?"

"She missed him. Besides, it was only a slap. It wasn't like he beat her up or anything."

"But bad enough for her to say that was it?"

"She was upset. But they decided to make up, and now they're more in love than ever."

More in love than ever.

Laura could picture the conversation, and it gave her a pang. She remembered what it was like to be completely immersed in guys and wanting to look like a magazine cover. Spending a half hour putting on makeup, figuring out what to wear. Talking to friends about boys boys boys, getting racier and, let's face it, dirtier, as they grew older. Getting drunk and crying and wishing that they could run away to Vegas and get married, that somehow it would all work out.

Her mind turning to her own tangled feelings about Tom Lightfoot. "You really think they're in love?"

Jillian shrugged. "She sure acted like it."

Laura could see them: two beautiful girls at the age where they were as close to perfect as possible, like living Barbie dolls, lying on beach towels on the deck, toasting their belly buttons in the sun and talking about "love." Getting each other worked up. A margarita turning to two, then three, turning the world into a fantasy.

Egging each other on, wanting what they could not have.

Shana, beguiled by the bright sun, the sparkling waves, the alcohol, the distance. Forgetting why she was scared. Thinking: *All I have to do is pick up the phone and call, and I can hear his voice.*

In her alcoholic haze, spurred on by a like mind, Shana would be lulled into a sense of security. *I'll call him and just hear his voice. That's all. Just talk to him. That couldn't do any harm, could it?*

And Bobby, who didn't strike Laura as stupid, would convince her that he should come and get her. A tarnished knight on a white horse.

Laura could see it; she'd fallen prey to the same kind of delusional thinking herself. God gave young girls beauty and brains and free will, but he also gave them peer pressure, insecurity, and a desperate need for validation from the other sex.

"When did Shana call Bobby?" Laura asked.

"Last night."

"Did you have margaritas then?"

"No. We were drinking gin." Defiant look: *We're grown-ups now.* "I've got to hit the head, all right? Be back in a minute." She ducked into the bathroom off the main room.

Laura found herself looking at the photos ranged along the walls. Most of them were family photos, blown up into eight-by-tens. One picture in particular caught her eye, two rows of boys and girls, four to a row, the boys in suits and the girls wearing white dresses.

She heard a toilet flush. Behind her Jillian said, "That was Natasha's first Communion."

"Natasha?"

"My little sister."

Laura was more interested in the girl sitting next to Natasha. "Is that Erin? Barbara Wingate's granddaughter?"

Jillian walked up and stared at the girl. "Uh-huh."

"You know her?"

"I *should* know her. She spent more time at our house than she did at her own. My mom babysat for Erin's mom when she was a doctor at the health center." She wrinkled her nose. "Little brat."

"Why do you say that?"

"She was always getting Natasha in trouble. Daring her to do things, and then Natasha would get the blame. She always liked to be the center of attention."

Laura remembered the listless child who showed only slight interest in her new horse. "Sounds like she was hell on wheels."

"You got that right. Finally my mom had enough and said she couldn't come to our place anymore."

"How long ago was this?"

She shrugged. "Oh, a couple of years ago. You know

what happened to her mom and dad, don't you? They died in a car accident. I hear Erin's with her grandmother now."

Laura nodded. "Erin's not doing too well these days."

"I'll bet. She worshiped her mom."

"No, I mean she's sick."

"Sick? What, does she have cancer or something?"

"They don't know what it is, but she's been sick for a while."

"Well, that's too bad. I remember she used to get hurt sometimes—kid stuff—probably because she was always doing something. One time she broke her arm. But sick . . . hard to think of her lying around in bed all day."

"Do you mind if we go out on the deck?" Laura asked. She thought that being outside would make Jillian more comfortable, bring the interview down to an intimate level—two girls talking. The idea of soaking up the sun and watching the water wasn't so bad, either.

"Fine with me." Jillian poured herself a drink from the water cooler but didn't offer Laura any, then led the way outside.

Laura asked her, "What do you think about Shana and Bobby, as a couple?"

Jillian sipped her ice water—Laura suspected it was the only drinkable water in the house—and looked out toward the gulf. "Well, you know, I don't know what she sees in him. But love is love, you know?"

"You don't like him?"

"It's not that," she said hastily. She didn't want to appear disloyal. "But he *is* a lot older. Some girls like older men, though, and there's nothing wrong with that."

"So the reason she left Bobby and came down here was because he slapped her?"

"Well, there was other stuff. She thought he wasn't really in love with her. That maybe he was stringing her along. But *that* worked out."

"What do you mean, it worked out? How did she know he really loves her?"

Jillian tossed her mane and shaded her eyes with a slim hand. "It really was romantic, you should have seen him. He didn't get down on his knee or anything like that, but he took her out here—I was in the house but I saw it all—and he gave her the ring."

"An engagement ring?"

"Yeah. She was so excited."

"You're sure it was an engagement ring?"

"She came in and showed it to me." Jillian made a little face. "It wasn't very big—you know, carat-wise? But Bobby never had much money and it's the thought that counts. Besides, he said it was just a first ring, you know? That down the line he'd get her something really nice."

"So off they went. Did they say where they were going?"

Jillian shrugged. "Back to Williams? That'd be my guess. I'm sure Shana wants to show everyone her ring. Plus, she said there was stuff she had to do."

"Stuff?"

"Uh-huh."

"Any idea what she was talking about?"

Jillian shook her head.

Laura tried another tack. "So what's going on with Shana these days? With the kids and everything?"

Jillian continued to stare out at the gulf, but her eyes narrowed. "She isn't much into her kids. Hardly ever talks about them. If *I* had a kid, I'd be talking about them all the time. I wondered what happened with the kids while she came down here and she said they stay with Ronnie and his parents."

Laura realized that Jillian didn't know her friend very well. Maybe it was the physical distance between them— Jillian living in Tucson now.

"Did she talk about Dan?"

"That was so awful. He was such a nice guy."

"She must have been pretty broken up."

"Oh, she was. One night we were out here, drinking margaritas, and she started telling me how awful it was. I mean, they were really, really close. He was more of a best friend than a brother, and she felt so guilty."

"Why would she feel guilty?"

Jillian shrugged. "I don't know. She was saying crazy things—we were both pretty drunk. How it was all her fault. Well, you *know* she didn't mean that."

"Did she say anything specific? How it could be her fault."

"No. Just that sometimes she hated herself, that she could have maybe done something—to save him? But when I asked her what she could have done, she didn't answer me."

"Do you think she was hiding something?"

"Maybe. She just got this scared look on her face and said she was sad because her brother was gone. And that was it."

"What then?"

"We went to bed. Well, actually, I went to bed. She sat out here awhile longer, just crying? I thought I should leave her alone, let her cry it out. She was still asleep on the chaise when I came out the next morning."

24

The drive back took over three hours. Once again Laura would be home late at night. Driving through the darkness through the Tohono O'odham reservation, she tried to figure out what was going on with Shana and Bobby.

They could be anywhere by now. But she was betting on Williams, which meant another trip up north.

She wondered if he really meant to marry her, or if it was a ploy to get her to go with him. From everything she had heard, Shana sounded like a user. Shana was a user and Bobby was a user. Who won when two users got together?

Laura was betting on Bobby.

As she got on I-10 to drive across Tucson, her mind turned to home, and to Tom. She realized that she'd been overreacting. The idea that he had suddenly fallen in love with a lost hiker—that sounded just a little bit paranoid. She hadn't talked to him for several days, and there was nothing to prove that things had changed between them, except for her own bad feeling. If she looked at it logically, from an investigator's viewpoint, there was no evidence that anything was amiss.

She needed to chill.

But when she got home, Tom was still gone. No sign that he had come back.

Where would he be now? Presumably, the hiker was in

the hospital for observation or out and going on about her life. Laura walked over to the cantina looking for him, but he wasn't there. Mina saw her and held up a hand, a signal that she would come by when she was finished serving other customers.

Tom obviously wasn't here and Laura didn't want to hear a lecture tonight. She walked back along the horse trail toward her house, stopping at the corrals.

Tom's trailer was back, but his truck was gone. His decrepit retired saddle bronc, Ali—named for Muhammad Ali—was in the corral.

Laura was relieved that Tom hadn't left for good. He wouldn't leave without taking Ali.

She went back to the house, which was still empty. Got into bed but couldn't sleep. Frustrated and angry that she was listening for him again.

She felt shut out. She wanted to know what was going on—if anything *was* going on. But there was no way to reach him. He didn't have a cell phone. He didn't have much of anything. He was the kind of man who lived his life the way he wanted to, and didn't worry about what other people thought.

Laura hated not being able to do anything about it.

She turned on the TV set. It was the same channel from last night, one of those movie channels where they repeated movies, because *The Sixth Sense* was on again.

Haley Joel Osment and Bruce Willis were back at the wake for the little girl.

The little girl handing Haley Joel the box.

The girl getting out of her bed and turning on the videotape.

The mother coming in with the tray, setting it down, pouring something into the child's food—all of it caught on tape.

Laura turned off the set. She remembered something Wendy had told her about Mrs. Wingate. How she haunted the Health Care Center, buttonholing the doctors, riding herd on them, never taking no for an answer.

An expert by now.

It seemed strange that Erin had suffered a setback at the soda fountain in Flagstaff while Laura was there. What were the odds of that happening?

The mother of one of the other girls said these incidents had happened a few times—twice? three times? So much so that it seemed unfair to the other girls.

If Erin was that sick, why did Mrs. Wingate insist she go in for extracurricular activities?

Maybe the activities were therapeutic.

But Laura also remembered what Jillian had told her about Erin: *Hard to think of Erin lying around all day.*

25

The first thing Laura did when she arrived at the Flagstaff airport was rent a car. It was on her dime, but that didn't matter. Whether or not she got reimbursed, she was fine with it. She didn't gamble, she didn't travel, she didn't buy herself expensive toys. Her job was her vice. She had no idea how long she'd be in Williams, but she sure as hell wasn't going to spend it riding around in Richie Lockhart's Starskymobile.

When Laura got in to work this morning, she found out that Richie was already on his way up to Williams. This was after the Williams PD informed him that Luke Jessup had turned up. Laura needed to go, too. There was the possibility that Bobby Burdette and Shana Yates had gone straight back home.

She called ahead to the Williams PD to let them know she didn't need anyone to come and pick her up. Something was lost in translation, though; Officer Tagg was waiting for her outside at the curb.

"I've got a car," she told him, holding up the key tab.

He looked at her morosely. She could almost hear what was going on in his mind. *Women: They can never make up their minds.*

Laura's conservation-minded upbringing had come out when she chose the car. Personally, she didn't like the new

American-made cars, although she never offered her opinion. If that got out she'd be universally despised by her squadmates; DPS bled red, white and blue. Laura had been razzed unmercifully when she chose her take-home car, the only Toyota in a pantheon of Excursions and Silverados. Drug dealers liked American cars as much as the cops did—which made a good argument that enforcing the law and breaking the law were, in some ways, two sides of the same coin.

Laura wanted another 4Runner—or God forbid, a *Camry*—but she got a Chevy Impala instead. Richie wouldn't have an excuse not to ride with her now.

The Impala was the color of freshly overturned dirt. She wondered what great marketing exec came up with the color. How did they describe it in the brochure? Coffee? Peat moss? Mole?

It was midafternoon by the time Laura pulled her suitcase into the same room she'd occupied only three days ago.

She dropped off her stuff and drove out to meet Richie, who was waiting for her at the gate to Unicorn Farm. When he saw her drive up behind him, he got out of his car.

"So you finally came to your senses," he said, nodding at her vehicle. "Didn't they have any Monte Carlos?"

"Didn't want to steal your thunder." She walked around to the passenger side and opened the door. "Shall we?"

He smiled but shook his head. "I would, but I can't leave this baby by the side of the road. Especially so close to a golf course."

Of course not. They drove across the meadow to the Wingate house. This time the wildflowers were shriveled and the grass had a decidedly brownish cast.

Laura was thinking about coincidences. Turned out Luke Jessup had been living in a trailer on Barbara Wingate's property, where he did odd jobs. He'd probably been up at the trailer when Laura came here last.

As they came up on the blue house, she noticed a beat-up ranch truck with the name "Unicorn Farm" painted on the doors, and a bumper sticker on the back that said, COM-MIT RANDOM ACTS OF KINDNESS.

Richie parked in the cleared space near the truck and got out, the sun haloing his white hair.

"You see a trailer?"

"No."

Richie glanced toward the barn. Laura followed his gaze, which had fallen on a stack of fresh lumber and rolls of shiny silver fencing wire.

"You think building a fence falls under odd jobs?" Richie said.

"If you're good enough."

Laura heard a noise and glanced toward the house. Josh Wingate had opened the door and propped the screen open. "We're in here."

Laura looked at Richie. "Did you call first?"

"Me? No."

She smiled. She never called first, either.

They entered the house.

"My mother is in the kitchen. You came to see her, right?"

"Actually—"

Laura shot Richie a look. Richie grinned, but didn't finish the sentence.

Josh Wingate was looking at Laura. He looked sheepish. "Just want you to know. My mom never mentioned he was here. And I don't talk with her about police business, so, well, anyway." He shrugged.

"It's fine," Laura said. "Is he on the property now?"

"I sent him out on an errand." Barbara Wingate stood in the doorway of the kitchen, holding a whisk.

She wore blue jeans and a starched white cowboy shirt, tail out, a green sweater tied around her shoulders, her red-gold hair pulled back in a ponytail except for a few feathery bangs on her forehead. The skin of her heart-shaped face just a little loose, but the effect was more charming than if she were twenty. Her fine deep-green eyes were wide and innocent. They reminded Laura of a doll's eyes.

She glanced at Richie. He was transfixed.

"Do you know when Jessup will be back?" Laura asked, deciding that she, at least, wouldn't be bowled over by the lady's charms.

"No, I don't. I was just baking a pie. Would you like to come in the kitchen? I have some wine open." She nodded to her son. "We have that Brie, Josh. Would you mind cutting some?"

She led the way into the kitchen: stainless-steel double oven, stove, and refrigerator, a long granite counter. A well-worn butcher's block formed an island in the center of the room. Everything bright, colorful, and inviting, like the ceramic rooster canisters ranged by height along the wall by the sink. Cozy.

Laura felt the air slice by her as Josh walked to the refrigerator. He pulled the door open with force, yanked out a crisper and pulled out a large Ziploc bag holding a block of cheese.

"I think they'd like the Brie better," Barbara Wingate said.

Josh's shoulders stiffened.

Mrs. Wingate ignored his reaction and said, "The other crisper. But that will be fine, too. You want to use the cutting board by the sink?"

Josh tumbled the cheese out onto the cutting board and pulled a knife out of the block near the sink with such force he could have been a samurai.

Barbara Wingate's back was to them; she was whisking egg whites while Josh knifed the cheese. "I have some red wine. Would either of you like some?"

"No thanks," said Laura.

"Thanks just the same," Richie said, then whispered to Laura, "That kid can really cut the cheese."

"Funny."

Mrs. Wingate did a few more things to the bowl of egg

whites and mixed it with something else until it looked like batter, then poured it into a pie pan lined with dough, did a few more things, then put it in the oven. Laura had never baked a pie in her life, had never even seen a person baking a pie, so she couldn't have articulated what she saw, but she did understand that Barbara Wingate was an expert at it.

There was already a warm smell, vaguely fruity, and it made Laura hungry. Did Barbara Wingate cook pies on a staggered schedule like they did on cooking shows?

Laura suddenly wished she'd paid attention in home ec—all the homey touches. Kind of like Martha Stewart, if Martha Stewart had an angry son.

Laura wondered what dynamics were in play here.

Josh placed the plate of cheese on the counter and reiterated, "I don't talk about police work with my mother, so she had no way of knowing we were looking for him."

"It's not a problem," Laura said.

"Just so you know," he said stubbornly. "It was a miscommunication."

"We got that," said Richie, taking a slice of cheddar.

Barbara Wingate sat down and joined them. "So you want to see Luke? It doesn't have anything to do with Dan's death, does it?"

"Not directly. We need to talk to him, though."

Mrs. Wingate's exquisite eyes held steady. More like Ann-Margret than Hayley Mills. She pushed her hand, palm up, under her chin, balanced on an elbow. "Josh has been so upset by what happened. With Dan. They were best friends—"

"They know all that," Josh Wingate said. He opened the refrigerator, looking for something, then slammed it shut and stood with his back to it, arms folded.

Barbara Wingate didn't seem to notice. "Luke's building a new fence for the corrals. He had to go get a new posthole digger, ours finally gave out. But he should be back soon."

An uncomfortable silence settled on the kitchen. Barbara

Wingate picked at a piece of cheese, stood up. "I have water crackers."

"That's okay—"

But she bustled over to a cupboard and brought them out, put them on another dish.

Outside, a truck groaned up the slight hill. It didn't stop at the house but went on up to the corrals.

"Here we go," said Richie, standing up.

As Mrs. Wingate walked them out Laura asked, "How's Erin doing?"

Barbara Wingate looked slightly bewildered. "Erin?"

"I was in Flagstaff the day you were all at the ice-cream parlor—the dance class. She wasn't feeling too well."

Barbara Wingate's expression clouded. "That was a scare. She's all right, except she's embarrassed. She felt we were making too much fuss over her, making her go in the ambulance."

Her lovely eyes sad.

"She's all right now, though?"

Josh, who had followed them to the door, said, "It's up and down. Isn't it, Mom?"

An undercurrent of anger in his voice. More than just anger over the Luke Jessup flap. She recognized it, had acted that way herself when she was a teenager. Almost as if Josh were trying to separate himself from his mother by challenging her. He was a little old for that, but family dynamics could be weird.

"She's been sick since she's been here," Josh added. "Even since Kathy and Mike died. All those trips to the Health Care Center, I guess it's just something my mother is going to have to live with."

Laura looked at Mrs. Wingate, who acted as if nothing were amiss. She'd make a good poker player. Cool and unruffled, those wide green eyes holding Laura's.

All those TV shows and movies and books that had taught Laura as a child: Beauty equals goodness. That kind of conditioning made it hard to think of Barbara Wingate making her own child sick.

But Laura had seen a lot in her three years as a detective. She'd seen people who could lie as easily as breathing.

And not all of them were cops.

When they got to the barn, Luke Jessup was already digging postholes for a new pen beyond the barn. He was as he'd been described: scruffy. His dark blond hair had been pulled into a long ponytail, which went well with the beard. As with many people who slept outdoors, it was hard to tell where his brown long-sleeved shirt ended and his dark complexion began. It was not a healthy tan, more like a combination of sunburn and grime compressed into one ugly color. But he handled the posthole digger well, and wore new yellow gloves.

Laura called to Jessup and he looked up. His eyes were electric blue in his dark face, aware and intelligent. She realized that if he cleaned up he'd be a good-looking man.

When he saw her badge he said, "You the detectives I'm supposed to talk to?"

"That's right. This is my partner, Richie Lockhart."

He set the posthole digger down and the three of them walked into the shade of an ash tree. It was warm already this morning, Indian summer holding, but Laura noticed that the edges of some of the leaves were beginning to turn yellow and gold. Fall was on its way.

Jessup removed the yellow gloves and wiped at his face. He was dripping sweat. Laura thought he must be a good worker.

They went over what he had seen, which didn't vary from Dave Soderstrom's account. He woke up to shots and saw a man walking around a tent, shooting.

"Did he seem calm?"

"Ma'am, I'm sorry, but it was way acrost the lake."

From that distance he couldn't tell what kind of clothes

he was wearing, although he guessed that it was a long-sleeved shirt and long pants, just from the shape.

"He left right after he was done shooting?"

"Uh-huh. Looked like he just jogged up the road."

"Jogged? You said 'walked' in the report."

"Seems to me he jogged. He knew firearms, though. The rifle was pointed at the ground."

"The rifle was pointed at the ground?"

"Yeah. The way he carried it, I could tell he knew his way around firearms. You know, casual."

"You didn't see the vehicle?"

"That was farther up near the road. He just disappeared into the trees."

Laura thought of something. "He didn't stop to pick up his shells?"

"Nope. Unless he came back later."

Unless he came back later.

"Did you stay around afterward?"

"Nope, I boogied."

"You didn't go to the tent to see if anyone was alive?"

"Ma'am, the way he shot into that tent, I knew there wouldn't be any point. Besides, I didn't want him to shoot *me.*"

"Why didn't you go to the police right then?" Richie asked.

"Somethin' told me not to."

"What do you mean, something told you not to?"

He kicked at the dirt. "I just thought I should keep it to myself. Police would find them soon enough."

Richie and Laura looked at each other.

"Where have you been all this time?" Laura asked.

He looked at her. "I was holed up in Miz Wingate's trailer."

"This whole time? What about church?"

He rubbed his neck. "I didn't make it to church this week."

"Why was that?"

"I was too sick. Must've been some kind of flu or somethin'. Couldn't barely move." He put his gloves back on. "I sure was glad I had some place to stay. Miz Wingate took care of me like she was my own mother, bringing me soups and stuff. I only started feeling better yesterday."

"How long have you been sick?"

"I guess I came down with it a day or two after I saw the shooting. Stayed up all night, trying to find out what was getting at the chickens."

"Chickens?"

"Something's getting in, because we've lost two since I've been here." He shook his head. "I reinforced that fence so well, hard to believe anything could get in."

Laura couldn't think of anything else to ask him, so she went for the tried and true. "Did you know Dan Yates or Kellee Taylor?"

"I seen Kellee around, and I knew Dan on account I met him a couple of weeks ago, right here."

Laura perked up at that. "On this ranch, you mean?"

"Uh-huh."

"Any special reason he was here?"

He shrugged. "He's a friend of Miz Wingate's son. The police officer. I know that much."

As Laura and Richie walked back to their respective cars, Richie said, "That Barbara Wingate sure is something."

"I know."

"Did you notice there wasn't any kid stuff around the house?"

"Kid stuff?"

He shrugged. "Hey, if it was my house, there'd be an *ant* trail to the kitchen—you know, backpacks, books, toys, Game Boys. That's one neat house. Everything in its place, like out of *Better Homes & Gardens*."

"So?" Laura didn't have children, so the world of children wasn't very real to her, kind of like the mysterious conjuring of Barbara Wingate's pies.

Richie shrugged. "It's just weird, that's all."

*   *   *

Following Richie back to the motel, Laura thought about Richie's comment on the house. Nothing to show a kid lived there.

Barbara Wingate, the perfect woman. Beautiful, kind, strong. More persona than person.

Was Erin just window-dressing on Barbara Wingate's stage set?

At the motel, Richie put the Club on his Monte Carlo steering wheel and slipped into Laura's brown Impala. He ran his hand along the dash. "*Much* better."

"Jesus."

"No, Jesus would drive a Monte Carlo."

Laura pictured that for a moment. It made her smile.

They spent the rest of the day looking for Bobby. They tried his house twice and his mother's house once. They tried his friends. Turned out he didn't have many. He had kept a pretty low profile for someone who had lived in Williams most of his life. They did learn, however, that he had quit his bread route.

"Something's brewing," Richie said as they ate dinner outside on the patio at Cruisers. "Why wouldn't he just come back home? Where are they?"

"Your guess is as good as mine."

"You think he's good for it? Dan and his girlfriend?"

Laura thought about the calls Dan made to Shana's cell. She thought about what had turned up on his computer: a half dozen ecoterrorism sites bookmarked, including the blog that contained the reference to the Earth Warriors. "He's the best bet so far," Laura said.

When they got back to the motel, Richie told her he was going to bed early. "I'm beat. The kids kept me up late last night."

She almost told him to put a sock in it; she knew the truth and didn't want to hear it anymore. But why bother? Clearly, it was important to him to maintain the illusion that he was happily married.

She guessed he was entitled.

*   *   *

   The next morning Laura walked to the *Williams—Grand Canyon News* building on Third Street, a couple of blocks away from the motel.

   Laura entered the small front office, half of it taken up by an old black printing press strung with fake cobwebs and decorated with skulls for Halloween. A counter ran along the left-hand side of the room, dividing the workspace from the entrance area. A thirtyish dark-haired woman with the name tag Lila Johnston smiled and said, "May I help you?"

   When Laura told her what she was looking for, Lila led the way into the back. "Let's go to the conference room," she said. "I think I can put my finger right on it."

   Laura pushed through the swinging door and followed Lila into a small room with a large table.

   "Just a minute, and I'll get it for you." Lila trailed a scent behind her—roses.

   As Laura waited, she looked out the window. An ash tree, its leaves just beginning to turn yellow, glittered against a crystalline blue sky.

   She felt guilty, spending her time on this. Time was slipping away and she was going off on a tangent. But she couldn't let it go.

   If what she suspected was correct, Barbara Wingate's granddaughter was a victim of Munchausen by proxy.

   Laura remembered the mother at the soda fountain in Flagstaff. What did she say about Erin's bad spell? It wasn't the first time? No, she said, *This is the third time this has happened.*

   Three times, just with the dance class.

   What are the odds?

   As Laura saw it, the question was, would Barbara Wingate make Erin sick just to get attention?

   She liked attention. No doubt about that. Everything she did was geared toward gaining it, every move calibrated for the right effect. Laura got the impression that Barbara

Wingate saw herself from the outside, just as other people saw her. Constantly aware of her effect on other people.

Laura wondered where the real Barbara was, or if she existed at all.

Lila reappeared with a heavy book full of newspapers. She leaned over Laura and the scent of roses was overpowering. "Let me see, I think that was the last week of March."

Expertly, Lila's lacquered nails flicked through the newspaper. And there it was. Mike and Kathy Ramey died in a car accident March 27, on their way home from a fundraiser in Flagstaff. Killed by a drunk driver not ten miles from home. Laura stared at the black-and-white photo of a mangled car.

She scanned the article. Mike Ramey, twenty-nine, and Kathy, thirty, were survived by a daughter, Erin. Both Mike and Kathy were general practitioners at the Williams Health Care Center.

Kathy was nine years older than her brother, Josh. Laura wondered why Barbara Wingate had waited so long to have another child. It could be she had been married to another man before. It was a small loose end but Laura could track it down if it turned out to be important. Right now it didn't seem to be. She looked for the obituaries of Mike and Kathy Ramey the following week, since the *Williams— Grand Canyon News* came out only once a week. The only other relatives mentioned in the obituary were Mike's brother and his wife and their three children. The brother was stationed in Germany.

Too far away to take Erin? It would certainly be disruptive. At least, though, there was family who could take her if need be.

Lila watched discreetly from the doorway as Laura looked at the obituary. There was nothing new there, except a suggestion that friends donate to the American Cancer Society in lieu of flowers. Laura also glanced over the obituary for Barbara Wingate's husband. He had died of cancer several years ago. He had been much older than she was.

Laura asked Lila if she knew Barbara Wingate.

"I wrote an article about her last year."

"Could I see it?"

Lila looked pleased. She found the article page quickly and spread it out for Laura. "I'll be in the front if you need me," she said.

The article, written last September, was a puff piece about Mrs. Wingate, cataloging the good works she had done teaching disabled children to ride and rescuing broken-down Thoroughbreds, her charitable work, her former career as a licensed practical nurse in Iowa. Touching lightly on her double tragedies.

Accompanying the article was a photo of Mrs. Wingate with one of her rescued horses, and another, smaller photo. In this one, she was teaching a catechism class to high school kids. A half dozen students sat in a semicircle of folding chairs, Barbara Wingate in the center, writing on a blackboard.

Looking radiant. In her element—the center of attention.

An interesting surprise: The student closest to the camera was Jamie Cottle. Laura thought it ironic. When this picture was taken, neither Barbara Wingate nor Jamie Cottle had been aware of the tragedies looming in their future.

She scanned the article a second time. One detail stuck out—the fact that Barbara Wingate had been an LPN—a licensed practical nurse.

Although Laura had dealt only tangentially with a case involving Munchausen by proxy, she knew the profile as well as anyone in the squad. Number one, people with Munchausen were almost exclusively women. And number two, they were very likely to have worked in the medical profession. They were often bright, articulate, knowledgeable about illness, and spent a lot of time talking to the doctors treating them or their children.

The term "Munchausen" was coined by a doctor in the 1950s to describe patients who faked acute illnesses and dramatized their medical histories. The doctor got the name from a historical account of the Russo-Turkish wars by a flamboyant German baron named Karl Friedrich von Münchausen, who made up fantastic stories about his time in the Russian cavalry.

Munchausen by proxy was worse. Instead of doing bad things to yourself to get attention, you did them to someone else—usually a child in your care. Laura remembered a recent case that received worldwide attention. A woman faked her daughter's cancer, convincing everyone—doctors, hospitals, even the child herself—that the illness was real. The child had been subjected to painful and traumatic bouts of chemotherapy and other radical treatments.

Laura went over what she knew about Erin. The incident at the soda fountain in Flagstaff, the fact that incidents like it had happened at least twice before. The day Laura had met Erin. The way the girl acted: listless, uninterested in the world around her. Jillian's portrait of a much different girl: one who was active to the point of breaking her arm.

When had that change taken place? After she moved in with her grandmother?

Be careful. If she acted on this, serious consequences could result. Erin could be taken away and put in a foster home. If she went ahead, she'd have to make sure she did everything right.

26

The Williams Health Care Center was four blocks over, on Seventh Street just south of the Safeway. One-story building, plate-glass windows along the front, the center's name in letters across a rock face outside. An ambulance parked to the left.

Inside, the place was small-town homey. Quilts on the walls, cornflower-blue chairs lining the perimeter of the common area on the left, a TV set mounted in the corner. Directly in front of her a long blond-wood counter angled back to an inside door, the length topped by plastic windows. Chairs pulled up to each window for patients to demonstrate their proof of insurance.

Laura had spent an hour on the phone with the doctor who testified in the Lynette Stokes case. Lynette Stokes was a Tucson woman who had cut her infant repeatedly and rubbed dirt and even garbage into the wounds to make him ill. In the long run, it had gotten her more attention than she'd planned for. The baby had been adopted by the assistant prosecutor on the case and was flourishing.

Laura expected the doctor to tell her she didn't have enough to go on. Instead, he suggested she talk to Erin's doctor and let him know her concerns.

"Most of these cases are based on circumstantial evidence," he'd told her. "Let me ask you this. How would you feel if you didn't pursue it?"

So here she was at the Health Care Center, mulling over what to say. She didn't want to go in with guns blazing. If it came to the point where it turned into a criminal investigation, she would take what she had to the Yavapai County sheriff's office, since Barbara Wingate lived in their jurisdiction. She was reluctant to do that now. She knew enough about small towns to understand that if locals investigated, whether or not Barbara Wingate actually abused her granddaughter, the presumption of guilt would stick to her like flypaper.

Laura asked the receptionist if she could talk to Erin Ramey's doctor.

The young woman glanced at the clock—almost noon. "That would be David Sanchez. You want me to page him?"

"Not if he's busy." Laura handed the woman—her nameplate said Renee—her card. "I'm always reachable by my cell—"

"It's okay. It's lunchtime, anyway."

Laura waited in the common area, listening as the young woman spoke into an intercom, then looked up brightly. "He'll be right here."

When she saw Dr. David Sanchez, her first thought was: *Doogie Howser.* He was very young, except for intense dark eyes that seemed to probe politely. He wore a white lab coat over chinos and bright white tennis shoes.

"You wanted to talk to me?"

"I wanted to ask you about one of your patients."

She saw the switch go off behind his eyes. "You must know that as a doctor, I can't tell you anything about my patients."

"I understand. I'll do the talking."

He looked at his watch. "There's a place on the corner that has good coffee. I can spare a few minutes. But don't think I'm going to let you talk me into saying anything."

They sat outside at one of two metal tables, in the shade

of the striped awning. Dr. Sanchez crossed his legs at the knee and took a sip of his coffee. "I'm not sure I should even be here."

"I understand that," Laura said. "I wanted to bring something to your attention that you might already know about."

He shifted legs. "What is that?"

Wary. Young, but oh-so-smart.

Laura outlined her suspicions regarding Barbara Wingate and her granddaughter, Erin.

Dr. Sanchez said nothing. He used the plastic stirrer on his coffee, which he took with cream and sugar.

"She *is* your patient?" Laura asked.

Her voice seemed to startle him. "What? Yes. In fact, she's—" He stopped. His chin went down, his lips closed. He checked his watch again. "Tell you what, I've got to get back." He reached over and tapped her awkwardly on the wrist. "We'll be in touch."

Laura watched him go, long-legged, his lab coat flapping around his trousers, the white so bright, setting off his dark skin.

Probably just a year out of med school, with a mountain of debt. Working at the Williams Health Care Center because it was the path of least resistance. Small towns were hurting for doctors. He'd probably gotten some kind of a deal, signed on the dotted line to get the financial aid he needed. So here he was, in Williams, and he had been thrown into the deep end. Two doctors dead. A big hole to fill.

And he had Erin Ramey. The child of the two doctors who had been killed.

He lived in a small town where everyone knew everybody else. Where Barbara Wingate was the quintessential good citizen. No doubt she had friends in every branch of Williams's small government.

Laura wondered if he would do anything.

Well, she'd planted the seed. It was up to Dr. Sanchez now.

*   *   *

David Sanchez stopped by to say hi to Erin and her grandmother and look at the chart. Seeing Mrs. Wingate in a different light, although she seemed the same. It was hard to believe she was anything but a concerned guardian.

Erin looked fine. She sat up in bed, drawing pictures of horses in the notebook she'd brought along with her. She loved to draw horses, and she was very good. The corner of her tongue stuck out of her mouth as she drew. Absolutely unconcerned that the bed she was sitting in was in the emergency room.

Used to it by now.

Half an hour ago Barbara Wingate had brought her in because the child was coughing up blood—the second time this month.

The tests she'd been subjected to amazed him. When he took her on as his patient, he'd called for all of them to be redone. And still, her chest X-ray showed clear lungs. The source of the blood was maddeningly elusive.

Pretty stern stuff for a guy just out of residency. But he planned to succeed where others had failed. It might take time, but he would figure it out. The blood had to come from somewhere. It wasn't from a nosebleed, it wasn't from her lungs, but there were many places to look. And he would look for them all.

Seeing her now, he felt a pang in his heart. She was a puzzle. So matter-of-fact. She didn't mind what they did. A tough little kid.

And the grandmother.

Now he looked at her in a new light. Her knowledge, the way she kept coming at him with new theories, constantly engaging him in conversation. As if this were her second home. He got the feeling she could talk for hours about Erin's illness. She made him nervous, too, just being around her. So much older, but there were times when he found himself attracted to her. Tongue-tied in her presence, which wasn't like him at all.

And the thing was, he knew she was aware of it. Not just

aware of it, but he could tell she enjoyed his attraction to her.

He didn't like the feeling. He already had a girlfriend.

He looked at the blood on Erin's blue-flowered hospital gown. She had tried to spit into her hand but it had gotten all over. She looked at him.

"You okay?" he said a little too brightly, ruffling her hair.

"Kind of. It tastes bad."

"I know. We just have to figure out where it's coming from, and then we can stop it."

"Uh-huh." Skeptical. Like she'd heard that a few times.

Mrs. Wingate watching him watch her. Her large green eyes seeming to catch and keep all the light in the room.

Suddenly, he heard choking sounds. Erin, leaning into her hand.

Without thinking, he reached into the top desk drawer, pulled on some gloves, and grabbed a slide and a Q-tip.

Blood poured out of her mouth onto her hands. It seemed like a lot, but it really wasn't.

He was right there with the slide. Why he didn't think of it before, he didn't know. Maybe it was as pointless as everything else he'd done, but it was worth a try. He scooped up some of the blood on the Q-tip and put it on the slide. Sandwiched it with another piece of glass. He would take it to the lab and have a Wright stain done just to make sure.

Erin was staring at him. He winked at her.

Thinking, *All this time, and I never thought to look at her blood under a microscope.*

Jeanette Moran was waiting for David to get off the phone. She wanted to firm up plans for tonight. She wanted to go to Doc Holliday's at the Holiday Inn for dinner, have the prime rib and all the fixings. After the day she'd had, having to put down three ailing animals in a row, she could use a good prime rib and some wine to go with it.

Being a vet wasn't all puppies and kittens.

Jeanette walked by the microscope set up on the long counter to the right, and stopped. She never passed a microscope by if she could help it. It was a compulsion with her. She had to take a peek, even if she didn't know what it was all about.

David got off the phone a short while later.

"What's this?" she asked, tapping the microscope.

He looked sheepish. "Just something I thought I'd check out."

"Like what?"

"I just got this dumb idea in my head, it's probably nothing."

"What dumb idea?"

He looked embarrassed. "I just wanted to make sure it was really blood."

"Oh, it's blood."

"I know."

Jeanette said, "So what is it?"

"What do you mean?"

"Is it from a lizard?"

"Lizard?"

"Or a bird. Maybe that's it. Does this have something to do with the West Nile virus?"

"What are you talking about?"

"Come *on*. You mean you don't know?"

"Know what?"

"This slide. It's got to be either lizard or bird blood."

If his girlfriend hadn't been a vet, David might never have known that the blood that came out of Erin's mouth was animal, not human. Or he would have found it out only after numerous tests and trips to the lab. He still couldn't believe it. He couldn't fathom how a woman would do that to her own grandchild.

He also couldn't imagine how a woman could do that to her own grandchild without the grandchild's cooperation.

Erin was nine years old. She'd have to know what was going on.

Nothing in his training could have prepared him for this. He was a doctor, not a psychiatrist.

When he saw the nucleated cells under the microscope earlier today, his first thought had been leukemia. Normal human blood cells did not have nuclei. According to his brilliant veterinarian girlfriend, only birds and lizards had nucleated blood cells.

The only nucleated blood cells in a human were abnormal. Which meant cancer.

That was the diagnosis that had stared him in the face, pending another round of tests for leukemia. But now Jeanette had provided him with another possibility.

Relief made his limbs momentarily weak. He didn't have to tell the grandmother that Erin had to be tested again for leukemia. He didn't have to tell Erin, either.

But now it looked as if that DPS detective might be right after all.

More and more, it looked like a case of Munchausen by proxy.

David tried to concentrate on his patients while he waited to hear from Jeanette, who had taken the slide to the lab her veterinary practice used. She was pretty sure she'd be able to find out what kind of blood it was, pretty quickly. As David tended to bee stings and wrote prescriptions for stomach ailments and gave people their annual checkups, he wondered what he would do if it turned out that the DPS detective was right. One thing he'd done—he'd sent Erin home, even though Mrs. Wingate had wanted her to stay overnight for observation.

When the phone rang and he heard Jeanette's voice, he still wasn't prepared for the diagnosis she gave him.

"Chickens," Jeanette said.

"Chickens?"

"Your patient has been spitting up chicken blood."

27

Laura was going over the autopsy notes on Dan and Kellee Yates when her cell phone rang. It was the sheriff of Yavapai County, Terry Langley. He was giving her a courtesy call to let her know about the status of Barbara Wingate and her granddaughter.

"We're investigating charges of child abuse against Barbara Wingate," he said.

Laura sighed: part relief, part guilt. It was never good to break up a family, but sometimes it had to be done for the safety of the child.

"You won't believe it," Langely added. "The girl, Erin, admits she faked spitting up blood. You know like they do in the movies? She did that with the chicken blood. Can you beat that?"

A void opened up inside her heart. "Why would she do that?"

"Kind of hard to explain. I talked to a doctor friend of mine at NAU who's worked with Munchausen patients, and he said there are all sorts of things that go into something like this. Apparently, Erin adored her grandmother. She lived with her the first year and a half of her life, when Kathy was in med school at Stanford, and we're pretty sure that Barbara was making her sick then. Erin eventually went to live with her mother—by that time Kathy and Mike were married—then her parents die, and presto! She's right back with her grandmother. You can see how she might pick up where she left off. To her, *that* was normal."

Laura was trying to follow this. "But wouldn't she know what Mrs. Wingate was doing to her?"

"On some level, sure. The way the doctor explained it to me, because she was with Barbara early in her life, feeling sick was what she was used to. So when she went back to Mrs. Wingate's, she took up with the familiar, I guess. And there was a good side to it. Seeing how her grandmother thrived on attention—and getting her own fair share. And her grandmother's approval."

Laura saw how it could happen. The void grew inside her. She wondered what kind of life Erin would carry with her from now on. If she was irreparably damaged or if she could find yet another kind of normal.

"We're requesting a psychiatric evaluation from the court, so maybe we'll know more soon." Langley cleared his throat. "We're also in touch with Child Protective Services. Things are moving pretty quickly now, thanks to you."

After he hung up, Laura walked over to Richie's room and knocked on the door. One look at his Woody Woodpecker boxer shorts and she started to laugh.

"Hey, I was just going to take a shower. What's up?"

She gave him the rundown. About Erin, about her grandmother.

"Just a minute." He disappeared into the darkened room. She heard the refrigerator open and close, and then a familiar *click-whoosh*.

He came back in jeans, holding two sweating bottles of Rolling Rock. "This calls for a celebration."

They sat at his little round table by the window, Laura seeking solace in the ice-cold beer and the buzz.

"I should have seen it," Richie said. "Especially after what Josh Wingate told me."

"What did he tell you?"

He leaned back, kicked the table leg with a bare foot. "Just that ol' Barbara tried to commit suicide a couple of weeks ago."

Laura straightened up. "What? When did you hear this?"

He shrugged. "Josh told me. One of those down times, you know. I don't think he meant to say anything, it just slipped out."

Laura couldn't believe her ears. If Barbara Wingate was that unstable, the sheriff's office needed to hear about it. "Does the Yavapai County sheriff know?"

"Hey, don't get your undies in a bunch. I called and told them soon as I heard. But they already knew. Matter of record."

"Langley didn't mention it to me," she said, thinking how a suicidal Barbara Wingate might affect Erin's precarious grip on reality.

"Well, he knows."

"I hope they'll take that into consideration."

"I'm sure they will. It's their job now."

"What do you mean by that?"

"Nothing. Just that you're so doggone conscientious."

"Aren't you?"

He started picking at the foil on the bottle neck. "Hey, I try. But for me, it's more like a job, you know? Something to support the wife and kids. Don't get me wrong—I like what I do. It's the best job I can imagine. But you—you're a true believer."

"What's wrong with that?"

He looked at her. "There's nothing wrong with it. You're a star, Laura. Sometimes I make fun of that, but you and I both know it's true."

"A star. Yeah, right."

"But you could make it easier for the rest of us, you know? Stumble every once in a while."

She wondered if he was putting her on. He'd proved to be a smooth liar. "You know, Richie, I wish you'd be straight with me. We are supposed to be working this case together."

"I *am* being straight with you. Sure, I like to joke around, but about this, I'm dead serious."

What the hell, she'd take it.

"I think you're a good cop," he added. "Always have. I just like to get your goat every once in a while. It's what I do, you know?"

He sounded sincere. Laura almost brought up his charade about his marriage, but they were sharing genuine good feelings for once and she didn't want to spoil it.

Richie held up his beer bottle and clinked it with hers. "No kidding, Laura, you saved that kid from God knows what. That's good news for everybody." He set his beer down and locked his stubby fingers behind his head. "We might not find Dan and Kellee's killers, but you sure as hell bagged Barbara Wingate."

Laura had just come out of the shower the next morning when the room phone rang.

Wrapping a towel around her, she tiptoed across the carpet to the phone, leaving wet footprints.

On the other end a voice said, "You fucking *bitch!*"

The venom in the woman's tone made her voice unrecognizable. "Who—"

"I know what you did—the people you talked to. People I *know!* And now she's gone. My little girl is gone!"

For a moment Laura was confused. Then she realized that Barbara Wingate was talking about her granddaughter. "Gone?"

Barbara Wingate's voice was shaking—more with anger than pain, Laura thought. "As if you didn't know. You called them."

"Called who? Would you calm down and let me see if we can—"

"CPS, that's who!"

"Child Protective Services?"

"Give yourself a gold star!"

The phone slipped from Laura's grip and she had to grab at it; she realized her hands were sweating. "Mrs. Wingate?"

"Why the hell couldn't you leave things alone, you vicious, conniving, meddlesome bitch?"

Ragged breathing. Laura started to say something, but didn't get a chance. "How could you do that to me? How *could* you do that? I hope you burn in hell!"

It was almost as if Barbara Wingate had stripped away every vestige of her humanity, and the gibbering creature underneath was nothing Laura had ever heard or seen under the living sky.

"Mrs. Wingate—"

She was speaking to empty air.

Heart pounding, feeling disconnected from her own body, Laura fumbled for the phone book, trying to find Barbara Wingate's number. The heavy book slipped off her knees and onto the cheap motel carpet. Her hands shaking, clammy with sweat.

The pounding had gone to her head. Suicide, she thought. The woman just tried to commit suicide. Barbara Wingate's beautifully constructed picture of herself had disintegrated.

Laura knew she needed to go out there. She pulled on her clothes, grabbed her keys and headed for the car, her urgency making everything go twice as slow. Fumbling for the car key, pulling at the door and missing, the handle snapping back and stubbing her fingers. Dropping the keys on the floorboards. Water from her hair running down between her shoulder blades.

Maybe it shouldn't be me, she thought as she drove fast out Cataract Road. Maybe I'm the wrong person to confront her.

But she had to go.

She punched in Richie's number.

"I'm worried about Barbara Wingate," she told Richie as

she drove under the railroad tracks. "Child Protective Services took Erin."

"Erin? Holy shit, that was fast. What—"

"Just listen to me. I think we're going to need some backup. She was hysterical on the phone and I have no idea what she might do."

"You think she'd try to kill herself again?"

"Jesus, I hope not." She hit the accelerator, sending the Impala into overdrive.

She fumbled for the END button and threw the phone on the seat, grabbing the wheel with both hands.

The meadow at Unicorn Farm was pale green-gold in the early morning light, glistening with dew. Laura had her window down and could smell the sweetness of the grasses, but rather than acting as a balm to her, it only emphasized the starkness of the situation. She opened the gate but didn't bother to close it, made good speed up the road.

In the pine shadows the house looked dark and shabby.

Laura pulled up just short of the house to the right, an unconscious move that had been trained into her. From here, anyone opening the door or looking out the window would not be able to see her.

Her eyes took in everything. The stillness. The pulled shades. The only movement the shadows on the house roof and the grass as a restless wind started up. She looked at the porch that ran along the front of the house. It was the kind of porch she'd seen often in rural areas; just a few inches off the ground, no railing, plank flooring, more of a boardwalk than an actual porch. Already she knew she would get on the porch and go left, making sure to stay under the windows, all the way to the front door on the left side.

She just had to do it.

She sat in the car, making sure she had all her ducks in a row, her plan solidifying in her mind. Felt the familiar surge of adrenaline, the "just do it," attitude starting to take over.

She should wait for backup. They wouldn't be far behind

her. But this woman was suicidal. She might already be dead. Or dying.

She slid across to the passenger side, her heart starting to pound. She felt something heavy and massive rise in her chest. Adrenaline like a wire through her, but more than that, something else, something wild and pulsating and buzzing in her mind, wanting to short out and go dark.

She recognized it, remembered it from the Chiricahua Paint Company: fear.

So fearful she had a hard time gripping the door handle. Fear beating like wings around her head, trying to blot out her vision.

Get a grip!

She needed to push it down. She needed to quiet the tremor in her legs, the way her heart seemed to shake loose inside her chest. She swallowed and felt the fear retreat a little.

Logically, she didn't think Barbara Wingate was a threat to her. Even so, she would take every precaution. Even so, she would be careful.

But she was surprised by her fear.

It had just shown up. In the blood thumping in her ears, the gnawing in her gut, the tremor in her hands, the dryness of her mouth.

Frank Entwistle: *You live in a glass house.*

Okay, then. Wait. Wait for backup. You can fade into the woodwork, you can stay back, stay at a distance, you can—

Screw that.

She opened the door and duckwalked over to the first porch post on the far right.

The restless shifting of the tree branches nearby covering the sound of her footsteps.

Feeling the fear lie down, waiting and attentive, but no longer a danger to her.

She stepped up onto the porch. It creaked slightly under her weight. Holding her breath, she made it to the house wall, crouched beneath the window. She moved toward the door, careful to step only where the boards were nailed down. Gun out and ready.

Halfway to the door, she stopped and listened. The restless shadows playing across the blue-gray planks.

Laura, preparing herself, letting the fear shrivel up into a ball inside, letting training take over. Collecting herself. Gun steady. She sighted up the line of the house with her bare eyes, looking for movement, fixing on the screen door. About to go forward.

A click. An acorn falling onto the roof, maybe, but metallic—

Suddenly she knew.

She felt it on the nape of her neck. Cold, alien. A small circle, a half-inch circumference.

The fear she'd been keeping under wraps broke loose and flooded her system as she realized what it was.

Barbara Wingate's voice broke the silence. "Don't move."

For a fraction of a second Laura was *unable* to move, unable even to think. Then her brain unlocked again. Remaining still was the right thing to do. But freezing from fear—that had never happened to her before.

She willed herself to stay still. Managed to crane her head a little to the side, felt the cold thing slide under her hair, pinch her skin, saw blue jeans and boots and a fawn suede jacket in the corner of her eye.

"I don't want to hurt you."

"Then put the gun down," Laura said.

"Only if you throw your gun away." Laura felt the gun press deeper into her neck. "Do it now."

Laura threw the gun.

"Turn around. Face me."

Laura did so.

"I want you to see what you did."

Barbara Wingate's face was haggard, mascara running in two tear marks down her cheeks. Her hair had pulled out of its neat ponytail, was as frazzled as she was, filaments of red-gold hair catching the sunlight like a halo. Her eyes gleamed with a crazy light.

Thoughts flew through Laura's head—Would she die? What was death like? Would there be nothing? Or would she *not* die? What if she became a vegetable? Who would take care of her if that happened? She had no one, not even Tom.

She tried to say something, but her vocal cords lost purchase. Stopped, her mind stuttering on one thought, one silly thought, Jay Ramsey's spinal cord injury.

Helpless. What would she do if that happened?

Stop it! Talk to her.

"Mrs. Wingate—"

In a flash, Barbara Wingate brought the gun to the side of her own head. "Don't *move!*" she shouted. "I'll shoot myself if you move at *all.*"

The cop in Laura moved back in and took command. The spell was broken. "Mrs. Wingate," she said carefully. "You don't want to do that. What about Erin?"

"Erin's gone." A tear coursed down the woman's cheek, dripped off her chin. She held the gun steady though. Her eyes had gone from crazy to steely.

Laura was aware she was holding her breath. "What do you want me to do?"

"They're coming, aren't they?"

"The police? They don't want you to hurt yourself. They want—"

"Fuck what they want! I want my daughter back."

If Barbara Wingate wanted to call the child her daughter, so be it. "If all this was a mistake, you've got to let them figure that out. I know you love Erin. You want what's best—"

"You don't know what I want! *I* want you to see what you've done to me. *I* want you to see it in living color." She bit the words off, one at a time. "I want this to stick with you for the rest of your life."

Talk to her. Talk was all she had. "Barbara, if you do this, you'll never see Erin again. Think what it will do to her. If she knows—how guilty she'd feel."

Barbara Wingate held her gaze. The gun muzzle steady at the place above her ear, the cold blue-gray metal dark against her hair. Her finger pressing—Laura thinking about the two pounds of pressure, all it would take.

"Think about Erin. This can be worked out. We can work it out, I can vouch for you. But you have to show them you're all right. You want that, don't you, Barbara?"

For answer, Barbara Wingate stared a hole through Laura's soul.

And pulled the trigger.

28

Laura had seen countless gunshot wounds, and they were ugly. She had been lucky enough not to see the act of murder or suicide—the moment a bullet crashed through the brain, obliterating everything that was human. She knew this time, though, it was going to happen, and she also knew she was powerless to stop it—there wasn't enough time. She flinched, seeing in the blink of her eye the explosion in slow motion, the angry cloud of blood obliterating one side of Barbara Wingate's face, gray matter and pulverized bone spraying sideways into the blue wall.

But she didn't see it, because it didn't happen.

Like film, time had stuttered forward. First frame: woman standing on the porch, gun to her head. Second frame: woman standing on the porch, gun to her head.

No gunshot, no smell of cordite, no blood, no thick wet sound as the woman collapsed onto the floorboards.

Just Barbara Wingate standing across from her, the gun at her head, her·face both defiant and triumphant.

Laura didn't wait for her to pull the trigger again. She lunged forward, using her weight to topple Wingate to the ground. Scrambled on top of her, grabbing one hand and then the other from behind. Placing her knee in the woman's back, jerking her arms roughly backward and cuffing her. Adrenaline quicksilvered through her veins; it was easy to drag Mrs. Wingate to her feet and force her the few feet to the car and shove her against the hood.

Rage like a red haze in her head.

Watch it. Don't lose it, she told herself. And so she was gentle when she nudged the woman's blue-jeaned ankles with her own foot.

"Spread your legs."

Barbara Wingate didn't protest. She was a lamb now. No tears, no shouting, just meek compliance. Laura patted her down, then reached down at her feet for the revolver lying in the grass.

She cracked open the cylinder and spun it: empty.

Feelings—relief and anger foremost—rushed through her, making her legs shake. She picked up her own gun and sat down on the low porch, keeping her gun trained on Wingate. "Don't you even think about moving," she said.

"Why? You think I care if you shoot me?"

"Brave words," Laura said, "from someone who never meant to kill herself in the first place."

She heard the familiar sound of someone gunning a patrol car. A sheriff's car, lights blinking, slewed into the drive.

"What's going on?" a deputy shouted.

Laura, still training her gun on Barbara Wingate, said, "Nothing. Now."

29

The sheriff's deputy—his name tag said Frank Gutierrez—put Barbara Wingate into the back of his patrol unit, then came to stand over Laura.

"You going to stay like that?" he asked.

Laura realized that she was still holding her gun in the same position, both arms shaking. Slowly, she let her arms down.

"What happened here?" he asked.

"I'm trying to figure that out myself."

The next hour went by quickly. Richie, Laura and three members of the sheriff's department entered the house, which was as neat as it had been when they were here two days ago. Nothing to indicate Barbara Wingate's state of mind: The beds were made, the girl's room neat as a pin.

In other words: perfect.

Framed prints on the walls, all with a romantic theme. Works by Maxfield Parrish, lords and ladies, beautiful maidens. Unicorns.

Richie went to interview Barbara Wingate, talking into the back of the police car. She kept her eyes steady to the front and refused to talk to him, except to say she wanted her lawyer.

The adrenaline that had helped Laura subdue Mrs. Wingate had not gone away. All it did was make her shake.

She went through the motions, looking through the house, allowing herself to be interviewed by both Richie and the sheriff's deputy, but her mind was on what she could have done to prevent this situation.

How did she allow Barbara Wingate to get the drop on her like that?

Laura realized she had not been sufficiently aware of her surroundings. She took for granted the early morning wind, the sounds and shadows. She had been so focused on breaching Barbara's house that she had succumbed to tunnel vision.

Hard to believe she had allowed herself to be ambushed like that.

From the start it had gone wrong. She had set this whole juggernaut in motion, and it had come back to bite her in the ass.

The sheriff's unit containing Barbara Wingate headed up the drive. Richie came up to her. "They're taking her to Flagstaff Medical for observation. They'll keep her on suicide watch, at least overnight."

"Then what?"

"She'll be charged with threatening and intimidation and probably released. Her son's on his way."

Suddenly, she needed to sit down. She opened the door to the Impala and sat on the edge of the driver's-side bucket seat. None too soon: The adrenaline that had sustained her was slowly slipping away. She felt incredibly weak.

Still seeing that gun muzzle pointed at her face, looking into that perfect, round black hole.

Richie surveyed the area. "I guess our work is done here."

"Yeah."

"Jessup turned out to be a dry hole."

"Uh-huh."

"Bobby and Shana are in the wind."

"I know."

"So what are you going to do?"

"Guess there's nothing else I can do, here. I'm going home."

"See you in Tucson." He thumped the roof of her Impala and walked to the Starskymobile, whistling. He looked like a man on top of the world.

Glad it was her and not him.

So what? He was up, and she was down. At this moment, she didn't give a damn. Numbly, she dragged herself back to the motel. She packed her suitcase. Put it in the trunk of her car and headed for the airport.

30

Laura barely saw the scenery as she drove Interstate 40 toward Flagstaff. Her mind was elsewhere.

She still felt the cold circle at the base of her neck. She couldn't stop thinking about her own reaction.

Paralyzed with fear, unable to do anything. Unable to think. It had been for only a split second, but in her job, a split second could last an aeon. A split second could mean the difference between life and death.

And she had frozen up.

Not only that, but even now, driving on the interstate, she was still scared.

Scared because she'd seen the intention in Barbara Wingate's eyes. The woman had thought about shooting her. It was in the tone of her voice, in the flicker of her eyes. It had been pure temper on Mrs. Wingate's part, because she'd already made sure the gun was unloaded. She'd already had her plan, and her plan was to scare Laura so badly that it would stay with her for a long time. But for a moment irrationality had taken over, and Laura had seen the resolve in her eyes.

The woman was far from crazy. But she had a bottomless well of rage, and that rage had bubbled up for a brief moment. If the gun had been loaded, Laura wouldn't be here now.

It had been Barbara's decision. Her life had been in Barbara Wingate's hands.

Laura slowed for the exit to I-17, aware of the trembling in her fingers. She had underestimated the woman. She'd planned her way to Mrs. Wingate's door, but she had not planned well enough. She had not considered that the woman could be outside, that she could come at her from around the side of the house.

Laura was alive now only because she'd been lucky.

The contained worry that had lived with her every day—the constant, nagging thought at the back of her mind that this day would be her last—had finally broken loose and taken over her body and her mind.

If it continued to happen, she would be useless for police work.

The possibility of dying in the commission of her job was real. It was something you figured into the equation. When you said good-bye to your loved ones in the morning, you made sure there was no unfinished business. Every day could end early. But you couldn't let it paralyze you.

Her legs were shaking. She had to pull over. She drove onto the grassy verge on the road near the airport, opened the door and walked out among the stolid ponderosa pine trunks. Tipped her face to the sun, felt it on her cheek, smelled the pines. A grasshopper catapulted out in front of her through the tall rust-red and gold grasses.

Alive. She was still alive. Time to appreciate that. Time to send up a prayer of thanks.

She'd made mistakes, but she was still here. When she got home, she would deal with what had happened today. She'd do things differently. She'd go to the eye doctor. She'd request counseling. She'd face what had happened today and make her peace with it.

And I'll straighten things out with Tom, find out once and for all where we're at. At least she had a second chance to do all these things.

She stood under a massive pine tree, feeling the shadows

play across her face, listening to the whiz of traffic, her fingers going automatically to the lip balm in her pocket. Suddenly thirsty for it, her lips feeling like the crevices in the Grand Canyon. So intent on the relief she craved that for a moment she didn't register the chirp of the cell phone clipped to her belt.

It was Shana. At first her words made no sense—she was on the verge of hysteria.

"Slow down," Laura said. "Take a deep breath and tell me again." Hoping the girl wouldn't hang up on her.

"He *left* me there! He tried to kill me, I thought I was going to die, I had to dig and dig and, oh Jesus! How could he do that? How could he? Troy, I told you, you're not going to do *anything!*" she said, addressing someone in the room with her. "He'd kill you!"

She was sobbing now, her voice breaking up on the cell, a male voice yelling in the background. Laura had the damn thing pressed to her head so hard it stung her ear, thinking how technology was a bastard. "Where are you? I'll come to where you are."

There was a pause.

"Shana? Shana?" Had she disconnected?

"I don't know if that's a good idea." Her voice dull.

"You said he tried to kill you. Is that true?"

A whimper.

"Shana, he could come back. You need to tell *someone*. You know you called me for a reason."

"I've got Troy."

"Who's Troy?"

"He's a *friend*." The old Shana, defiant.

"Tell you what," Laura said quickly. "Just tell me where you are. I'll come out and we'll talk if you want to or we won't. It'll be up to you. Where are you staying?"

"If Bobby knew I talked to you— Would you shut up, Troy? Shut *up!* I can't hear myself *think!*"

"Bobby can't do anything to you while I'm there. Are you at home?"

Another pause. "I'm in Flagstaff."

"That's a coincidence. I'm over by the airport." Laura tried to make her voice sound warm. She'd never met anybody so suspicious, so perverse. "Where are you?"

Laura heard the phone drop on a table or counter, and Shana's voice. "*You* tell her."

Someone snatched the phone up, and she heard a young man's voice, angry. "Look, I don't know who you—"

"Will you *just* tell her where we are?" shouted Shana.

Laura drove south on I-17 to the exit for Kachina Village and Mountainaire. As she came off the ramp she spotted the convenience store Shana had told her about. She drove to a T intersection and turned right on Kachina Trail. Kachina Trail wound up onto the pine-covered bluff above. Asphalt turned to cinder, the dust rolling up under her tires and hazing the green backdrop of pines.

Streets on the left, pine forest on the right, dropping down to glimpses of grazing horses on a meadow near the freeway. Up ahead, cars and trucks lined the road, parked around the house on the corner. A family walked across the road, the woman and daughter in pastel dresses, each of them carrying a wedding present, which went well with the flower arbor near a man-made pond, and the radiant blond girl in a wedding dress.

Laura turned at that corner, Moenkopi. The rest of the street, with a few exceptions, wasn't as nice. She drove by dented mailboxes, mobile homes in various states of disrepair, cars on blocks, and the ubiquitous pines that still managed to look beautiful even in this setting. Up on the right a waist-high chain-link fence wrapped around a yard mostly taken up by a decrepit school bus and two snake-headed pit bulls.

A faded turquoise mobile home sat far back on the lot, a slender young woman sitting on the warped wooden stoop, one arm resting on her knee, a long cigarette between her negligent fingers. Her wheat-colored hair a straggle, a man's long-sleeved shirt unbuttoned over a Neapolitan-colored striped tube top, dirty jeans and boots.

It took Laura a minute to realize it was Shana, and that the chocolate in the Neapolitan on the tube top was dirt. Laura walked up to the gate.

The dogs raced to the fence, sticking their noses through the spaces in the links, their eyes golden and unknowable.

Shana looked in her direction, flicking an ash from her cigarette out to the side. A young man sat up from a weight bench, wiped his face with a pink dish towel, and sauntered up to the gate. Tank top, tats, earring. He had black hair and haunted eyes with dark smudges underneath, and a heavy chain looped from his belt to the front pocket of his jeans. He unceremoniously dragged the two dogs by their collars around the house to a shed, and pulled the door closed with a metallic shriek.

Giving her the evil eye, he opened the gate.

Laura walked in, avoiding a rusted Weber grill lid lying on the path to the door.

Shana remained on the stoop, tangling her fingers into her hair and pulling it back and around her neck so that it fell over one shoulder. Laura noticed dark roots, maybe because the hair was dirty.

Laura said, "Mind if I sit down?"

Shana sighed, took another drag from her cigarette. She was trying to appear as if she didn't care, but Laura could see her arm was shaking.

Troy had followed Laura up to the trailer and stood there, looking from one to the other. "You don't have to tell her anything," he said.

"Troy," Shana mumbled.

"You called me," Laura said, keeping her voice low and reasonable. "You must have a reason."

Shana dug into her hair again. Laura noticed her nails, which were ragged and in some places cut down to the quick, rims of dirt underneath. Ridges of dirt in her knuckles, too.

"You said you had to dig. I guess you weren't kidding. What's that all about?"

Troy stood over them, arms crossed, glowering. "Look, you want her out of here—"

"Nuh-uh," Shana said wearily. And then she started talking.

At the house on the corner the wedding was in full swing. The handsome young couple stood under the white lattice arbor reciting their vows. As Laura slowed for the turn, Shana said, "Wait a minute."

Laura let the car idle. Shana stared out the window, her expression wistful. Laura thought that if Shana cleaned up she would look a lot like the bride.

Over the rushing water in the pond and the rattle of quaking aspens at the edge of the bright green lawn Laura could hear the murmur of the reverend's voice. She glanced at Shana, who was twisting the cheap engagement ring Bobby Burdette had given her back and forth on her finger.

After a few minutes, Shana sat back, all animation gone from her expression.

Laura said, "Shall we go?"

Shana looked straight ahead. "I don't see why I have to go to the hospital. I'm fine."

"We have to get you checked out, Shana. You could be dehydrated. You're sunburned and you said yourself you were pretty sick when you got to Troy's."

"So I threw up. Wouldn't you, if someone did what Bobby did to me?"

"The sooner we go, the sooner we get this over with."

As Laura put the car in gear, Shana muttered something. Laura asked her what she'd said.

"*I* never had a wedding that nice."

The hospital in Flagstaff kept Shana overnight for observation. As Laura suspected, the girl was dehydrated and needed to have her fluids replenished. The abrasions she had received in digging herself out of the makeshift grave Bobby Burdette had made for her also needed tending.

Shana protested, but weakly. Laura got the impression the girl liked the attention. Laura had already called Shana's parents and they'd broken land speed records to get here. Laura talked to them in the waiting room. Mostly to allieviate their fears, but she didn't touch on what Shana had told her about her harrowing experience of the last few days.

Laura did not tell them that she feared Shana was involved in something dangerous. She still had to figure out if this was a crime of domestic violence or if there was more to it than that.

She found a motel just up the street from the hospital on Business Loop 40—old Route 66—and had a dinner salad at the motel coffee shop.

She'd been debating most of the day whether to call Richie, who would be back in Tucson by now. Shana had called her specifically, which indicated trust to some degree, but she'd been vague about exactly what happened to her in the desert north of Phoenix. Richie's presence would introduce another element into the equation, and it might not be a good one. Still, Laura knew she had to let him know what was going on. She needed to let Jerry Grimes know, too.

Sitting out by the pool, steam rising from the heated water. Staring at the tall mountain overlooking Flagstaff and listening to the sigh of car tires of the traffic plying Business Loop 40, Laura called Richie at the office and left a message, repeated the same with Jerry Grimes. The coward's way out.

The hospital released Shana at ten thirty the next morning. She was ready for show-and-tell. She had enjoyed the sympathy and attention at the hospital, and when Laura suggested they go looking for the hole where she'd been buried, she jumped at the idea.

For the moment, the horrors of being left for the better part of three days in a boarded-up hole in the ground had receded, replaced by the idea of an adventure. This didn't mean she wasn't rude to Laura. Her first instinct, as always, was to withhold certain key pieces of information, and force Laura to drag it out of her.

Laura had not cared much for Shana from the beginning. She thought she was spoiled and self-centered, and dealing with her had been maddening. She was at turns sullen or defiant, and had never once broken out of that mold. But Shana had lost her twin brother. And now the man who supposedly loved her had buried her out in the middle of the desert and left her to die.

Shana's self-esteem had always seemed fragile to Laura, but what must it be now?

The drive down I-17 had taken them down from ponderosa pine to juniper and grassland, and finally back to the Sonoran Desert. The desert baked under midday sun, but it was beautiful to Laura's eyes. Her country. She felt a pang, missed her *nidito* in Vail.

Missed Tom.

As they approached the exit for Rock Springs, Shana broke her silence. "I have to pee."

Laura turned into the parking lot of the Rock Springs Café.

Shana shoved the door open and stalked across the parking lot to the old pueblo-style trading post. Laura noticed a pay phone out front; probably where Shana had called her ex-boyfriend to come pick her up. Burdette had taken Shana's cell phone when he buried her in the desert.

Laura gained the shade of the building and decided to check out the general store while she waited for Shana. She wandered between the half-empty shelves in the old store, past stacks of Rock Springs T-shirts and a few curios. She heard a familiar sound, though, and followed it to a dark room that looked like somebody's basement except for the beer banners strung under the ceiling, neon beer signs, and the old-fashioned mahogany bar against the back wall.

Up above the bar was a TV simulcast of a horse race at Turf Paradise. The familiar sound was the race caller, his voice getting more urgent as the horses swept around the turn and flashed under the wire.

"What can I getcha?" a gray-haired woman behind the bar asked, setting down a napkin.

Laura's gaze didn't move from the horses, now galloping back after the race. "I'm just waiting for someone."

"Okay."

Laura watched the Thoroughbreds coming back, and was surprised at the longing she felt. Nothing was more beautiful to her eye than a Thoroughbred at the top of its game.

She still missed her mare Calliope, even after all these years. Jay Ramsey's brother had given her the phone number of a woman who owned one of Calliope's colts, but so far Laura hadn't done anything about it.

Inertia. She had done nothing for her own life, only for her job, and even in that she had been screwing up.

"What are you doing?"

Laura looked around, feeling unaccountably guilty. Shana stood in the doorway, arms crossed, looking pissed off.

"Waiting for you."

"I don't want to be here all day. Troy and I are going to dinner tonight."

The sun's glare after the darkness of the bar made Laura squint. "Where to?" she asked as they pulled out of the parking lot.

"That way," she said, pointing to the right. South on the access road, in the direction of Phoenix.

Shana leaned against the passenger door, as far away as she could get from Laura, her face pensive.

"Stop! You went too far."

Laura braked, backed up along the dirt verge.

"I think that's it," Shana said. On the right was a dirt road, a post-and-wire fence pulled taut across it, a metal sign attached saying NO TRESPASSING.

"This was where he took you?"

"Uh-huh."

Laura got out, pulled up the wire loop connecting the weathered gatepost to the fence, and dragged the gate across the road. She drove through and glanced at Shana. Shana ignored her, so Laura had to get out and close the gate behind them.

"How far?"

"I don't know. I'll know it when I see it, though."

They started up the road, two tire-track paths worn around a hump of dirt, rocks and low bushes in the middle. It was slow going in the low-slung car, which almost bottomed out when the road became part dry creek bed. "This is somebody's ranch. Did you see anyone?"

"Some guy picked me up and drove me to the trading post." She added, "He asked me if I wanted to have a ball."

"What?"

"He was joking. Some old cowboy, had to be at least eighty. He said Rock Springs Café was famous for its mountain oysters. Have a ball. Get it?"

Laura wondered how many hitchhikers the old cowboy had regaled with that one. "You're lucky he came along."

Shana didn't say anything, but just kept twisting her engagement ring. Laura didn't know anything about carats, but she thought the diamond on this ring had to be one of the smallest ever made. The last size down before you got to a chip. Bobby Burdette hadn't gone to much expense to get Shana to go with him. Even for window-dressing, the ring was unbelievably cheap. But she also knew that in Shana's mind it was still an engagement ring.

Laura thought that Shana had a habit of expecting both too much and too little at the same time.

They drove for what seemed like a long while, up a long hill encrusted with rocks and cactus.

"I think that's it," Shana said, pointing at a ghost of a road heading off into the brush. Laura glanced at her odometer. They'd come two and a half miles.

They followed this road over another couple of hills and then down into a wash.

"It was near the wash." Excited now.

They got out of the car and followed the wash east. Hot, probably ninety degrees out here, and Laura could feel the sweat beading in her hair. Glad that each of them had a bottle of water. Shana looked at several spots, but there was no disturbed ground, no indication of the makeshift grave where she had been trapped for so long.

At last Shana stopped. "Maybe it's the other way."

An hour and a half later, it became clear to Laura that Shana had no idea where they were or where she had been buried.

"You sure it's around here?"

"It's here somewhere. Why, do you think I'm lying? Because I'm not!"

"Why'd Bobby bring you out here?"

Patiently, Shana went through the story again. How, when he picked her up in Rocky Point, he said they'd drive back up to Williams and they'd tell her parents they were getting married. How, on the way up, he had turned off at Rock Springs, asking her to go on a little detour with him, because he wanted to show her something.

"What did he want to show you?"

"He said he had some pot stashed around here."

But when he led Shana to the place in the desert where he said the marijuana was, she had gotten the shock of her life. He had showed her his "fort," telling her it was just like the kind he used to dig in the ground when he was a kid.

"It was plywood," Shana said. "He piled dirt on top of it, a lot. I could hear him shoveling it over me—"

She shuddered and started to cry. Adventure had suddenly turned to reality.

Laura hated herself for disbelieving Shana even for a moment. She found herself opening her arms and letting Shana into their circle, felt the girl's hot tears coursing down her own neck, her sobs coming from her depths.

Above her, Bobby's muffled voice telling her she had water, she had food, she even had toilet paper. Telling her he had to have her play hostage, but he would be back soon, and then they would get married.

She just had to do this for him.

Her fear was real. Her torn, ragged fingernails were real. She couldn't find the hole, but she had been there. She had faced the dark alone.

Bobby had been true to his word, Shana told her. He'd left her a case of bottled water, a twelve-roll of toilet paper, and some energy bars. But no light.

She had, literally, dug her way out.

"The thing I don't understand," Laura said as they drove back toward Flagstaff, "is why he'd do that to you."

Shana twisted her ring again.

Laura let her own left hand drop to her side, drift into the pocket of her slacks. She felt around for the button on her portable tape recorder and turned it on. What she was doing was well within the law. She did not have to inform Shana she was taping her, or ask for her permission.

All's fair in love and police work.

Laura said again, "It's just hard for me to understand. What do you think he was trying to do?"

Shana just stared ahead.

"I mean, if a guy was going to marry *me*—"

"He told me he was coming back." Defiant.

Laura said, "I guess he wouldn't have said it if he didn't mean it, would he?"

"He meant it."

"Don't you think he'd be worried, though? About you, being down there?"

"He was coming back for me."

"Is that what it felt like when you were down there? Weren't you scared?"

"Of course I was scared! Wouldn't you be?"

"Do you think he feels bad about scaring you? I mean, look at you. Your nails. All that dirt—that fort could have caved in on you."

"It *did*."

Laura didn't say anything, let the horror of it sink in. In her agitated state, Shana would likely deplore a void and would probably rush to fill it.

Shana was still looking out the window when she said, "He shouldn't have done that to me."

Laura said, "You're right. It wasn't fair."

"I could have *died* in there."

"You're lucky you didn't die," Laura said. "What I can't understand, is why he did it. He said he wanted you to play hostage. What does that mean? Do you think it was a game?"

Silence. They were headed up the long grade to Cordes Junction, passing some cars as if they were standing still. A car was parked in the breakdown lane, hood up—Laura had seen many cars over the years blow up on this grade. She glanced at Shana. She could almost see the wheels turning. Laura said, "I think it must have been a game. But what was the point?"

Shana turned on her. "I don't know, okay? All I know is, he wouldn't try to kill me."

Up ahead a tanker truck and a semi took up both lanes. The same trucks that had borne down on her like the hounds of hell on the flats had now slowed down to a crawl at the top of the grade, their taillights blinking steadily. Laura would have to slow down, lose her momentum.

Laura glanced at Shana, whose arms were crossed, fingers tightly gripping her sides. Shana wanted to be reassured. She wanted her belief to be validated. "I'm sure that killing you wasn't his intention," Laura said. "He left you the water and the food. But what if something happened to him and he couldn't make it back?"

"I was able to get out, wasn't I? He didn't bury me that deep. He probably did that on purpose. Made it easy for me to get out."

"Was it easy?"

Shana was trying not to cry. But she was losing the battle.

Laura said, "When do you think he was coming back? Today?"

There was a long pause, and then Shana said something so faintly Laura wasn't sure she heard it right. But she thought she said, "Never."

They hit Camp Verde, drove over the Verde River, past the cottonwood trees along the river, past the RV park water tower and the JESUS IS LORD sign, and up the double-laned hill.

Laura said, "Does this have anything to do with the Earth Warriors?"

Alarm in Shana's voice. "What's that?"

"We know about the Earth Warriors—about the SUVs."

"I don't know what you're talking about."

"Maybe that was what the hostage thing was about."

"No way." But she sounded unsure.

They were up on a plateau now—ranch country. Pale yellow grass sheared down to almost nothing, lots of prickly pear, red volcanic earth and rocks running in dried rivulets through the grass, cowpens on the right. Laura weighed Shana's inflections, sensing a change. Most of the guys she worked with were better at reading body language. They said the eyes were the windows to the soul. But Laura was more sensitive to tone of voice, to the way people constructed their sentences—she could almost always tell if someone was lying by listening to them talk.

Laura said, "You know what I think? Bobby is using you

to put forward his own agenda. I think he's the one who cares about the environment, not you."

"That's not true. I was in the group long before—" She caught herself, shot Laura a nasty look. "You tricked me."

"What am I supposed to think? This guy just buried you alive, and you said yourself you didn't know if he was going to come back. I've had bad relationships. I know what it's like to get shit on."

"We're getting *married*. Did you ever get someone to marry you?" Looking pointedly at her ring finger.

Laura made a quick decision. She reached down into her pocket and turned the recorder off. "Once. But it only lasted seven months."

"What happened?"

"He betrayed me." Not the whole story about Billy Linton, but close enough. "He told me he loved me, said we were going to be together forever, but that didn't last. I realized he was just using me."

That was an out-and-out lie, of course, but it suited her needs.

"Bobby's not like that."

"Dan didn't like him, did he?"

"So what?"

"Maybe he knew what kind of person Bobby was. Do you think he ever talked to him—you know, as your brother to your lover?"

"How should I know?"

"Dan looked out for you, didn't he? How do you think he felt about Bobby?"

"What's it matter to you?"

"I'm just saying, I've been there. I know what it's like to be betrayed. I know what it's like when your friends and family are telling you to slow down, maybe this guy isn't the best thing since sliced bread, and then you go on your merry way and all of a sudden you're in too deep. I know *I* got in too deep."

"Thanks for the story of your life."

"Well, we might as well be honest with each other. We have enough in common. Dan didn't like Bobby, did he? He was worried about you. I know about big brothers—"

"He wasn't my big brother. We were twins."

"He was worried about you, maybe thought you were getting in too deep with the Earth Warriors. I mean, the way things are these days—what you did isn't just *monkey wrenching*. After nine-eleven? The government means business. We're talking, lock you up and throw away the key. If you were Dan, wouldn't you be worried?"

"Shit," Shana said, starting to cry again.

"I understand you feel bad. But you shouldn't. You were only doing what Bobby wanted you to do. I know it wasn't your idea to burn those SUVs. But Jesus, you could be in such big trouble."

"Are you going to arrest me?"

Laura answered by saying, "I personally don't think it was your fault. I think Bobby used you, and Dan knew about it."

Shana said nothing.

Laura added, "I bet he was really worried. I wonder if he confronted Bobby on his own? Sounds like something a big brother would do."

"He didn't." But there was no conviction in Shana's voice.

"How do you know?"

"I just know, that's all."

"The way I see it, Dan knew what you were doing. Or he suspected. And Bobby has a hot temper—"

"You don't know that." But she sounded even more unsure.

"You do. You guys have a tempestuous relationship. Fight and make up, fight and make up. I've been there. I know what love's like. It's almost like a drug, it feels so wonderful. And when it's bad, you get so mad you can't stand it, but, Jesus, you feel so alive. All those highs and lows."

She let that sink in.

"Like when Bobby buried you. I think Bobby got worried that you weren't going to go along with him, especially because of the bad blood he had with Dan, and I think he was going to teach you a lesson. Put a scare into you."

"That's not true—"

"I mean, think about it. With Dan gone, without him to look out for you, you're all alone. Isolated, you know what I mean? Dan's not there to give you advice, you've got nobody to help you, nobody to *take your side*. And all of a sudden you're in this big mess, and you end up buried out there somewhere in the desert. The ultimate betrayal."

Shana turned in her seat and shoved her hand out. "See this? This is an engagement ring! We're going to get married, we love each other." And she started crying again.

Laura said, "You know that's not true, don't you?"

"It *is* true!"

"He's never going to marry you. You know that. You're not a stupid person. He might not have meant to kill you, but you know the score. You said yourself he was never coming back.

"Maybe that's why he made it easy enough for you to escape. So he didn't have to face the fact that he was a killer. If you got out, great. If you didn't it was your fault. Either way, though, you lose. If he gets away with whatever he's doing, if he's using you as a hostage and this is something really bad, guess who's going to end up holding the bag?"

"Me," Shana said, her breath hitching.

"Bingo."

Laura could feel Shana turning toward her. She could feel Shana wanting her protection, wanting her comfort. There was a time in interrogations that this happened, and it was magic. Laura felt the thrill course through her, a top-of-the-world high. She was on the horse now and riding it for all it was worth. "I'm looking at this from the outside, Shana. And I want to ask you something. When do you think he dug that little grave? When do you think he salted in the supplies? Before he bought your engagement ring?"

Shana didn't say anything, but she was still crying.

"When did he plan that? When you called him and told him where you were? When he went to the store and bought your ring? When he came to pick you up?"

"I don't *know!*"

"What did he say to you when you were driving up here? When did he tell you about the pot?"

"Right before we got there."

"And then he shoved you in that hole. Like you were a pile of garbage. He shoved you into that hole, pushed on your feet, boarded it up behind you. Took a shovel and *buried* you, Shana. Does that sound like someone who wants to marry you? Someone who loves you?"

No answer. But Laura knew she had won this round.

"But what I want to know even more than that is: How much did Dan know? If Bobby was willing to bury you alive, and you're his girlfriend, what would he do to someone he didn't like so much?"

She caught Shana's gaze, held it.

"What would he do to Dan?"

By the time Laura reached the Kachina Village–Mountainaire turnoff, Shana was asleep. Crying jags generally made people sleepy.

She awoke just as I-17 turned into Milton Road and the traffic slowed. She looked at Laura, startled. "You missed the turnoff."

"I'm hungry," Laura said. "Aren't you?"

She'd struck a chord. But Shana said, "Troy and I are going out for dinner."

"There's a Wendy's." Laura turned in to the drive-through. Shana didn't object, and ordered a double with everything and fries. She attacked the food as if she hadn't eaten in days, which was pretty close. Laura kept going, backtracked on Business Loop 40 past some cheap new motels and some older, seedy ones. Before Shana was through eating they were driving through the rolling gate to the DPS District Two office on Kaibab Lane.

"What're we doing here?" Shana asked.

"I have to go in for a minute. You want to come along?"

Shana shook her head. "I'll stay here."

"You've got a better bladder than I do." Laura got out and started toward the pale yellow mobile home on the far side of the enclosed area, where the Flagstaff detectives worked.

She heard the car door open and Shana's footsteps behind her. "Wait."

They walked up the steps and went inside. Desks were ranged along the opposite wall, delineated in some cases by short partitions but mostly just by personal possessions—a cowboy calendar, a poster of an American flag, family photos. All the desks empty—it was past five and everybody had either gone home or was out working cases. Laura picked the one with the least clutter and said, "You go first." The nameplate on the desk said Z. BROWNING. She hoped he wouldn't mind her commandeering his space for a few minutes. She led Shana to where the bathroom was, making sure she got a good look at the last chair, face-out from the wall, complete with handcuffs and leg irons. She nodded toward Z. Browning's desk. "I'll be right here, okay?"

Shana nodded wearily.

Laura pushed a couple of files to the side so she had a good area to work, took some papers out of her briefcase and set them right in front of the chair. The door to the outside opened and a young redheaded Highway Patrol officer stuck his head in. "Can I help you?"

He saw the badge clipped to her belt and said, "Oh. Sorry," and ducked back out.

Laura moved the chair slightly to the left, so that anyone coming in would be able to see over her shoulder. She placed the diagram of Dan and Kellee's tent on the desk, along with the list of shots the couple had taken and the damage that had been done to flesh, bone and sinew.

She sensed rather than heard Shana come back into the room.

"What's that?"

Laura put her arm across the paper in a half-assed attempt to hide it. "Are you ready to go?"

"That's the tent, isn't it? Danny's tent."

Laura cleared her throat. "Yes, it is."

Shana leaned over her. "What are those numbers on the left?"

Then she gasped.

Laura stood up hastily, picking up the papers and stacking them. "I'm sorry, Shana; you shouldn't have seen that."

"Let me see."

"It's not pleasant."

"Let me see." Her voice like steel.

Laura sighed and put the page back on the table.

Shana stared at it a long time. Then she sat down in the chair and covered her face. "Shit," she said.

Laura gave her time.

"He *obliterated* them!" She started to cry.

"It's my fault. You shouldn't have seen that."

Shana's voice shook. "How could he do that?"

Laura said, "I don't know."

Shana looked at her through red-rimmed eyes. "Did they know what was happening?"

All the times Laura had interviewed Shana over the last week, and finally she was asking this question. Finally, it had come home to her. For the first time, Shana wasn't concerned about herself or her feelings. She was thinking of her brother.

"Dan tried to protect Kellee," Laura said, carefully picking her words. "The second round came so fast, I don't think he had time to think. Either one of them."

"That was the shot that killed them," Shana said.

"Yes."

They sat in silence.

Finally, Shana said, "You think it was Bobby."

Laura said nothing but continued to hold Shana's gaze.

"You do, you think Bobby did this." She crossed her arms, rubbing them with her fingers.

"It's important to know what *you* think."

"He couldn't do that. He loves me. He wouldn't . . ." She trailed off, staring at the desk. The page was gone but she was looking at something. Perhaps it was her own bleak interior landscape.

Laura said gently, "He buried you alive, Shana. He's capable of anything."

"Maybe."

Laura thought she would finally get Shana to talk— really talk. She could feel it, they were on the brink, the way an Olympic diver feels at the moment he's about to leave the board, toes on the edge of the high dive, tensed for the spring. That was where Shana was.

And then, just like that, it was gone. Shana blundered to her feet, her eyes angry. "I don't want to talk to you anymore."

"Fine. But do you mind if I give you some advice?" She didn't wait for the girl's answer, but stepped close to her so they were face-to-face, getting into her personal space. "If I were you, I'd get as good a lawyer as I can find."

Shana stared at her, her sullen expression turning to shock.

"Come on, Shana. You and I both know you're tied up with the Earth Warriors. I told you before, this is post-nine-eleven. It's a different time. Terrorism can get you put away for a long time. If you're smart, you'll work out some kind of deal. It's the only way you're not going to spend your best years in prison."

Shana's mouth set in a stubborn line. "Can I use your phone? I need to call Troy and have him pick me up."

"Absolutely."

*   *   *

After Shana left, Laura put in a call to the U.S. Attorney in Flagstaff, but got his voice mail. She left a message, tracked down his administrative assistant, and got his home phone. She reached his voice mail, and left the same message—asking him to call her back as soon as possible.

Laura thought that by using the carrot and the stick she could get Shana to give up the Earth Warriors in exchange for no charges being brought. Shana wasn't particularly forthcoming, but she did have a healthy sense of self-preservation. She would tell what she knew because, despite her protestations to the contrary, Shana always came first.

Laura was pretty sure the prosecutor would agree with her request. But time was slipping away, and she had no idea where Bobby Burdette was.

She checked her e-mail before going to dinner. There was one that stuck out, a post from Peter Sage, the blogger who had mentioned the Earth Warriors. He gave her Janet Weir's e-mail address. Janet Weir was the woman who had sold a house in Ojai for the man named John, leader of the long-defunct Earth Warriors.

Laura ordered a dinner salad at the motel coffee shop, her mind still on her interview with Shana, and what it might mean to her investigation. Was there really a link, or was she trying too hard to make one? She had just speared her last leaf of iceberg lettuce when she remembered to check her phone, which she'd turned off during dinner. There was a message from a lawyer named Marty Gaar, who represented Shana Yates. She wanted to meet Laura at the U.S. Attorney's office in Flagstaff tomorrow morning at eight o'clock.

Shana's self-preservation had indeed kicked in. She had worked it out all by herself.

31

Laura started the next morning already at a deficit. The clock radio failed to come on, and she hadn't slept well, waking at midnight and drifting off around three A.M. Looking terrible from the lack of sleep, she got some ice from the ice bucket and applied it under her eyes with a washcloth while she downloaded her e-mail. There was one e-mail she had to read. It was a reply from Janet Weir, the artist and real estate agent who had sold a house for the head of the Earth Warriors. Janet Weir supplied Laura with a name: John J. Traywick. Janet had lost track of him a long time ago, but was sure he had moved to Arizona.

Laura arrived at the U.S. Attorney's office five minutes late, her hair still wet. Chuck and Louise Yates sat beside a sullen Shana Yates, who appeared scrawny and haunted next to the colorful Marty Gaar. Marty Gaar favored chiffon and color, and wore shoulder pads that made her look like a linebacker—a five foot tall linebacker. Reading glasses hung from beaded chains on her ample breast.

Jon Service, a Flagstaff resident FBI special agent Laura knew from when he'd worked down in Tucson, sat opposite Shana. He stood when Laura entered the room and gave her a flicker of a smile. His eyes were clear and blue but carried the burden of the job in the fleshy pouches underneath.

Laura liked Jon; he seemed easygoing but missed little,

and there was something comforting about his stolid bulk. What she liked best about him was the fact that he didn't act superior. Laura had no doubt that somewhere deep inside, hardwired into him from Quantico, there was the belief that all other law-enforcement agencies—and their officers— were inferior, but to his credit, Jon didn't show it. Laura understood this because she had the same mind-set regarding the local agencies she worked with, and she strove not to show it, either.

Jeremy Sharp, the U.S. Attorney, joined them. Short, balding, and young, he had soft features, pale skin, and startling black hair. In his call to her last night, Jon Service explained that Jeremy Sharp and Marty Gaar were good friends who shared a love of antiques—for a couple of years they'd worked together as prosecutors for the Coconino County attorney's office. Their friendship had apparently played a role last night in expediting this deal.

From the moment Sharp first spoke, it was clear that both the U.S. Attorney and Marty Gaar had done all their homework and were already in agreement. There must have been a flurry of faxes and phone calls last night, clearing the way for Shana to tell her story.

Forgoing the preliminaries, Shana's lawyer announced that Shana wanted to bring Dan Yates's killer to justice, and had decided to tell them everything she knew to achieve that end.

Laura was now allowed by Marty Gaar to ask her questions. Shana answered in a monotone, but she didn't evade. Every time she got that stubborn look on her face, Marty Gaar would nudge her.

She spoke as if she were reciting a memorized piece for a high school class. Yes, she was a member of the Earth Warriors. Yes, she had participated in the burning of the SUVs and Jimmy Davis Ford.

Yes, she thought that Bobby Burdette killed Dan and Kellee.

"Why do you think that?" Laura asked her.

"Because Dan figured it out about the SUVs. Bobby was worried he'd find out about—"

Marty Gaar stopped her by placing her plump freckled hand on the girl's skinny brown one. She looked at Sharp.

Sharp nodded.

Gaar said, "Go on."

Suddenly, a light wavered at the edge of Laura's right eye. She concentrated on the air right next to Shana's face, which shimmered in and out of the light. Made herself focus.

Shana took a deep breath. "You want me to tell them about the trucks?"

"You have to," her lawyer told her.

Shana started twisting her ring again. Lights blinking. *Concentrate.*

"Bobby told me about this plan they had." She looked at Marty, and Marty nodded.

"Who had?"

"Bobby, Jack, and Glenn. They weren't going to do anything dangerous," she added quickly. "They just wanted it to look that way."

Laura glanced at Jon Service, nodded. Let him do the questioning.

"Who are Jack and Glenn?" he asked Shana.

"They run the Earth Warriors."

"Do you know their last names?"

"Jack Taylor and Glenn Traywick."

The name Jack Taylor was maddeningly familiar—someone important, someone she had met, but she couldn't remember when or where she had met him. The damn *bling-bling*ing at the edge of her vision was making it hard for her to think. The name Traywick, though—that she had seen in an e-mail just this morning. John J. Traywick.

John, not Glenn.

Brothers?

She wrote down the three names: Jack Taylor, Glenn Traywick, and John J. Traywick. Looked at each name in turn, the lights flashing like shining salamanders, wrapping their tails around her vision. Laura ignored them as best she could, trying for a connection. When it wouldn't come, she looked at Shana. "What were they going to do?"

"Have you ever heard of the WIPP project?"

"No."

"It stands for Waste Isolation Pilot Plant. It's that place down in New Mexico, near Carlsbad? Where they bury nuclear waste? They truck low-grade plutonium from the Nevada Test Site to WIPP all the time."

Plutonium. Laura was aware of the smile frozen to her face.

Laura knew where this was going, even as Shana's voice droned on. It fit the kind of guy Bobby Burdette was. A creep who drove a lime-green Dodge Challenger and who buried his girlfriend with bottles of Dasani and LUNA bars.

He planned to hijack one of the trucks.

And do what?

Laura's mind kept darting ahead and circling back. Shana was speaking too slowly for her racing mind. But she assimilated it.

Bobby Burdette and some other Earth Warriors had managed to work their way into the Nevada Test Site, which contracted out the trucking of the transuranic waste they shipped to New Mexico.

That was news to her: The NTS contracted out the transporting of nuclear waste. Had the world gone crazy?

The plan was harebrained: steal a truck carrying the waste and drive it to some place in the boonies, abandon it there and then call in the media—

Film at eleven.

The way Shana laid it out, it seemed so simple. Too simple. Laura didn't see how they could pull it off. Not unless they had someone on the inside. She glanced at Jon. The lights in the corner of her eye still going but more of an annoyance now.

Jon said to Shana, "When are they planning to do this?"

"I don't know. Soon. But it's not that big a deal."

"What do you mean by 'not a big deal'?"

"They weren't going to *do* anything with it. They just wanted to take it to some remote place and the media would show up. . . . It's for a good cause. People need to know how dangerous this stuff is."

Laura wanted to say something, but didn't want to step on Jon's toes. It was his interview.

"What if something happened?" Service asked. "Something Bobby didn't plan on?"

Shana looked at him. "Those things are indestructible."

Laura wanted to shout, *Then what's the goddamn point?*

Jon said, "The Earth Warriors are driving these nuclear waste trucks for the government?"

"Uh-huh. Well, technically, for Fleet Trucking."

"And these trucks carry plutonium?"

"It's called transuranic waste," Shana said. The expert. "Technically, it's plutonium, but it's not real bad stuff— mostly just by-products like rubber gloves and clothing that's been contaminated, you know, beakers and stuff."

So it's just a little *bit of nuclear waste,* Laura thought. She remembered seeing the story about the waste shipments on the news. She had seen pictures of protestors standing on the freeway bridge in Albuquerque, their signs taped to chain-link fences over the underpass as the trucks passed underneath, on their way to Carlsbad, New Mexico.

The trucks going right through the center of Albuquerque. For that matter, they came through Flagstaff, too.

Laura knew from her own experience that a lot of bad stuff—hazardous waste, dangerous pharmaceuticals, low-level nuclear waste—was sent over the roads every day. In fact, she had helped guard two shipments of hazardous waste last year. She'd been in one of the security cars that had leapfrogged from exit to exit, checking the area, then catching up again. When certain types of dangerous materials were being shipped by train or by highway, every member of the DPS throughout the state was on call.

And that was what didn't make sense about this scheme. There were too many safeguards. Hazardous waste was periodically checked, whether it was shipped by train, ship, or truck. Anything radioactive was escorted by at least two law enforcement officers and tracked by the Global Positioning System, TRANSCOM.

"Where were these friends of yours going to park it?" Jon asked.

"On the Colorado River."

The Colorado River, which supplied California, Nevada and Arizona with their water. That gave her such a jolt she just stared at Shana.

"It wasn't that big a deal," Shana said. "We weren't going to hurt anybody."

Laura thought of Dan and Kellee Yates lying dead in their tent.

And then the piece of the puzzle—the one she had been waiting for—fell into place. Now she remembered who Jack Taylor was.

32

Normally, this was the kind of morning Mark lived for. Driving here in the suspended breath of dawn, tracking the pink glow of the rising sun over the Amargosa Mountains, the sun spilling over and spreading across the desert valley like an incoming tide.

It seemed like a routine day, too, the two of them passing through the gates of the Nevada Test Site and driving over to the section of Area Twenty-five they'd been to half a dozen times before. Parking in the lot and putting the sunshade up in the window.

Except the car they parked here was a junker Dell had bought for a couple hundred bucks. Mark's new Ford truck was miles away in Kingman.

Mark and Dell got out and walked toward Glenn Traywick, who was sitting on the tailgate of his truck having his breakfast outside a tall corrugated-tin warehouse. A flatbed semi was backed into the mouth of the cavernous building. The truck bore the logo of the company Mark worked for, Fleet Trucking.

Guided by a mobile loading unit worker positioned on a scaffold, a crane inside the building was in the process of lowering a fourteen-pack of transuranic waste drums into one of three Trupact II canisters on the truck. The canisters, which Dell liked to call Trupact Shakurs, were tall and round, eight feet around and ten feet high.

The drums were bunched into tightly packed cylinders of seven, one on top of the other, which gave the thing the visual effect of bundled dynamite. Which wasn't far from the truth, if you thought about it.

They were halfway to Glenn's truck when Dell clapped Mark on the shoulder. "I'm gonna go talk to Teddy," he said, and headed toward an office building to the left of the parking lot. Teddy and Dell played pool for money in the tiny rec room that had been set up for workers during the off shifts. Mark didn't like that, but what could he say? "Be sure to be back by nine. That's when we're leaving."

Dell turned, started walking backward. "That's two and a half hours away. Why'd you want to come out so early?"

"Just want to make sure everything's okay," Mark said.

He knew what his cousin was thinking, because he said it often enough: *What a pussy.* But Mark couldn't help it. He'd been careful all his life, and wasn't about to change now. He wanted to talk to Glenn before he left, and as it was he was cutting it close.

As he approached, Glenn looked up from the bear claw he was eating, grinning. "Hey, kid. What's up?"

What's up? His life was over as he knew it, that was what was up.

Glenn took a sip from his Styrofoam cup of coffee. "There's coffee up at the office, you want it."

Mark was in no mood for coffee. It would go right through him, and he was feeling queasy enough as it was. But there was a kind of thrill, too, as if someone had tugged on a little thread in his groin. Not a carnival-ride feeling, exactly, but the excitement was catching. He was about to change his life. And maybe that was just what was needed.

Glenn's face was pink in the early morning light, and he squinted and tugged down the brim of his Glenn Electric cap. "You might as well relax. You've got a long time before you go."

"I just wanted to go over it with you one more time. To make sure we're on the same page."

Glenn slid down from the tailgate. "Sure. Why not?"

Mark started for the truck.

"Son, you're barking up the wrong tree," Glenn said. "That's not your truck." He started walking around the big warehouse. Mark followed, feeling the way he often did around Glenn, like a little brother trying to keep up.

"There's your truck," Glenn said.

It was another Fleet truck. The only difference was, the three canisters lined up on the flatbed were closed up now, the tops looking like close-fitting French berets, little buttons on top.

Glenn said, "We did it early, so I could do the inspection work myself."

The inspections had been the trickiest thing, Mark knew. As a supervisor with the MLU—the mobile loading unit—Glenn Traywick oversaw the four-step process and sometimes did it himself. "It's all taken care of," Glenn said. "The assay, headspace gas sampling, glove box exam, radiography."

Mark knew there were four steps, but didn't really understand what they were except in the most general terms, so he took Glenn's word for it. "Seems like a lot of work to me, considering they're supposed to be empty."

"Well, people around here like to make sure. Let's go over this one more time. Where are you headed?"

"Texas A and M."

"Which one?"

"Come on, Glenn, I'm not stupid." But he added, "College Station. Outside Waco."

"Uh-huh."

Mark and Dell were supposed to be carrying empty canisters to Texas A&M, where an MLU team would load the nuclear waste into the Trupact II canisters from their lab there. It had been just luck—or Glenn's finagling—that they had three empty waste casks here at the Nevada Test Site, because otherwise the casks would have gone out of the Waste Isolation Pilot Plant, at Carlsbad. This was, after all, a WIPP project.

The casks themselves were reusable. Because they were going out marked empty, there would be no police escort. It was the only way something like this would work.

Mark felt a flutter in his stomach as he looked at the tall casks. "Which one is it?"

Glenn walked up to the canister immediately behind the cab and rapped on it. "That's the one."

Mark flinched. He didn't really like the idea of pounding on one of those things, even though they were supposed to be damage-proof. He'd never gotten used to towing this stuff, but he had done it, because this was the last time.

A month in Kingman, keeping a low profile with Dell, and then he'd go to Indiana to be with his daughter Sarah. And Rhonda couldn't say anything about it, not if he was willing to relocate to be near his daughter.

And so that was what he thought as he looked at the tall canister, which seemed to swallow the light of the beautiful Mojave Desert morning. *Think of the endgame.*

Maybe they could stop this craziness once and for all, make the people in this country stand up and take notice.

Glenn checked his watch. "You might as well go get yourself some breakfast, maybe play a video game or something. Get your mind off it. I've got to get going, myself. Have to be in Salt Lake by this afternoon."

He turned to leave.

"Glenn?"

"What?"

Mark could tell he was annoyed, but he plunged ahead anyway. "What about the checkpoint at the border?"

"Don't worry about it."

"But—"

Glenn looked disappointed in him. "Look, if you don't want to do it, we can send Dell out by himself."

It took Mark right back to the days when he was in high school, when he went along just to be part of things—always the fifth wheel. He remembered the time Jimmy Hollings had taken them all for a ride in his new Camaro, cranked it up to a hundred miles an hour, and there he was, sitting in the back, keeping his mouth shut but desperately wanting to scream at the top of his lungs, "You're gonna get us killed!" He had survived that night, but the stupid thing was, the next time they asked him if he wanted to go, he went. Now he'd been offered a chance to get out, which would have been the commonsense thing to do. But he heard himself say, "They won't send Dell out alone. You'd have to get another driver."

"I know of somebody. Might slow us down a little, but we'll still get out today. Thing is, you've got to make up your mind. Then we can come up with an excuse."

"I'm going," he insisted. "I just want to know what's ahead of us."

"You've got to trust me, Mark. There aren't going to be any problems at the border. You'll sail right through. You'll see."

Mark wanted to say something else, like the fact that the state inspectors at the California border were equipped to do the same tests Glenn had done this morning. Like, how many people were involved in this, anyway?

But this time he kept his mouth shut. He just watched as Glenn strode briskly over to his truck, climbed in, and peeled rubber out of there.

As if he wanted to get away from here as fast as he could.

The closer they got to the new port of entry a few miles inside the California state line, the worse Mark felt. The inspection station on State Route 127 had been erected specifically to monitor the waste trucks going from the Nevada

Test Site to the Waste Isolation Pilot Plant site in New Mexico. Mark and Dell had been through it many times in the last three months, but this time their load did not match the manifest.

He hoped Glenn was right about the inspectors.

To be fair, Glenn had been right about everything else. He had gotten Mark and Dell the job with Fleet Trucking easily. He had supplied their fake identities, and despite all the warnings about how scrupulous the DOE was about background checks, both he and Mark had sailed through. Glenn was someone you could trust, and Mark always felt better when he was around. But he wasn't around now, and here was another hoop to jump through.

He tried to calm himself by looking at the desert. To most people the Mojave Desert was as barren as a moonscape, but to Mark there was nothing more beautiful. He loved the subtle colors of the mountains, which ranged from black to plum to five shades of blue to purple to pink. The light seemed to shift like a kaleidescope as the day went on. He loved the road, loved the open space. Now he tried to fill his eyes with the stark beauty—the alluvial fans that spread out at the base of the mountains and froze into place, biscuit-colored, dotted with sage, saltbush and creosote. More colors: silver, gray, and olive green. He had spent a lot of time around here looking for rocks, on the high mountain passes in Death Valley off to the west, the Funeral and Amargosa mountains.

He had studied this area; the geology, the biology, the history. He knew what he was looking at. From an early age, he'd always been the kind who wanted to label things. His ex-wife said he was anal-retentive about it.

He knew, for instance, that this area was all basin and range. He knew what the denizens were, and the makeup of the rocks. He had found rocks in the mountains near his home, stones he had cut and polished and made into earrings and bracelets and necklaces for Sarah.

This place was one of the loneliest on earth. The only

signs of man were the power lines marching across the landscape from Boulder Dam and the black ribbon of road ahead of them, which at this time of day dipped in and out of the dead zone where mirages melted the road and blurred separate peaks together and pulled them back apart like taffy.

Indiana would be nothing like this.

Something wailed inside him. He'd already put his lapidary equipment into storage. He might never get back here to retrieve it—he knew that.

And he'd already returned his desert tortoises to the government. That had been the worst.

But he would see Sarah grow up. He would start a new life. And he, himself, would be different after this.

He would have made a difference to the world.

"Here we are," Dell said.

Mark had been through the inspection process probably thirty times in eight states, but today was different. He felt as if something full and viscous were blocking his throat. How would he act? He wasn't good at deception, never had been. He kept reminding himself that Glenn had paid the guy off, but what if there was a last-minute change in personnel? What if this was a trap?

His heart started to pound. His stomach felt like it was snarled in piano wire, cutting the top part of him off from the bottom. He felt like the top half of him could float away if he didn't watch out.

I'm going to blow it.

They drove into the truck lane.

The state inspector wore a dark blue uniform and matching baseball cap, and sunglasses like Bobby Burdette's. The desert sunlight bounced off his badge.

Despite his fears, Mark was expecting to be waved through. Glenn had always been right before, and Mark had put his faith in that.

But it didn't happen. They were directed to park over on the right.

His breathing got shallow. His hands were sweating, and beads of perspiration ran down his face.

"Stay cool, man," Dell said. "I'll do the talking."

Mark wondered if he would ever see Sarah again.

Dell looked cool. Twenty-eight years old and he acted like nothing could hurt him, like he was a superhero or something. He was the coolest liar Mark had ever seen.

Dell handed the inspector the clipboard with their itinerary. Mentioned casually that, as the guy could see, the casks were empty, on their way to Texas A&M. Even joked about it. How he thought Texas was "bigger than shit but no better."

Mark thought that was a little much.

Still, it looked like they would be waved through.

But the inspector surprised them by asking them to get out of the truck and walk over to the trailer while they did a level-one inspection and checked the load with a radiation detector for leaks.

This wasn't the way it was supposed to happen! They'd know, the minute they got to the first canister behind the truck cab.

As he and Dell waited on folding chairs in the shade of the trailer, Mark wondered what it would be like to be handcuffed, taken away in a squad car, booked.

In this post-9/11 world, he knew they'd throw the book at him.

He tried to fill his eyes with the desert. The desert was impassive, her face beautiful. He remembered the one time he had ridden this road on a bike, part of a tour in what seemed like another life. That had to be seven, eight years ago? Sarah was only a baby then.

Sarah. The idea that he would never see her again—

Someone cleared his throat nearby. Mark looked up, trying not to betray the fear he felt.

"All done," the inspector said, handing Dell the clipboard. "Have a safe trip."

When Mark stood up, his knees nearly buckled with relief. Dell gave him a funny look as they walked to the truck.

Pussy.

Mark didn't care what Dell thought. He had come through. He had passed the test.

And Glenn Traywick had not let them down.

33

It was still early when Jon Service's take-home car, a navy Taurus, negotiated the curves along Oak Creek, flickering in and out of the shadow cast by the Mogollon Rim. The few stretches of road where the sun reached the pavement were dappled with the shade of oak, walnut, wild grape, and sycamore. The sycamore turning rusty, the walnut trees and cottonwoods tinged yellow-gold.

Glimpses of Oak Creek, at turns brown and hammered silver, rushing over the rocks below.

But Laura was preoccupied by the idea of transuranic waste casks and crazy people like Bobby Burdette and the creeping fear that maybe those casks weren't as indestructible as they'd been made out to be.

At least the bling-bling was gone. She'd ridden it out, and as usual it had gone away. Whatever it was, the lights didn't stick around much longer than twenty minutes, and then her vision returned to normal.

She could live with that.

Jon Service's car smelled of pine air freshener. If Laura hadn't already known that Jon was a devout Catholic, it would have been clearly evident from the inside of the car: Rosary beads hanging from the rearview, a stick-on rendering of Christ in the garden on the dashboard. He took the curves capably and fast as he talked into his headset.

Laura thinking: *Jack Taylor.*

Jack Taylor, John Traywick.

Jack was a nickname for John, wasn't it?

All the way down 89A along Oak Creek Canyon, she thought about how easily she'd been taken in by Jack Taylor. Who wouldn't be? There was no way she could have seen this coming. He was the grieving father of a murdered girl; that was the context she'd seen him in. But apparently, Kellee's father was also the head of the Earth Warriors.

"Keep trying," Service said into the headset, then looked at Laura. "We've got a task force, but we're still working on the warrant."

"This is *terrorism.* How hard can it be?"

"You want the happy-crappy version, or the awful truth?"

Laura shielded her eyes as the sun hit the back window of the VW microbus ahead of them—it had appeared out of nowhere and was going approximately twenty-five miles an hour. The Taurus put on the afterburners and swooped by the microbus to catcalling hippies and middle fingers.

Laura said, "He'll know the minute he sees all of us what's going on. Is there a place down the road we can park? I'd rather not tell the world about it."

"There are a few places."

Laura tried Richie again, who was on his way up to Williams from Tucson. He was having his own problems. He'd been playing phone tag with a judge in Williams, trying to get a search warrant for Bobby Burdette's house.

Sometimes it seemed as if they had to do their job hogtied and blindfolded.

Jon turned into a clearing at the entrance to a private cabin, which was hidden behind a tall fence with posts carved into totem poles. A Coconino County sheriff's car was already there. "Taylor's Creekside Cabins is just around that curve," Jon said.

They gathered there for a short parlay, then walked down the road.

The cabins appeared around a blind corner, drowsing in a patch of sunlight. Megumi Taylor was out front, tending the flowers that aproned the office. She wore a floppy straw hat, pink blouse, old jeans and gardening gloves. When she saw them she smiled and waved her trowel.

Laura glanced at the sheriff's deputies, nodded for them to stay back. She approached Megumi. "Mrs. Taylor?" she asked. "I need to talk to your husband."

Megumi's sunny smile turned to confusion. She knew immediately that something was wrong. Laura wondered what she knew.

Megumi glanced from Laura to Jon in his navy suit and tie, to the deputies standing behind them on the road. "Is this about Kellee?" she asked.

"Is Mr. Taylor here?"

Megumi stood. "He's at cabin eight. I can call him." She reached for her walkie-talkie.

"That's okay," Laura said. "In fact I'd prefer it if you wouldn't call him. Where is cabin eight?"

"Up the hill on the right—the far cabin. The guests who stayed there last night left early. They came in late last night and they left even before we opened up the common room for our continental breakfast. That doesn't make sense, does it? Somebody spending all that money and coming to a beautiful place like this and not bothering to see—"

She stopped suddenly, realizing she was babbling. "Nothing's wrong, is there?"

"We just need to talk to Mr. Taylor."

"Okay, then."

Laura nodded to one of the deputies. "Why don't you stay with Mrs. Taylor?"

They walked up the winding road to cabin eight, Laura thinking about Megumi's reaction. Shana swore that Megumi and Kellee didn't know about the Earth Warriors; Jack had purposely kept them in the dark to protect them. But it was clear Megumi suspected something. Either that or she had a really good antenna for trouble.

An electric cart was parked down below the rustic cabin, the short bed behind the seats piled with sheets stuffed into pillowcases. The cabin door was open and a vacuum droned inside, along with the blare of a TV set.

Laura kept her hand close to the holster riding on the waistband of her jeans. She noticed that Jon and the deputy were also ready.

All of them hyperalert.

They went in under cover of the vacuum. The television was turned up loud, so it could be heard over the noise—an old gangster movie starring Jimmy Cagney.

Wearing one of those button-down long-sleeved shirts they sold in Cabela's catalogs, Jack Taylor vacuumed around the other side of the bed, his back to them. Unaware, even though he should have noticed the change of light in the doorway. In his own world, or just pretending not to notice? Laura couldn't take a chance, so she moved fast. Cuffs ready, she caught up to him in a couple of strides, reached around his left side and grabbed his free hand, snapping the cuff in place just as Jon Service's voice cut through the vacuum noise and the movie: "FBI. Freeze."

Jack Taylor stiffened, his back still to her. Turned his head slightly and saw Special Agent Service, gun at the ready.

Laura reached around and shut off the vacuum.

Taylor stared at Jon in bewilderment as Laura took his other hand and cuffed it to the one behind his back. She steered him around the bed and marched him outdoors.

"What's going on?" He sounded puzzled, scared, and innocent.

Special Agent Service read him the Miranda rights. Inside the cabin, there were shouts and gunfire. Laura recognized the dialogue; it was from the movie *White Heat*. The police commissioner yelling into a megaphone, exhorting Jimmy Cagney to give up.

Laura leaning Taylor or Traywick or whatever his true name was against the side of the cabin, asking him if there was anything sharp in his pockets, anything she should know about.

Inside cabin eight, Jimmy Cagney was shooting back at his tormentors and the chemical tanks around him.

Laura knew how it ended. Pretty soon he would yell, "I made it, Ma! Top of the world!"

And go up like a Roman candle.

34

"I'm willing to talk," Jack Taylor said.

His shoulders had slumped and his hands had gone slack.

Laura had never heard a suspect say that before. She'd heard people come in and confess to things they had not done, but this complete capitulation took her off guard. So much so, in fact, that she almost suggested he get himself a lawyer. She stopped herself, however. She glanced at Jon, who raised his eyebrows and smiled.

Taylor added, "I *want* to talk."

"Why is that?" Jon asked.

His voice was resigned. "I'm glad you caught me. I was thinking about turning myself in, anyway."

That left Laura nonplussed.

"I've been doing a lot of thinking the last few weeks, after—" He swallowed. "After what happened to Kellee." He turned his face to Laura's and she saw the agony in his eyes. "This was my thing. I kept my wife and daughter out of it. I did my best to protect them both. You can ask my wife. She didn't know anything about it." He looked up at the sky, and Laura saw his eyes shine with tears. "I'll tell you everything you want to know. It's the least I can do."

They walked him down to the sheriff's car, now parked at the entrance to the motel, and placed him in the back.

Laura said to Jon, "He seems sincere. While we're waiting for the warrant, we should question him here. We have no idea what kind of time line they're going on."

Jon produced a tape recorder from his suit pocket.

"You get everything?"

Jon played it back. *I want to talk. I'm glad you caught me.*

"That takes care of one headache."

They took him to the small room off the office where the continental breakfast was served. The room was paneled in pine, with gingham curtains and homey plaques on the walls, at odds with the dark, disturbing slashes on a canvas in the hallway titled *Pico Central.* Janet Weir's signature was scrawled in the right-hand corner.

The long table by the wall had been cleared away except for the coffee, for which Laura was grateful.

Laura and Jon sat him down at one of the little round oak tables near the communal TV.

Jon turned on the tape recorder and gave his name, date, the name of the suspect, read him his rights again. "Do you agree to waive these rights?"

"Yes, yes!" he said impatiently. "I already told you that. Where's my wife?"

"She's been asked to stay in the house. A deputy's with her."

"She had nothing to do with this. Nothing. I never told her what we were doing. Never. Kellee and Dan didn't know either. I would never put my wife or child in jeopardy in any way, I would never do that. I love them."

And so he told them about the Earth Warriors—in fits and starts. Laura noticed he would give them a piece of information, almost offhandedly—and then work his way back to the rationalization that he was not a bad guy because he would never expose his family to this kind of thing.

He told them he had headed up the original Earth Warriors from 1968 to 1972. They'd been on the run since their biggest coup—the torching of a ski resort under construction in the Sierra Nevada. In Jack Taylor's parlance, he had "just walked away. I decided that it wasn't worth it. No matter what we did, it was only a drop in the bucket compared to the destruction that was happening all over the country. I wanted to settle down and have a family, and I knew they'd chase me to the ends of the earth, so I changed my name and left California."

A little melodramatic, Laura thought, considering she had not been able to find anything on the old Earth Warriors except for one blog. Then he launched into an impassioned diatribe on the Kyoto Accord, the Endangered Species Act, ANWR, SUVs, a dozen other acronyms.

It was hard not to roll her eyes. It wasn't that she didn't agree with him on some things, but it seemed as if he was using them as a justification for his own behavior. She noticed that for all his willingness to come clean, he had told them precious little about the actual plot to steal a truck from the Nevada Test Site. Interviewing Jack Taylor was like wading through quicksand.

"Kellee was such a good little girl. Her mom died when she was five. I raised her by myself for five years—she was a real daddy's girl. When Megumi and I started seeing each other, she didn't sulk. We became a perfect little family. And now I've ruined it all." His voice broke.

When Jon patiently brought him back to the subject at hand, Jack managed to slip away yet again. His first wife dying of breast cancer, his little girl getting the brain tumor, what it was like to watch your daughter get sick and nearly die.

"It was fate," he said. "She was meant to be taken from us, and she was." More tears. His hands, now cuffed in front, dangling uselessly between his legs. "My sweet little girl. She was ill-fated from the very beginning."

Jon asked, "Do you have any idea who might have wanted to kill her?"

"Why would *I* know?" He looked horrified. "It can't

have anything to do with *this*. I kept her out of this. She didn't know—"

Jon Service leaned across the table and looked him in the eye. "Dan Yates knew about the arson at Jimmy Davis Ford. If you think there could be a link, I need to know."

Taylor leaned away, confused. Shook his head. "No way. I would never expose either of my two girls to this." He shrugged, added almost serenely, "It was fate. She was meant to be taken from me."

Laura wanted to hit him.

Patiently bringing Taylor back from each evasion, Jon Service took him through the plot with skill and aplomb. Eliciting from Jack Taylor how Bobby Burdette had been hired to help fix up some of the older cabins on the property, how they'd have a few beers together afterward. How Jack told Bobby about his past as the head of the Earth Warriors in the sixties, under his real name, John Traywick. It was on those beery nights they hatched the plot to take a truck carrying nuclear waste from the NTS facility, but only to expose the real dangers—a government run amok.

"Homeland Security," Jack Taylor said contemptuously. "What a joke. If you knew half of what I know . . ."

Warming to his subject.

The plan was to take the truck to Lake Mohave on the Colorado River and leave it in the marina parking lot at Cottonwood Cove. "That would throw a scare into anybody." You know the Colorado provides water for three states? Imagine if something happened to that truck and it got into the water, think about that." Smug.

Laura had heard that with plutonium, the real danger was if it was released into the air. At least that was what she'd heard on the Learning Channel.

Laura could see he was starting to enjoy himself, elaborating on his story, throwing around words like "Trilateral Commission" and an old one—"the military-industrial complex."

"Laughlin's just downriver. Can you imagine the panic

that would cause? Maybe the Stepford Americans will finally catch on, see what their government is doing to them."

A couple of anonymous calls to the media, and the truth would be known.

Jon said, "Is Glenn Traywick your brother?"

Jack Taylor didn't answer.

"Is Glenn Traywick involved?"

But on this issue, Jack Taylor would not be moved. "I want my lawyer now," he said serenely.

What Laura wanted was to wipe that supercilious smile off his face. She regretted that there were laws against police brutality.

They walked him back to the car. Behind them, Megumi stood in the parking lot, still in her floppy hat. Her whole world crumbling around her.

But Laura noticed she did not come up to talk to her husband. Instead, Jack Taylor's wife gave them a small wave and walked straight-backed up the steps into the general store. Holding the hurt to herself.

As they approached the sheriff's vehicle, Jack Taylor stopped and stared at the deep blue sky above them, inhaling the fresh mountain air. "There's more you should know."

"Yes, sir?" Laura asked.

"If I were you, I'd move fast."

Glenn Traywick was almost to the North Las Vegas airport when he punched in the number for Michelle's work phone. He'd already tried her home and her cell, with no luck.

"Trecor Business Machines, may I help you?" It was Michelle, her voice crisp and professional.

"I thought you'd be home by now."

"Don't worry, be happy. I'm all packed. Everything I need is in the back of the car."

"What about the moving van?"

"Been and gone."

He checked his watch. "I should be in Flag by eleven thirty. You know where to go?"

"Like, you never took me flying before," she said in her best imitation of a Valley girl.

He ignored that. Sometimes Michelle could be maddening. "I want you to be ready to go. Just in case things go south."

"I'll be there, love-pucky. Don't you worry about that."

"You were careful not to pack too much? You put it on the scale, didn't you? It can't be over a hundred pounds."

"Been there, done that."

"I want to be in Calgary by the time this shit hits the fan."

"Next stop, the Loon Lake Lodge. Just you, me, and the loons."

"We're gonna be famous."

"Unknown, but famous."

"That's the plan." He saw the sign for the airport up ahead. "I'm at VGT. I'll see you soon."

As he walked out to the red-white-and-blue Cessna C-175 tied down closest to the fence, Glenn decided that the preflight would have to be minimal—check the oil, drain the sumps, and go. He didn't have to file a flight plan for his trip to Flagstaff, but at some point between Flag and Calgary he'd have to, by law, if he was going to get into Canadian airspace. He'd debated flying in under the radar—literally—but that meant taking a lot of chances he was not ready for, flying through tight valleys at low altitudes.

He was too old for that.

He'd decided to file his flight plan at the last place he stopped for gas, hop over the border and ditch the plane the minute he got there.

If everything went according to plan, he would be in Canada before they found the truck. Jack had promised him some lead time. Still, he knew he was cutting it close. If any one of his coconspirators got caught and implicated him, he could be looking at Royal Canadian Mounted Police along with customs in Calgary.

All these thoughts whirled in his mind as he taxied out toward the runway, automatically checking his gauges and tuning to ATIS for the latest in flying conditions and runway information.

He switched to the tower frequency. "Cessna N21993 is ready for takeoff," he said, pleased to hear that his voice was rock-steady. "Departing North, have numbers."

By the time Mark and Dell turned off on the dirt road outside Micaville, California, Glenn Traywick had been in the air almost an hour.

As Mark and Dell drove out to the abandoned hangar, a coyote crossed in front of them fifty yards up, a rodent hanging from its jaws. It stopped and gave them a look, its shiny gold eyes bright and knowing, then trotted off.

"The trickster," Mark mumbled.

Dell looked at him. "What'd you say?"

"Coyote. The trickster. That's what they're called by the Indians. Maybe it's a bad sign."

"Bullshit."

But Mark was still puzzled about what had happened at the port of entry. He'd assumed that the inspector would look at the manifest, then wave them through with a wink and a nod. But they'd gone over the truck for almost twenty minutes, and he'd seen the guy with the radioactive detector checking the casks.

Maybe they were just making it look good. He shouldn't let it bother him. They got through okay, didn't they?

The hangar was only a few hundred yards from the road, rising out of the creosote like a giant's mailbox, sided with corrugated iron painted white. A row of many-paned windows, either opaque from the white paint or broken, ran along the sides. No sign of anyone, but that was the point. Bobby would be waiting inside with his rig.

The wind had sprung up by this time and funneled dirt

from under the truck's wheels into the ceramic blue sky. They turned into the vast clearing that faced the hangar, feeling sandblasted. Bobby Burdette's semi truck was backed in, and Bobby had somehow managed to pull the huge sheet of army-green canvas up to the scaffold. He hopped down and directed Dell to back in. Wind whistled through the broken windowpanes.

Mark didn't like Bobby Burdette, but he had to admit he worked fast. He had the GPS computer out of the dash of the Fleet truck and into the decoy semi in two minutes flat.

They put stolen plates on both trucks. The canvas used to cover the canisters took some wrestling, but thanks to the scaffolding Bobby had brought along, it wasn't as bad as he'd thought it would be.

Still, the casks were tall and the canvas fell short on either side. "Reminds me of Dana's little kid," Dell commented. "Runs around the house in a T-shirt and a bare butt."

It was a trick to tie the canvas down, and Mark wondered if the wind, which now buffeted the hangar like an angry boxer, would get under the tarp and pull it loose.

Mark opened his mouth to say something, but shut it again. It wasn't his problem now. He and Dell were basically home free. All they had to do was continue along the route in the decoy semi to give Bobby some time, then ditch it in Seligman, where Dell had a car stashed.

After that they'd melt into the woodwork. Dell had a friend who had a "safe house" in Kingman where they could stay for a couple months until things calmed down, and then he would fly to Indiana using his own name.

It sounded really simple. But as his dad's favorite poem said, "The best-laid plans of mice and men gang aft aglay."

Bobby was still struggling with the last of the tie-downs when he said, "You guys better go. If anybody's looking at TRANSCOM, you've been standing still almost forty minutes."

Suited Mark. He and Dell climbed up into the semi and

drove out. His last view of Bobby Burdette was in the side-view mirror: arms folded as he leaned against the big front grille of the rig, cocky as ever.

Mark and Dell were almost to the outskirts of Baker (Home of the World-Famous Giant Thermometer!) when they were nearly run off the road by a Corvette pulling out of a side road right across their grille.

"Did you see that motherfucker?" Dell said.

Mark watched the car dwindle quickly in the side mirror, remembering all over again his terror at the hands of Jimmy Hollings. Older, wiser now, he shook his head. "I sure wouldn't want to be in his way when he goes off the road."

35

The once-quiet Highway Patrol Division Two office was buzzing with the hyperactivity of a beehive.

Jon Service had been on the horn since they arrived from Oak Creek Canyon, putting together the task force and setting up a roadblock west of Searchlight, Nevada. Although a helicopter had already been dispatched to take them to the staging area outside Searchlight, the flight itself would take an hour. Jon was coordinating what resources were available on the ground—a logistical nightmare involving three state jurisdictions, several federal and local agencies, and the area itself, which was in a remote desert area lacking in law-enforcement resources. Already, the Department of Energy, the ATF, and the Nuclear Emergency Search Team—NEST—were organizing their own people and heading out to Searchlight.

The other resident special agent, Darcy Clayborn, had been dispatched to Jack Taylor's house to oversee the removal of his computers and any other information he would have. She stayed in constant contact with Jordan Benteen, an FBI intelligence analyst who was working Rapid Start, a computerized clearinghouse which collated information coming from other sources. He was ensconced at one end of the conference table in the common room of the DPS Highway Patrol office—the yellow-brick building facing

Kaibab Lane—which had more room to spread out in than the detectives' modular unit. Ranged around him were a cell phone, two laptop computers, a laser printer and a fax machine. The table awash in paper. Two identical road maps were tacked up on the bulletin board. One, marked in black, followed the regular Fleet Trucking route. The other, in red, showed the planned route of the hijacked truck.

The routes were identical until they reached Searchlight, Nevada: south from the Nevada Test Site to Baker, California; east on Interstate 15, exiting onto 164 going east to Searchlight. There, the truck was supposed to turn south on 95, which would take it to Kingman, Arizona, and Interstate 40 going east. But instead of turning south, the hijackers' plan was to continue straight through Searchlight on 164 to the Colorado River and Cottonwood Cove.

Jon got a call on the speakerphone from Las Vegas Metro Police Department SWAT team offering their services. Jon told them to stand by; he'd get back to them ASAP.

Laura said, "I bet they liked that."

"Can't be helped. I have to clear it with the SAC."

That would be Special Agent in Charge Damien Peltier. Laura had worked with him before. "He's still here? I thought he'd be running Homeland Security by now."

"They must think *we* need him." He sat on the edge of the desk, one leg over the other knee, swinging. "Still, I don't want to burn any bridges—we might need Las Vegas SWAT for point control."

"Point control. That'll make them happy." Laura looked at the blackboard, where she had been putting up information in list form. Something about the stark white chalk against black made the information stand out for her.

Two trucks had gone out of the Nevada Test Site this morning, one of them loaded with transuranic waste headed for Carlsbad, the other carrying empty canisters to Texas A&M. TRANSCOM was tracking both of them, and so far, both of them were following the prescribed route.

Information was being collated on the drivers of both trucks and the trucking company contractor, Fleet Trucking. They had names, but little else at the moment.

One of the two trucks—the one carrying the waste—had already turned south on 95 at Searchlight.

"It has to be the other truck, then," Laura said.

Jon said, "The other truck is carrying empties."

Laura looked at him. "All HazMat loads are escorted by police. What about empty trucks?"

"I don't know."

Laura was already looking at another item: Jack Taylor had used a credit card under the name John Traynor to rent a semi truck. She tapped the paper with a fingernail. "Why would he rent a semi?"

Jon stood up, ponderous as a bear—looks were deceiving. "Maybe they moved the waste casks to the semi. No, scratch that." He glanced at the digital photos of a truck carrying the Trupact II waste casks. "Even if it was a flatbed, which this one isn't, they'd never be able to switch those things out in a hurry—it says here it takes four hours to load those things and tie them down properly."

Laura went over and stood behind Jordy Benteen, so she could follow the GPS location on one of the laptops. She knew she was missing something. Maybe looking at the Global Postioning System notations would help, but Jordy had the log data up: All numbers—latitude, longitude, altitude, speed.

"Jordy, could you pull up the map?"

"Sure thing." He switched to the map, zoomed in to a fifty-square-mile area. On the map were two dots, belonging to the two trucks in question.

He clicked on the second dot and a window came up, listing the ID number of the truck, its destination and projected arrival time.

"You can forget changing out the casks," Laura said. "There's no way they stopped for four hours."

Jordy said, "That's the interesting thing. I did some

calculations—what time they left, how long it would take to get to Cottonwood Cove? It looks like this second truck must have stopped somewhere. There's a discrepancy of almost forty minutes."

Laura looked at Jon. "They stopped for *something*," she said. "But what?"

Jordy said, "That's why they're so far behind the other truck. But that's not the weirdest thing. Somebody at TRANSCOM caught this—for a couple of minutes earlier this morning the truck disappeared."

"What do you mean, disappeared?"

"Once a GPS is up and running, it doesn't stop, even if the vehicle shuts down. Say somebody goes to the restroom— the thing keeps going. Which is weird if the truck just disappears like that."

"Do you know what could cause this?"

He shrugged. "I guess if it was disconnected."

She had a fleeting thought—two disparate items joining up—then noticed the look on Jon Service's face. He was intent on something behind her.

She heard knuckles cracking. She knew that sound.

It was the sound of all the air being sucked from the room.

36

One of Bobby Burdette's favorite stories was about Jim Thorpe, the Indian guy who was considered one of the greatest athletes of all time. On his way to the 1912 Olympics, Thorpe sat on the deck of a ship for hours on end and stared at a bar he'd set up, every once in a while getting up from his deck chair to raise it a little. When a reporter asked what he was doing, he said, "I just broke the record for the high jump."

Maybe the story wasn't true—Bobby didn't know—but it sure resonated with him. He had a stack of books at home that said if you wanted to be successful, you came up with a plan, and then you visualized yourself going through it. There was one book that said that just by thinking your way to what you wanted, you actually changed the molecules inside yourself, so that your whole body became a missile launching itself toward success.

That sounded a little far-fetched. But he knew there was power in positive thinking.

Driving through the dull-brown-and-gray Mojave, it would have been easy to get bored, but Bobby was looking at other things, things inside his head. He was picturing his plan, step by step.

He saw himself driving up I-15 into Vegas.

He saw himself parking the truck outside the Blue Lagoon Hotel and Casino.

He saw himself walking up the street to the Mirage, going upstairs to the roof, where he'd have the truck perfectly in his line of vision.

He saw himself calling the Blue Lagoon, asking to speak to the manager, the manager coming to the phone. He saw himself calmly and intelligently explaining the situation to the manager, telling him that the phone he was talking on was also a detonating device. He could be pretty persuasive when he talked—he had that ring of authority, had always been able to talk his way into or out of anything. "That Fleet truck out there, just out your window?" he'd say. "Those are Trupact II canisters on the back. Look it up. Call the Department of Energy, call the Nevada Test Site, you'll find that a truck with Trupact II casks went out today, headed for Carlsbad carrying low-level nuclear waste. Except they're not going to Carlsbad. They're right here at the Blue Lagoon.

"There are three places on that truck wired with dynamite. I set them so they'll penetrate the first tank. I can detonate it with my cell phone. You understand what I'm saying?"

He'd outline the dangers of transuranic waste, especially on a windy day like this.

"It's not that it will kill anyone," he'd say. "Not now, anyway. That's gonna come down the pike—lots of types of cancer you don't even know the names of. People are gonna inhale, and that's what's going to get them.

"But that's not even the worst of it, right?"

The manager stammering now, because he understands what Bobby's getting at. It isn't the potential loss of life ten, twenty years down the line. No, that's not how casino owners think. They think in terms of the bottom line, they think in terms of stockholders, they think in terms of the next *business* cycle.

So Bobby lets that sink in and says, "You know what happened at Chernobyl, right?"

By this time the manager's shaking in his Guccis.

"They put a fence around it. They got everybody out of there and they put a fence around it, around the town, around the area, and nobody can go in for hundreds of years.

"Think about it. All these casinos. *Your* casino. Think about all the money that changes hands every day. Think about what would happen if Las Vegas didn't exist anymore."

Then the kicker: *How much is a million dollars compared to that? One lousy million dollars. I know what you're gonna say. "How can we lay our hands on money like that?" But you know that would be bullshit, right? You have that in petty cash right now. If there's one place you can get your hands on cash, it's Las Vegas.*

It was a perfect setup. The truck in the parking lot, Bobby with the phone at—as Dick Cheney would say—another undisclosed location, and plenty of money downstairs and all over Las Vegas.

"What I want is real simple," he'd say. "If you do what I ask, it will be one of the simplest transactions in the world. All I want is one million dollars. If you can't scrape up the money on your own, you can always call some of your friends. I'm sure you can come up with a million in no time." He'd list a few interested parties: the Mirage, Mandalay Bay, the Bellagio, the Luxor. They'd all have a stake in this.

And so he would make his demand: the million dollars, wired to a Swiss numbered bank account, which he would have to get confirmation on. Once the money had been successfully wired, he would take off in the car he had stashed in the Mirage parking lot.

He knew, though, that they would try to cheat. Even for a million dollars, which should only be the cost of doing business when you're trying to save Las Vegas from becoming a ghost town—even then. He'd learned that about folks, especially rich folks. Especially corporations. They liked to hold on to their money. The more they had the more they begrudged the loss of even a penny. The casino guys, they'd think they were being really crafty, trying to put one over on the poor white guy with dirt under his nails. It could manifest itself in many ways: They would try to stall him so a bomb team could come out and defuse the bombs. Or they would enlist the police to make a hotel-to-hotel search in this immediate area. Or they would try to do something with the wire transfer itself—although that was pretty much foolproof.

Still, he didn't trust them. Hence, the hostage.

Sometimes, the human factor was the only thing that could change the equation. The fear that a woman might be buried underground, left to die under a pile of earth—anybody could relate to that. Or at least the fear that the Blue Lagoon Hotel and Casino would be seen as putting the value of their bank account over the value of human life.

If *that* came out, their lagoon would dry up into a tadpole pond.

Bobby's eyes tracked a jackrabbit as it loped across the desert, the same dull gray-brown as the landscape it ran through. Las Vegas, for all its billion lights and shows and waterfalls and fake-looking grass and the maddening chiming that went on day and night, could be as dead as this desert in a week. He pictured it: refugees in Armani suits with PDAs, running off the Strip like rats.

Bobby knew he had to keep it between him and the casinos. He knew they wouldn't want the media there any more than he did. Last year an al Qaeda operative videotaped casinos as possible terrorist targets. When the city fathers were notified that there were terrorists casing the place, they stuck their heads in the sand like ostriches. They didn't want to hear about it. They didn't want the bad publicity, didn't want to discourage so much as one overweight, flip-flop-wearing, Hawaiian-shirted tourist from unloading his paycheck here. That was their answer: Ignore it and it will go away.

So he thought his chances were pretty good for getting away clean, if he kept it between himself and the Blue Lagoon.

Something his mother always said popped into his mind: Think positive. Coming from her, that was a joke. She never had one positive thought in her life, but she made that her mantra. As in: The trouble with you is you don't think positive. You don't aim high.

High enough for you now, Ma?

Well, he was going to think positive. Like the song said, he was going to put on his sailing shoes, and he was going to sail all the way to Mexico. He wasn't going to think about all the ways it could go wrong. He was going to set those happy, success-oriented molecules in motion.

Bobby was still thinking about all of this, and starting to feel really good about his prospects when he came up over the rise and saw the line of cars in his lane up ahead.

37

"So what have we got?" Special Agent in Charge Damien Peltier said as he pushed past Laura into the room.

Laura looked at Jon. His demeanor had undergone a change. He seemed polite—attentive, even. But the light had gone out of his eyes; they were still blue marbles in his head. As he gave the rundown, his voice was as flat as his eyes.

Peltier was short, slender, with black hair and a narrow nose whose flared nostrils always seemed to sniff out something bad. Elegant ringed fingers always in flight, the black hairs on the backs of his pale knuckles catching the light. Laura had once heard Jon call him Captain Queeg, because he focused on minutiae at the expense of what was important.

Plus, he was a little bit crazy.

In early 2000, he'd been one of the supervisors who had ignored warnings of potential terrorists wanting to fly planes without learning to take off and land at an Arizona flight school. For that oversight, he had been promoted to special agent in charge, Phoenix division.

Jon got about a paragraph into his description of events when Peltier raised his hand. "We don't have time for this," he said. "I want the boiled-down version."

Jon started over, using short sentences. He outlined the

basic points, but there were big gaps in between. Peltier seemed to like it; he cracked his knuckles when Jon was through. In Peltier-speak that meant rolling up the sleeves and getting to work.

Peltier glanced at Laura. "Good the way that worked out—thanks for the tip. As soon as the helicopter gets here, I'll be setting up house at the command post. We'll be out of your hair pretty soon, so you can get back to your routine."

FBI-speak for dismissal.

Laura knew better than to get in a pissing match with him over that. But she wasn't going to back down regarding her own case. "You're not in my hair," she said in as pleasant a voice as she could muster. "Although we have our own interest in Bobby Burdette. He's suspected in the murders of two people. We'll be working the case from here."

He smiled, but his little currant eyes glinted hard. "Of course you need to follow your case," he said. "What you need to understand, though, is that we have a nuclear emergency here. You can go ahead and do your thing, but I just want to be clear. Don't expect us to hold your hand through all this—we're busy trying to avert a disaster."

"I wasn't aware until now that the two cases weren't linked."

"Priorities," he said briskly. "You know how that works." He turned to Jordan Benteen, dismissing Laura. "When's that chopper going to get here?"

"Any minute, sir."

Peltier put his hand to his chin like *The Thinker.* "You picked the right place—east of Searchlight. Good job, figuring that out from here. But I think we should be a little closer. We're moving the command post two miles back toward Searchlight—about six miles east of town instead of eight." He walked to the map and tapped the Route 164 east of Searchlight. "I've got FBI SWAT on their way now."

"Las Vegas Metro offered a SWAT team."

"We've got that covered. Did you call for helicopter surveillance?"

"No," Service said. "We don't want to spook them. We've got them on satellite."

"We're going to have to have a real show of force—we want them to give up right away, realize there's no way out. I want every law officer within a thirty-mile radius right there—behind the roadblock—make sure they don't get to the Colorado River. We can't afford to let these guys think they can run the roadblock and get away with it."

"We should have somebody on 95," Jon said. "Just in case the truck turns south."

"Why would they do that? They're going to the Colorado River."

"They probably won't, but—"

He tapped the map again. "I want everyone at the roadblock on 164. Is there anything else?" He looked from Laura to Jon.

"DPS is sending a negotiator," Laura said.

"A negotiator?" He looked at her. "Why?"

"A hostage negotiator, in case—"

"We don't need one."

"I would advise you to have one there," said Service.

"Well, we're not having a DPS team. This is going down in Nevada. We don't want any more jurisdictional headaches than we need. As it is, everybody and his brother's coming to the ball."

"You could get a team out of Las Vegas," Laura said.

He glared at her. "This is really not your business, Detective." He turned to Jon. "I talked to our SWAT commander not an hour ago. He seems to feel we don't need a hostage negotiator. So we'll leave it at that."

Suddenly, there was the familiar whopping of helicopter blades. Damien Peltier's white teeth showed, half grimace, half smile. "There's my ride. Jordan—pack up your tent."

Service said, "I think you should keep that unit on 95."

Peltier ignored him. "Let's go, let's go. Everybody get a

move on, let's make this quick." He saw Service filling his briefcase. "Jon, we're going to need you here. You're going to be coordinating the info coming in on this end."

Jon's face turned a dull red, but he said nothing.

"You two go ahead and coordinate your efforts." He glanced at his watch. "Just remember you're a guest here, and don't trample all over her homicide—you've got to work and play well with others, be sensitive to her *needs*."

He picked up his shoulder bag. "Let's show some chivalry. Just because there's a truck full of nuclear waste headed for the Colorado River doesn't mean we can't give the locals a hand."

Grabbing up his briefcase, he strode briskly out of the office, calling back over his shoulder, "Look busy!"

38

California Highway Patrol officer Jess Harding walked along the row of cars, occasionally stopping to talk to one motorist or another, what they called in his job being "officer friendly"; presenting a good face to the citizenry and doing his bit for public relations.

Some motorists were impatient, downright pissed-off at the delay, and some were philosophical—one family was playing Trivial Pursuit in their big new SUV, windows rolled up and air-conditioning on. Despite the heat and the wind, a number of people were standing in the road, straining to see the wreck, which was still smoking.

"What happened up there?" asked a guy in flip-flops, shorts, and a T-shirt emblazoned with an eagle head and the words PROUD TO BE AN AMERICAN.

"Car accident. We're close to clearing the road; shouldn't be long."

Actually, it would be a while. The tow truck was waiting to remove the wreck of the Corvette, which had been reduced to a black, wheelless hulk. But the other vehicle, which had escaped the fire, was dead center in the roadway and they were waiting for the Jaws of Life to extricate the driver.

"What happened? Did anyone get killed?"

"I don't have that information, sir."

But of course he did. The driver of the Corvette was toast. The other guy was alive but didn't look like he'd stay that way. How it looked to him, the Corvette must have been going at a high rate of speed when the old ranch truck pulled out in front of him going in the same direction and—boom!

CHP officer Jack Sheedy was measuring the scene and marking evidence for any criminal charges and when it got to court. There would definitely be a lawsuit from someone. Jess continued up the line, deflecting questions and putting a cheerful face on it. The last vehicle in line was a semi truck.

When he got to it, he grabbed the mirror and stepped up on the running board. The driver rolled down the window.

"Where you headed?" Harding asked.

"Flagstaff," the driver said. He nodded to the cars in front of him. "What's going on up there?"

"Accident. Speeder in a sports car ran into some old guy turned right in front of him."

"What time frame're we looking at?"

Harding decided to be a little more honest since this guy was a trucker. "Looks like an hour and a half, at least."

"Guess I have time for a smoke, then."

"I could use a cigarette right now myself."

Guy shook out a Camel but Harding declined. "Can't," he said, feeling strangely apologetic. As Harding stepped down, he saw the silver tanks under the heavy tarp. "Looks like giant beer kegs under there. That would be something, huh? What are they, anyway?"

"Milk."

"Milk?"

"PET milk."

Harding shook his head. "Haven't heard that name in years. There's still a market for that stuff?"

"Uh-huh. Especially in France."

"France." He laughed. "Figures." He had one foot back on the running board, which offered him some lumbar support. He would rather bullshit with the truckers or play officer friendly with the citizens than sit in his car, even though standing for long periods made his back ache. "Where you coming from?"

"Tonopah."

"That's where this stuff comes from?"

The guy looked at him, sunglasses dark and glossy. His mouth turning up at the corner. "Dairy farm."

A blast of wind buffetted Harding, fluttering his uniform pant legs. Wondering whether the guy was putting him on, or just making a joke. He laughed. "Dairy farm, what else? Must be hard getting milk into those little cans, huh?"

Silence. Guy just sitting there, serene behind his dark glasses. Clear he had no sense of humor, so Harding didn't bother to explain his joke. He could still hear the echo of his own laugh, tinny all by itself. He patted the cab door, said, "Hey. Take it easy." He started back up the line of cars again, the wind coming hard now and slapping him sideways, carrying with it the smell of charred meat, and Harding could swear he felt those dark glasses staring at his back all the way.

39

Richie Lockhart already had his telephonic warrant and was on his way to Bobby Burdette's, but decided to stop by the Williams police department as a professional courtesy. As he parked on the street he saw Josh Wingate talking to the chief out in the parking lot.

"You need any help executing that warrant?" Chief Loffgren called out.

"Oh, so you know about it."

"Talked to the judge. Jungle drums." He clapped Officer Wingate on the shoulder. "You might want to take Josh along. Might be good to have another eye."

Why not? Richie didn't want to do it by himself, and he had been impressed with the way Wingate had handled himself at Cataract Lake. He nodded to to the young officer. "Come on."

Josh Wingate detached himself from the car he'd been leaning against and followed Richie to his Chevrolet.

"You ever execute a warrant before?" Richie asked.

"No, sir."

"Just do as I tell you. The occupant won't be there. But we gotta maintain the chain of custody, any evidence we gather, so the main thing I want you to do is follow my lead, do exactly as I say—and wear gloves."

"Yes, sir."

They drove out Seventh to Edison Avenue and turned right.

Josh Wingate was quiet. Glancing in Wingate's direction, Richie saw that the kid was staring straight ahead, his face impassive. Richie had noticed that he had been very helpful in the past, even though he had this nervous energy, like static electricity. Not today, though. He'd thought he was doing him a favor to bring him along, but the kid was like a bag of laundry sitting on the passenger's seat.

Then he realized. Of course. Family troubles: His mother had gone off the deep end, nearly taking Laura Cardinal out when she tried to kill herself a couple of days ago. Of course he'd be shaken up. Barbara Wingate off to the loony bin. His whole world turned topsy-turvy.

"Everything going okay?" he asked.

Josh Wingate mumbled something Richie couldn't decipher.

Richie decided to pursue it. He needed to know this kid's state of mind. If he was preoccupied with his own problems, he would be useless at the house, which was a crime scene and needed to be treated as such. "I heard about what happened with your mother. She all right?"

"She's okay." Staring out the passenger window now.

"Heard they took her in for observation. She out now?"

"Yes, sir." Flat voice, flat expression. Holding on to a lot of pain, trying to keep it inside. Richie knew all about that, only he hid his pain by joking. He remembered in happier days when his wife had season tickets to the Arizona Opera, and dragged him along. One of them was *I Pagliacci*.

Laugh, clown, laugh.

What he wouldn't give to have her drag him to one more opera. "How about Erin? She okay?"

"My brother-in-law and his wife are coming for her next weekend."

"They're from out of state?"

"Germany."

"*Germany?*"

"He's stationed there."

"Oh. So they're taking her to Germany?"

"Looks like it."

"You okay with that?" he asked. A regular Dr. Phil.

"I'm *glad*."

He didn't sound glad. He sounded mad. Pissed-off at the world, but then, Richie didn't blame him. With a witch like that for a mother, who wouldn't want to see his niece go as far away as possible? Making her sick like that. Germany was as good a place as any.

Richie glanced at Josh Wingate again. Profile carved in stone, eyes forward, hands loose on his lap. A thousand miles away.

Richie stopped the car. "You interested in working this scene with me?"

Josh Wingate swiveled his head to look at him. "Yes, sir. I want to."

Richie thought about it. The kid was depressed—big-time—but Richie could use the help. Reluctantly, he put the car in gear, wondering if he was making a mistake.

And throughout the afternoon, Josh zombie-walked through the search. Nothing you could put your finger on. He was precise, he was obedient, he was careful.

But he wasn't there.

Look busy. Laura glanced around the room, which had been reduced to herself, Jon, and an off-duty dispatcher brought in to help. At the moment, she was cleaning up coffee spills on the table. Priorities, as Special Agent in Charge Damien Peltier would say. "Well, we have enough people for a lemonade stand," Laura said to Jon.

Jon Service glanced at one of the laptops. More messages coming in. He sat down and started logging them into Rapid Start, Laura looking over his shoulder.

There was new information on Glenn Traywick. He had been at the Nevada Test Site earlier today, but left early, supposedly on his way to Utah.

Laura knew he was Jack Taylor's nephew. Although Jack Taylor wouldn't implicate him, they already knew he was part of the scheme. But she'd seen his name written down before: on the old refrigerator door at Taylor's Creekside Cabins. The brochure for flights over the Grand Canyon. "Traywick has an airplane."

Jon looked up from the computer. "He does?"

She described the brochure, the red-white-and-blue plane.

"If ever a guy could use a plane, he could," Jon said.

Ten minutes later, Laura got the information from the FAA. "He keeps it here in Flag, at Pulliam Airport. A Cessna 175." She gave Jon the call letters. "A plane with those call numbers left North Las Vegas Airport earlier this morning. He didn't file a flight plan."

"You think he's coming here?"

"I don't know."

A search turned up the information that Glenn Traywick had owned a house in Flagstaff for fifteen years, but had sold it eight months ago. His current address was an apartment here in town. More good fortune: The apartment manager lived across from Glenn Traywick, and was on nodding aquaintance with Traywick's girlfriend, Michelle.

"Do you have her last name?" Laura said into the phone.

"No. She's not on the lease. Know where she works, though. Trecor."

"Trecor?"

"Trecor Business Equipment on Milton Road. My brother buys all the stuff for his business there—he has a telephone software company."

"Have you noticed anything unusual about either of them recently?"

"Does moving out of the apartment count?"

Laura grabbed the phone tighter in her fingers. "Oh, that counts."

"Moving van was here all day yesterday. They sure had a lot of stuff for a small apartment."

"Did they skip out?"

"Nope. Michelle came over yesterday. Said there was a death in the family and they were going to have to leave town, break the lease. She was nice about paying up—they lost the security deposit and a few months' rent."

"That was yesterday?"

"Uh-huh. But she left today with the last of her stuff."

"When was this?"

"Quarter of eight in the morning."

When Laura hung up she asked Jon when Glenn Traywick was last seen at the Nevada Test Site.

He was staring at the computer. "It's in here somewhere. Where's Jordy when you need him?"

"Out playing cowboy with Clint Eastwood." Laura grabbed the phone book, punched in the number for Trecor Business Machines, and found out that Michelle, whose last name was Cantey, had worked there most of the morning. About ten minutes ago she'd left on a personal errand, and wouldn't be back for the rest of the day.

It was clear to Richie early on that Bobby Burdette had taken all his personal information with him. As the hours ground on, working his way through dirty clothes, cupboards of canned goods, a refrigerator full of cold cuts turning brown and condiments that must have been here for a decade, he realized that Burdette hadn't been here for a while.

And he wasn't coming back. The place felt stale, closed-up, but it was more than that. The minute someone left a house for good, you could tell. It was like the house itself had given up. He had left a few things behind—a ratty old couch, a bed and bedside table, some mismatched kitchen chairs. And, surprisingly, a new wide-screen TV, and combination DVD player and VCR. Worth at least two grand.

Who in his right mind would leave something like that?

But even if Richie didn't know the circumstances, didn't know what Bobby Burdette was planning, he would have known he wasn't coming back.

Suddenly, Josh Wingate said, "Hey."

Richie looked over to where Josh Wingate was standing in the kitchen, at a door that looked like it was to a pantry. "There's a basement down here."

His blood quickening, Richie went to take a look. Looked down into the dark. Cement walls. Ten steps down before a blind corner, a lightbulb on a cord halfway down.

Richie remembered what happened to two police officers in that little podunk town in Florida when Laura Cardinal was down there serving a warrant.

"Don't go down those stairs," he said to Josh. "I'm going to call the Bomb Squad."

Getting one might take a while, this being Williams.

At exit 337, Jon Service turned right on West Shamrell Road and drove through a parklike area: New blacktop winding through vacant land dotted with pines. They passed an industrial park and turned onto Grumman, a short road dead-ending at the chain-link fence to the airfield. The only place to go was a parking lot on the right. The parking lot belonged to Wiseman Aviation. According to the information Laura had gotten over the phone, Wiseman Aviation was an FBO—a fixed-base operation—a combination filling station, rest area, and concierge service for the airplane-flying public. This was where Glenn Traywick would come in to pick up his girlfriend, if he showed up at all.

A beat-up red car old enough to be called a Datsun baked in the sun. Michelle's car, from the apartment manager's description and the number on the plate.

"She's here," Laura said.

"Unless she's been and gone already."

As Laura approached the door on the right side of the large, aluminum-sided building, every sense was alive.

Laura tried to project calmness. She didn't want to spook Michelle. They wanted to intercept her quietly.

They walked through the long entry hall, which ended in double doors to the tarmac. The lounge opened up on the right: a grouping of brown leather chairs, a Santa Fe–style coffee table, a fireplace in the corner. A woman sat with her back to them, luggage at her feet. Blond hair with dark roots pulled into a ponytail under a white visor cap, pink sweater over manufacturer-faded blue jeans, running shoes. Big busted and big in the hips, but she had a narrow waist. She was leaning forward. When Laura came around the chair she realized she was petting a sleek black cat who made passes around her legs like a bull with a cape.

Laura liked Michelle immediately, but that didn't stop her. She glanced at Jon, who seemed to slip like smoke around the other side of the chair.

"Michelle Cantey?"

The woman looked up. For a moment Laura thought she was going to bolt. Then she heaved her shoulders and sighed. "What do you want me to do?"

"I'm with the FBI," Jon said, showing her his shield. "We'd like to talk to you for a few minutes."

"Talk away." Her words belied her nervousness, which was evident in the stricken look on her face.

Jon glanced around the small room. "It would be better if we talked outside."

"Fine." She stood up and reached down for her bags.

"You can leave them here." He nodded toward the receptionist. "They'll watch them."

"My mother's photo albums are in there."

"They'll be fine," Laura said.

They walked out into the sunlight, Michelle between Laura and Jon. Michelle was saying, "I don't know what you think I've done."

Laura aimed her toward Jon's car.

"Am I under arrest?"

"No," Laura replied. "Do you want to be?"

That got her mouth working, but she didn't say anything. At the car, Laura said, "Do you know why we're here?"

"Not really."

"You're meeting Glenn Traywick, isn't that right? He's flying in?"

"Yes, as a matter of fact he is."

"How long before he gets here?"

"Any minute."

"How does that generally work? Will he gas up?"

Michelle stared at her, and then at Jon. Reluctantly, she said, "I think he said he'd top off the tanks and we'd load up and go. But I don't know what you think he's done."

Laura remembered seeing a sign for services in the lounge that listed both full- and self-serve. "Self-serve or will they fill up for him?"

"Could you at least tell me what you think he did?"

"How about you tell us where you're flying to?" asked Laura.

She shook her head and asked again if she was under arrest.

"No."

"Can I go, then?"

Laura said, "I'll go with you."

Laura and Michelle went inside. Jon remained in the parking lot, waiting for the Coconino County sheriff's office deputies to arrive.

Laura and Michelle sat down in the lobby. Michelle pulled out a paperback book from her bag. The book was called *Blood Is the Sky,* and the cover showed a sunset over a lake, a float plane coming in over the trees. It looked like Alaska or Canada. Michelle tried to read but Laura could tell she was having difficulty making sense of the words.

"Where are you headed?" Laura asked, keeping her tone conversational.

"I don't have to tell you."

"No, you don't. But you're obviously making a move."

Michelle stood up. "I have to use the bathroom."

"What a coincidence," Laura said. "So do I."

While he waited for the Bomb Squad, Richie Lockhart went back to look at the new TV set. If Bobby Burdette was really gone, why did he leave something like this?

Next to the TV was a cheap veneered cabinet for storing DVDs and videotapes, that heavy dark-wood Spanish style reminiscent of the seventies. Nothing was in it. Did Bobby take everything with him or give it away? With his gloved finger Richie pushed the button for the DVD player—the holding tray was empty. What the hell, punch the VCR eject button, too. This time the machine hummed as a videotape appeared.

Richie knew then that Bobby had left him something.

He pushed the tape back in and hit REWIND. It was already rewound, so he turned on the TV and hit PLAY.

Josh Wingate came and stood just inside the door to the kitchen, watching. "What's that?" he asked. The first interest he'd shown all day.

"I guess we'll find out."

Ambient sound. The scene was this living room—the couch Richie was sitting on now. Bobby Burdette walked into the frame, sat down, and cleared his throat. Richie noticed he was wearing a short-sleeved shirt, jeans, and white tennis shoes, and that his hair was still wet from the shower.

He held a piece of notebook paper in his hand, creased in fourths. He cleared his throat again, looked at the camera, and smiled, showing yellowed teeth.

"If you're watching this, I'm either in Mexico, or I'm dead." He waited a beat, giving his audience time to assimilate this. Looked down at the paper and up again. "You probably saw it on the news. Whatever happened, I did what I set out to do. I'm not going to apologize, because there's nothing to apologize for. If someone forced my hand, then they paid the consequences. It was a lack of judgment on their part."

He paused to look down and commit more words to memory.

"I did not mean anyone any harm. If circumstances turned out not the way I wanted them to be, I regret it, but I gave the people in charge a clear choice. I hope that they will take this seriously, because there's *absolutely no reason for anyone to get hurt.*"

He scratched his neck and let the paper fall to his knees. "I am not the kind of guy who bluffs. Bluffing is not in my makeup. If you understand that, we get along fine. So," he said, leaning forward. "I hope they took it seriously. If they did, then everything turned out all right for everybody. If not, they underestimated me big-time. I'm sorry about that, but they knew what they were dealing with. I do not back down. *Ever.* That's the way I am.

"My only request is that you send a copy of this tape to my mother, Mrs. June R. Burdette. All my possessions I give to her, unless you confiscate everything for the government. But that's not my problem anymore. Wherever I am, I'm where you can't reach me."

He got up off the couch and headed for the camera. Then the screen turned snowy.

Richie glanced at Josh Wingate, who stared rigidly at the screen—an intensity he hadn't seen all day. Richie asked him what he thought.

"Guy is tough," he said.

"You think he's tough? I think he's a coward."

Josh looked at him. "Whatever it was he did, he went through with it, didn't he?"

40

Approximately six miles east of Searchlight, Nevada, on a side road just over the first low hill on Nevada 164, Damien Peltier waited at the command post. The command post was invisible from the road until someone was right up on it. Behind him, the road continued on to Cottonwood Cove at Lake Mohave, dropping from three thousand feet above sea level to six hundred.

The roadblock had been set up three-quarters of a mile beyond the command post, just over the rise of a second hill. There was a spotter up by the road. When the target went by, two FBI vehicles from the command post would fall in behind him.

At the roadblock, the SWAT team would be waiting. The team included two snipers: one for the driver and one for the passenger. Even in this godforsaken area, there were enough stunted trees and brush to camouflage them. The rest of the roadblock would be parked around and on the road, but would allow for a driver to thread his way through if he had to—slowly.

Safety First.

Peltier glanced at the navy-blue Suburbans parked one in front of the other on the dirt road—ready to go. He tried to stifle his impatience, but it was hard.

It had been hurry up and wait. Everything was planned

down to the second, but this wind was getting to him. He hated waiting. That was something he'd had to do a lot of when he was a kid. His harried and forgetful mother, who had eight children, had always left him for last when it came to picking up her brood from their various after-school programs. Consequently, he would have to cool his heels consistently for a half hour to an hour, and often she would forget to pick him up at all.

Now he made sure that he never had to wait much. As the SAC of the Phoenix metropolitan area, he had others do his waiting for him. But somebody forgot to tell Mark Anthony and Jerry Lewis that.

Mark Anthony. Jerry Lewis. Those assholes at Fleet Trucking—a company that contracted with the Nevada Test Site to move nuclear waste—had not even bothered to check out obviously fake names like that.

The wind rattled the canvas awning of the ramada, shuttling dirt into the phalanx of police vehicles, pelting them and the men outside them. The dirt hit him, the exposed parts—his hands, his face. It felt as if he'd been shot with a BB gun.

When he first got here, the sky was blue bisected by a jet contrail. Now the sky was cataracted over, making the desert dishwater dull. He hated it out here. Too barren, too much open space.

He shaded his eyes with a hand, listening for the spotter to alert him by radio. He had made the decision not to evacuate Searchlight. From what he knew about these two morons, all they wanted to do was make a point. Too cowardly even to stay with the truck—just leave it there and call the news affiliates. He just didn't respect them. Ecoterrorists were not about to go to the wall for their cause. He wasn't dealing with survivalists, and this wasn't Waco.

It was a tough decision, but he was used to making tough decisions. He had always been able to look at a problem and see the answer quickly. He prided himself on his decisiveness, his ability to boil things down to their essence, so it was perfectly clear what action was required.

Evacuating the community on such short notice would have tipped off the drivers of the truck. You couldn't do something like that quietly.

He walked over to Jordan Benteen, who was sitting in a plain-wrapped vehicle, hunched over his laptop.

"How are we doing?"

"They're just getting to Searchlight now."

Another blast of wind. He could taste dirt in his teeth. Suddenly, something flew into his eye.

"*Dam*mit!"

He leaned in to the car, his back to the wind, pulling his upper lid over his eye, trying to dislodge the grit. He blinked several times, but he could feel it in there.

Jordan said, "Uh-oh."

"What's the matter?" He was pulling on his eyelash, bringing his lid down like a roll-up shade.

"It looks like—"

"*What?*" he shouted. "What's going on?"

Jordan Benteen said, "They turned off."

For a minute it didn't register. Then he felt his stomach drop several stories. "What do you mean, they turned off?"

"It looks like they turned south."

"*South?*"

"You can see for yourself."

"South? Why would they go *south?*"

"GPS doesn't lie, sir."

"You must be mistaken."

"Take a look, sir."

Squinting, one-eyed, he looked at the computer. "This thing is hard to see. Where's a map?"

Benteen reached across the bench seat and grabbed a map, already unfolded and awkward to wield. It took him a few moments to find the place. "It's 95. They're going south on 95. Toward Cal-Nev-Ari."

Where had he seen that name before?

On the map back at the DPS substation. Some godforsaken outpost on State Route 95.

He had to think fast—there was no room for error.

"Are there any side roads that can take us down to 95?"

"It doesn't look like it."

Shit.

He wasn't worried about catching them. That would not be a problem. But coming at them from only one angle—from behind—might encourage them to run with a truckload of nuclear waste.

He lowered his head so that Jordy could look him in the eye, and enunciated clearly. "I don't care what you do, how you do it, but we've got to get our people out in front of them.

"You'd better goddamn *find* a road."

Glenn Traywick taxied his Cessna toward the FBO ramp, his mind already ticking away—how he would do this. It would be cheaper to get self-serve, and normally he would do just that. He hated to spend more than he had to. He was in a hurry today, though, so he would ask the lineman to bring the fuel truck. While the plane was being fueled, he could go in and get Michelle and they'd be on their way.

He hoped she wasn't fudging on the weight issue. That was all he needed. That woman had more designer clothes than a Liz Claiborne outlet.

Glenn slowed down, expecting the golf cart to come out any minute. He needed the guy to come out and park him. He'd debated calling ahead and requesting a spot at the jet line, which was right in front of the door, but decided against it. So he had to walk a little farther—he wouldn't be signaling the fact that he was flying in. Better to just get in, get out, fly right under the radar. But where was the lineman?

Then he saw the guy come out of the FBO building, get into the golf cart and tootle his way.

He stopped the plane on the tarmac, the engine still running, waiting. His mind already spinning ahead to Loon Lake. To the lodge he had bought with the down payment from his uncle Jack. That was the great thing about Jack; he took care of his obligations.

Once they got out of the U.S., it would be fine. He had his new name, his new passport, his new lease on life. If his girlfriend didn't bring all her clothes and sink them right here.

He noticed the guy in the golf cart looked ill at ease driving. He didn't look like any meet-and-greeter or lineman he had ever seen. He looked like a cop.

Suddenly, Glenn had a bad feeling. He knew from experience that he needed to trust his bad feelings. The guy might or might not be a cop dressed as a lineman, but he wasn't taking any chances. Michelle would be disappointed, but she could meet up with him later. He started to turn the plane around, just as he saw something dark in the corner of his eye.

A cop car coming through the gate, onto the tarmac.

He sat there in his plane, where he had always felt invincible before. Still in command. He looked at the vintage dash, the flight instruments, the shiny finish of the wing outside his window, the sun and the blue sky shining on his lap. His little kingdom. The only place he truly felt free. And now the cops were here and he'd never fly this plane—or any other—again.

He still had time to move forward, turn the plane around. He could taxi the plane around but there were more police cars. It would be like driving his way around an amusement park. He could cover some ground, but in the end, the gates were closed and he wasn't going anywhere. No way could he take off without some runway.

He shut the engine down just as the cop car came up and blocked his path. Two sheriff's deputies opening the doors, guns trained on him. He glanced at the guy in the golf cart who was just now getting out, holding up his badge, accidentally knocking the length of red carpet the people at Wiseman Aviation always rolled out for their customers, knocking it onto the tarmac, where it rolled out in a parody of welcome.

41

Richie waited for the Bomb Squad to go through the house. When they gave him the okay, he headed for Bobby Burdette's basement.

Josh got a ride back to Williams PD with the Bomb Squad. To tell the truth, Richie was relieved he was gone. He had the place to himself, now, and in a way he enjoyed that.

The head of the Bomb Squad, Bill Slade, had already told him what was down here. A washer/dryer combination, a water heater, a workbench that had not been used for a long time, and a gun cabinet.

Richie looked at the guns: a Mini-14 with a folding stock, a Remington 870 shotgun—also with a folding stock—an old .30-caliber M-1 carbine, a Winchester model 70 .270 rifle, an S&W Model 19 6-inch, and a Raven .25 autoloader.

Nice stuff, even to his uneducated eye. He checked the shotgun to see if it was unloaded. It was. He sniffed the barrel; it smelled of gun oil. All of Bobby's guns were well cared-for. He found ammo, too; bagged and labeled the gun and the ammo as evidence.

Then he called Laura. When he heard her voice, he said, "I've got a twelve-gauge shotgun here. A Remington 870."

"Oh," she said. "That's great." The way she said it

warmed him: an undercurrent of excitement in her voice, almost gleeful. They'd had their differences but this was something they both wanted.

"Hope we can nail him," he said.

"Me, too."

Feeling expansive, he added, "That was good work, finding that cartridge."

She laughed. "It was luck more than anything."

"Yeah, well."

When they disconnected, he had a big smile on his face—a good day's work.

Hard to see in the dust and wind, which had cast a bluish pall over the landscape, but Mark Sproule thought he saw lights ahead. "Is that a cop car?"

Dell looked up from the motorcycle magazine he was reading. "Looks like it."

Yes, definitely a cop car. Headlights blinking back and forth, blue and red lights on the roof.

Mark's foot hovered over the brake. He shifted down.

"What are you doing?" Dell demanded.

"We have to stop."

"Why don't you just run it?"

Mark looked at Dell. Twenty-eight years old and he thought he ran the world. He wasn't going to get Mark killed over this.

"It's probably nothing, anyway," Dell said. "He probably stopped some speeder."

But Mark knew. And a few moments later, when he saw the lights in his side mirror, he was sure.

They had the truck, they had the drivers. The drivers were currently sitting inside the Las Vegas Metro car that had come up from Laughlin.

Special Agent in Charge Damien Peltier leaned in to the Suburban to grab a bottle of water. The dryness getting to him, his eye still gritty. Jordy sat inside, working on his computer.

Great, how it had worked out. Even if they had to pursue, even though they couldn't find a road down to cut them off. The Las Vegas Metro unit had come in handy after all.

Making the streets safe for tourists in Laughlin.

"Mission accomplished," Peltier said between drinks.

"That's what Bush thought."

Peltier looked at Jordy. Always suspected he was a liberal. "What do you mean by that?"

Jordy nodded toward the truck, sitting on the desert verge, taillights blinking. "That look like an NTS truck to you?"

42

"Everybody wants a deal," Laura said to Jon, after a fruitless half hour of trying to finesse Glenn into talking. She had co-opted the tiny conference room off the hallway at Wiseman Aviation, rather than taking Traywick back to DPS. The room was mostly taken up with a table and chairs, but it was self-contained and private. Laura added, "His lawyer's on the way. How are you doing with Michelle?"

"Nada. She's cooling her heels in the county jail, though."

Laura wondered where she had gone, what her life would be like now. "They've got the truck, at least," she said.

"*A* truck."

"*A* truck?"

"It sure as hell isn't *the* truck. They were driving a regular semi. It's completely empty—Jordy told me just a minute ago."

Laura suddenly remembered the half thought she'd had before everything hit the fan: the forty-minute time lapse and Jack Taylor's rental of a semi truck. "A decoy," she said.

"That's what it looks like."

"Then where's the *real* truck?"

*   *   *

The real truck, Fleet Trucking number fifty-seven, had finally cleared the wreck outside Baker, California, and was on its way to Interstate 15 going east.

As Bobby Burdette drove into the outskirts of town, he saw a yellow Dodge Challenger up on blocks in somebody's yard, and felt a twinge of remorse.

Maybe he should have found a place to store the Mean Green, so he could retrieve it if he ever got back here.

But he wasn't coming back. He had himself a white Toyota Camry—there were about a million of those on the road—waiting in the parking lot of the Mirage Hotel and Casino. The Camry would take him straight down to Mexicali, and once he was over the line, he'd be home free, with a million dollars in the bank and the cash he'd liquidated from his accounts. Not a huge amount of money, but he'd be able to live comfortably. Find himself a nice place down near Cabo, live the simple life. Margaritas on the beach, maybe get him a little sailboat.

If Cabo was too obvious, there were plenty of little fishing villages down the coast where you could disappear, as long as you could support yourself. Nobody was going to be checking passports in places like that.

Still, he'd miss the Mean Green.

He remembered one of his girlfriends had a poster in her apartment that said: IF YOU LOVE SOMETHING, SET IT FREE. IF IT COMES BACK IT'S YOURS; IF IT DOESN'T, IT NEVER WAS. Or something to that effect. Every agency in three states would be looking for the Mean Green. If he was lucky, some poor sap had already taken the car and was driving it God knew where.

He was fine with that. He had a new life and he couldn't afford to be sentimental. He loved the Mean Green, but if it was meant to come back to him, then it would. Otherwise, he hoped whoever took it enjoyed it while he could.

An outside observer, privy to Bobby Burdette's thoughts, might be surprised that Shana Yates, the woman he had slept with and lied to, did not enter into his mind at all.

"Sir?"

Damien Peltier wanted to bite Jordan Benteen's head off. "What is it?"

Staring at the semi truck that wasn't the truck he was looking for. Tasting grit in his teeth. Gearing himself up to interrogate Mark Sproule and Dell Anders, thinking about the best way to go about it, but having a hard time concentrating because of this goddamn wind.

"Call for you."

"Who's it from?"

"CHP officer. I think you should listen to what he has to say."

"Oh, you do?"

"He says it's important. In light of what's been happening."

Peltier grabbed the phone. "Who is this?"

The man identified himself as CHP officer Jess Harding. "You're looking for a truck with those nuclear canisters on a flatbed?" he asked.

Peltier grunted assent.

"There was a wreck just north of Baker on 127. Took a long time to clear it—"

"You need to get to the point."

"There was a trucker there who got caught on the wrong side of the wreck. Something not right about him. Talked a lot of bullshit. It was like he looked right through me."

Despite himself, Peltier felt a surge of excitement. "Yes, go on. What kind of truck is it?"

Harding described it: a tall load on a flatbed, most of it covered with a large tarp, like the kind the army used. "But I could see the tanks—three of them, the tarp didn't cover them. At the time I didn't think much about it, but I've seen tanks like that before. The ones that come down here on the way to Carlsbad."

Peltier might or might not have thanked him before tossing the phone back to Jordan Benteen.

This was his chance to shine. He knew how to lead, he knew how to cut through the bullshit, and he knew how to make spontaneous decisions. He thought about what Harding had said about the man. The way he described him. This did not sound like the eco-pussies he'd been dealing with. This guy sounded like he had left the reservation.

"We need two things," he said to Jordy. "We need a helicopter with a spotter. We need to cover I-15 and every other road out of Baker." He paused, remembering Jon Service's suggestion earlier today. He had made one decision then, but now things had changed. "Talk to the people with Las Vegas Metro. We're going to need a hostage negotiator."

Glenn Traywick's lawyer arrived and met with his client while Laura and Jon Service cooled their heels outside at a picnic table under the pines. They had been waiting almost two hours at this point. At least they had company; the Wiseman Aviation cats, Stealth and Cessna, were in the hospitality business just like their owners.

"Where's Sharp?" Laura asked, watching as a plane took off.

"He's got a meeting, but he should be here soon."

"What do you think Glenn Traywick meant by that? Saying he had something we really needed to know?"

Jon shrugged. "Could be anything."

"But the *way* he said it." She folded her arms. "Like it would solve everything. Like he was going to give us something that we'd be very grateful for."

"He could just be bullshitting—at this point we've got it all figured out, with or without him."

But Laura wasn't so sure that was true.

Just then a man in a suit holding a briefcase came out the double doors and motioned them inside. Jeremy Sharp, the U.S. Attorney.

"That's our cue," Jon said, holding the door for her as she walked back inside.

The first time he saw the helicopter cruising over the freeway, Bobby thought it was police, monitoring the traffic. The second time it came over, he started to have a bad feeling.

He noticed, too, that the freeway traffic was lighter than usual. No, he realized—not light—nonexistent. At least on the lanes coming from Las Vegas.

A momentary panic, as he realized that there were no cars coming his way.

He glanced from one side mirror to the other, saw the cop cars and dark Suburbans coming up fast, headlights winking back and forth, lights on—completely silent.

Ahead were orange cones, marching off down an exit.

Something blinking dark and light up ahead in the whirling dust, a mirage.

The cars behind him, swift and silent.

The helicopter flying overhead again, looking like a giant navy-blue dragonfly. Another helicopter, clearly marked—this one from a TV news affiliate.

A clear path ahead, the road all to himself, leading to a dead end of more Suburbans and black-and-whites.

He thought about Mexico.

He thought about the money.

He thought about the Mean Green.

Run it, a voice inside his head urged.

He knew he wouldn't be able to thread through the vehicles ahead of him. He knew he wouldn't be able to get past SWAT, who stood like black stick figures behind car doors, aiming high-powered weapons at him.

He could run it, and fail. But if he stopped, maybe he could play one more hand.

He still had the explosives, strapped around the first tank.

He still had the plutonium.

And Las Vegas was only thirty miles away.

He shifted down, the engine dropping into a low-pitched whine. Shifted down and down and down.

Ready to deal.

43

Bobby was thinking: Better make sure they call the right phone. Otherwise—

Boom.

Glad he'd bought two different kinds of cell phones. Two different colors. Using a ballpoint pen, he wrote the good cell phone number on the back of the truck manifest. Making the number as big as he could, going over it several times to make the letters dark and thick.

He held it up to the window and waggled it.

"Sir, throw the keys out of the truck."

Guy talking into a bullhorn, just like in the movies. For answer, he waggled the paper some more.

Silence.

The wind worried at the windows, chortling at him. Dust shuttling across the now-deserted patch of asphalt of I-15 north. The lights winking two hundred yards ahead. Black-garbed SWAT team members. The FBI Surburbans, just like in the movies.

He wondered where the snipers were. He knew he was in the crosshairs right now. The only thing stopping them was the fact that he was sitting on a shitload of transuranic waste, the biggest fucking hostage in the world.

"Throw your keys out now!"

Or what? You'll take away my phone privileges?

He walked the sheet of paper along the top of the dash, one corner up, one corner down, up and down.

He heard "Yankee Doodle Dandy"—the phone. The right phone. If it wasn't, of course, he'd never know it.

He picked up.

"We want—"

"I don't care what you want," he said, keeping his voice whisper-quiet, barely audible. Whoever was on the other end—and he was pretty sure it was the head honcho—would have to listen hard to hear him. All his concentration would be on trying to understand what Bobby was saying, rather than jumping ahead in his mind, finding a way to outsmart him.

"Listen to me. I'll only say this once. I have a load of transuranic waste right behind this cab. I have explosives strapped around it. If you come near me, I'll blow myself and this rig sky-high. Don't think I won't do it—I've got nothing to lose. If I go, I'll go fast. The rest of you—it's gonna take a while, you'll probably end up in a hospital bed with a tube up your nose and a bedpan under your ass. I'll let you think about that, and you can call me back."

He hit END.

Shocked silence. He could almost feel it. They had all that hardware, all those Suburbans, all those *professionals,* but he, Bobby Burdette, he was the one who was calling the tune.

The phone rang again. A different voice. Calm, reasonable.

Oh-ho, Bobby thought. When they get all calm and reasonable, they're really scared.

Laura and Jon resigned themselves to more waiting. The U.S. Attorney and Glenn Traywick's lawyer—broad-shouldered, gone-to-fat man wearing black-framed glasses and a graying ponytail—were cooped up together in the tiny conference room, hashing out a deal.

Jon's phone chirped. He listened intently, his face going from relieved to concerned.

Laura trying to read what was going on, listening to his side of the conversation.

"They're sure? *Dam*mit. But they are talking to him—that's good. They're going to need hi—"

Then she saw his face sag, the pouches around his eyes become more pronounced. He looked at her, but didn't see her.

Laura stared at him, stared at the phone he held in a death grip to his ear.

"ANFO," he said.

"ANFO?" Laura asked.

He fluttered his hand at her—*Be quiet.*

ANFO. It stood for ammonia nitrate-fuel oil.

"That's what he *says,*" Jon said. "He could be bluffing, but . . . Yeah, all right."

He closed the phone and stared at Laura.

She'd already put the pieces together, but he told her anyway. "They caught up with Bobby Burdette. He's strapped explosives to the tank with the plutonium in it."

Just then, Jeremy Sharp came out of the conference room.

Peltier could see from here that the hostage negotiator wasn't getting anywhere. Although SWAT didn't show it, he knew they were getting disgusted. Going on two hours out here in the heat and the wind, that asshole holding them *all* hostage.

From where he stood, the LVMPD negotiator didn't know his ass from a hole in the ground.

"What's he *doing* in there?" Peltier demanded.

Jordy said, "Waiting us out."

"He thinks we're going to go away?"

Jordy shrugged. "Maybe he doesn't know what he's going to do. I guess that's where the hostage negotiator comes in."

"SWAT wants to move. They think they can get him, with nobody else getting hurt."

Jordy didn't reply.

"If it wasn't for that damn N-waste—"

"Heard a good one the other day."

Peltier wiped sweat out of his eyes. "Yeah?"

"What's the difference between a SWAT team and a hostage negotiation team?"

"I give up."

"SWAT says, 'Hey, it's been ten minutes. He's not gonna ever give in.' Hostage negotiator says, 'Hey, it's been three weeks. I think we're making progress.' "

Peltier laughed out loud.

The lead hostage negotiator, Frank Handley, was laying out how easy it would be. Bobby might not even get that much prison time. He could serve it in Arizona, where he could see his mother.

That didn't sound like much of a treat.

Handley and his team had done their research. They'd talked with Bobby Burdette's mother. From what Peltier gathered, the woman had real contempt for her son. She said something to the effect that they shouldn't worry, he wasn't the kind to go all the way.

She called him a quitter.

Everybody here hoped she was right.

Peltier's cell rang. It was that DPS detective, Laura Cardinal. She started to talk, just as the other phone rang—the one from Bobby Burdette. "I can't talk to you now," he said brusquely, and cut her off.

"What'd he say?" Jon asked.

Laura was still looking at her phone. "He said, 'I can't talk to you now.' "

"Maybe they're at a turning point."

Laura heard the faint *thwop-thwop-thwop* of helicopter blades. "DPS helicopter's here," she said.

"Let's go. We'll tell him when we're up."

* * *

When they were settled in the helicopter, earphones on, Jon said to Laura, "Do you believe it?"

"I want to."

"So do I."

Laura thought about Traywick's demeanor. He'd clearly wanted a deal. The thought of spending the rest of his life in prison had to be daunting.

He could just as easily be lying. Hard to tell.

They would know, at some point soon, if it was a lie. Right now the people at NTS were double-checking their transuranic waste canisters, making sure all of them were accounted for. They had people crawling over all of them, doing tests, checking them for radiation. There was a slew of things they could do, she'd been told. The other truck, the one that had gone ahead, had already been checked out. Its load was intact. All three canisters were radioactive.

She pictured Glenn Traywick's face. He had seemed preternaturally calm, matter-of-fact. Hands clasped in front of him, waiting for the signal to talk. His lawyer clearing his throat. "Go ahead."

A big pause. Like he was setting up a punch line. And what a punch line it was.

"I never switched the canisters."

Laura not quite understanding. Watching his lips move, not getting what he was saying.

Jon stiffening beside her, at full attention. "What are you saying?"

"I thought Burdette might do something—guy's crazy as a shithouse rat. I didn't trust him, so I decided not to switch canisters."

Jon said slowly, "You're saying there's no transuranic waste in those canisters?"

GLENN ELECTRIC, the bill pulled down over his red forehead. "That's what I'm saying."

The room quiet, almost a void, as they considered this.

"He doesn't know?"

"Nope. Nobody knows." He paused. "Except the five of us here."

When they were up, Traywick stowed in the seat behind them, Jon tried Peltier. He got Jordy Benteen, who must have been answering Peltier's cell.

"I've got good news."

"You just saved money on your car insurance?" Jordy deadpanned.

Jon laughed. "Better than that."

He told him.

"Empty?" demanded Peltier as he came on the line. "Are you shitting me, Service?"

"Glenn Traywick never switched the canisters."

"How do you know that for sure?"

"Well, I guess we don't. Yet."

"What'd he tell you?"

Jon went into chapter and verse. How Glenn Traywick didn't trust Bobby Burdette, thought he was a loose cannon. Thought that if he were cornered he might do something dangerous. Since the object of their scheme was to scare the public, just having one of those trucks in their possession would be enough to do the job. They would make all the cable news channels, and this would help them achieve their goal: to prove how dangerous nuclear waste was, and how easily it could be hijacked. How foolhardy the government was to go back to nuclear testing and building more nuclear power plants, after a moratorium of twenty-five years. Glenn Traywick told him they didn't need to endanger people any more than they had to. They just needed to make their point.

Traywick had also told them he loved fishing the Colorado River. He would never take a chance that it could be destroyed for generations.

Never. On that point he was adamant.

Now Peltier said to Service, "I checked with the California port of entry. They swear they checked those canisters for radioactivity. That would explain how they got through." His voice wary.

"Empty canisters, just like on the manifest."

"Hard to believe, though."

Jon said, "We should hear soon. There are only so many Trupact II casks, and now every one of them's been accounted for." He added, "We'll talk some more when we see you."

"What?"

"We're bringing Traywick. Just in case Burdette wants to talk to him."

"What do you mean, *we're* bringing him? Who's 'we'? You're not bringing that woman, are you?"

"Can't not bring her. It's her helicopter."

44

Bobby Burdette had gone to another level. Maybe his molecules really *had* rearranged. Whatever it was, he felt serene, like it was meant to be. He wondered if soldiers felt this way when they met the enemy. Probably, they didn't have time to think at all. But he did.

Maybe it was more like facing execution. Every sense heightened. Every feeling like a razor cutting into you. Feeling *everything*. Really living, for the first time.

The two helicopters up above were for him. On this day, he was the most important person in the world. What he did in the next few hours would change the U.S. economy, let alone Las Vegas and this godforsaken desert.

Imagine, Las Vegas turned into a ghost town. A fence around it to keep everyone out. All those pricey casino resorts bulldozed back into the earth. And he was the one who held that potential in his hands.

It was up to him. Everybody else out there in their black outfits and fancy SUVs, with their radios and high-powered rifles and helicopters—all of it was just window dressing.

As he talked on the phone with the hostage negotiator, he saw himself from the outside. He was in complete control, even having a little fun with the guy. Saying one thing and then another—contradicting himself. Telling him the most amazing stories. How he saved his sister from a crazy killer when he was just four years old, when he didn't even have a sister. How he was a paratrooper in the army. Stuff they could check. Total bullshit.

He saw his picture on the news. Hoped they didn't use his mug shot from his stint in prison. He saw them poking into his past, talking to his mother, the neighbors. *He always was quiet.*

"It's not worth killing yourself for," the negotiator said. "You agree on that, don't you?"

"You have a point."

Enjoying this.

"Look, here's the bottom line. Nothing's happened yet. If you think about it, all that's happened is you're sitting in that truck, you haven't done anything—"

Suddenly, he heard another voice. "Let me have that."

Interesting. Bobby viewing it from his serene place, where he felt like he was riding on a magic carpet and at the same time the adrenaline was rushing through his veins— two distinct feelings at once.

Better than the best pot in the world.

"Burdette, we know something you don't know," the voice said briskly.

"And what is that?" Smiling inside.

"Your friend Glenn double-crossed you, buddy. You're not sitting on any transuranic waste. Those canisters are empty."

For a moment he felt the good feeling flying up beyond his grasp. Grabbed at it, like the string to a kite.

"You're lying," he said.

"Glenn Traywick's on his way. He can tell you himself."

"That's bullshit."

"It's the truth. You'll see that. Look at the SWAT team. The whole game has changed. They want to take you out and now there's no reason not to."

He squinted through the windshield at the SWAT team, the cars. They looked no different to him, but for the first

time, he felt a hairline crack in his confidence. "I don't believe you."

"We're not gonna wait long now. You can talk to Traywick, and if that doesn't work, you're toast."

Bobby hit END.

Prick!

They were trying to mess with his head. What an obvious lie. He should have been prepared for that.

Traywick wouldn't have the balls to switch tanks.

Would he?

Bobby didn't know Traywick well enough to be sure. It
didn't make sense, though. It had to be a trick.

But he could feel it, in his gut, a kind of tiny wailing
sound, like someone calling from the bottom of his soul.
Asking him if he'd done all this for nothing.

45

Laura had been relegated to the back of the unit. She could see the truck, but that was about it.

All the units were far enough back from Burdette's truck that damage from even a big explosion would be minimized. If it was just an explosion. She hoped Glenn Traywick had been telling the truth.

Bobby Burdette had heard what Traywick had to say.

There was no reply.

Calls to his phone were left unanswered.

It had been an hour since the last time they tried. She knew that Peltier was about to the end of his patience. The sun was sinking like a bloodshot eye beneath the western mountains, turning them pinkish purple.

What was he doing in there?

The wind swatted at her like an angry cat. Hopefully, when the sun went down the wind would die out.

She leaned against one of the vehicles. Thirsty, tired, sweaty, her eyes watering from the wind. Her back starting to ache. She had put lip balm on her lips probably five or six times since she'd been here, but it didn't seem to do any good.

Did Bobby Burdette believe them?

She had no way of knowing.

The hostage negotiator had taken to using the megaphone, but there was no answer.

It was quiet except for the wind. When the sun went down it would be cold, too. Someone had set up lights, which made things eerier, the shadows stretching out along the road. It felt like a stadium. And this was the sport.

Peltier pacing back and forth, looking at his watch. Suddenly he stopped, looked at Handley, the negotiator, and made a cutting motion to his throat. He strode over, took the megaphone.

"Bobby Burdette, throw out your keys and come out, hands on your head. Come out *now!*"

No reply.

"If you don't come out now, we will take you. I have two snipers on you. Throw out your keys! Do it now!"

Silence. The truck standing there in the glare of the high-density lights. Immovable. Light flaring off the windshield, making it opaque. Impossible to see in.

"Throw out your keys! Do. It. Now."

Laura was aware of an almost imperceptible movement among the SWAT team, like a breeze through a cornfield. And then, stillness.

"Bobby Burdette—"

The rest of Peltier's words were drowned out in the explosion.

46

The shock stayed with Laura long after the debriefing, which took them well into the night. The memory still raw, the way they cleared out—fast—a panicked rear guard action. An orderly retreat. There would be cleanup, but not by them. There would be crime-scene investigation—but not by them.

The incredible media circus.

The hours at the FBI headquarters in Vegas. All of them—including Peltier—seemingly lost and trying to focus. Shocked. His arrogance gone. And through it all, the scene kept replaying itself in Laura's mind. She had seen the detonation before she had heard it: the almost incremental rise of the truck's hood in slow motion, lifting up along with the top of the cab, starting to settle into new, less-familiar lines—before distintegrating into spouts of shooting flame and boiling black smoke, an oily miasma filling the red-stained sky. The sound deafening.

Debris raining down, all of them enveloped in smoke. Laura's first panicked thought was also the one that stayed with her: *What if Glenn Traywick lied?*

And another question: What could they have done different? That was the big question, and one that had no answer.

For Laura's part, she thought there was nothing they could have done to make it turn out differently.

Bobby Burdette's big moment had come, and he had not flinched from it. He'd had his chance at immortality, and he took it.

Everything she had been told about him this long day backed up that hypothesis.

Laura boarded the DPS helicopter just before dawn, weary to the bone. The word that had come in from the cleanup crews was good. There were small traces of radioactivity, but nothing commensurate with a tank of transuranic waste. But even so, the fear had worn itself a path into Laura.

Flying back in the pure pink light of dawn, the desert floor warming to the sun, the shadows deep, the land below them like a nubby blanket of sage, Laura could see the trucks, the tankers, the men in white suits and masks, the piles of white plastic bags. Working their way through the charred ruins of the Fleet truck and the Trupact II canisters.

The canisters were intact. Bobby's explosives, it seemed, hadn't made a dent in them. They lay like beer kegs after an all-night party, scattered on the desert earth's surface.

Not enough explosive to do the job. Bobby Burdette must have known that.

When Laura got to Flagstaff, she checked into the motel, closed the drapes, stripped off all her clothes and crawled under the sheets. She did not wake until late that evening.

She was hungry, but when the food came at the same coffee shop she'd eaten at before, it didn't look good to her. Looking down at the steak and potato ("watch out, the plate is *hot*") she called her house and got her machine. Needing to talk to Tom after what had happened. Still seeing Bobby's truck disintegrating, then turning into a missile.

No one there to pick up. This was the third time she'd called and left a message.

When her cell phone rang a few seconds later, she grabbed it. "Tom?"

"Uh, no. This is Brandon. Brandon Terry." Dan Yates's roommate. "You wanted to talk to me?"

Laura swallowed her disappointment and asked him a few questions, more to wrap things up than anything else. He had little to add to Steve Banks's account of the day Dan and Kellee left for Las Vegas.

"There's nothing that stands out?" she asked wearily, feeling like a broken record. How many times had she asked that question?

"I can't think of anything. . . ."

"Well, thanks for—"

"A friend of his showed up later that day. Is that the kind of thing you mean?"

"When?"

"I don't know, I was just getting ready to go to class. Quarter of eleven, maybe?"

"Which friend was this?" Laura picturing thirty-eight-year-old Bobby Burdette, all swagger and dark glasses.

"I don't know. Probably someone he knew from class."

Class?

"Can you describe him?"

"He was my age—"

Laura straightened. "Your age? What did he look like?"

"Just your average guy. I do remember he was upset, though. Really mad he missed Dan. You could tell he was pissed."

"What did he say?"

"I don't know. He was just upset. The way he acted."

"Did he give you a name?"

"He did, but I can't remember it."

Laura asked him a few more questions, but he couldn't think of anything else.

A kid looking for Dan. It could mean nothing. *Probably* meant nothing. But she'd give a great deal to know who it was.

47

The ophthalmologist was cute. Not good-looking—cute. He was in his mid-thirties, and had an open, friendly face. His brown hair flopped in a bang over his forehead as he scooted around the darkened room on his little rolling chair, his quickness and the lab coat reminding Laura of some long-ago movie starring Groucho Marx.

He asked her to recount the last couple of instances when her vision went haywire. She did. A stickler for detail, she even told him about the ice.

"Ice? Oh, for those circles under your eyes." He had been looking at her chart on the low table by the door. Now he zoomed across the space between them, looming up close to her face, his eyes searching. Shining a light on her face. "You know we can fix that."

"What?"

"Just a little snip here and pull this tight—it's a simple operation."

Laura felt something shake loose inside her. If he was talking plastic surgery, the prognosis couldn't be that bad.

"I used to do that kind of work, but now I'm strictly ophthalmology. But I know a good man who could do it. Let me know if you want his name. Insurance doesn't cover it, though. . . ." He tapped the chart against his knee, thinking.

She wanted to scream, *What's wrong with my eyes?*

"You probably want to know what's going on."

Duh.

"You've got ocular migraines. It's obvious—it's either that or a brain tumor."

"I *don't* have a brain tumor?"

He shook his head. "Not likely."

He told her about ocular migraines. They were like migraines, but instead of giving her headaches and nausea, they caused a halo effect around her vision. "Harmless, but a pain in the ass. Stress brings them on, so if you can eliminate stressors, you're home free."

How simple it sounded. Eliminate stressors. Right.

"Also, if I were you, I'd stop using ice. No wonder you got ocular migraines—you must have frozen half your cranium."

Laura had made the appointment from the Tucson airport and gone straight there. She'd debated going home, but there were too many things she had to do, so she drove back to DPS afterward.

Richie gave her the bad news as soon as she came in.

"The shell cartridge doesn't match Bobby Burdette's shotgun."

She assimilated this.

"He had other guns."

"None of them were twelve-gauge."

"He could have ditched it."

Richie nodded. "But that's like looking for a needle in a haystack. Anyway, the dirtbag's dead, so it's a moot point."

"Swell." She walked to her desk. Five or six While You Were Out slips sitting there waiting for her. She looked through them all, hoping one of them was from Tom.

No such luck.

She sat down, feeling oddly disconnected. From the place, from the other detectives, from the world. At least her eyes were all right.

She closed said eyes now, feeling disoriented. That familiar tightness in her chest. The need to know what was going on with Tom, needing to pinpoint the source of bad feelings rising up in her throat. Maybe it was just what she'd seen: Bobby Burdette's truck rearranging itself in the air over the Mojave.

She sat there for a few minutes. Remembering the billboard she'd seen on the way to the airport in Flagstaff this morning: CHOOSE LIFE.

The people who paid for the billboard were referring to abortion. But it made her think of Bobby Burdette. He'd had an image to protect; he'd seen himself a certain way. She thought that the picture of himself was more important to him than the reality.

Given that, it was easy to see why he had killed himself. In his mind, he'd had no choice.

But she did.

She walked downstairs to Jerry's office, knocked on the doorjamb. Jerry stood up from his desk, grizzled and smiling. "Congratulations are in order. That was some wild ride you went for up there. Looks like you closed this case and then some."

"Looks like it." Although now she wasn't so sure. "What I came in to ask you—I'd like to take a couple of days off. I haven't had much sleep—"

Jerry sat back down, his blueberry eyes assessing. "I think that's a good idea. You've been through a lot."

"So, it's okay? I can leave now?"

"I think you should."

Laura turned back at the doorway. "I think I'm going to need some counseling, too."

She was almost to the turnoff to Vail, to the Bosque Escondido and her reunion with Tom Lightfoot—however that might turn out—when her cell rang.

It was the chief of police in Lordsburg, New Mexico.

"Laura Cardinal? I understand you know a Jamie Cottle from Williams, Arizona?"

"Yes—"

"We have him here at the jail. He asked to talk to you."

"Jail?"

"He was stalking a schoolteacher named Richard Garatano."

Laura saw the Wentworth Road exit sign come up, then flash by. She glanced across the median at the mesquites, the road arrowing through the desert toward home.

She pushed the 4Runner up to eighty.

It was only another one hundred and forty miles or so to Lordsburg, if she kept going straight on I-10.

48

By the time Laura got to Lordsburg just over the state line, the lowering sun was hanging on by its fingernails, staining the world red under streaky dark high clouds, the glow almost blinding in her rearview. Red suffused everything: the houses on the outskirts dotting the high grassy plain, the reflective signs, the bargain motels, fast-food places, truckstops. The town seeming to stretch out on the left side of the interstate like a giant motherboard. Car lights flashed on as she took exit 22, drove under the overpass, and tracked her way up State Route 70 to Wabash Street.

She gave her name and badge number into the speaker set into the plastic window dividing the police department from the public. A few moments later Chief Daniel Farnsworth himself met her in the small lobby and led her back. Chief Farnsworth was a tall man, a rancher. Square face, square hands, the wrinkles webbing his sure-shooter blue eyes like a badge of honor. He smelled of nicotine and Juicy Fruit.

"Kid is something else," he said as he led her to the interrogation room. Laura looked in the window: The boy inside, looking small and helpless, even though he was tall for his age. His dark hair flopping over his face.

"You said he was following Garatano?"

"I'd say 'stalking' is more like it. We confiscated a twelve-gauge shotgun from the gun rack in his truck."

"Truck?" Laura asked. "He owns a car."

"It's registered to his parents."

"What exactly was he doing?"

The chief summarized the events of the last day and a half. The first time Richard Garatano noticed Jamie Cottle was when he went to the Pizza Hut with his wife and baby boy. He sensed the kid watching him. When he got a good look, he knew right away who it was.

Apparently, Cottle had followed him around in Williams, too. Ran into him a lot, never said anything, just gave him the evil eye.

"When Garatano saw Cottle here in Lordsburg, it threw the fear of God into him. He called us. By the time we got there, the kid was gone. We didn't take a report. Last I checked, a cat can look at a king."

Laura smiled at that. "Do you know Mr. Garatano's history?"

"We do now. I talked to the Williams PD yesterday. Bad situation." He paused a beat—poor kid, let him rest in peace. "Anyway, two nights ago, Cottle spent the night in his truck outside the Garatano residence. Garatano twice asked him to leave, and Cottle told him what I just told you: 'A cat can look at a king.'"

Garatano was now teaching at Royal's Academy, a charter school here in town.

Jamie Cottle had parked outside the school and stayed there all day. When Garatano came out, Cottle got out of his truck and asked him if he'd found another boy. "This was when school was letting out and there were lots of kids around to hear it. According to Garatano, Cottle threatened him, said he better not touch another boy or he'd regret it. Since there were witnesses, we had enough to bring him in for questioning. It was a clear threat."

"How did he react when you brought him in?"

"He seemed happy."

"Happy?"

"Said he wanted to make Garatano's life miserable, and it looked like he was succeeding.

"As I understand it, he's got a real beef. After what happened to his brother. Jesus." He touched his nose. "Chief Loffgren and I go way back. He said this kid had a crush on the girl who was shot up there a week or so ago? She was killed by a twelve-gauge shotgun, wasn't she?"

"Yes, she was."

The chief shook his head. "That kid could be in a heap of trouble. I know he asked for you, but I wouldn't cut him any slack if I were you."

"Don't worry," she said. "I won't."

Jamie Cottle looked up when the door opened, his expression interested. Again she was struck by his clear-eyed intelligence. His face open, and yet she knew that he had plenty of secrets roiling underneath.

"You came," he said. "I didn't know if you would."

"Looks to me like you're in some trouble."

His smile dropped. "Not so much. I didn't do anything."

"Stalking someone isn't nothing."

"And pedophilia is? What about drowning someone?"

That stubborn look again.

"You don't know that. You don't know what happened."

"I know my brother's dead and that bastard is walking free. Even got himself another job teaching the kiddies."

Laura set her recorder on the small table between them and switched it on. Gave her name, rank, his name, the location, the date. Then she read him his rights.

"I called you for *help*," he said.

"I am here to help you. But you have to tell me the truth. Why have you been following Mr. Garatano?"

"Isn't it obvious?"

"How did you find out he lived here?"

"I've got my sources. I'm not stupid."

"So when did you get this idea? To come out here? What did you think you would accomplish?"

He leaned forward. "Have you ever lost anyone? Someone in your family? Well, I have. I think about my brother *every day*. Why should that—that *prick* walk around, enjoy the sunshine, enjoy going to the Pizza Hut for Christ's sake, have a whole life, after what he did to T.J.?"

He looked her in the eyes, his gaze daring her to argue. Laura said, "It's not up to you to dispense justice."

"Dispense justice? Are you kidding? They didn't even charge him. The only thing that happened was, he lost his job. And now he's got another one. Teaching *kids*. You call that justice?"

He was drawing her into an argument she couldn't win. "You had a twelve-gauge shotgun in your truck. Have you fired it recently?"

"Oh, is that it? You still think I killed Kellee, don't you? What's your theory? I shot them both in a jealous rage? Is that it?"

On the offensive. For a moment she thought he'd shoot out of his chair at her.

"You honestly think I would kill her? What, you think I shot her and her boyfriend, then I drove out here to shoot the teacher? Like some kind of rampage? Is that what you think?"

"You have to see it from where I'm sitting."

"No, I don't. Because you're wrong."

"Then why are you here? Enlighten me on that. Why did you come all this way? Just to bother him?"

He stared at her, his face pale. Two pinpoints of color on this cheeks. Eyes like stones.

"You don't believe me, do you? You really think I killed her."

Laura thought: *You only get one chance with this guy.*

"Jamie, you know how it is. I have to ask you questions, but we're all on the same side."

He folded his arms, glared at her. "I thought I could trust you, that you of all people would understand, but I can see you're just like the rest of them. I'm not talking to you anymore. I want a lawyer."

From that point on, there was nothing she could do. Jamie Cottle had a very strong will. When his lawyer showed up, the game was over.

As Laura left, he gave her one last resentful look.

In his mind, she had betrayed him.

She drove home that night.

Spent most of that time thinking, working things out, as she flashed past the few small towns strung out along the freeway, a sprinkling of lights here and there. The road unraveling before her. Weary, but her mind alive.

She thought about Jamie Cottle, about what his world must be like now.

When his brother died, it had acted like a lit fuse. So much rage—outrage. There was a moral component, as if it had been all done to him. His brother had died but the insult was to him. Yet even after his brother's death, he'd still had something tethering him to the world. He had his family, and he had Kellee.

His relationship with Kellee had all been fantasy, but it had been real to him. Was this the reason he didn't spend all summer following and threatening Richard Garatano? Had his love for Kellee made the difference?

Then his fantasy—perhaps the only thing sustaining him—was blown to bits. He knew Kellee and Dan were an item; he saw that every day. But Laura guessed that Jamie Cottle had nurtured in his mind the idea that Kellee and Dan would split up. When they got married, it changed the equation. To Jamie's mind, marriage would be seen as permanent. Their wedding had to be a terrible blow. Something he couldn't deny, something he couldn't gloss over.

Brandon Terry had described the young man showing up at Dan's apartment as agitated.

Angry.

49

Laura thought: *I'll know in a minute.*

She turned onto the loop road. Glanced at the corrals, but the moon was under cloud tonight and she couldn't see shapes, just a dark mass. Couldn't tell if his truck was there or not; it was too far away.

She drove up the dirt road, through the wash and up again, to the curve. Her house, *mi nidito,* on the right.

The house was dark.

She glanced at the digital clock on the dash: almost one A.M.

He'd be asleep by now.

She parked out front and pushed through the iron gate. Walked up onto the old brick portal. A cricket chirped somewhere.

Laura unlocked the door and was confronted by pitch black. She reached to her right and flicked on the light—a white ceramic globe on the ceiling, held in place by wrought iron. Pretty funky—it came with the house.

She tiptoed through to the bedroom, letting her eyes adjust.

The bed was made. It looked same as it had when she left three days ago. She looked over at the answering machine on the bedside table. Blinking manically—too many messages to count.

She turned on lights. No need to creep around because there was nobody to wake up. She walked into the kitchen, looking for notes. There were none. Checked the refrigerator. A few condiments. Not even the beer he liked. Nada.

He had not been here.

Where *was* he?

Too late to go to the cantina. Too late to ask anyone. The whole place was sleeping.

She went back in and played the messages. She didn't like the sound of her own voice, which sounded tentative and increasingly desperate.

She walked over to the closet they shared together. His stuff was still here. That was a relief.

What do you think? He's going to walk out on you? Why would you think that?

Something going on, but what?

Tom was a free spirit. He had mentioned going down to Mexico, a working ranch where sometimes he hired on to round up cattle. The owner was a friend of his from way back. Laura had his name and number in her address book.

She found the page, started to punch in the number.

One in the morning.

Screw it.

She pulled off her clothes and crawled into bed, sure she wouldn't get a minute's sleep, everything running around in her head like a hamster on a wheel.

The phone woke her.

She reached across the empty side of the bed. She had been scrupulous to keep to her own side, a habit she had gotten from sleeping with Tom.

"Hey there, Sleeping Beauty. Rise and shine."

It was Richie.

"What time is it?" she asked. Full sunlight across the bed, the floor: late.

"Noon."

"Noon?" Then she remembered. Jerry had given her some time off. She didn't have to go in. "What's up?"

"Just your genius partner, making another brilliant deduction."

"I'm not coming in today. Didn't Jerry tell you?"

"He said something about that, but I thought you might change your mind."

"Why?" Wishing he'd just come right out and say what he had to say. Everything had to be a production.

"You sure took a hell of a lot of photos of the scene, you know that?"

"So what else is new?" *Get on with it, so I can get off the phone and do some gardening—or something.*

"I think this time, your anal-retentiveness just may have paid off."

Will you stop talking in riddles?

"That's something about you, Laura. You always play it by the book. You *over*do it. Shit, I looked at these photos and I could follow everything you did. It's kind of a chronicle."

"How good for you."

"I even have a photo of your footprint. There's an oldie but a goodie. A little dramatic, maybe, but effective."

Laura remembered clearing the dirt, planting her foot in the ground, telling Officer Wingate to do the same. "So?"

"Just so happens, I think I got a photo of the shooter's print, too."

Laura felt something bump in her chest. "Really? Something turned up?"

Remembering the scene, how the guy had brushed away the prints, using a push broom. Probably did it in the dark, maybe with the headlights on, missed something—

"Yup, you got a partial. Almost all of the sole. Size eleven."

"A partial. So he covered it up but he missed some."

"Uh-huh."

She thought of Jamie Cottle in Lordsburg. Could he be a

size eleven? "Too bad we don't have anything to compare it to."

"Oh, yes we do."

Laura hung up the phone, feeling as if she'd been in an elevator that had dropped ten stories. How had she missed it? She went over it in her mind, how trusting she'd been. It felt as if she'd been duped. Betrayed.

What a great judge of character you *are.*

She had to go in right this minute. Now that they knew who they were dealing with. She started for the closet, eyeing her navy and black pantsuits. *Pick a card, any card.*

She'd missed it. She had missed it completely. But her camera hadn't.

Pulling the jacket off the hanger, she had an idea. One more nail in the coffin.

She went into the den, got her purse, grabbed the memo pad she had used most recently, and found the number. Punched it in. "Please be there. Please, please."

A young man answered.

"Is this Brandon?"

"Hold on."

When Brandon Terry answered, she asked him one question.

He couldn't be absolutely sure, he said. But he thought the guy, the kid who came looking for Dan Yates that day, was blond.

At DPS, Laura and Richie went over the photographs, paying particular attention to the photo of Josh Wingate's shoe print, putting it side-by-side with the partial. The print had been partly brushed over but the tread was clear.

"It could be an old print," Laura said. "From before that night."

"Yeah, it *could.*"

"The guy didn't just cover over his own prints, he covered up all the prints that were there before him. You know that."

"Josh was the one who found them—Dan and Kellee." Richie's voice holding his excitement. That great feeling when you were finally at the finish line, you'd followed up on all the dead ends and then, finally, you broke through. Laura always thought of that moment as the satisfying sound of a car door closing—*kachunk*.

Signed, sealed, and delivered.

But she didn't feel good about it this time. Richie could say all he wanted about her dogged police work, but she had missed it completely. Because Dan's and Kellee's killer wasn't Bobby Burdette. It wasn't Jamie Cottle.

Their killer was Josh Wingate.

Laura looked at Richie. "One thing I don't get is, why?"

50

Earlier in the day

Josh had been driving around most of the night, waiting for dawn.

Now, the sky getting lighter, he went back to his place. Ruckus greeted him at the gate, wanting to go.

"Want to go for a ride, huh?" he said. Tears pricking his eyes. He wiped at them with the sleeve of his shirt.

He went through the gate and got the leash from where it sat on the old grill, Ruckus wriggling, making it hard to hook the leash to his collar, especially because the tears were coming again.

Men don't cry. He knew that, but he figured this time he was allowed. Ruckus was the only friend he had left, and now he was, in a sense, betraying him, too.

He let Ruckus jump in the cab with him instead of the back, where he usually stayed. Found himself stroking the shiny black Labrador coat, over and over, Ruckus licking his face, his tail thumping against the passenger door of Josh's new Nissan.

Josh drove the few short blocks to Seth Janney's house. Seth had always liked Ruckus, and Ruckus got along well with Seth's dog, Coalie. They had come from the same litter.

Seth's truck was parked out front but the house was

still. Coalie barked behind the fence. Josh took Ruckus over to the gate, opened it, unhooked the leash and left it on the fence. Squatting down, he held the dog's face between both hands and planted a kiss on his nose. "Gonna miss you, bud." Tears falling down on the perfect black face. Ruckus looking at him, his soul clear in his brown eyes. The reason Josh had no use for churches: If dogs didn't have souls, then there wasn't much of a point, was there?

He wondered where he'd go. If he'd go anywhere. It might be just like sleep. He hoped that was the case. Just a long sleep, where you never felt anything again.

He gave Ruckus one more pat, then took off.

Leaving his best friend behind.

Back at the house, he took a shower and changed into his uniform. He had the uniform dry-cleaned yesterday, had ironed the creases into the legs himself, polished his brass, cleaned his weapon. Now he turned on CNN and got online.

The television was full of the story of Bobby Burdette. There was a reporter standing outside his house, talking about how his neighbors didn't know him well but thought he was all right.

Josh opened up his Web site, thefoundling.com. He didn't know why he'd named it that, except it sounded good. A foundling was a found baby. Maybe that was why he chose it. He wasn't adopted but he felt the way an adopted baby must feel—apart. Separate somehow. He didn't have many friends. In fact, his best friend, Dan, had not been just his friend but his lifeline. When Dan went away to college, it had been hard to deal with. He always felt he didn't fit into this family. His sister was strong, always knew what she wanted to do, but Josh had been aimless and unfocused until he realized he wanted to be a cop.

The last blog, the one no one would be expecting, was ninety-nine percent finished. He'd written it like a diary, complete with times. He entered the time now: 6:03 A.M.

What was he going to write? He wanted it to mean some-

*thing. He wanted the few people out there who followed his
site to understand what he was doing.*

And why.

"Where you going?" Richie asked as Laura headed for
the stairwell.

"I just remembered something," she told him. "Be right
back."

Laura walked down to Evidence and checked out one of
the boxes she'd taken from Dan Yates's house.

Her pulse quickening as she rummaged through it. She
found the cigar box and signed for it.

Her mind half putting it together earlier, when Richie
mentioned that strange day at the Wingate house, the day
they had interviewed Luke Jessup. Richie remarking on
Josh's resentment of his mother.

But something else tickled Laura's memory.

Something Luke Jessup said.

She started up the stairs with the cigar box, stopped on
the third step. Retraced her steps to the Evidence Room and
asked for another piece of evidence. Filled out the forms.

Back up the stairs to the squad room.

Richie got up from his desk and followed her to hers.
"What're those?"

"Some of Dan's things. Greeting cards, letters."

He looked over her shoulder as she lifted out a stack held
together with a rubber band.

She spread the cards out on the desk.

"See anything in common?"

"They look like pictures I had in a book when I was little."

"What kind of book?"

"Fairy tales. Passed down to me from my grandmother."

Laura looked at the cards. All of them appeared as if they
had been painted or drawn long ago, possibly at the turn of
the last century. She'd had a book like Richie's when she

was little, too, lots of pictures like this. Snow White and Rose Red. Sleeping Beauty. Rapunzel.

A fantasy world of beautiful maidens and mean-spirited dwarves. Good versus evil.

"You remember seeing anything like this recently?" Laura asked.

Richie frowned. "Uh-huh. Somewhere."

"How about Barbara Wingate's house? Unicorn Farm?" She remembered the print in the bathroom, the maiden with long flowing hair.

"So?"

Laura opened a card. She felt Richie's breathing on her neck. The card was blank inside, but written in beautiful calligraphy were the words, *Nothing can keep us apart.*

Richie said, "So?"

Laura opened another card. *We were made for each other.*

"Heartwarming."

Laura produced the textbook Kellee had with her at the campsite, *Oedipus Rex.* She opened the book and gestured to the facing page.

Kellee Taylor, with a phone number underneath.

Richie looked from the card to the book. "Different handwriting. Dan was getting love letters, but they weren't from Kellee."

Laura reminded him about the day they went to Unicorn Farm: Luke Jessup outside by the barn digging postholes. "Remember what he said? Dan came by Mrs. Wingate's house a week before he died."

Richie looked at her. "You're thinking, why go to Mrs. Wingate's house? Why not cut out the middleman and just go see his best friend? Tenuous, though. Tenuous is a word, right?"

"Uh-huh."

"Could be nothing." He tapped one of the cards. "Could have been a girlfriend from way back."

But Laura had that feeling, the same feeling Richie'd

had when he saw the photographs lined up together. That feeling of inevitability, when it couldn't be denied. That solid *kachunk*.

Barbara Wingate loves fantasy art. She even names her ranch Unicorn Farm.

Dan comes to town, visits Barbara Wingate, not Josh.

A week later, Josh shows up at Dan's place, "agitated." Mad at his best friend.

Laura knew that Barbara Wingate saw herself as a beauty. She'd seen the way she used her looks for effect. She had a flirtatious quality. Her awareness of men always front and center.

Laura had seen the fantasy Barbara, the lovely, star-crossed creature who had borne so much adversity with grace and dignity. Even Wendy, the night clerk at the Pioneer motel, had fantasized about being like her when she was a little girl. Barbara Wingate was the composite of the perfect woman. Gentle, kind, beautiful, but with a tragic air. Strong enough to prevail through tragedy, but the kind of woman men liked to protect. A princess, a maiden, thrown to the wolves and in need of a champion.

The romantic ideal.

But Laura had seen the mask slip. She had seen what was behind the mask—a cold, calculating evil that had could have taken her life.

A maiden in need of a champion.

Was Barbara Wingate capable of seducing her son's best friend?

Laura was willing to bet the answer was yes.

Josh found himself driving again. The blog had been good—if shocking. He had decided to be completely truthful about everything, even the parts that would normally have embarrassed him. He wanted everyone to know how deeply he had been betrayed, by both his best friend and his mother.

She had to be held accountable.

People wouldn't be expecting it. They were used to a little philosophy, commentary on this crazy modern world. But he'd said it right out:

Have you ever seen true evil? I mean looked it in the face and recognized it for what it is? I have. And you know what? It's a face like any other.

And here's something you might not know. The face of evil belongs to my mother.

All those years, his friend Dan and his mother, leading a double life. Pretending to his face that they weren't fucking each other. His best friend. He felt it all over again, the rage building up, so when he stopped the truck outside the entrance to Cataract Lake he was glad again.

He sat in the truck, staring down through the trees at the lake. Remembering.

He'd thought it was just going to be another dinner at his mom's. But when he got there she was in her nightgown. He had to admit she looked beautiful, younger than her age. And tragic.

She'd played that part before.

His mother was a lot like this lake—beautiful but there were bad things underneath, things that could snag you and take you under, like it did with that kid and his teacher—

Another *case of statutory rape.*

He forced himself to remember, her coming up to him, wineglass in hand—half in the bag—telling him before he was even through the front door that she had taken a whole bottle of pain pills. Swooning against him—

He didn't know if that was part of the act. But dutiful son that he was, he'd driven her to the Health Care Center. They had pumped out her stomach. Telling him it was good he arrived when he did, because otherwise she would have died.

He doubted that. His mother's will to live was remarkable.

She'd asked him to come to dinner at six. Probably took the pills at five till.

He stayed at her house for a few days, as the doctor suggested, to keep an eye on her. Nurse her back to health.

Sitting in the truck now, he laughed.

She was fine the next day, as if nothing had ever happened. But she stayed in bed, asking him to bring her things. A tray of food, and she asked really nice if he'd get some flowers from the garden and put them in a cut-crystal vase so she could see them.

Pretty soon she started crying. He felt he had to listen. And pretty soon she had told him everything.

In duplicate. In triplicate. Every detail she could think of. Her tears turning to rage at Dan, that rage transferring to him. He could have sworn she got off on it. Got off on telling her son that all this time, all this fucking time, for years, she had been fucking his best friend. That all this time he had been a dupe, and how did he like that?

We love each other, *she'd wailed.* He doesn't want that girl. He's just doing it because he knows no one would accept our love. He doesn't love her, he loves me.

Me me me.

She enjoyed shocking him. He could tell. Enjoyed his hurt, even enjoyed his rage. "You want to hit me?" *she'd demanded.* "Go ahead. I deserve it. I love you, and I'm sorry I hurt you. You must hate me!"

How he had wanted to hit her.

He remembered getting out of there. He couldn't stand the sight of her. He remembered driving around. He'd always liked to drive, it had always calmed him. But this time it only made him madder.

He'd worked his shift, acting as if nothing happened. There was a lot of sympathy about his mother. How everything was too much for her, the death of his older sister, raising her granddaughter by herself, how much she had suffered.

And after shift, he drove around some more. He drove all

the way to Wickenburg and back, not seeing the scenery, not seeing anything except her face when she told him, the satisfaction lurking behind her tears. He drove to Flagstaff, looking for Dan, wanting to punch him out, wanting some closure. But Dan wasn't there.

It made him feel impotent. All this anger and nobody to hold accountable.

Exhausted, he had gone home and slept, for hours.

When he woke up it was night. He drove to his mother's farm. He would tell her what he thought of her. He would get it out of his system, at least. But her house was quiet, the lights out.

Driving home on Cataract Lake Road he spotted Dan's truck.

Seeing his mother's face as she twisted the knife: One of our favorite places was Cataract Lake. We'd tryst there.

Tryst there.

After the shooting, he'd planned to drive to one of his own favorite spots, just a place out in the wilderness, and take his own life.

And he would have, if it wasn't for Ruckus.

If they weren't found right away, if he wasn't found right away, Ruckus might do without water and food. He would be trapped in the yard. Talk about betrayal. The idea of his only friend dying of starvation or lack of water kept him from killing himself.

He would have to find a place for Ruckus. Unlike his mother, he didn't betray those who loved him. Even a dog.

When he got home, the phone was ringing. He let the answering machine pick up.

And got the shock of his life when he heard his mother's voice. Alive and kicking. Calling him because she was worried about him.

Richie made the call to the Williams PD.

Laura listened to his side of the conversation. From the tone of his voice, she could tell he was met with skepticism.

Better have a SWAT team just in case.

He hung up and looked at her. He appeared weary around the eyes. "They're on their way. I told them how dangerous he is—both of them—are."

Laura nodded.

"Here's an interesting tidbit. Josh Wingate has a twelve-gauge shotgun. It's one of his service weapons. What do you bet we finally get a match?"

"I guess we'll know soon." Laura looked at her watch. Even if they could get a plane now, it would probably be another two hours before they could get there.

By then, the arrest would have been made.

"What about the mother?" Richie said.

"I wouldn't worry," she said. "She's handled him so far."

One more thing he had to do: mail the letters. Unlike his mother, he faced his responsibilities.

The pile of letters was on the seat next to him: one for the chief, one for Dan's parents, one for Kellee's parents. One for Erin.

He didn't know where to send Erin's letter in Germany. Jeff, Michael Ramey's brother, had given him the address but he'd been a little distracted lately and had lost it. He could look through his mother's address book; she'd have his address.

He pictured that, looking through her address book, while she made him lunch.

51

Since she couldn't do anything, Laura went home to officially start her vacation. For the first time in years she felt
disconnected from her work. It had consumed too much of
her time and energy. Nice to think about puttering around in
the garden, going for long hikes, spending time with Tom—
if that was still a viable option. She turned on the TV while
divesting herself of her work clothes. That was how she
heard about it—on the news. The phone started ringing at
the same time, but she turned the ringer down and sat on the
edge of the bed, mesmerized by the scene, watching as the
tech with the Coconino County medical examiner's office
wheeled a gurney out of the blue house where Barbara
Wingate lived.

Surprised that she wasn't surprised.

The reporter, a brunette with a wide mouth, talked over
the buzzing in Laura's ears. Laura caught the words
"murder-suicide."

Suddenly it hit her, smashing into her stomach, a double-
cut to the throat.

She remembered Josh Wingate that first day, how she
thought he was trying to be a good cop even though he had
lost his best friend.

Tears spilled out of her eyes and down her cheeks and
onto the coverlet. Her chest ragged, and suddenly she was

sobbing, as if a dam had given out and all the hurt and pain of the world poured out of her soul.

That was the state she was in when Tom Lightfoot found her.

They lay tangled together on the bed, Tom stroking her wet face.

"It's okay, Bird," he said, holding her eyes with his. Stroking her as if she were a frightened animal.

She had let go, let the tears pour out. She realized at some point the tears weren't for Barbara Wingate or Josh Wingate but for herself. Something was gone, something she couldn't quite recognize, but she knew it from the shape of its absence. Gone from her life.

Making love to Tom had been wonderful at the time, comforting beyond belief, but now she felt stale. Stale and incredibly weary and sad.

Tom looked in her eyes, said the right things, but she could almost feel the division between them, as if it were physical. Making love had been an illusion. Something was going on. It was in the way he looked at her, his eyes not quite focusing on her. Focusing *around* her.

What was it—pity?

She felt her heart close up. Had to get out of the bed. She got up and trailed the sheet to the bathroom, suddenly not wanting to be naked in front of him.

Weird.

She looked at her face in the mirror, the puffiness under her red-rimmed eyes. The ophthalmologist saying, *We can fix that.*

She closed the door to the bathroom and put the lid down on the toilet and just sat there, wondering what was going on. Tom had made love to her. It was like any and every other time, more or less. And yet she knew it was over.

After a while she got up and took a shower. Washing him away. She wrapped herself in a towel and walked back out into the bedroom.

He was sitting on the edge of the bed in his jeans, no shirt. Staring at the floor.

Looking like a man who dreaded what he was about to do.

"You're leaving, aren't you?"

He looked up, his face immobile. Eyes sad, but she could see the resolve there.

"It just isn't working out, is it?" she said. Trying to sound flippant, like it didn't hurt her.

He didn't say anything.

"It was a mistake. This whole living-together thing. You're a free spirit, I knew that. You need your *space*. You like your lifestyle just the way it is, thank you very much, you don't need anybody and neither do I."

She sounded bitter to her own ears.

He stood up. "Bird—"

"Don't say it. Just get the fuck out."

She walked past him, ripped a shirt off a hanger in the closet, pulled on the slacks she'd just gotten out of from work. Forgetting her underwear. Screw it.

She took her shoes and her car keys with her, put the shoes on out on the porch. Yelled back into the house. "When I get back, you'd better be gone."

Then she drove off the Bosque Escondido.

On the road through Vail, she wondered where she should go. Back to work? No. No way.

She got to the freeway exit, found herself on I-10 going east. Back toward Lordsburg. After Lordsburg there was Deming, then Las Cruces. From there she had a choice: continue east to Alamogordo, or south to El Paso.

She didn't stop until she reached El Paso.

52

There was a place in El Paso Laura had hoped to find—a little park with a water tower where she and her parents had stopped for lunch on one of their road trips, when she was eleven. There'd been a boy in the park, and it was clear he was attracted to her. They spent maybe a half hour together, and never saw each other again; the first time in her memory she'd felt that rush through her system, that attraction to the opposite sex. Better than any drug. But what good had that attraction ever done her?

She found two water towers but no park. Wondered why the hell she'd driven all this way, what had gotten into her head. After a night at the Motel 6 reading supermarket tabloids, watching reality shows, and eating bad Chinese takeout, she drove back home, no clearer in her mind about Tom, except that she wanted him back. The house was empty, though: Every trace of him gone. She walked to the corrals. His pickup gone, his trailer gone, the old bronc, Ali—gone.

Following the horse trail back to her empty house, she reached a patch of low-hanging mesquite. And there was Frank Entwistle, sitting on a tree stump.

"How you doing, kiddo?"

"How do you think?"

He had his vermillion blazer folded over his knee. The

one he wore to court almost every day of that terrible summer when Ricky Lee Worrell went on trial for the deaths of her parents. "What are you going to do now?" he asked.

Laura shrugged. "I'm going to counseling." Counseling, as far as she was concerned, was just a word right now. Something she'd have to go through, and hopefully, come out better on the other side. She had no idea what it entailed, and had no desire to know. Just Do It. Starting on Monday.

She hoped the counselor could do something about this stone in her gut, but she wasn't optimistic.

Frank crossed one knee over the other. He wore white loafers—old man's shoes.

"He didn't dump you. You know that, don't you?"

Laura crossed her arms to keep the tears down in her chest where they belonged. "It sure feels that way to me."

"You want to know what I think?"

"Sure, why not? I'm sure everybody'll have an opinion."

He looked unusually serene today, the way he had appeared in his coffin. Like an old warrior who had finally earned his rest. "He wanted you to be the one to feel it, not him."

"Hey, I was the one who wanted the relationship."

Entwistle gave her a look. "You really think that?"

"Look, I gave myself freely. I wanted to make it work—"

She stopped. That wasn't exactly true.

Frank stood up, folding the vermillion blazer over his arm. "You liked the idea of having someone and you tried to make him fit. He could have been anybody. Don't you think he knew it?"

Laura didn't have an answer for that.

"Tell you what, you weren't all wrong—wanting someone to love." He winked at her. "Don't give up on it."

And she was alone again.

53

Richie called her a week later. All the pieces were falling into place; she could hear it in his voice.

He told her about the blog on Josh Wingate's computer, left up for them to read. "Kind of like a suicide note."

A suicide note from the technological age.

He gave her the details: Josh had used the same twelve-gauge shotgun he'd used on Dan and Kellee to kill his mother and then himself. "She was making him lunch," Richie added. "Shot her point-blank in the face—a real mess. Kind of a shame, she was such a looker."

There he went again. Laura inwardly groaned. Just like Richie to say that.

"Then he put the gun in his mouth and used his big toe to blow himself to kingdom come." He paused. "Something interesting came up on another front. Jamie Cottle was in a Catholic youth group run by Barbara Wingate."

"You mean the catechism class?"

"Nah, more like a youth group, after school. According to one of the kids I interviewed, those two were thick as peas in a pod. Wonder what they talked about."

"I'll bet she wanted him to keep trying for Kellee."

"Oh, yeah, that makes sense. Big-time. Stoke up his fantasy, get him fired up. Couldn't hurt, I guess. Maybe Kellee would have tumbled to him. Persistence can wear a person down. That's how I got my wife."

Laura didn't want to go there, so she said, "Barbara Wingate could be manipulative."

"Uh-huh. She manipulated herself right into an early grave."

"So. How are things going?"

"Believe it or not, we all kind of miss you. You are coming back, aren't you?"

Laura held on to the phone. She looked out the window at a roadrunner crossing the back patio, a lizard dangling from its beak. Beautiful around here, but enough was enough.

Already wishing she was back in the squad bay, bantering with the guys, feeling the electricity as she zeroed in on an answer to a particularly tough case.

Missing it like it was a ghost limb.

"Laura? You there?"

"Oh, yeah," she told Richie. "I'm here. And you don't have to worry—I'm coming back."

Big-time.

"A complex, multi-layered, nail-biting superthriller."

—New York Times bestselling author Michael Prescott

DARKNESS ON THE EDGE OF TOWN

J. Carson Black

Laura Cardinal, a detective with the Arizona Department of Public Safety, is called to a crime scene in the town of Bisbee. The body of a teenage girl has been discovered-bearing all the signs of a serial sexual predator, and calling to mind the murder of Laura's schoolmate 18 years earlier.

0-451-21391-2

Available wherever books are sold.
penguin.com